THE FIREPROOF MOTEL

Logan:
Hope you enjoy this
local Tale

Naples, Fl

THE FIREPROOF MOTEL

Arthur Barry

To order additional copies of this book, contact:
Xlibris Corporation
1-888-795-4274
www.Xlibris.com
Orders@Xlibris.com
40891

DEDICATION

This book is dedicated to Melissa, Tigger, and the Fool on the Hill.

ACKNOWLEDGEMENTS

I want to express my heart felt appreciation to Dr. John Skilling M.D. for his help and support in the earliest stages, or birth if you will, of this novel. Additionally, I want to thank Don Kinney for his emotional and spiritual guidance, and Eric Furry for his invaluable critical and editorial assistance. God bless you all.

Prologue

Two figures dressed in black clothing scurried in the darkness down an unlit road paved with coral rocks and broken shells, a narrow flashlight beam lighting their way. A chorus of crickets and bullfrogs serenaded them from the surrounding marsh. It was 3:00 a.m. on a balmy Southwest Florida night in mid-March, and stars shone bright over the Everglades. A scrubby forest of slash and longleaf pines, cabbage palms, saw palmetto, and myrtle bushes sheltered them from the view of the house they were seeking. The dwelling was set back from the road about fifty yards. The first man carried a candle in one of his pants' pockets, matches in the other, and a pistol under his belt. The man following him carried a roll of duct tape. They were on a mission from a devil with a badge.

As they approached the intersection of the driveway and the road, the first man, holding the flashlight, raised his hand to signal caution; they stopped for a moment, and he turned off the light. The house was dark, and there were no cars visible. "Bueno," whispered the light bearer. The two compatriots were of Mexican heritage with coffee-colored skin and raven black hair. The lead man spoke to his fellow countryman in Spanish. "It looks like there is nobody here, Omar."

"OK, Carlos, let's do it."

Approaching the house with caution, Carlos turned off the light. He didn't want to alert any of the gringos who came here to drink and gamble. One or more might still be inside, having passed out from too many *cervezas* (beers) or that sour mash whiskey they seemed to prefer. The house was built up on posts about four feet off the ground; a hip-style roof covered the one-story frame building like a four-sided hat. An open porch ran the length of the front wall. Visibility being almost zero in the night, Carlos risked the flashlight again. A black snake slithered under the house, almost over his boots. He drew a deep breath of surprise but stifled his cry of disgust. A ripple of revulsion ran down his spine. He really *didn't* like snakes.

Ascending the steps while holding the railing, they tested each one to ensure quiet. They didn't want any surprises. Walking across the porch, Carlos tried the door; it was locked. Padlocked shutters secured the windows. No big deal. Carlos signaled Omar to move to the side of the door and put his back against the wall. The big deputy called "Tiny" had given Carlos a .38 revolver. It was some cheap Brazilian job, but they didn't need anything fancy. He pulled the gun from where it was tucked, under his belt at the small of his back, and told Omar to hold the light. He knocked loudly on the door. They waited for any signs of life. There was none. Thank *Dios*! Carlos didn't think he could shoot anyone. The two men planned to scram to Carlos's pickup, hidden up the road, if there was an answer. Omar put the beam on the padlock; and Carlos pulled the hammer of the pistol back, pointed, and fired. Flame shot from the barrel into the darkness, and a deafening boom echoed through the night. For just a few moments, the cacophony of sound coming from the enveloping fen halted, and there was utter silence. The two looked at each other briefly, shrugged, and began to pull the shutters apart.

Like multitudes of illegal immigrants, these hapless men were trying to survive and feed their families in the United States. But Carlos and Omar had been caught with their dicks in the wind by that jackal of a deputy in the middle of a small transaction involving a certain illegal weed smoked by legions of the Americanos. In fact, as far as Carlos could tell, just about every local teenager was hot for good bud. This gringo sheriff, who had them by the short hairs, was dangerous and frightening—*malvado* (evil). He and his partner, the *Capitan*, could send them back to Mexico, put them in jail, or worse. The hulking deputy might even take their children and do *Dios* knows what. There were rumors in some of the camps and barrios about torture and sexual slavery. Carlos shuddered, dismissing these distracting thoughts, and began prying the window up with his pocketknife. He clamored through and turned to get the flashlight from Omar.

"Rápido, Omar," he said. "Let's get it over with!"

There were a dozen card tables set up in a large open room. Used decks of cards were scattered like yesterday's news. Full ashtrays were at each table along with empty and partly full bottles of beer or liquor. Thousands of poker chips were stacked like drunken partygoers on each table. Obviously, the cleaning lady was a no-show. Carlos found the wrench for the propane cylinder by the stove. He opened the vented closet where the tank stood and duct-taped the vent opening. Turning clockwise to loosen it, just as the deputy told him, he undid the nut connecting the copper tubing. The gas was now flowing into the room.

"Omar, close the window!" Carlos pointed to the window they had come through. Omar went over and pushed it down. Carlos lit the candle and put it on the floor near the wall opposite the gas line. "Get out, Omar! Pronto! Go! Go!" Disengaging the two dead bolts in the door, Omar pushed it open; and the two rushed out, closing the door behind them to let the gas build up. They flew down the steps and back down the road through the tenebrous woods, flashlight beam darting like a firefly in the night. Before they could reach their concealed vehicle, an earthshaking explosion rocked the still night like a monstrous thunder clap. A fireball mushrooming above the surrounding treetops illuminated the two desperados as they raced for their getaway truck. Collapsing back into the place where a house once stood, the roaring flames, like a colossal bonfire, drove back darkness. Just as they reached their truck, poker chips cast skyward by the explosion fluttered down on the duo like a multicolored snowfall in the Land of Oz.

1

The white-with-green trim Baron County sheriff's patrol car sped east in the balmy twilight down County Road 846 toward Bella Villa. The large gold sheriff emblems, a five-pointed star on the doors, and its off-white color with green trim distinguished this car from the others on the road. The driver had been granted a special request to have the blue-and-red light rack, designated for county police vehicles in Florida, removed from the roof and less conspicuous ones installed behind the windshield mirror and rear window. There was little traffic heading east to impede its progress. On the Gulf of Mexico, just twenty miles west, the sun was close to setting after delighting residents and tourists alike with another perfect seventy-five-degree March day in Southwest Florida. A large billboard proclaiming Bella Villa as the "Tomato Capital of the World" welcomed motorists at the city limits. It was often said the sign should read "Alligator Capital of the World" as well.

A group of Mexicans stood silently at the edge of a tomato field so vast its end could not be seen in the fading light as the cruiser passed. These were the migrant workers whose poverty was exploited for the cheap labor the growers needed to bring in the crops. They were hard and usually uncomplaining worker bees, desiring a shot at the American Dream, if not for themselves, at least for their children. They watched with sullen faces until the taillights were small dots of red light. One of the older men with white stubble on his careworn face crossed himself and mumbled a prayer in Spanish. A few of the men whispered, "El Diablo," and also crossed themselves.

The cruiser pulled up to a convenience store on the outskirts of Bella Villa with a faded sign proclaiming it to be Crayton's Market. Deputy Sergeant Edwin Harris, also known—or mostly known—as "Tiny," emerged from the car; his six-foot-two-inch frame carried 275 pounds of massive muscles with a thick waist and barrel chest. He was an imposing figure under any circumstances, but add the cement gray uniform, badge, and gun belt with the 9mm Glock holstered at his side and he became a titan. Scanning the usual congregation of local crackers, "porch pundits," an exclusive all-men group of provincial philosophers and local gossips, Tiny made his way toward the stairs. The yellow bristle of hair on top of his blocklike head seemed to glow like embers in the rays of the setting sun, which backlit the colossal cop as he lumbered toward the porch. He wondered if he should ask old Harold Sasser what he knew about the report of child neglect leveled at the store's owners, Bud and Mildred Crayton, but he dismissed the notion and settled for a nod at the men and a curt. "Gentlemen."

Tiny spotted Bud almost immediately as he walked into the store. The lighting inside was dim by supermarket and modern convenience store standards. This market had the usual coolers lining one wall, filled mostly with beer but with a couple of shelves relegated to soft drinks and one for milk and dairy. The coolers were old, and the glass smudged. There was a dinginess to the atmosphere; rows of molding old shelves, arrayed with a variety of canned and packaged goods, as well as lots of candy and chips, stood too close together in the dim light. The smell of mint mingled with the musty odor of age. A distinguishing feature of Bud's market was the meat counter in the back, where you could buy just about any kind of meat that walked (or swam) with four legs. Although illegal, Tiny knew poached alligator tail was a house specialty. Bud, a crusty man with red hair going gray, was behind the register to the right as one walked in, ringing up a sale for a twelve-pack of Busch Lite. Bud spit a wad of mint Skoal chewing tobacco into a coffee can after completing his sale. The customer, a squirrelly old coot wearing a beat-up Marlins baseball cap, gave Tiny a frightened glance as he scampered out the door.

"Bud, Bud, Bud. How you doin', *Bud-dy*?" Tiny boomed. With a broad smile stretching his lips, he approached the register. He was trying to figure how to exploit this potential opportunity to enrich himself by adding another tribute payer to his little fiefdom. He felt a little irritated for not knowing about this situation before it was reported and the months of revenue he had most likely missed. Now there existed a child abuse offense, reported by another deputy no less, and the delicate and irritating cover-up process that would have to ensue. Oh well, no use playing with a spent pud.

"I'm not going to mince words, Mr. Crayton." Tiny's voice assumed an official police business tone. "There's been a report of child neglect, and I'm here to investigate until child welfare can look into the case." *Which will be never*, Tiny thought. "Where are your three children right now?" Tiny pulled a small black notebook from a pouch on his belt and squinted at a page. "Says here you have a boy age nine, a boy age seven, and a girl age four."

Bud's leathery narrow face scrunched up in fear underlaced with malice. His eyes darted and glinted with a coyote's cunning. "It's awl lies and foolishness," he said. His accent was a unique Southern drawl from a rural part of southern Florida, an accent so severe most Northerners could grasp a mere fraction of what he said. "They're with the wife, probably getting their dinner fixed right now." This sounded more like "Thar weeda wyfe, probly gettin' thar deener feexit rhyet nahw."

"Let's go have us a look, see what's cookin', hmm?" Tiny smiled and raised his almost-invisible blonde eyebrows. The overhead light reflected from the shaved sides of his large noggin, but somehow, it made his thick flattop of blonde hair look dirty. His head seemed to sit neckless on his broad shoulders as he nodded it toward the back of the store. There was a door behind the meat counter leading to the living quarters.

"Now y'awl wait just a minute thar, Mr. Dep-uty, sir," Bud said in his cracker accent; his lips made a defensive pucker, the scorn in his tone cut like a rasp. "Don't y'awl need a warrant or somethin'? I mean, y'awl can't come in here with accusations and go a bustin' into my home!"

"I'll show you a warrant," Tiny said, grabbing Bud's puny bicep with a massive paw and squeezing it *hard*.

"Ow!" Bud squeaked and tried to pull away, but Tiny dragged him like a recalcitrant puppy toward the meat counter and the door at the back of the store.

Josh, age nine, cringed like a beaten dog at the sound of his father's voice yelling and coming closer. He was thirty-five pounds, all skin and bones, with hollow cheeks and wispy light brown hair. He wore only a pair of filthy, ragged shorts. There were red sores on his back, chest, arms, and legs. He wore a dog collar around his neck with a chain and padlock attached. He was in a small antechamber between the store and the living quarters of the house. The other end of the chain was locked to a bar running beneath a bloodstained bench where Bud Crayton did his butchering. He had peed his pants again because he was unable to hold the flow back. The sky beyond the small grimy window had gone almost dark. He had been chained here with his younger brother, Kevin, age seven, and his sister, Alice, age four, since the early morning. Just after awaking, his screaming mother, Mildred Crayton, beat him with her husband's belt, buckle side to the flesh, because he was "whinin' like a whelp" for an apple. "You brats will learn grad-itude and o-bedience," she snarled. Fact was all three of the kids had eaten only a small bowl of cold oatmeal each since yesterday morning and didn't have the energy to whimper, let alone be rebellious. Yesterday, while grabbing at a scrap that had fallen from the butcher table as Bud cut meat, Josh had received the bottom of his father's boot on his fingers for his trouble. When he yipped in pain, Bud put the toe of his boot to work on Josh's rib cage. It wasn't hard to see his ribs either as they protruded through his taut skin.

His younger brother and sister were chained together in a similar manner to the other end of the bench. Neither his brother, Kevin, nor his sister, Alice, weighed better than twenty pounds on a good day. They hardly had the energy to breathe or lift an eyelash. They were in the final stages of terminal starvation. Josh sensed this and knew he was not far behind. He fared slightly better than them by developing a feral cunning that provided him with a few more calories than the other two, allowing his brain to still function—somewhat. His thinking was muddied and sluggish, however, and a physical malaise had taken over. Soon, very soon, he would join Kevin and Alice in a death-presaging stupor. Even now, flies landed on the open sores of the two starving and abused siblings, infusing them with the maggots that would accompany them to death's dooryard.

Yesterday, a policeman had seen him. Or was it the day before. He couldn't remember. Mildred had left the front door of the house open a few minutes; and contriving to worm his way around furniture without being spotted, he was able to stand out in the sunlight squinting, just as a sheriff's patrol car passed. The red-and-blue lights on top of the car came on, and it pulled to the side of the road. A man in a gray uniform with a badge got out and looked at him. His mother came out, grabbed him by the arm, and yanked him back into the cavernous house. Josh didn't know much about the workings of the world, but maybe there was some hope the man in the car would come back and help him and his brother and sister. He vaguely remembered something he heard when he caught a glimpse of morning TV about uniformed men called "policemen" helping little kids. Neither Josh nor his siblings had ever attended school or been out of the house for that matter. Sometimes, his parents left for short periods, but the children were chained to the butcher's bench, with a cup of water each.

During such intervals, Josh led brave discussions about escape. He told them about how they would steal a boat and go down the canal they could glimpse through the back window until they came to where a beautiful lady in a white dress lived. She would take them in and feed them all the bread, meat, fruit, and sweet cakes they could hold. They would go to bed in a clean room with no spiders and black ugly bugs that bite you in the night. Maybe, everything would be all right if the man in uniform came back to help.

As if in answer to the child's unspoken prayer, the door swung open, and a very large man in the same uniform strode into the room with Josh's father firmly in tow. Josh sucked in air as his heart raced in new hope. Surely he and his brother and sister would be saved by the compassion of an outside world, represented by the imposing and portentous presence of this lawman. Salvation had at last arrived!

Tiny grabbed the door handle and twisted it. The unlocked door pushed open into the meat-cutting room. Tiny began to cross the room, dragging Bud to the door opposite, which provided entry to the house part of the building. He caught a movement out of the corner of his eye to the left at floor level. He stopped and looked down at Josh, over at Kevin, and finally, at his emaciated sister, Alice. At first, he could only stare in amazement. He had witnessed many acts of neglect and abuse in the past nineteen years in this slop pot of a town, but this had to be one of the worst. Yet no sense of indignation or moral outrage stirred in the massive deputy's heart. This was merely another opportunity, which, if played correctly, would bring more illicit dollars into his personal coffers.

"What have we here?" Tiny shook his enormous head sadly and clucked in disapproval for appearance's sake as he let go of Bud's arm. Mocking Bud's accent, he said, "Looks lyk sam miss-traited yunguns." Tiny walked over and looked at Josh, shaking his head. He cast a look over at Kevin and Alice, still shaking his block of a noggin. "I'd say from the looks of 'um, you and your wife will be spendin' most of the rest of your sorry lives cuttin' meat at the state prison in Raiford. Most folks just a' soon see ya'll fed to the gators."

"Deputy, listen here, we didn't mean no harm," Bud said. "I heared y'awl could be a reasonable man. Ain't there someway to help the kids here and yourself too in the bargain?"

Tiny pursed his lips and scrunched up his face. "Problem is, this is something that's already been broadcasted on the police radio. I'm the investigating officer, and I'll have to file a report." Tiny took a moment to look at the children, still shaking his head. He stared directly at Bud. "Tell you what, pardner, you promise to get some chow into these rug rats, and I don't care if it's dog food, long as they put on a few pounds, and I'll report the kids are OK."

Bud's face lit up, and a smile began to appear between his stubbly lips.

"Naturally, there is the matter of my 'fixin' fee," added Tiny. The smile faded from Bud's lips, and his face took on a prunelike worried countenance.

"Fee? How much y'awl talkin', Tiny?" Bud used the deputy's nickname and moved a little closer in a conspiratorial huddle. "I reckon we can find somethin' for yer help."

"Well now"—Tiny rubbed his chin with thumb and index finger—"I figure a case this dire, where it's already been reported and all, is gonna run a minimum of 10K, *Bud-dy*."

"Ya'll mean ten thousan' dollars!" Bud gasped.

"Yup. 'Course you can pay in installments. Say, a thousand a month, startin' tomorrow—same time as now. If you don't have the money, you lose the kids, the store, the house, and you go to jail to boot. Fact is, I got to arrest you tomorrow night if there ain't the green in your miserly hand. And by the way, your ugly wife will be charged with a crime as well. You go talk to her and make up your mind. I got business elsewhere right now."

Bud stood stupefied, his mouth working at inarticulate sounds as the deputy left the room. He turned and looked malevolently at the cause of all his problems, Josh. He snarled and walked over and gave the cringing youngster a hard kick to the stomach before going into the house to give his wife the bad news. They would have to scheme on ways to hoodwink the deputy out of the money.

The hulking sheriff passed through the store and out the screen door to the porch. The chattering came to a sudden halt, and the only sound was the *whoosh* of the passing traffic. Tiny eyed Harold Sasser and asked with a grin, "Played any cards lately, Harry?" Harold was visibly flustered, which greatly amused Tiny.

"Of course not, Deputy. Don't do any gamblin' now days."

"That right?" Tiny raised his brows in mock surprise and nodded once in feigned approval. "Stay well." He went down the stairs to his cruiser.

Once on the road, he mulled over the incident in his mind, turning it this way and that, trying to get a perspective on all the angles. Certainly that weasel Bud and his scumbag wife would try some bullshit to not pay their dues. They would soon learn the folly of crossing him. Still, when all was said and done, they would pay. And he could be almost certain they would have his grand tomorrow. He could use some of that moola to buy something special for his recalcitrant little love bug, Mona. Lately, she was a regular toothache with her whining and complaining. If she wasn't such a sweet young dish, he'd dump her back into the hands of that drug-lovin' Haitian whoremonger Andre. Let him farm her out to the migrants to feed his heroin habit. Speaking of dope, he was overdue for his protection money from Carlos and his sidekick Omar out at Rainbow Pines, or in his vernacular, "Pissed on Pines" Trailer Park. Of course, there was Captain Post and his mismanaged gambling racket. Not to mention the county commissioner, Constance Valentine, a real pain in the ass with her unquenchable thirst for Hispanic boys. Still, she was rich, filthy rich, with all that under-the-table developers' money. There were hundreds of thousands in offshore accounts that needed constant trimming by yours truly. And Judge Thomas, with his sweet tooth for underage girls, was a necessary, if not distasteful, chore in his portfolio of shakedowns. Tiny didn't mess much with the big boss, the high sheriff of Baron County, John Gunther. Then again, he left Tiny alone as well, even covered up for him. "Knowledge is power" was his high school slogan, but they left out the money part. Peeking into closets and exploiting what he found was Tiny's area of expertise, and the top cop liked his drink and women. Who didn't? But the really big fish was Rooster Babcock out at the Red Rooster Ranch. "Insuring" his operation was going to be more lucrative than all the others combined once he had his bumbling captain on board. Yeah, his plate was full all right, and soon, his offshore accounts would be as well.

2

About a mile south of downtown Bella Villa on State Road 28, Carlos put on his left blinker and steered his beat-up '79 Ford pickup into the parking lot of the Fireproof Motel. An ancient neon arrow with the letters spelling the name pointed at a relic of fifties Florida motel architecture. It looked as if the single story L-shaped block structure with severely faded pink paint was being swallowed by the encroaching swampland. Saw palmetto, bottle palms, date palms, and screw pine palms testifying to south Florida's benign winters were scattered in the courtyard. Both Carlos and his passenger, Omar, looked exhausted and a little hungover. They wanted to do their business and depart pronto. They likedl the motley group of gringos who had taken up residence here, but after last night's escapade with fire, they had no appetite for socializing, especially with folks who didn't speak much Spanish. Carlos spoke enough English to get by. Omar spoke even less.

"Ah, bueno," said Carlos. "He's here." Carlos pointed to a man in khaki shorts with his walnut-colored hair in a ponytail. Jamie Dorr was in his late thirties and healthy looking with a glowing tan face. Already twice divorced with a child by each woman, he decided to come out of the closet while living in Burlington, Vermont. Soon after, he moved into an apartment with a male lover of twenty. They had a hot and intoxicating relationship for six months before deciding to nest in Southwest Florida. Following a turbulent year in which his boyfriend twice beat up on him after they had both indulged in too much boozing, Jamie called it quits and moved into this motel. He met the owner, Morris, at the interior design shop where he worked. The genteel old-timer wanted to give his motel suite a Southwestern motif. At that time, Jamie mostly delivered supplies to contractors in the dozens of swank country clubs that abounded in Southwest Florida. Jamie waved and smiled broadly at the two Mexicans. They pulled into a nearby parking slot.

"Buenas dias, amigos," Jamie said. He stuck out his hand and shook each of theirs as they got out of the truck. "Come inside."

"Uno momento," said Carlos. He walked back to the truck, grabbed a gym bag from behind the seat, and followed Omar and Jamie through the open door.

The interior was a single room with a double bed to the right of the doorway in the middle of the room. An air conditioner hummed noisily from the window frame. The obligatory TV sat on a counter at the center of the opposite wall. A boom box also sat on the counter next to a picture of Jamie's son and daughter. An easy chair on the left side of the bed faced the TV, and a small table with two simple padded straightback chairs was to the right of the bed. A narrow bookcase with three shelves crammed with horror and mystery novels occupied a niche in the wall by the table. Another table, with a shelf, adjacent to the TV, held a small microwave oven and a one-burner hot plate. Under the shelf was a small refrigerator with a dozen small handmade Mayan Indian doll magnets. An oil painting of a volcano near Antigua Guatemala hung above the bed. A poster over the microwave featured two hunky men in Speedos walking on the beach, holding hands with the slogan COME OUT at the bottom. A doorway across from the microwave led to a cramped bathroom.

"So, amigos, how are things?" asked Jamie.

Carlos yawned and, in heavily accented English, replied, "Not so good, Hymie. That loco sheriff ees much trouble for us. We are scared for our *familias*, our childrens."

"Yeah, he could pose a real problem," Jamie agreed. "I don't think he's on to me yet. After this deal, we should kick back a month or two and see what's shakin'."

"Tal vez," replied Carlos, "maybe." He didn't dare mention to his gringo business friend that the monster Tiny was already extorting money—half of their profits—to keep them from getting busted and was likely to take a dim view of any curtailing of sales.

"OK," Jamie said, becoming animated. "Let's see what you brought me this time. Bring the bag over to the table here."

"Bueno," said Carlos as he put the bag on the table and opened it.

Jamie reached in and pulled out a sample. He sniffed deeply. "Ahh," he sighed, "*primo* bud."

Morris Kline bought the Fireproof Motel in the late seventies with the intention of fixing it up and retiring after selling it for a hefty profit. As it turned out, the company he worked for in Connecticut for thirty-two years went belly-up after a half dozen of the top executives borrowed it into bankruptcy. However, these same top dogs managed to sell their stock and to pilfer through "forgiven" loans, tens of millions of dollars apiece, before any mention of financial problems hit the media. They exited the stage with golden parachutes letting them down in the courtyards of their gingerbread multi-million-dollar Florida mansions. Morris, on the other hand, was left with nothing but his heavily mortgaged house and the motel in Florida. So he sold the house, took what little cash was left, and moved to Florida with his wife of fifty years, Ida. He had a small two-bedroom cottage built on land adjacent to the motel for them to live in while they oversaw day-to-day operations.

For Morris, now seventy-seven years old, a life of daily routine and exercise kept him physically, mentally, and emotionally steady. Every morning, he would awake and proceed to the kitchen where he pulled the blinds to let in the sunshine. Next came his twenty-minute morning bicycle ride followed by breakfast with his wife, usually cereal with bananas, and the newspaper. Afterward, he was off to visit with his cronies on Harry Sasser's lanai about twenty minutes west. They all drove together another twenty minutes to the beach for an hour-or-so walk before returning to Harry's for ice tea and more gossip. At twelve thirty, Morris took his leave and would return home for lunch, usually borsch and crackers. After lunch, he would read the paper some more and nap. Often, he and Ida would go to the pool down the street at his brother-in-law's condo. Afterward, supper out at a local family restaurant or, perhaps, a drive to a favorite Napolis eatery like Mel's diner. The evening was spent in front of the telly. Starting with network news and *Wheel of Fortune*, Morris would go on to spend the night watching every news magazine or crime show on the lower channels. Jay Leno was the late-night choice on the bedroom TV before sleep.

Morris paid little attention to his guests as long as their rents were paid on time. That is not to say he didn't like most of them or care about them. After all, most had been here for a couple of years now, like Jamie Dorr. It's just that he really didn't care to get involved too deeply in their respective lives. He suspected Jamie might be smoking some of what he and his buddies called "wacky tabbacky." But as long as they didn't bother anyone, why should he care? Be friendly, and don't ask about what you don't want to know. That suited him just fine.

On the other hand, if Jamie was involved more heavily, say selling the stuff, wouldn't that have implications for him and the motel? Morris didn't particularly care to see the Mexicans in their beat-up old truck stopping by. Today, at the insistence of his wife, who claimed a deputy had been stopping in the dooryard, he opted to forgo his morning constitutional with his pals in order to see if the sheriff's department was watching the motel. "That sheriff got out of the car for a minute or two," she said. "He was a *very* large and scary-looking man." He sounded like the same deputy Harry had told him about, a potentially very dangerous man to have poking around in your sphere. No, Morris didn't like the "vibe" as Camilla called it—not a bit.

Camilla Valentine and her husband, Robert, lived in the only two-room suite in the motel. They had a one-year-old baby boy named William who they called "Billy." Camilla's mother was Mexican, but her father was an American who spent a lot of time playing and surfing on the Mexican coast. He was fond of reefer and Mexican beer. He met Camilla's mom in a bar in Puerto Vallarta. A year later, they were married, and Camilla was born. She looked mostly like her mother, thick dark hair and light coffee-colored skin, but had her father's green eyes. She grew up in a "hip" surfer subculture. She was well-educated although most of it was self-taught. While not part of any identifiable clique, she and her husband both were "deadhead" kind of people. Robbie, especially, loved his weed and liked to trip a lot. Since becoming pregnant and caring for an infant, Camilla didn't have much inclination to get bombed.

Camilla was outside weeding her vegetable and herb garden when she saw the sheriff's patrol car pull up. Her garden took up a little more than a 150 square feet of what posed for lawn area in the center of the motel's U-shaped driveway. She stopped working for a moment to gaze at the car, thinking it was just a deputy turning around in the motel's driveway. It wouldn't be the first time. But this particular squad car was being operated by one Sergeant Edwin Harris, a.k.a Tiny, no ordinary patrolman.

Tiny got out of the car for a moment and scanned the motel. He was wearing a black tee shirt and dungarees. A sheriff's star was on his belt as was his 9mm Glock handgun. For a long moment, he fixed on Jamie's room. His appraising gaze soon found Camilla where she knelt, trying to blend into the landscape. A chill skittered mouselike down her spine, raising goose bumps where its tiny feet touched flesh. This man had an aura that was bloodred. An almost-palpable malevolence shone from his eyes as they were unmasked from dark sunglasses. A fleeting smirk distorted his face as he put his sunglasses on and got back into the cruiser. Blue-and-red lights flashed as if to mock her, and the car was gone.

Camilla went back to her apartment to tell Robert about the cop with the red aura. He was on the bed with Billy on his lap watching cartoons. Robbie had thick shoulder-length blonde hair and a wispy goatee, a handsome face with large blue eyes, and a nice smile with dimples. He was short, about five six, with a stocky muscular build. Billy, almost a year old, was a smaller version of his father, except with his mother's dark hair. He was sucking on a baby bottle with juice in it and pointing at the TV. They looked so sweet together. Maybe she shouldn't say anything to disturb the mood. If only Robbie would get a job, a real job, she almost reflexively started to think, they wouldn't be so dependent on his crazy mother, who happened to be a very prominent and wealthy local figure. She was one of three Baron County commissioners. What jobs Robert did get were usually bones thrown to him by his mother. Robert didn't like any job that lasted more than a month or two. "Don't want to get tied down, have to answer to some jerk of a boss," he said. "Those rich capitalists live on the blood of the working man. All their money and power comes by riding on our backs. I don't want to be somebody's mule the rest of my life."

Camilla often wondered what he did want to be. They certainly couldn't live forever on scraps from his mother. Camilla knew she would be the one going to work, and soon. They needed to get a decent car first. If only Robert would approach his mother on this subject, as much as his mother disapproved of their lifestyle, she would surely help with a car. Robert's father's Mercedes and his VW convertible were sitting around unused. Constance preferred the comfort of her Lexus. Robert's father was almost two years dead now. He was old when Robert was born, almost sixty. His second wife, Constance, was more than twenty-five years younger than him, just over thirty, when they got married. Now in her early fifties, she was often in the company of important men, usually many years younger. Camilla also suspected Mrs. Valentine of cradle-robbing young Mexican boys.

There was a time, about six months ago, she and Robert went to the house unannounced on the pretext of bringing the baby for a visit, but really for Robbie to get a handout. The smell of bread toasting lured Camilla to the kitchen. There was a gorgeous Mexican stud, about sixteen or seventeen, without shirt or shoes on, drinking coffee and eating toast. He flashed a mischievous yet charming smile at her. Later, Constance told Camilla the lad was helping the gardener, and she felt sorry for him because he brought nothing to eat, so she let him help himself to some coffee and bread. Call it women's intuition or anything you want, Camilla wasn't buying the story.

"Robbie," Camilla said, "a sheriff's car just pulled into the driveway, and a big guy got out and was looking at the motel." She left out the aura observation.

"Yeah? So?"

"I don't know . . . he just made me feel creepy," she said.

"Was he built like Arnold Schwarzenegger, only bigger, and have blonde hair with a dorky flattop?"

"That's him," she said.

"Uhh . . . ohh."

Morris saw the squad car pull into the driveway. By the time he got to the small vestibule serving as office and put on his Velcro tied sneakers and opened the door, the car was pulling onto the highway, blue lights flashing in the rear window. This ruffled the old man's feathers enough for him to make a point of going over to see the Valentines. He noticed Camilla leaving her small garden patch. He waved at her and flashed his most charming seventy-year-old smile. He liked Camilla quite a bit. But she didn't see him. She was returning to her suite with a frown, concentrating on some disturbing thought. He opened his mouth to shout a greeting but decided to just hoof it over to Jamie's room and ask him if he was having any trouble with the law. It was only at that moment he noticed the old Ford pickup in the driveway outside the room. Funny, he didn't see it until now. It must be those Mexicans he suspects were involved with drugs. He hesitated a moment, suddenly unsure of himself, and decided to go see Jamie after they left. His stomach rumbled irritably, and he belched banana into the Florida morning.

"Dios mió!" gasped Omar. "Look!" He had the curtains pulled slightly apart and was pointing out the window. Carlos and Jamie took a peek just as Tiny was getting back into the car. Jamie pulled the curtains together as the blue lights winked at him. He broke out in a cold sweat, moisture coating his forehead and temples in a light dew.

"That's one ugly son of a bitch," he whispered.

Toad, who was still drunk from the night before, but up for a little hair of the dog, opened the door of unit number 108 just in time to see the farewell blue flash as Tiny left the motel. "Pigs are onto somebody," he mumbled to himself and took a swig from his half-gallon bottle of Popov, now only two fingers full.

A Vietnam veteran on partial disability for posttraumatic stress disorder, Toad was a professional drunk. And he took pride in his profession. He did take leaves of absence, however, to sample some of the sober life. In these interims, he read profusely and was a fountain of knowledge on every conceivable subject. These reading jags provided fodder to blather on about when lit. He could go on for hours on any topic, repeating his points over and over once the alcohol overtook the senses. But of his army service, there was one thing no one doubted, he was no stranger to the killing fields.

Toad came to Florida from Maine, by way of Alabama, Mississippi, and Georgia, with his buddy, Brian Sutter. They were planting trees way out on paper company clear-cuts, camping with the other planters at different sites in a variety of rigs. Some had fancy trailers or RVs, but most had just vans, while others were in tents. Brian had a van converted to a camper he and Toad shared. Most days, the planters would assemble just after sunrise, packing the saddle bags they carried on their backs full with loblolly pines, plunking them in the ground with a long-handled tool called a hoedad—a tool resembling an adz. They would swing the hoedad over their heads and "plunk," make a divot, put a seedling in the ground, stomp the earth around it, and move on. They were paid two to four cents per tree planted, so everyone hustled. This went on all day, resulting in each planter putting in many thousand trees. Sometimes, Toad just hung back and buried a few hundred trees, had a smoke, and went back to the bundles to resupply his bags.

The weather had come off bitter cold the last winter; even as far south as they were, the bare ground was frozen solid. It had been that way for a week, and the planters were getting extremely restless. One afternoon, after getting paid for the previous week (paychecks came at infrequent intervals), they lit out for town to get some supplies and just kept going. Toad wanted amphetamines, so they went to Macon, Georgia. They scored a few crummy diet pills from a dude who claimed to be part of the Allman Brothers' entourage. From there, they went to Jacksonville, Florida, and Daytona Beach. They headed to Fort Lauderdale but decided to turn west and cross "Alligator Alley," U.S. 75. In ten days, they were broke. By chance, they stumbled onto the Fireproof Motel just as the last of their money was spent. Brian lucked into a roofing job in one day, and Toad had his eight-hundred-dollar-a-month disability check forwarded down. They both rented their own room by the week and decided to stay put. After all, everything Toad needed was right here, including a dope dealer next door and half a dozen liquor stores within fifteen sun-filled minutes of his cozy foxhole.

After another mini swig of vodka, Toad sat down and rolled a cigarette out of a package of Bugler rolling tobacco. He clicked a Bic, lit the ragged end, and inhaled deeply. First thing he should do, he figured, is go over to Jamie's and see if he had any weed. If so, he better buy some right off in case Jamie boy got busted. He might need a stash to tide him over a potential dry spell. If Jamie didn't know about the pig stoppin' by, he would inform him. Toad poured a shot of the booze into his coffee cup, took a last drag from his butt, and watched as Carlos and Omar got into their truck to leave. "Rut roo, rig rubble," he said, imitating cartoon characters.

Brian Sutter, Toad's tree-planting partner, was shingling a roof on Flamevine Circle, a street in a middle-class part of Bella Villa, about the time Tiny pulled out of the motel driveway. It was the same kind of neighborhood he grew up in but much farther north—Coventry, Rhode Island, to be exact. He was the only child of a single mom; he never met his father, but there was a regular parade of stepfathers to abuse him. He was lean and muscular and stood five feet eleven inches. With his coal-colored black hair and azure eyes, he had the same kind of handsome and compelling appearance many young soap stars did. True, he was going on twenty-six, but he could pass for twenty with his smooth boyish face. He made it through a year at the University of Maine in Orono before deciding college wasn't his thing. He did meet a lot of interesting people there, however, including Toad.

Brian's real passion was his painting, especially the watercolors. Jamie liked his artwork a lot, saying he should try to sell some at the flea market. Brian didn't think it would go too well in Napolis where the taste was for the traditional landscape and seascape kind of stuff. His work was kind of abstract. Still, one of those dizzy rich dames might shell out a hundred clams for one of his paintings, if he was real friendly. Jamie said he had charm, lots of it, and a real sweet and winning face. Of course, Jamie might say something like that just to get naked with him, but he did think of himself as pretty good-looking. Anyway, a hundred bucks was pocket change to a lot of those gals, or guys for that matter.

Brian was half-done shingling the roof and hoped to finish today so he could get paid. His boss usually paid him by the job, but only when it was finished. There was the matter of a new master brake cylinder for his van to attend to. Besides, the food-and-beer money was running real low. If all went well, he could go see Jamie tonight and score some bud. He liked to get a buzz on with the weed once in a while. He wasn't like his crazy buddy, Toad, who smoked, drank, and ate anything that got you fucked up. At least not *yet*. Although, he must admit, he drank far too much. Standing up to stretch a moment, he glanced at the road and noticed a sheriff's patrol car creeping by, the markings on the Crown Victoria unmistakable, despite the lack of bubbles on top.

Tiny drove down Highway 28 about half a mile after he left the motel and pulled off on a gravel road to the right. There was an old barn near the road that would provide cover for him while he waited for the Mexicans' old pickup to come by. They had to come this way to get to the other side of town where their dump of a trailer park was. He didn't know if they saw him or not but guessed it wouldn't make much of a difference. They were supposed to meet him tonight when he was officially on duty. He didn't think they'd expect him to stop them in broad daylight when he was supposed to be off duty. He admitted it was a bit risky, but he had to find out for sure if the clown at the motel was selling drugs. If he was, it meant they were holding out on him. That was something he would *not* tolerate.

About fifteen minutes later, the Ford pickup carrying Carlos and Omar rumbled by. Tiny slammed the cruiser into gear and flew after them, lights flashing. Carlos caught sight of the blue-and-red flashing lights. "Sheet!" he blurted.

The truck pulled over, and Tiny parked behind it. He didn't bother to radio this one in. He got out of the car and walked up to the driver's window. "Buenas dias, amigos," he said, grinning. "How are the taco twins today?"

Carlos began to perspire, a sheen of moisture appeared over his eyes. In an instant, sweat drenched his shirt and dripped down from his temples. Mopping his forehead with a handkerchief, his stomach twisting in knots, he smiled and replied, "Buenas, Señor Tiny."

"Guess you boys know about the fire out on the east side of town last night. It appears to have been an illegal gambling place. Fire marshal says it was arson. Good job of it too. But mostly, what I want to know is what you boys were doin' back at the motel."

"We visit our amigo, señor." Carlos did the talking, as always.

"And what amigo would that be, pray tell?"

Carlos looked at Omar then shrugged. "Hymie."

"Hymie? Who the fuck is Hymie?"

"Only an amigo." Carlos was trembling; he felt the pressure in his bladder.

"Okay, okay, get out of the truck!" Tiny dropped all pretense of being on official police business. "I want to look behind the seat." He opened the door and grabbed Carlos by the arm and yanked him out of the seat. He pushed him past the front of the door. "Get your hands on the hood, head down. Don't move. You too, shit face!" he yelled at Omar, who was already half-out of the truck. He went to the driver's door and reached behind the seat where he found a plastic bag from Publix Supermarket. Inside the bag was a wad of hundreds, fifties, and twenties. Tiny estimated there was over three thousand dollars. He took three hundred dollar bills and put them in his front pants' pocket. He didn't want to take too much because he wanted to make sure they brought enough of the capital back to their supplier to reinvest and make more money for him. Tonight, he would find out who their main man was. Now, he needed to be on his way in case a road patrol passed. He didn't feel like making up any stories to satisfy the curiosity of his fellow deputies. He put the bag back behind the seat.

"You boys can get back in and go. You try to hold out on me, again, and you won't have to worry about going to jail, you will be talking directly to Saint Peter. *Comprende?*"

Both men nodded and eased back into the truck.

"By the way, good job last night. I'm recommending you both for promotion." Snickering like a preteen who just farted, Tiny returned to his patrol car.

Neither Tommy Nelson nor Julie Moore, resident musicians, saw or heard anything on the morning Deputy Harris pulled into the driveway. They were sound asleep in each other's arms. Having played a gig at the casino about two miles from the motel; it was after three in the morning when they hit the hay. Later that morning, they were to brunch with Camilla and Robert Valentine at the First Watch in Napolis, so they set their alarm for ten thirty in the morning. Tommy got up to pee just before the alarm sounded, so he shut it down. Thick copper-colored hair, cropped in a ragged mop, framed his round and joyful face. No sense waking Julie with an obnoxious buzzing when he could let his fingers do the waking, with pleasure for both of them. There was only the faintest of hangovers misting his senses this morning. Last night was a light booze performance and a particularly good one. He drained his radiator, flushed the toilet, and snuggled back into bed, arms around Julie's slender waist. He began gently rubbing her tummy. "Eez time to geet up," he said, doing his imitation of Spanglish.

"Umm, I know," Julie purred. "Just a few more minutes." She turned toward him, her long blonde hair covering her sweet elfish face.

"I'll give you a few more minutes, all right, while I molest you." Tommy's hand slipped down from her belly to the curly thatch below.

"Oh, you bad, bad man," Julie purred. "Umm, I'm going to molest you right back." And she reached between his thighs for a handful of his manhood. A mock evil smile revealed straight chalk white teeth. "See, you're not so tough." Tommy moaned with pleasure.

Special Agent Mike Nolan pulled into the Fireproof's driveway around lunchtime of the same day Tiny paid his most recent visit. Morris and Ida were just finishing their borsht with dollops of low-fat sour cream. They were discussing whether to have fruit and Graham crackers for dessert or maybe some chocolate chip cookies. The federal cop surveyed the scene standing by his ten-year-old LeBaron convertible, preserved in near-mint condition. Nolan had studied surveillance photos of the motel, but this was his first visit. He was an undercover officer with the joint federal, state, and county drug enforcement task force; but technically, he worked for the feds in the DEA. A robust man of thirty-two, he stood almost six feet and weighed 180 hard and ready pounds. He was an ex-Navy SEAL with a black belt in karate. His training made him a formidable adversary with half a dozen major busts in the last three years.

He already knew the two Mexicans, Carlos and Omar, were doing some pot dealing with the guy named Jamie who lived here. He was after bigger fish. Still, he had to start somewhere, and this was as good a place as any. Nolan figured he'd check in here and stay awhile. Dressed in dungarees and a Quicksilver tee shirt with longish brown hair the color of aged oak and a headband, he looked like just another workingman or, perhaps, a low-budget tourist. He walked up to the Kline's cottage, which had a sign in red letters designating it as the OFFICE. He rang the bell.

Rising with a mumbled protest, Morris went to the door. Opening the door, he faced Mike Nolan, who stood in the sunlight, an infectious smile dimpling his cheeks.

"Good morning, I'm looking for a room. The sign said this was the office."

"That's right," said Morris, grinning a little despite himself. "You got your man."

"Do you have anything available? The vacancy sign is out."

"Yes, we have a room available. How long will you be staying?"

"I really don't know to be honest. I'm in between jobs right now but have some good prospects over in Napolis. I just can't afford to stay there. Everything, even a sleeping room, is exorbitant. But I can pay you a week in advance, providing it's reasonable, and we can go from there."

"We get thirty dollars a night, but the price is one fifty for a week," said Morris. "If you're staying a month or more and we do have some longtime guests [glossing over the fact he had *all* longtime guests] we bring that down to one twenty."

"Sounds good to me," said Nolan. Fishing in his pocket, he brought out exactly one hundred and fifty dollars in fifties. Having done his homework, he already knew the price.

Morris raised his gray eyebrows with an "ain't that some coincidence" expression.

"Seems like you have the exact change, minus several kinds of taxes, which comes to ten dollars more."

Nolan looked a little chagrined. He forgot about the money that paid his salary, or maybe he just didn't think a shit-for-sheets operation like this would even bother with taxes. "Sure thing," he said, fishing in his other pocket. He pulled out a money clip and peeled off a ten.

"OK," said Morris, "let me show you your room, and I'll bring over your receipt." Morris reached inside the door and pulled a key from a row of hooks just inside. "I'm givin' you the end unit so you can have a little privacy. There's a small refrigerator and microwave in the room, as well as a telephone for local calls. You'll need a calling card for long distance. We have cable with HBO. I get HBO so I can watch *The Sopranos*. Ida, that's my wife, she don't care much for it, but I like a good crime story. I'll bring fresh towels and a change of linens with your receipt. We provide maid service on Friday mornings for our weekly guests. More than that, you got to pay our housekeeper to come in. Her name is Camilla. She happens to live over in unit 105." Morris nodded in the direction of Toad, who was snoozing in the chair on the porch outside his door. "That's Toad. He's a full-time resident here. Don't do much but drink as far as I can tell, but he hasn't caused us any trouble *yet*." They had arrived at the door, and Morris opened it. "You want to look at the one next door?"

"No," Nolan replied, "this'll do just fine."

Tiny drove his cruiser in the warm Florida afternoon sun to the Bella Villa sheriff's headquarters. An eight-foot alligator sunning itself on the banks of the canal to his right scrambled back into the water as if startled by something or, perhaps, spotting a meal nearby. The herculean deputy's first order of business when he came on duty at three this afternoon was to have a private tête-à-tête with his shit-for-brains captain. His bungling and inept handling of the illegal gambling racket was threatening to bust open all his other operations. Problem was, the captain had a gambling addiction himself, which compromised his ability to manage the accounts. Now, Tiny was forced to step in and help the dumb critter out like his operation last night with burning down the house. Much more of those kinds of tactics could bring the heat right back at them. Tiny pulled his cruiser into one of the Sheriff Only parking slots outside the double wide modular building that served as the Bella Villa Division Headquarters of the Baron County Sheriffs' Department. He squeezed his large bulk through the front door.

"Afternoon, Maria," Tiny greeted Maria Chavez with his finest smile. Maria was the second-shift dispatcher, a fine-looking Mexican with a full bosom inside her deputy uniform.

"Hey, Sergeant. What's new?"

"Same old, same old. Is the captain in?"

"Unless he sneaked into the bathroom to smoke crack, he should be slavin' away in his office." Maria was quite the jokester.

"Knowin' the captain, I should check the men's room first," said Tiny, "or maybe see if he snuck out to the casino." Maria chuckled, shaking her head while returning to business. He knocked on the door with a small plaque inscribed CAPTAIN POST.

"Come in," a muffled voice responded.

Tiny walked into the crowded office, the size of a master bedroom in an average home but crowded with filing cabinets and tables overflowing with paperwork. The captain's desk was relatively clean. Benjamin Post, an African American around fifty, resembling Morgan Freeman, the actor, with flecks of white in his natty hair and bifocals, looked at Tiny over the tops of his glasses. "Well, Sergeant, what do you have going today?"

"Apparently, Captain, that arson case last night was a card and craps house. I'll be interviewing the owner within the hour. I'd like a warrant in case I need one to search his house."

"Already done," replied the captain, shoving a folded paper across the desk. "Compliments of Judge Thomas. We can send a message to these operators, but we both know we have to hit the ringleader. Rooster Babcock is hauling in a king's ransom out at the Red Rooster Ranch."

"Speaking of which, my informant tells me there's a craps-and-cockfighting joint out on the Reyes road." By informants, Tiny referred to one Lucas Alvarez, who pretty much supplied him with most of the skinny on underground activities. Alvarez was a functioning alcoholic who wrote for *El Milagro*, the local Hispanic news and views rag. A substantial portion of the publishing money came from Saint Anne, the local Catholic Church. "My guess is they don't pay our protection fees either."

The captain grimaced and shifted uneasily in his seat. He leaned forward, his voice low, just above a whisper, and he said, "It's growin' too fast around here. Things are getting out of control. I'm going to have to let a few independents go, maybe bust them and haul them into court to be fined."

"I think there might be some reluctance to operate outside your supervision after last night," Tiny said. "Rooster is a cock of a different color. He's the one been settin' these guys up to operate. He's not paying near enough for his 'insurance,' considering what the bastard's pullin' in."

"That's for damn sure," said Post.

"I'm taking care of your little problem"—Tiny leaned over the captain's desk, bringing his face within two feet of the captain's—"but I want in for a full 50 percent from now on. You're losing control, and it's gonna bust wide open if I don't help you get a handle on things. Besides, those pretty girls you like taking to the Registry Resort in Napolis, they're putting up a fuss for more pesos, and they have to be taught not to bite the hand that feeds them."

"OK, OK." Post held up both hands palms outward in front of him. "We can split the money these operators pay for safe passage. It's getting too big for me to handle anyway. But there's another thing I wanted to pass along. I received a highly classified memo—'for my eyes only'—from our top dog, Sheriff Gunther. The feds, along with a state task force, are putting an undercover DEA officer in our stomping grounds. They won't give me any more information than that. Apparently, they're on to something and don't want us in on it, or maybe there's just too much heat from citizens' groups."

"Not to worry," Tiny said. "We'll get a make on this chump soon enough. We'll hand him a trophy to take home, let him bust a couple losers. He'll be gone like he was never here."

"Hmm . . . maybe so." The captain grimaced and fidgeted with his pen. "I think Gunther is getting squeezed by someone to step up the busts here. Maybe we should let our boys in gray do their jobs for a few weeks."

"Once they get a taste, it'll be hard to rein them in," said Tiny. "No, we best keep our troops on a short leash and feed this DEA creep a few of our wounded deer and let it go at that. No need to put the mule in the shed now. The dough is just beginning to roll in. I'm planning an early retirement in the Cayman Islands with a big house on the beach and lots of pretty women. So trim the mainsail and steady as she goes, Captain."

"Right, right, carry on, Sergeant."

3

Tiny's head swam with all the possibilities, as well as the problems, that loomed before him. The potential for harvesting a fortune in a short time, after years of laying the groundwork, was becoming a reality. Just a little patience, determination, and a ruthless disregard for petty notions like life, liberty, and justice were needed. He was like a great blonde spider that, having paralyzed its victims and wrapped them in webbing, could now drain them at his leisure. Sure, there were some loose ends that needed mending, but he thought, *All in good time*. Yea, he was feelin' good. Maybe a quickie with Mona would be just the ticket to kick off a lucrative workday.

Having made up his mind, Tiny picked up his cell phone and pressed a quick dial number. The phone rang five times.

"What is it, Tiny? I'm about to go out shopping," Mona finally answered in a petulant tone like an exasperated mother.

"Well, get *unready*," replied Tiny. "I'm on the way over and want to see you." To himself, he said, "See you *then* fuck you."

"Tiny, you know I don't like it when you just come over like this. You should call the day before, at least, and make a date with me."

"What are you—a fuckin' doctor?" Tiny's neck and face were getting red. "You got somebody else with you now?"

"No, it's just that . . . well, you know I like to have time—"

"There *is* somebody, isn't there?"

"No . . . I mean yes . . . but it's just Janice, she stopped by to pick me up."

"OK," said Tiny, "put her on the line."

Tiny was less than a mile from Mona's by now and closing in fast.

"She's already in the car waiting for me—I gotta go. Bye." And she hung up on him.

Mona fled the apartment to see if her visitor, Ron Badger, owner of the local King Burger and a plethora of other properties, had escaped yet. She flew downstairs in time to see his powder blue Cadillac Seville pulling out of the driveway. She whispered a short foxhole prayer to speed him on his way, but too late. Tiny arrived just as the Caddy was pulling away and zoomed in front of it with blue lights flashing, blocking his getaway. The burly deputy was out of his car in an instant, red face puffed with anger. Tiny stopped dead in his tracks when he was as far as the gold grill of the Cadillac. Realizing who it was, Tiny fought to regain control of his rage. A misstep here could cost him dearly, but a hand well played could reap unexpected dividends. He would tend to Mona shortly.

Regaining some composure and stepping to the Caddy's right front window, Tiny assumed professional decorum. "Sir, may I see your driver's license and registration please."

Ron Badger was a small-town big shot accustomed to deferential treatment from the powers that be. Despite being almost literally caught with his pants down, he viewed Tiny with obvious disdain. "Officer, I assume you have some reason for stopping me. I really don't have time to be playing cops and robbers with you today. State your purpose, or I will be on my way . . . pronto."

Tiny's eyes flashed with an almost-uncontainable rage. This pip-squeak had the temerity to patronize him. "License and registration," he snapped.

"OK, OK, but Captain Post will hear of this, I assure you." Badger thrust the documents at Tiny.

"This is what Captain Post will hear, Mr. Badger, sir." Reaching through the open window and pulling on the businessman's seat belt, he gathered sufficient slack to wrap it around his throat, then pull—hard.

Badger began to gobble in some unknown language. A moment later, he made a gargling noise as his last breath came and went, his face turning from red to purple. Just as his eyes began to roll up in his head, Tiny let go of the strap, opened the door, and yanked Badger out of the car. He leaned the middle-aged, balding citizen against the Caddy and slapped his face while the man gasped, struggling for breath. He entwined his powerful fingers in the Rotarian's knit golf shirt sporting an embroidered pelican and pulled him to within two inches of his face. They were practically lip kissing. "Now, Mr. Badger," Tiny said, "let's talk about how you have been soliciting prostitution despite being a happily married, church-goin' man. And about exactly how much it's worth for you to keep your reputation intact."

Tiny ascended the stairs to Mona's apartment after fifteen well-spent minutes with the busted Badger. "Man, that Janice sure changed since last I saw her," he chortled as he went through the door. Grabbing Mona by the arm and pulling her off the couch, he slapped her tearstained cheeks once on each side, quick and sharp. "Now you listen to me, bitch. I'm not here to do sloppy seconds after that nasty burger man or anyone else for that matter. You're my property, and I ain't sharin'—got that? Next time I'll run you in on prostitution and racketeering charges and make them stick. You'll be doin' a year at the county lockup if you're lucky. Now go clean your nasty pussy up and expect me later." He released her arm; a red mark where his fingers held her would later turn deep purple. "And make sure you have a good meal ready." He turned and left her sobbing on the floor in a disheveled heap.

Tiny headed east on State Road 848 for the Baron County Youth Correctional Boot Camp. He was the former director of this much-touted facility and knew most of the guards. In addition to getting his cruiser washed and waxed and his shoes shined, it was a great place to pick up department gossip. He approached the cement block guardhouse about fifteen minutes later and was waved through by the guard who knew him by sight. The facility was set on about five acres of dry hammock surrounded by swamp. A chain-link fence topped with barbwire curls enclosed the interior two acres. There was a single-block dormitory building with thirty bunks. A separate building, equally drab, served as the cafeteria and administrative office. There was a large central courtyard for assembly and drill. In the center of this court was the "pit and post" yard. A wooden fence eight feet high enclosed this infamous four-hundred-square-foot area of punishment. This was the brainchild of Sergeant Edwin "Tiny" Harris.

It was to this post that uncooperative cadets were brought and chained naked, sometimes for an entire day, while red ants and mosquitoes had their way. Often they arrived already well softened up by blows dealt by Tiny and a couple of the more sadistic guards. The pit was also used on occasion to bury alive troublesome inmates. A straw inserted in their mouths provided air to these unfortunates. In most cases, there was no further rebellion from alumni of the "post and pit" playground. In fact, quite often they became Tiny's secret agents in exposing those who dared plot or speak against him and his staff. On the outside, they snitched on their comrades.

Tiny parked in front of the cafeteria building and wandered over to the post yard to see if there was a recalcitrant cadet meditating on the righteousness of obedience. To his amusement, there was a butt-naked white boy, head shaved nearly to the bone and chained by the neck and feet. He looked half-dead with his head lolling listlessly, face swollen and bruised, and red welts turning deep purple on his legs and body. It was unusual for Caucasians to be disciplined at the post due to family connections, not that most of the smart-ass spoiled bitches didn't deserve it. The Hispanics and Blacks, on the other hand, were fair game for everyone. Most likely, this wreck of a human was some unwanted foster child who had been passed from home to institution to home ad infinitum and would end up in the state prison a couple of years from now. Tiny called these poor slobs "biscuit bitches." Just shake 'em and bake 'em. Yeah, he missed this place a little.

He turned away, shaking his head, and made a beeline for the office of Sergeant Samuel Troy, head honcho. Sam was Tiny's assistant in the days when he ran this fun house and an apt pupil. Tiny walked through a door to a small antechamber with a desk and two chairs next to it. The clerk was a rookie guard who looked like he just got discharged from the army. He was just getting ready to leave from the looks of his spotless desk. His car keys were in his hand.

"Yo, Tiny, what's up?" the turnkey greeted.

"Same game," Tiny replied. "Where's Sam?"

"In his office, go ahead in. I'm splitting for the day."

"Have yourself a good night," Tiny said, striding to the sergeant's door. "Oh, on the way out, grab one of your young maggots and have them run a hose over my cruiser, wash off some of the trail dust, huh?"

"Right, will do," the deputy said, walking out.

Tiny knocked on the door with the rectangular black plastic plate with the name Sergeant Samuel Troy engraved in white. He opened the door without waiting for a reply.

"Hope you're not jerking off in here, Sammy boy," Tiny said.

"What the fuck?" Sam looked up from his desk. "Hey, Tiny! What brings you out to Camp Swampy?"

"Hey, yourself. What's the scuttlebutt hereabouts, amigo?"

"Oh, same old shit, different day." Sam shifted a little in his padded desk chair and leaned back on its rocker. He was a flat-faced, mean-looking man in his thirties with extremely close-cropped black hair and dark eyes set deep in heavy-lidded slits. "I did hear something the night before last while having a few with Gunther, not that I make a practice of drinking with that lush. Some high sheriff that slob is, half in the bag all the time. What the hell, the upstanding folks of Baron County elect him to office over and over. Sheriff for life."

"Yeah, he's a real wiener, all right," Tiny offered in way of shared sentiment.

"Anyway," Sam continued, "he's getting pretty loaded and starts talking about how there's a fed up in our territory now, undercover, gonna bust up some dope ring. He goes on about how some sheriff department personnel aren't gonna look too good when all is said and done. Then he starts laughin' and carrying on, sayin' those deputies out in Bella Villa aren't 'fireproof,' and that really busts him up like he made some great joke. After that, he looks real serious, like 'poof' he's sober, and says, 'Ain't no way I'm going to let my department look bad. That reflects on me.' He finishes his drink and leaves toot sweet."

"No names?" Tiny smiled indulgently, indicating what a fool the top dog was, but secretly, he was a little worried.

"Nope, just that this hombre was going to 'seal' the fate of some bad guys. And when he said 'seal,' he raises his voice an octave and starts cacklin' like an old woman."

"Well, how about that shit," Tiny replied. "Guy's not dealing with a full deck, I suspect. I'm off to run down some leads of my own and keep the good folks safe from the scumbags of society. Speaking of which, you want me to have one of Andre's girls come by?"

"Not tonight. I gotta go home and eat with the wife and kids. They've been raisin' hell about me neglecting them, and I don't want any domestic disturbance, if you know what I mean."

"Fair enough," Tiny said, walking toward the door. "Thanks for the update."

"Keep it on the road," Sam replied.

Tiny drove through the gate of the "these boots are made for walking" juvenile camp, mulling over what Sam had told him. Good ole Simple Sam hadn't connected any dots, but it was now clear to Tiny there must be a new guest at the always-fabulous-and-fantastic Fireproof Motel, and he better find out who it was, and soon. He picked up his cell phone and dialed Captain Post.

"Post here," the captain answered.

"Captain, advise delay on executing search warrant."

"What's up, Tiny?"

"I think it's better we go together and deliver our new insurance pricing to Rooster Babcock. We'll go in civvies as interested parties, do a little gambling ourselves. Let him know we're on the job."

"Ten-four, I take your meaning. I'll clear my calendar for Friday p.m."

"Oh, one other thing—"

"What is it? Tell me quick, my wife and I have a dinner date with the Badgers."

"Ha ha, that's funny," Tiny said.

"Whaddaya mean?" The captain got all flustered.

"I mean that dumb fuck, Ron Badger, was screwing Mona this afternoon. Now I have to clean her pussy out with degreaser."

"Oh, Jesus! What did you do?"

"Do? I beat the shit out of him. He looks like those burgers they serve at that slop box he owns."

"You're joking, right?" But the captain was clearly fretting.

"Yeah, just joking." Despite enjoying this little torture, Tiny had a lot of ground to cover, so he gave it up. "But I did put the fear of Thor's hammer in him. If he says anything, just shrug it off. But I seriously doubt he'll have the nerve, especially if his wife is there. No, I think you can depend on him not bringing up the subject."

"I hope so," Post said. "I don't need trouble with the mayor and councilmen right now."

"There's one more thing I need for you to do right now," Tiny said. "Call off those stakeouts on the Old County Road. They might get lucky and pop a small-time dealer. That would upset my master plan for overall law enforcement. You catch the drift?"

"Done," the captain said.

Mike Nolan was out cruising in the crisp March night, top down, listening to his police scanner. He heard through the intercar babble that patrols on the Old County Road and Route 29 were to be curtailed. He figured this would be a good area to check out. He was half-convinced before coming to Bella Villa there was a bad cop somewhere in the pack. All the signs pointed to someone pulling strings to keep drug busts minimal while returning the offenders to the streets within a few months. He decided to drive north on Route 29 past the Old County Road and turn around at the county line five miles north. On his way back, just as he was approaching the Old County Road from the north, a Crown Victoria was turning right onto that particular road. In his headlights, Nolan noticed the gold sheriff's star on the driver's door. He drove past the road, executing a quick U-turn almost immediately, went back, and turned right, following the patrol car. When the cruiser turned right into the Rainbow Pines Trailer Park, Nolan drove by and U-turned again. He pulled to the side of the road, being careful not to go too far off. There was a steep bank running into the canal adjacent to the roadbed. Most of these canals were teeming with alligators out in this neck of the woods. He listened for communication from the car but heard nothing to indicate the officer had stopped or had official business here. Usually, the only cops driving patrol cars without roof lights, other than a handful in special traffic patrol, were lieutenants or higher brass. Certainly, none of them lived here or would be making a routine patrol through the park. He waited a few minutes, and when the car didn't come back out, he decided to drive in and check things out. He pulled his Glock out from under the seat and pumped a round into the chamber, "just in case." He put the car in gear and drove into the trailer park.

Tiny headed north on Route 29 and, a few miles out of Bella Villa, turned right onto the Old County Road. A half mile later, he made another right into the Rainbow Pines Trailer Park. Throngs of Mexicans filled the narrow dirt road that made a circle through the park. Bearing left, there was barely enough room for his cruiser to pass between the trailer homes and the parked cars lining the road. Brown waves of humanity moved aside to make way. Dirty-faced little *niños* fled before him, screeching, "La policía esta aquí, la policía!" They pushed and pulled at one another, making a game out of what their *padres* feared. The men scowled and glowered but quickly turned their faces as Tiny passed. They all knew this was *el carro del diablo*, "the devil's car." And every man, woman, and child recognized the hulking form behind the wheel. They were plenty used to bad and corrupt cops where they came from, but to confront such malevolent evil here in America, where they came to escape such things to try to earn a living and a future for their families, seemed somehow much worse. It was like taking the tapestries of their hopes and their dreams and turning them into toilet paper. If they were on the dung heap on their native soil, they were buried in it here.

Tiny pulled up to a sixty-foot mobile home holiday, parked in a cranny where the road curved sharply to the right. This was the luxury residence of Carlos, his wife, his two brothers, and God knows how many kids. There was no yard, just the dusty road, and, perhaps, a place to park one car. Many of the trailers shared water and sewage connections. There were many days the backflow of raw sewage turned parts of the dirt road to mud and filled the air with the effervescent stench of raw sewage. This elegant community did without playground, swimming pool, or clubhouse.

Carlos and Omar were sitting on the wooden stoop in front of the trailer. They stopped talking and watched the cruiser pull over in front of the trailer. Tiny stepped out in the gathering darkness, a big shit-eating grin on his gringo face.

"Buenos natchos, amigas," he began, insulting both their language and them. "We need to talk. But we need to make this look good for everybody's sake, so how 'bout you step over and put your hands on the hood please." Carlos and Omar, looking both frightened and sulky, did as they were asked. Tiny frisked both of them. "Get in the car."

"OK, my little *fajitas*, talk to me," Tiny said once inside the cruiser. He turned the air up a notch and the music on the radio off. "Money for Nothing" by Dire Straits was just beginning. "I need to know the guy you're buying from. Is he Mexicano? Does he live here? Speak to me!" Carlos looked at Omar and shrugged his shoulders.

"Señor, maybe he will keel us eef we say anythings."

"Maybe I'll do worse than *keel* you if you don't. Now listen here, don't be fucking with me because I'm running a short fuse tonight, and I don't want to listen to any shit. You tell me right now who this guy is. Don't fret about him hurtin' you 'cause I'm here to serve and protect, remember? Besides which, I'm going to see to it you boys stay in business. You need extra *dinero*, don't you? I'm not gonna take food out of the mouths of babes, so lighten up, huh. Now, let's hear *un nombre*, a name, if you please. Carlos?"

Carlos didn't understand most of what Tiny said but knew what was required of him.

"Just first name. Mario. Hombre Negro. He black man. Live in house at 19 Barentwoed."

"Burntwood?" Tiny answering his own question.

"Sí," replied Carlos, "Barentwoed."

"OK, that's what I want to hear, cooperation. Remember, we're a team. I'm cutting you two *chinchillas* free. Have a nice night. *Adiós!*"

As soon as the two Mexicans were out of the cruiser, Tiny put on his red and blues. Burping the siren and fishtailing a 180 degrees, spewing gravel in all directions; he scattered the small crowd of men and boys who had gathered nearby. Grinning maniacally, he sped with reckless abandon out of the park.

Nolan entered the park but had to stop his car almost immediately due to the large number of children milling in the congested dirt road. They looked curiously at him and began to point and scream in Spanish. They ran up to his car smiling, peppering him with questions in a language he could barely understand when spoken slowly and deliberately. A couple of the braver boys began climbing into the car, shrieking with delight. The others seemed to be shouting encouragement, egging them on. Nolan tried to keep them out, repeating over and over, "Por favor, niños. No. Permiteme passar." He didn't want them anywhere near his gun and was growing increasingly nervous and impatient. At last, two men strolled over to the car. They were both smoking and holding beer cans. The taller one wearing a black cowboy hat barked something at the boys, and they fled from the car, regrouping a few yards away.

"Whatchuwant, gringo?" the taller man asked.

"I'm looking for Carlos Santana," Nolan lied. He felt like an idiot. If these guys listened to Santana, he could be needin' a "Black Magic Woman" real soon.

"Maybe, you make wrong turn," Black Hat said.

"Yeah, maybe I did," Nolan replied. He didn't want to start a ruckus and alert Harris if that was him in the patrol car.

"Niños!" The exiled cowboy clapped his hands twice, and the kids scattered. "You can back out, señor."

"OK. Thanks." Nolan, deciding discretion was the better part of valor, put the car in reverse and departed Rainbow Pines.

Tiny drove back toward the center of Bella Villa. On the north side was a small middle-class community of one-story stucco homes on quarter-acre lots. There was enough backyard to put in a pool, if you could afford it, and still have a little lawn space. Southwest Florida lawns, consisting mostly of St. Augustine grass, were mostly for show rather than any useful purpose like a place for the kids to play. Children of all ages in Baron County, wherever they lived, rich or poor, played on the streets. Sidewalks were almost unheard of, bicycle paths nonexistent, road shoulders a steep bank leading to a canal. Community planning, if there was such a thing, considered only the right of way of the automobile. Pedestrians, bicyclists, children, and animals were inconsequential. Tiny drove past two abandoned cars that had been left on the roadside for weeks. In no other place in the continental United States, except Baron County, were broken-down autos left to just sit indefinitely like roadside sculptures. Even in prestigious Napolis, the junkers were left untowed. Finally, he turned right onto Burntwood Drive. He had no trouble finding 19 among the nicely numbered mailboxes.

Tiny drove past once just to scope out the scene. It looked like a quiet neighborhood. He couldn't remember any complaints about this particular address. Everything looked quiet. Most of the blacks in Baron County were of Haitian origin and lived in project housing. This Mario could be a deep Southern fried chicken, possibly from Atlanta or Charleston. More likely, he was a Northerner, a refugee from Detroit or New York or, worse, a Yankee black man from Massachusetts. He decided to pull into the driveway and run a check on the plate and see what he could get out of the onboard computer. It was fully dark now, so he pulled in with his headlights off. He got out of the cruiser with his flashlight and got the plate numbers. Getting back in, he checked to see if anybody noticed. There was no sign from the house. Running the plates, it took him less than five minutes to find out Mario, last name Stevens, was from Hartford and had a clean driving record. But as luck would have it, there was an outstanding warrant for failure to pay child support the last two months. That was going to make things a lot simpler. Disregarding protocol on calling backup, Tiny got out of his cruiser and made for the front door.

Tiny rapped on the door, right hand on the grip of the 9mm.

"Yeah, who's there?" said the voice from inside.

"Sheriff's department," Tiny said. Long pause.

"Who you looking for?" the same voice said.

"Mario Stevens. I have a warrant from Connecticut. Open the door!"

The door opened promptly, and a medium-built but muscular African American, about five feet nine inches, wearing a sleeveless white tee shirt and gym shorts, stood before the hulking deputy, frowning. He was holding a paperback in his left hand.

"Are you Mario Stevens?" Tiny asked in his best cop voice.

"That's me."

"There's a warrant from Connecticut," Tiny informed him. "Failure to obey a court order to pay child support." Mario tried to look past Tiny who blocked the entire doorway.

"Damn that woman," Mario said. "I paid her in cash when I was up there a couple months ago."

"That's a matter for you and the courts to decide," Tiny replied as he pushed past Mario into the house. "You and I have other business right now."

"Hey! Wait a minute!" Mario shouted. "You can't come bustin' in here like that! I still have rights!"

"The only right you got is to go to jail if I choose to bring you right now," Tiny said. "Maybe I'll search your house, see what I can find. I'll bet there's drugs here all right."

Mario was looking at Tiny now with a spark of recognition. This was the bad cop, El Diablo, Carlos and Omar had spoken of. That's why there was no paperwork or backup. This was a shakedown. Mario smiled and said, "I know who you are. You're the cop named 'Tiny,' am I right?"

"Been talkin' to some known drug dealer name of Carlos, have you?" Now Tiny was grinning as well. Not the kind of grin that means happy either. It was more the grin of an angry Doberman.

Tiny glanced around the sparsely furnished living room. A caramel brown leather couch with matching La-Z-Boy faced an entertainment center with television and stereo. A poster of Snoop Doggy Dogg adorned the adjacent wall. A coffee table with magazines and what might be pot and cocaine residue was in front of the couch. A poster of rapper Mr. Big was on the far wall.

"Hey, Holmes!" Mario shouted back into the house. "Meet Tiny."

Another African American, bigger than Mario, but not the size of Tiny, appeared around a corner holding a 9mm Colt Commander.

"Hey, nice piece!" Tiny being real friendly. "They make those right in Hartford, don't they?" While the two partners in crime exchanged glances, Tiny stepped behind Mario with surprising quickness, put his left arm around his throat, and squeezed hard. Mario's face went all red and ballooned out as his air supply went to an instantaneous zero intake. Using Mario as a human shield, Tiny drew his weapon and fired it from his hip without a second's hesitation. The bullet caught Holmes in the left thigh, knocking him off his feet. Before he could recover enough to get his gun pointed at Tiny again, he was slammed with two bullets in the chest. The rounds passed through the man, splattering the wall behind with blood. Holmes's eyes rolled up in his head as he listed to port, exhaling his last breath. The adrenaline was flowing in Tiny. He brought the butt of the handgrip on the Glock down on the back of Mario's head. Mario reeled, stupefied. The smell of gunpowder permeated the air. Tiny got out his handcuffs and, twisting Mario's arms behind his back, slapped them on. The deputy backhanded his prisoner a hard blow to the cheek, knocking him to the floor. Then Tiny lunged through the kitchen door, gun leveled, grasped in both hands. Panning first to the right, now left, he raced from room to room. Nobody else was present. Tiny returned to the living room. He was alone with Mario and the deceased Holmes.

"Look at all the trouble you caused me, boy," Tiny said. "Now I gotta call a bunch of busybodies to come investigate this shooting and fill out no end of forms and paperwork. I ain't got much use for you Yankee niggers comin' down here and takin' shit over. You and I are going to talk later about business. Way I see it, you owe me some protection money. After all, I just saved you from Holmes there."

"You ain't getting shit from me, pig." Mario coughed and spit bloody phlegm on the floor. He pushed himself into the nearby La-Z-Boy.

"This dance is just beginning, my natty-haired friend," Tiny said as he hauled him out of the chair and flung him into the wall. Mario's head hit the Sheetrock hard enough to bust a hole through it. His legs gave out, and he collapsed to the floor, blood smearing his forehead and temple. Dazed, with arms still cuffed, Mario lay still by the damaged wall. Tiny kicked him in the side. There was the sound of breaking bones as ribs cracked, and Mario cried out in agony.

"You'll see things my way when you're looking at twenty years or more behind bars," Tiny informed him. "Your black ass won't be worth a pack of Camels inside. Now, I'm taking off these cuffs, and you best mind your manners while I call backup. Once the dust settles here and you're back in business, you and I will talk. Hey, pardner?"

4

Toad arose from a restless sleep. Constant nightmares broke through the alcoholic stupor he induced almost every night. Visions of the Vietnam jungles still haunted his rest. The unseen enemy seemed to be everywhere. A muddy path turns into a bloodbath around a bend as unseen snipers assail his troop. Often, it is impossible to tell friend from foe. A serene village suddenly becomes a death trap. Allied Vietnamese soldiers harbor Vietcong spies. An apparently harmless civilian tosses a grenade into your midst. Green Army lieutenants are put in charge of combat-hardened troops. These recent West Pointers or ROTC graduates often give orders foolishly, compromising their squads. Those officers who listened to their NCOs were likely to make it back to base to fight another day. Those too cocky or unadaptable were likely to go missing in action as often as not, killed by the Americans they commanded. These horrific executions add more fuel to the dark dreams—nightmares that haunt so many of the veterans who made it back home.

Sitting up in bed, Toad picked up a half gallon of Popov Vodka and took a long swallow. Putting on his dirty denims (he never wore shorts and rarely did laundry), he ventured out the door, bottle in hand, into the bright Florida sunshine. There is something magical about early mornings in Florida, especially winter mornings when the air is often crisp as an autumn day in New England. The rays of the early-morning sun warmed Toad's left side as he plopped in the rocker outside his room. It was a wicker chair he picked up for a song at a Goodwill store. He fished out his rolling tobacco, placed it on the plastic table next to his liquor, and began the ritual of rolling a morning smoke. The vodka was beginning to work its own kind of black magic, steadying his shaking hands and bringing on a mellow feeling. He took another gulp and lit his cigarette. Another addiction satisfied. More mellowness. Life was good, at least right now. For today, he had another bottle, still uncorked, and a can full of tobacco. He thought there was a joint or two of pot kicking around as well. The nightmares were fading with each passing moment. Toad was looking forward to this day at the Fireproof Motel. Anything could happen today—or nothing. Let the dice roll. Maybe, if he could borrow fifty bucks from Brian against his veterans' disability check, he'd exercise the old schlong with a hooker tonight. Yeah, sounds good. Go easy on the drinking so he could get it up. He picked up the bottle, poured a large dose into a coffee cup, and sipped with discretion, like a gentleman. No sense being greedy. He inhaled some more smoke. *Lookin' fine, good buddy, lookin' top notch.*

Carrying a large backpack on his spare six-foot frame, John Vaughn walked into the parking lot of the Fireproof Motel. His close-cropped brown hair, receding to form a modest midlife peninsula, was wet and sticky. Sweat glistened on his temples like beads of sap on spring pines. He was hot. He was tired. He was dirty. Time for a little R & R in the "civilized" world. John Vaughn disdained the modern world and its gas-powered conveyances. Automobiles were the nemesis of mankind and the natural world. Of all the products of industrial society, these ubiquitous, gas-guzzling fuming metal and plastic future junk heaps presented the greatest threat to man and nature. The entire culture of Western civilization seemed to wrap, like tread around a tire, in the obligatory expansion of the cement and macadam passageways marring the earth's surface like inflamed varicose veins. No place was too remote to be despoiled by these insidious ribbons of disease. Everywhere, these paved corridors from hell were jammed with speeding juggernauts, operated by half-crazed humans, driven by an unstoppable culture of self-mobilization. Fueled by greedy oil interests and industrialists, buoyed by propaganda mixing necessity, prestige, and fear into a frenzied cauldron of bubbling black death, people drove themselves with compact discs blaring into the abyss.

It had been a harrowing mile walk for the intrepid outdoorsman dodging cars going at least twenty miles an hour over the fifty-five posted speed limit. These highways and byways became like minefields to countless thousands of animals every night. They were roadkill annihilated trying to cross the blacktop, the powerful beams of headlights illuminating their deaths. Huge sections of the planet Earth had become uninhabitable by any creature and impassable by any means but these painted powerhouses. Most of these one-to-three-ton equipages were carrying a single person. They had, in fact, become extensions of the individual, like some monstrous prosthetic appendage. Even minimal passageway for pedestrians or cyclists was not afforded. Motion denied. They were fair game. Here in Southwest Florida, you rode the road onboard or swam in the canals with the alligators.

John put his pack on the concrete pavement at his feet and knocked on the office door of the motor hotel. As long as there was a shower, bed, and TV, this place would be just fine. He had no desire to set foot once again on the inhospitable and dangerous "die-way" he just trudged to look for better accommodations. Besides, he was sure this cozy oasis would fit his purse. An elderly man with close-cropped white hair circling an almost bald crown came from around the right side of the building. There was a look of puzzlement on his tanned face.

"Can I help you?" Morris asked.

"I'd like a room for a week or so," John replied in a voice with the timbre of cement sliding down a metal shoot. Morris looked at the backpack by the man's feet and his well-worn hiking boots. He scanned the parking area, a little perplexed.

"Where's your car?" Morris asked.

"No car."

Morris raised his eyebrows and squinted a little. "You have an ID?"

"Yeah, I have a Florida State ID. And I'll be paying cash in advance."

"Just yourself?" Morris was eager for the cashola now but did not want any surprises.

"Just me."

"OK, let's go inside, I have a room with your name on it."

After registering the wayfarer, Morris led the scruffy Vaughn to room 110 on the corner of the L, adjacent to the storage and tool room, sharing the corner with Julie and Tommy in 109, and one room away from Nolan in 112. Room 111 was vacant.

"Good Morning, Mr. Toad," Morris said as they passed by. Images of a toad speeding in a stolen motorcar caused him to grin as he recollected the story he read to his grandchildren from *Wind in the Willows*. Toad squinted at them through a cloud of cigarette smoke as they passed, nodding a greeting. Morris turned the key in the lock, opened the door for Mr. Vaughn, and waited for his approval.

"This'll do just fine," Vaughn grunted.

"Okay, here you go, enjoy." Morris handed John Vaughn the key and departed.

Vaughn walked inside and locked the door, and propping his pack against the bed, he opened the top flap and lifted out a black metal cylinder, twenty-two inches long and about an inch in diameter with the last four inches becoming twice as thick. This part bore the inscription, Survivor. Next came a plastic camouflaged rifle stock about a foot long with a six-inch metal piece extending from beneath it with the inscription "New England Firearms." Finally, he extracted a small plastic piece, ten inches long, shaped so the barrel would fit into it. This piece contained a hole with a turnscrew about a third of the way down. He pushed one end of the metal barrel against the stock at a forty-five-degree downward angle until there was a slight *click*. Then he lifted the barrel into a horizontal position, resulting in a louder *clink*. Picking up the grooved plastic piece, he placed it under the barrel, wedging part of it into the stock. After turning the knob screw until it was tight, he pushed a thumb button next to the hammer on the stock; and with a noticeable *clunk*, the barrel dropped down, again at forty-five degrees, opening the magazine. Vaughn pulled a twelve-gauge shotgun round loaded with 00 buckshot from a pocket on his pack and pushed it into the gaping chamber. He flicked his wrist, and the barrel snapped shut. John Vaughn was now holding a loaded twelve-gauge shotgun, capable of killing anything from briar rabbit to black bear. He always stocked an assortment of loads to meet any contingency.

Vaughn placed the loaded shotgun on the shelf over the small open cubicle next to the bathroom, which served as the only closet. He stretched, walked into the bathroom, turned on the hot water in the shower/bathtub, and began to remove his sweat-dampened and dirty clothes. It was sure going to be like a little bit heaven getting under the stream of hot water.

Camilla and Robbie lived in a two-room suite. There was a separate bedroom and bathroom in addition to the same living room/kitchen area as the other rooms had. The living area was furnished with a cream-colored cloth couch and matching La-Z-Boy opposite the TV. Over a small desk in the middle of the wall opposite the outside entrance was a large picture, encased in glass, of the Three Wise Men looking toward a glowing star in the shape of a cross. The small bedroom had a double bed against one wall with Billie's crib on wheels next to it. A closet and bureau were at the other end of the room. Next to the bureau, on a small table, a thirteen-inch TV dominated the room much of the time. The bathroom was between the living area and the bedroom.

Baby Billy was screeching with the annoying shrillness of a flute being played by a precocious monkey. Robert came out of the bathroom rubbing sleep from his eyes. Camilla was changing Billy's diaper while Saturday morning cartoons pranced across the TV screen. "Robby, we need another box of Pampers, there's only one left. How much money do you have?"

"I dunno, maybe fifty bucks." Robert shuffled over to the dresser like a zombie in an old horror flick. He opened his billfold. "Let's see, I have . . . exactly fifty-three dollars. And there's seventy-seven cents on the dresser."

"That's just fuckin' great!" Camilla's usual angelic temperament was on vacation. "And just how the hell are we supposed to buy diapers and food and pay the rent, not to mention fix that heap we're driving."

"Don't worry, I'll come up with something." Robert opened the top dresser drawer, closed it, and opened the second and third. "Where'd I put that bag of weed? That's some awesome sinse, mon."

"I'll give you some sinse, mon," snapped Camilla. "If you don't get a job and some money, I'm going to move in with your mother. Maybe I'll find a sexy Mexican dude to help me in the sack while I'm there." She put Billy on the bed and gave him a Graham cracker to gnaw on. Afterward, she sat on the bed and stared with pursed lips at her husband.

"I'd get a job waiting on tables," Camilla said, "but to be honest, I don't trust you alone with Billy. For God's sake, Robbie, we have a child to take care of here! All you seem to care about is your pot and beer. I can't live like this!"

Camilla sobbed and burst into tears, accompanied by the wailing Willie. Robert Valentine collapsed onto the double bed, arm over his eyes as if fending off invading phantoms.

"OK, OK," Robbie said, at last sitting up. "Listen, tomorrow, we'll go to Napolis and visit my mom. I'll ask her for a couple C-notes to get us by and Dad's VW. Once I have reliable transport, I can find a job, easy. There's tons of work in Napolis. Maybe one of her developer friends can turn me on to a construction job. Why don't you give her a call and set it up."

"I can do that," Camilla said, suddenly waxing hopeful. She picked up Billy and began pacing, his little head on her shoulder, his cheeks tearstained but blessedly quiet for now. "She'll want to see her bootiful grandson anyway. It's been a while." Robert sighed and went to the fridge to get some juice but pulled out a can of Budweiser instead and popped the top.

Tommy Nelson got out of bed, leaving Julie to snooze, and slipped into his boxers. Heading to the bathroom, he took just enough time to grab the remote and flick on the TV. He liked watching cartoons on Saturday mornings. They were so crazy; he hardly believed what he was seeing or hearing at times. He guessed most parents had no idea what their kids were being exposed to. If nothing else, these animated features must induce vocabulary growth. Many words were new to Tommy, and he had an *almost* college education. A lot of the cartoons presented morality plays: how virtue overcomes corruption, why justice outshines ruthlessness, how self-sacrifice supplants selfishness, the value of generosity opposed to greed, and, almost always, the meaning of friendship. Tommy supposed there were many adults, at all levels of society, who could learn a thing or two watching some of these parody parades designed to captivate children's attention.

Tommy emerged from the bathroom to find the evil Carmen plotting to usurp all power from the governor by hypnotizing one of his assistants, only to be thwarted by the unexpected arrival of the Buckateens, a motley group of three shabbily dressed and ill-groomed teenage boys and one likewise adorned female. A few minutes later, Tommy muted the volume, sat down with his guitar, and began strumming a tune from his vast repertoire.

"Hey, Julie! Are we going out with Camilla and Robbie today?" No reply. He stopped strumming and tried again, a little louder. "Yo, bitch, get yoah lazy fat ass out da bed and speak at me." A loud groan emanated from under the covers as Julie rolled over. All that could be seen of her was a blonde mop covering the top half of a pillow.

"Meow," wailed the tomcat. There was a responding moan from beneath the bedclothes. Tommy put down the guitar, poised himself like a cat, and jumped on top of the moving lump with a feline shriek. "Tommy Tiger will eat you alive, you poor, helpless little girl!"

They were in Jamie's renovated room. Two new wall adornments brought the otherwise plain motel room to life. The largest occupied half the wall above the bed; it was an embroidered wall hanging of a Guatemalan village with several women dressed in their indigenous garb, long dresses with bright colors, carrying baskets on their heads. One of the women carried an infant in a sling. In the background, an active volcano was belching smoke, lava coming down the sides. None of the ladies seemed concerned. The other was a large Bev Doolittle color-print calendar, hanging above the writing table. The face of a Native American could be discerned from the pattern of rocks, fallen leaves, butterflies, and multicolored ferns.

Brian's mind raced with conflicting thoughts and emotions. He was sitting up against the headboard in Jamie Dorr's bed, smoking a Camel. His blue eyes were almost spellbinding in their brightness, set off by his thick coal black hair. His face was almost smooth, just a fine down for a morning beard. Was he really gay? he thought. He just made love with another man. Or was it love? Maybe it was just lust. There was a fair amount of Myers's Rum shared between them last night, not to mention a gram of Baron County's finest coke. He wondered if there was any of the evil white powder left. He finished his cigarette and went to the dresser. Unba! There was still one line left! How could such an oversight occur? He picked up the rolled dollar bill and put an end in his nose, bent over, and inhaled the magic dust. Magnifico!

Jamie watched Brian do the coke through slotted eyes without saying a word. He watched Brian sip some Myers's from the bottle and chase it with a glass of water. Watching Brian's well-formed and smooth naked body was giving him an early-morning hard-on. He waited for Brian to get back in bed and smoke another morning cigarette. The lad was thinking, thinking too much. Confusion has its cost, amigo. When Brian snubbed out the butt, Jamie rolled over with catlike laziness and stretched out his left arm, his fingers touching Brian's thigh. He rubbed it sensually, then put his hand on Brian's hard tummy and rubbed. Switching hands, Jamie moved his right hand along the inner thigh to Brian's now-tumescent joystick. His capable hands soon had the overgrown boy moaning with pleasure. Placing his own throbbing member against the furnace of flesh writhing at his fingertips, Jamie brought their roiling carnal juices flowing over the dam to the valley below.

Nolan walked out on the small porch in front of his room and stretched. The air was a little crisp but warming fast in the midmorning sunshine. "Another beautiful day in paradise," as the Napolis Country Club set oft repeated. Spotting Toad sitting in front of his room, a plume of tobacco smoke swirling around his homely hairy head like clouds around a mountain peak, Nolan decided to go over and introduce himself. Hell, he might as well get started with the losers closest to home. He checked his pockets to make sure he had a pack of Marlboros on board and headed over. Toad's room was at a diagonal from his in the other part of the L shape of the motel. Nolan walked across the small courtyard and passed Camilla's garden. There were tomatoes ripening on the vine with an abundance of salad greens, broccoli, and squash. There were flowers of every color throughout the small fenced plot. A vine laden with large white blossoms ran up the fence like the resurrection, transforming the wood and wire barrier into a beautiful botanical display.

Nolan waved at Toad and approached with his hand outstretched. "Morning, my name is Mike Nolan," he said. "I'm right over there in room 112."

"Toad," grunted the wary veteran. Toad wasn't paranoid; you have to care about something or someone enough to have a little fear, and he really didn't give a shit.

"Pleased to meet you," returned Nolan, fishing for a Marlboro. He put one between his lips and proffered the pack to Toad who took one. Nolan offered a light from a red Bic lighter. Holding straggling wisps of hair away from the flame, Toad craned his head forward to the light. He took a long toke, sat back, and exhaled a volcanic plume of smoke. His eyes were a swampy mixture of dark greens and browns, but there was an intelligence lurking beneath that put Nolan off a bit. "So how long have you been taking in the Florida sunshine in these elegant quarters?"

"Long enough to get a pretty good buzz on." Toad tipped his bottle and just wet his whistle, followed by a long drag on the Marlboro as he assessed the new kid on the block. *Two new kids,* he thought, remembering the newly arrived outdoorsman. *What was his name? John, wasn't it?* Nolan gave a brief snort and a smile in response.

"Speaking of buzz ons, you wouldn't know where I could score a little bud for recreational purposes, would you?" Agent Nolan figured he might as well get right into it as long as he had this ex-army derelict on the line. He had done his homework and knew this booze sponge was a Vietnam veteran, 101st Cavalry Lance Corporal, on a partial disability for mental disorders. The guy was a regular army fuckup who couldn't cope with the working world when he was discharged. He just wanted to cop a buzz and collect enough to get by on. Still, he scored high on intelligence tests and could prove to be a real live wire if ignited.

Toad reached down and pulled a leather bag from somewhere below the table, opened it, and pulled a half-burnt joint from a sack. "Sit down. I'll burn this with you. It's the last of what I have, but I don't like to save anything for tomorrow when tomorrow may just never come."

"I hear you there." Nolan fished for an out now. "Truth is, I got to go meet someone about a job in about an hour, and I'd rather wait 'til later." Nolan reached in his pocket and pulled out a money clip and peeled off two hundred-dollar bills. "How about I give you this to score something for me, and I'll split it with you since I don't know anyone here yet." He held the money out to Toad who was already sucking on the lit joint, inhaling deeply, holding his breath, coughing like a badly tuned truck as he exhaled the cobalt-colored THC laden smoke.

"Good stuff, huh?" A wan smile flickered on Nolan's lips.

"Yup," said Toad as he extended a soiled hand and grasped the money between nicotine-stained fingers with long grimy nails. Nolan couldn't help but notice, with some satisfaction, the look of greed and anticipation that passed across the troglodyte's face when he saw the possibility of getting free drugs appear before him.

"I'll come by tonight around eight, if that's all right. You need anything from town?" Nolan played being the neighbor, knowing Toad didn't have wheels.

Fucking narc. Toad, thinking of how to play this guy, noticed the bulge by his inside left ankle under the denims. *Snub nose .38, probably Smith & Wesson.* "Pick me up a large Popov and some Bugler, if you don't mind. I'll pay you Tuesday after I go to the bank." Warning lights were flashing in Toad's altered, but not addled, gray matter. *Could be a bust going down, but not likely real soon. Still, no sense looking a gift horse in the mouth.*

"Forget it," Nolan said. "This one's on me. Later." He departed.

"Later," Toad replied. Then under his breath, he added, "Asshole." He watched Nolan move toward his room across the courtyard. *Military training, probably Special Forces*, he mused.

When Nolan drove off about thirty minutes later, Toad got up and ambled over to Jamie Dorr's room. He was anxious to share his encounter with Mike Nolan, resident narc, with the petty drug-dealing resident queer. Maybe Nolan was legit, who knows? The waters were too muddied to tell friend from foe anymore. Noticing the front window drapes were slightly parted as he walked by, he paused. There was a light on by the bed. Practiced at being a shadow (who knows what evil lurks in the hearts of men, the shadow do), Toad stooped a bit to peek, to see what he could see. What he saw were two naked men sitting up in bed, talking and smoking. *Ah-hah*, he thought, *just about what I expected.*

Brian took a drag on his Marlboro Lights and exhaled slowly. "I really like you an' all, Jamie, but I don't know about this sex thing. It all seems so mixed up. Like okay and right in one way, then all wrong and crazy in another." He shook his head from side to side and took another long drag from his cigarette, exhaling the smoke and staring into the cloud as if it held the answers to five millenniums of homosexual guilt and consternation.

"It's a society thing," Jamie said. "It's all about trying to control people through religion and guilt. Take that away and what've you got? Two people who care about each other getting down. How bad or wrong can that be? In some places, we'd be hung for what we're doing even if we were a man and woman. It's all a big cultural bunch of bullshit. Sure, I agree, it's really hard—maybe impossible—to shake off all the pollution they've pumped into our heads—but we've got to try to be happy despite the bigots." Jamie reached over and touched the top of Brian's hand and rubbed it gently. He could feel a faintish and sluggish stirring in his groin.

"It did feel good," Brian said, an impish smile working its way across his lips. "Let's do it again, see if we can *really* burn in hell."

Toad took a long swallow from the Popov jug and went to the door after the peep show was winding down. He knocked gently, trying the knob, hoping to catch the boys by surprise, let them know the Toadmeister didn't miss a trick. *Damn, locked,* he thought. He knocked hard, twice. Jamie and Brian sat up in the bed, still a little stuporous after their last round of lovemaking. They looked at the door as if the gestapo were about to bust in, then scrambled into their denim shorts tossed on the floor by the bed in the heat of seduction. "Who is it?" Jamie managed as soon as he'd zipped up.

"Toad" came the reply from the other side.

Jamie gave Brian an "oh, brother" look and said, "Just a minute." When they had on their shirts and Brian disappeared into the bathroom, Jamie opened the door. "Hey, Toad. What's up?" Jamie was not the least thrilled to see the intrusive Toad, especially with the vodka bottle. Before he could trump up an excuse to get rid of him, Toad barged into the room looking around.

"Is Brian here?" he asked, knowing full well the answer.

"Yeah, he's in the bathroom." Jamie resigned himself to the unwelcome intrusion, at least for a few minutes. He hoped he could recapture the energy with Brian afterward, but he feared not.

"Thought so. I stopped by his room earlier, and he wasn't there," Toad lied.

"That's because he was probably here." Jamie thought, *No way am I going to give him a clue about Brian and me.* But he knew Toad well enough to figure he knew plenty already. Toad could smell sex on you like a dog. He seemed to soak up the leftover carnal vibes like a salacious sponge.

"So you need something from town? I'll be going in later," Jamie offered, avoiding any attempt at hospitality, knowing even the offering of coffee could be an invitation to spend the day with a tipsy, rambunctious, and possibly violent Toad.

"No, I'm set. How 'bout a shot for some pot?" He proffered the jug of clear distillate to Jamie. Jamie was shaking his head and waving his hand as if to ward off evil spirits when Brian came out of the bathroom.

"Morning, Toad." Brian gave a faint smile and nod to the army veteran and looked away. His face would have given away the story of the past few hours to any but the most obtuse observer, and Toad noticed *every* nuance even through a veil of intoxication.

"Interesting morning," Toad began. "Mind?" he asked, fishing a roach from the ashtray on the bureau by the television.

"Knock yourself out," Jamie said with a resigned shrug.

"Don't mind if I do." Toad lit the roach away from his full beard, sucking noisily on it. He coughed out the smoke and held out the burning ember pinched between his index and thumb nails. Jamie and Brian both declined.

"We got a new guest in 110," Toad began when his breath returned. He began to pull out his Bugler, but Brian held out his pack of smokes. Toad put his tobacco away and shared the world of cigarette lights with his erstwhile planting partner. Toad's lighter appeared like a magic trick, and both men began blowing smoke screens with the look of gratification nicotine addicts get when lighting up fixed on both their faces.

"Really," said Jamie, walking over to the window and peeking through the same small gap in the drapes Toad had used earlier to look out at the parking lot.

"He's on foot," said Toad, watching Jamie. "No car. He was carrin' a backpack, so I don't think he's here on foot because his car broke down. Looked like he's been roughin' it outdoors for a while."

"Is he white?" Brian asked for no apparent reason.

"Oh yeah, he's a white guy." Toad seemed to pick up on some unspoken meaning in Brian's question. "And if he's been living out in that swamp, you can be sure he's carrying a long knife and possibly some kind of firearm."

"Guess we'll find out soon enough, huh?" Brian said, pouring a half glass of orange juice and handing it to Toad, nodding at the vodka. Toad topped off the tumbler with vodka and handed it back to Brian.

Oh, Jesus! Just what I need, Brian getting fucked up and crazy, thought Jamie. Brian was a wild card when he drank too much, and once he started, things could become unmanageable fast. Jamie needed to get Brian away from Toad as soon as possible.

"Brian, let's go to Napolis and get some breakfast at Perkins—I'm buying." Jamie picked up his wallet from the night table.

"There's something else I wanted to tell you," interjected Toad. He took a pull from his jug.

"Yeah, what's that?" Jamie was moving toward the door, trying to get the show on the road and not caring if he was being rude.

"I think that guy in 112, his name is something Nolan . . . Mike, that's it . . . Mike Nolan. I think he's a narc, so be careful with him."

"Fuck him," said Brian, finishing his screwdriver.

"Why do you think that?" Jamie was a little interested, but more interested in getting Toad out of the room and away from Brian.

"Vibes," Toad began. "And he gave me this." Toad pulled the money from his pocket and showed them. "Told me to score some weed with it. Acted more like he wanted to know where riffraff like me got dope than he wanted some to smoke."

"So what d'ya want from me?" Jamie was looking at Brian, gesturing toward the door with his head.

"Some pot. What else you holdin'?" Toad cast a glance at the cocaine-stained mirror on the dresser. "I'm certainly not going to tell him where I got it, and it'll be interesting to see what he does with it."

"I don't give a shit as long as the money ain't marked." Jamie walked through the door and held it open like a doorman. "I better take it to town and clean it up. But I can't get you anything 'til later." Toad, who was leaning against the dresser, started toward the door.

"You coming with us, Toad?" Brian asked, oblivious to Jamie's obvious discomfort. The Popov was percolating in his brain cells by now. Jamie shook his head no as Toad turned to look at Brian. A puzzled expression crossed his new lover's face.

"Nah, thanks though," replied Toad. There was a faint smile beneath his whiskered face. "But as long as you're out, mind picking me up a liter of vodka? I can pay you Tuesday when I go to the bank."

"No *problema*," shot back Jamie as he locked up. "*Adios*." As the pair departed for Napolis in Jamie's Civic, a pair of blue Irish eyes were smilin' from a copse across the road from the motel.

5

Pablo Rodriquez blew out seventeen candles on his huge birthday cake iced with a generous amount of chocolate frosting. He was celebrating his *compleanos* in the great hacienda of the widow Constance Valentine. Pablo was an extraordinarily handsome young man with the looks and build of a young Antonio Banderas. He could easily have been an underwear or bathing suit model. Dressed in suit and tie, he could have been pictured with a gooseneck martini. But Pablo grew up in one of Bella Villa's poorest Latino barrios, the Rainbow Pines Trailer Park. Still, he spoke pretty good English, having spent eight years in Bella Villa's school system. Pablo knew he wasn't here to be a gardener and part-time houseboy for the great lady. Andre, Bella Villa's most ostentatious pimp, had personally chosen him for this job. And the deputy, El Diablo, had driven him here in a sheriff's patrol car. The money he received for each month here was more than his family earned in a year working in the tomato fields or mopping the floors of the aristocrats in Napolis. In one year, he would have enough money to go to any college he chose. With the help of Señora Valentine, he was enrolled for a year of prep work at a local community college. Besides, the wealthy widow wasn't bad looking for her age.

Constance came around the table, face glowing beneath a layer of carefully applied makeup. Her shoulder-length chestnut hair was styled beautifully in a series of waves and trusses so complicated as to defy description. If she had any gray hairs, they were certainly not visible. Renoir would have described her figure, somewhat round, as voluptuous. She was adorned in a silky maroon evening dress bought in Paris two months ago. A fortune in gold and stones adorned her wrists and neck. She stood behind Pablo and placed a bejeweled hand over his, guiding a pastry knife to the cake.

"Happy birthday, my sweet!" Constance placed her cheek next to his, at first coyly, letting the heat of her internal furnace transfer to his smooth brown skin. Her breasts pressed against his back. She kissed him on the cheek. It was an old drill, but she didn't tire of it. This was her third boy since the death of her husband, and there had been plenty while he was still alive. She had grown a little too emotionally fond of the last one, Francisco, and he of her. There was a nasty scene when it came time for him to go. That brute of a deputy, Tiny, had to be called in to clean up the mess. She would be more careful this time. She placed her left hand along his jawline, turning his mouth to hers. His lips were full and soft. She felt a slight tremble. "Easy, darling. Come with me." She took his hand and led him to the guest bedroom nearby with a double bed. Swinging the door closed behind them, she put her arms around the boy's neck and pressed her lips to his. Burning with passion and anticipation of this seduction, she unfastened his shirt buttons and rubbed his smooth chest. A growing hardness pressed against her groin. She encouraged it with her expert fingers. Her dress fell to the floor even as he fell to the bed on his back. She undid his belt and pulled off his pants. Without ceremony or any further fooling around, she pulled his jockey shorts down his muscular legs and over his feet. Constance took a long drink with her eyes of the man-boy lying before her, his love machine at full attention and ready. Her own juices were flowing. He was hers now. She would have him again and again, each day for days without end. She was practically swooning as she sat on top of him, her fingers rubbing his nipples as her lips came down on his, inserting her tongue in his mouth. It was true what that former secretary of state once said at a party, "Power is the greatest aphrodisiac." The commissioner's mind went blank, all thinking swallowed in dark wet pleasure.

Judge Henry Thomas paced the floor of his rented Napolis condominium with a Dewar's on the rocks, same as he always drank. And he always seemed to drink quite a bit on these occasions. Thank God, his wife had flown to Santa Fe to visit her mother and siblings. If he wanted, he could return later to his country club home in one of Napolis's most prestigious gated communities. After all, at fifty-seven, he had earned millions on real estate deals before being elected as district judge. He could pretty much do as he pleased now. The only fly in the ointment was that repulsive and blackmailing deputy sheriff, Edwin Harris. But if not for him, it would be impossible to keep a lid on his meetings with the young girls he so desired to help. Yes, that was the bottom line, wasn't it? He craved only to help these emotionally distraught and abused children. They would come back and thank him in the years to come. There was no sin in the little touching he did. Didn't they encourage him? Yeah, sure they did, practically begged him for his attentions. He took a long swallow of his Dewar's, jangled the ice, and went back to top off the glass.

This appointment would take place like the rest. A deputy chosen by Harris would bring a girl caught in the middle of a nasty custody case or involved in the criminal court system for some reason. Usually, it was a problem relating to drugs. Acting as a friend of the court, he would take charge of arbitration and hold "interviews" with the girl in the privacy of his apartment. He justified the apartment as an expense relating to his work in and for the court system. The deputy would conveniently leave for two or three hours to get coffee and donuts or whatever. The important thing was that Judge Thomas was left absolutely alone with the young and unfortunate blossoms of womanhood.

The judge picked up the file of the girl he was seeing tonight. He opened to the first page. There was always a file photo there. "Let's see." He read out loud, "Jane Austin, thirteen years old, taken into state custody on November 12 when both parents were arrested for possession with intent to distribute marijuana." He shook his head and couldn't help chuckling a bit to himself. Maybe it was the scotch. The good judge had been no stranger to the wicked weed himself when he was younger. No real harm done there. The laws were insane to be sure, but he was sworn to uphold them; and that he would do, that he would surely do in the case before him of little Ms. Austin. The photo showed the face of a delightful, smiling young girl with big bright blue eyes and dimpled cheeks framed with blonde tresses. *Norman Rockwell*, mused Judge Thomas, *my favorite*.

The doorbell rang. The judge removed a small canister from his sport coat pocket and sprayed a mist into his mouth. He walked over and answered the door. A young deputy stood before him, appropriately humble before the great judge. Obviously, he had no clue. Everything was in order.

"Judge," he began, "I brought Jane Austin. Sorry I'm a little late. Traffic this time of year. You know how it is."

"Not a problem, Deputy. Hennessey, is it?"

"Yes, sir."

"I was busy with the young lady's file and didn't notice the time myself. My interview will require about two and a half hours. Can you come back in that time to return the girl to juvenile hall?"

"Absolutely, Judge."

"Has she had supper, do you know?" Thomas acting concerned.

"Oh yes, sir. I picked her up right after," replied Deputy Goody Two-Shoes.

"OK. See you later." The judge closed the door. A moment of silence for the innocence of childhood was observed while the deputy departed.

"Am I going to be able to live with mom and dad again soon?" unplain Jane asked. She was dressed in blue jeans and a white cotton blouse.

"Do you want to?" the judge answered with a question. He looked at the girl. Delicious. Peaches and cream, this one. No fooling around.

"Yes." She shifted uneasily from one foot to the other. *Like a scared and helpless fawn*, thought the judge. He took a seat in a large easy chair near the wet bar. Across from him, there was an entertainment center with TV and stereo. There was a couch of black leather, a small table with four chairs. It was a small place, one bedroom. A place just for work. A couple of watercolor beach scenes adorned the walls. The Dewar's had appeared in his hand again.

"Come over here." The judge spoke with authority but smiled. The girl was trembling with fear. She approached the chair. He put down his drink on a small table. He could feel the implacable stirring in his groin. He reached out his hand and took hers. He pulled her over. "Sit." He put his arm around her slim waist and pulled her onto his lap. "If you please me, I can make it so you're with your mommy and daddy *very* soon." He slipped his hand under her blouse, rubbing first one budding breast, then the other. The girl was in shock. Frozen like a deer in headlights. The judge worked quickly and expertly on buttons and zippers. She was naked in his lap in a matter of seconds, sitting on top of his fully hard gavel. *Now is the time of judgment, and I am the one and only judge. The bringer of all delight. The binder and the unbinder. In my hands shall you prosper.* The litany cascaded through the judge's intoxicated mind while his fingers did their dirty work. Soon, pleasure supplanted all thought as he plunged into her soft, downy dark wetness. Power *is* the greatest aphrodisiac.

When the judge came to, lying naked on his bed, the girl was in a fetal position on the floor, whimpering. He glanced at the clock on the nightstand. It was almost time for the deputy to return. Thank whatever dark powers ruled heaven and earth he had resurfaced in time. He put on a robe and picked the girl up. Without patience or ceremony, he dragged her to the shower and stuck her under the faucet, cranking the cold water. He watched her try to escape the stream, coming alive now. He too was coming alive, a rising below the equator. Watching her squirm was a great sport, but time was of the essence. No shenanigans. He added some hot water and handed her a washcloth, making sure she cleaned up thoroughly. He took on the job of drying her off, copping a few last feels to titillate himself with when she was gone. He brought her clothes in and bade her dress quickly. The judge went to the bar for an eye-opener of a different sort. Calling the girl over, he used an electric dryer on her hair. The doorbell sounded. It was Deputy Goody Two-Shoes.

"Sir, I've come for the girl," he said.

"So you have," said the judge. "And in good time."

The deputy and the girl departed with papers from the judge's desk, appropriately stamped, instructing the juvenile authorities to return the girl to her parents, pending a final interview with him. There were a host of other girls on the docket. The judge disrobed; and thinking of toweling off the girl, he laid down for a solo session with the only instrument he knew how to play.

Two weeks after Tiny's run-in with Mario, Brenda Andrews, a junior at Baron High School in Napolis, arrived at the Bella Villa's sheriff's station. As part of the Explorers, a program to introduce teenage cop wannabes to law enforcement, Brenda was to spend a weekend hanging out with a deputy sheriff. Since Tiny was in the final days of administrative leave while investigators finished up their report exonerating him from any malfeasance in the shooting of Homeboy, he was the perfect choice to escort the nubile Brenda.

"Welcome! Welcome!" Captain Post was holding out his hand, being Officer Cordial. "I want you to meet our best deputy." He led the young lady by the arm into his office where Tiny was waiting, decked out in his newest uniform, minus gun and badge. He extended his huge right mitt.

"Pleased to meet you, Officer Harris," Brenda said. A shiver ran through her. After all, she had read about the Goliath-like sergeant's escapades in the *Daily News*.

"My pleasure, entirely," responded Tiny. "Call me Tiny, all my friends do. Isn't that right, Captain?"

"Yeah, that's right," Post said. "Look, I've arranged for you two to use my unmarked car. It will be less conspicuous as Tiny is still technically off duty."

"Great," began Tiny. "I have a perfect duty patrol for us to make tonight and still get Cinderella home before midnight. And next weekend, we can go on a special trip together." Tiny led the demure high school student to the car. "Let's begin with some coffee and talk, wha'd ya say?"

"Sounds like a plan," replied the enthusiastic Explorer.

On the following weekend, Tiny picked Brenda up at her house in his Jeep Grand Cherokee. He told her she could accompany him to the state prison at Starke where he was going to interview a prisoner about a current drug investigation. She came bounding out of the front door of her white stucco home clad in denims and a simple blue blouse. Her hair, the color of sunset but darkening into the dusk, was in a French-style braid. She looked as fresh as a spring shower. Indeed, spring was already in the air in Southwest Florida.

"We'll head up State Road 27 and stop in Avon Park for some shooting practice," Tiny said when she was seated and buckled up. "There's a terrific range there. Like I told you on the phone, I've been fully vindicated and reinstated, so I need to practice up a little. Have you ever shot a gun?"

"Not really, just my dad's shotgun, once," Brenda replied.

"OK, then we'll start at the beginning. If you're going to be a police officer, you need to get familiar with guns of all sorts." Tiny was being the teacher now.

"Ready, willing, and able, sir," Brenda said, sounding like a recruit.

"*Willing* is the key, my dear." Watching the girl hold his .38 Smith & Wesson and the 9mm Glock was getting the sociopathic deputy all worked up. After the shooting, they had lunch before resuming their trip. Tiny turned onto a gravel side road five miles north of the shooting range.

"What's up?" Brenda was becoming nervous at the side trip and the speed Tiny was driving.

"I've got to make a quick stop up here, about another mile, to talk with my subject's brother." Tiny stared straight ahead, concentrating on his driving. There was nothing around but endless orange groves on one side of the road and forested swamp on the other. A canal ran along the right side to provide drainage for the roadbed adjacent to the swampland. An alligator, sunning itself on the side of the road, splashed into the canal with a speed belying its lazy manner. Another mile down the road, Tiny pulled over to the left and parked next to a wooden shack with a small porch and an old rocker.

"I'll go see what's up." Tiny was suddenly all police business. "You stay put unless I signal it's OK." Tiny walked up the steps, Glock at the ready. He banged on the door. No answer. He opened the door and barged in. It was a migrant picker's shack as he was well aware. There wouldn't be anyone here for another couple of weeks. He signaled for her to come in, holstering the gun.

"What's going on, Officer Harris?" Brenda was getting nervous. Her girl radar was beeping noticeably now.

"Tiny, remember, call me Tiny," he said, coming down the steps. "You *are* my friend, right?" Tiny moved around the Jeep as quick as a gator coming out of the water to snag a fawn on the bank. Grasping the girl by the arm, but not gently, he pulled her from the Cherokee. "I said come on in. Obeying a superior officer is lesson number 1 after all." There was no escaping the vicelike grip of those huge digits. Brenda dug in her heels, but it was as useless as trying to stop a bulldozer.

"Tiny, no! What are you doing?" Her pleas fell on deaf ears. There was nobody at home in Tiny's head now. "Stop! Tiny!" In the door and onto a dusty cot, she was propelled. Her mind was going blank now, in shock, as she realized what was happening. There was a *ripping* sound, and her blouse was torn off. She flashed on the alligator by the canal. *What was that feeling? Her pants were off. She thought about what somebody had told her about alligators, or had she seen it on TV? They grab their prey and drag it underwater where they rotate with it, around and around, until it is drowned. Afterward, they stuff it in an underwater hole to let it ripen to taste.* Brenda's head seemed to be on a carousel spinning madly out of control. She felt an unwelcome hardness between her legs and lost all consciousness.

Tiny exploded in an unusually prolonged and mind-bending orgasm. He literally blanked out for a few moments. The girl lay beneath him like a warm and pretty doll. *Mine, all mine,* he thought. Power is the *greatest* aphrodisiac.

Julie Moore and Tommy Nelson arrived in Napolis about a year ago on a whim. They found employment for a few nights, here and there at nightclubs, but were quickly depleting their relatively meager reserves when they stumbled into the casino job. It required a changing, or at least postponing, of their dream of living near the beach. But what the heck, they were only twenty-five minutes from Wiggins Pass and Vanderbilt Beach. Besides, the casino job paid well, was steady, and included a free dinner and two complimentary drinks. Julie substituted at both the elementary and high school quite often as well. She had a degree in social studies from the University of Rhode Island. All in all, they were pretty fat. And they were very much in love.

Julie pulled her Toyota Corolla up in front of 109. Toad and that guy, John Vaughn, who had roosted next door, were out in front of Toad's room smoking cigarettes and talking. Toad had the obligatory bottle of Popov next to his chair and was drinking out of his trademark coffee cup. Julie waved.

"Yo!" she said.

"Yo, momma," shot back Toad in his best voice from the hood.

"Yo momma yoself, white-bread." Julie liked Toad OK, but usually kept her distance. His drinking and carrying on were a bit much. And she sure as hell didn't want Tommy hangin' out boozing with him. She was apprehensive enough as it was about Tommy getting sucked down the alcohol gutter. For some reason, maybe it was the way her students seemed to be wild all day, she felt like having a little pop of the Popov to unwind. Maybe she could get some of the skinny on this Vaughn guy and the other dude, Nolan, in 112.

"How 'bout buyin' a pretty gal a drink, cowboy." Julie smiled winsomely, always the consummate flirt.

"Not a problem." Toad played the bartender.

"Orange juice and ice?" Toad fished a red plastic cup from a box under the table next to a small blue-and-white Playmate cooler.

"I got Bud too if you want a beer," offered Vaughn in his diesel voice.

"Thanks"—Julie flashed the shy outdoorsman a sly smile—"but a screwdriver sounds like just the ticket."

"Two dudes having a drink is OK," remarked Toad, handing Julie her heavily laced orange juice, "but add a pretty gal into the mix and you gatta pah-ti."

"Why, thank you, if that's a compliment, and fuck you if it's not." Julie sipped the drink. "Whew, strong one!"

"So you have been with the wee steen-kers or the me teen-kers?" Toad was being the flip host while rolling a smoke.

"Oh, I went five rounds with the third-graders," Julie said. "They were extra crazy today. It's hard walking into someone else's classroom and figuring out what to do. Half the kids *no hablan ingles*—they don't speak English. It seems like most are from single-mother homes and the rest have alcoholic fathers. No offense to present company."

"No offense taken," responded Toad, a small smile peeking from beneath the whiskers.

"I ain't no alky," retorted Vaughn, visibly disturbed by the reference.

"It's just that there are so many family problems compounded by ethnic and cultural diversity," continued Julie. "Trying to run a traditional school with standardized testing and a woefully understaffed faculty is ridiculous. I mean, they really think the school system can perform miracles with children in the time they spend on campus. The real miracle is the schools do as well as they do."

"I hear you there," said Toad, blowing out a galaxy of smoke from his home-rolled cigarette. "I went to school where everyone was white and mostly middle class, and I thought *it* was totally fucked up."

"Soo, John, what is it you do?" Julie asked, wanting to change the subject.

"I kinda just drift around." Vaughn shifted uneasily, staring out at the garden, looking like he wished he were a rabbit hiding under the giant zucchini leaves. "Live mostly out in the woods."

"Really," Julie said. "Like, how do you mean? You live in a tent or a box and eat snails?"

"Yeah, somethin' like that." Vaughn was visibly uncomfortable but beginning to warm up to the feminine attention. "See, I was married for two years . . . found out she was sleepin' the whole time with my best friend. You know . . . like that Jethro Tull song, 'Locomotive Breath.' Anyway, I figured I best put some distance between me and them before somebody got dead. I was working regular as an electrician at the time, and I had some money saved up, so I cleaned out my account and split. All I took was a change in clothes, a small fishin' pole, and my Survivor shotgun. I camp out in the woods and live cheap, shoot or catch my food, hit the grocery and fast-food dumpsters, work odd jobs or do migrant work occasionally . . . I get by. Besides, I'm not so crazy 'bout returning to the rat race and all its trappings. I'm especially in no hurry to own one of them killin' machines, again, that everyone tears around in." He nodded toward Julie's Toyota. "It's like there were never such things as trains and buses the way this country's gone car crazy."

"How long you figure on camping here at the Fireproof?" Julie was both curious and concerned although the automobile reference didn't make even a blip on her radar. John Vaughn made her a little uncomfortable somehow, but not in a scary way. She took a long drink from her red cup.

"Heck, I don't know." Vaughn reached down to the cooler and pulled out a beer. "It feels pretty good here right now. I've been out there"—Vaughn nodded toward the pine forest hammock separating the motel from the Everglades—"for quite a while. I'm thinkin' I'll take advantage of the special monthly rate they got here and stay that long anyway. Think some things out in the air conditioning, away from the insects."

"What's a Survivor shotgun?" Julie didn't know doodly-squat about guns but felt uneasy somehow knowing Vaughn had a firearm. She looked at Toad who appeared to be taking a mini siesta, beard on chest.

"Hold on, I'll show you." Vaughn rushed back into his room quick as a lizard scooting under a rock. *Didn't think he could move so fast,* Julie thought. She sipped the Popov screwdriver. When Vaughn returned, he was carrying a short riflelike gun with camouflaged plastic stock. The barrel was pointed at the ground.

"This here is the Survivor twelve-gauge shotgun," Vaughn said. He thumbed a button by the hammer and jerked up a little with his right arm and shoulder. The barrel cracked open, and a yellow plastic shell ejected part way from the chamber. Vaughn plucked it out and placed it on Toad's table. "This gun'll kill any size game from squirrel to 'gator. Knock a full-grown bear on its ass. You put in the size load you need to do the job. This here is double-aught buckshot, magnum load." Vaughn picked up the three-inch-long plastic shell about three-quarters of an inch round and handed it to Julie. "That right there will kick ass on just about any living thing, and you don't have to be a great aim, just point and shoot." He handed the gun to Julie. She took the gun, still broken open, and looked down the barrel from the chamber side.

"My god," she said. "This looks like a miniature cannon."

"That's exactly what it is," replied Vaughn.

"You carry this around like this wherever you go?" Julie asked.

"Naww," Toad, returning to life, half-croaked, half-barked, answered for Vaughn. "It breaks down."

"Breaks down?" Julie looked Vaughn with a puzzled expression.

"Yeah," Vaughn said, reaching for the gun. "Let me show you." Vaughn flicked his arm, and the gun snapped shut. "You start with the gun like this. First, you unscrew this knob below the barrel on the plastic stock piece." A moment later, the weapon was in three pieces, four if you count the screw.

"I see," Julie said. "Pretty cool."

"Think I'll put it away like this for now, be harder for someone to make mischief with or steal, and I can whip it together fast enough in an emergency." He took the disassembled gun back to his room. Julie was feeling a little better about Vaughn; he wasn't really any threat at all, especially after volunteering to put the gun away unassembled. The vodka was really hitting her now. She decided to go back to her room.

"I gotta get back to my place, thanks for the drink." Julie smiled at Toad, who grinned back, nearly toothless, through his beard.

"Anytime you want to play with guns, mine is always loaded." Toad winked obscenely at her.

"Yeah, sure thing, Toady." Julie, accustomed to Toad's drunken one-liners, turned to go back to her room. "Bye, John!" she shouted over her shoulders.

"Bye." Vaughn stood, waving as she walked away, the delinquent schoolmarm.

6

Driving east in his Grand Cherokee, Tiny was meeting Captain Post at the intersection of county roads 846 and 858. From there, they would head south on 858 in Tiny's Jeep to attend a cockfight at the Red Rooster Ranch. Afterward, they would attend to business with the proprietor, Rooster Babcock. He reviewed what he knew of the man. He was allegedly a retired developer who moved here about a dozen years ago from Alabama. He had bought a 250-acre spread on the Baron-Hendry County line. The land was half swamp and gators. But the other half was dry hammock with good pasture and some orange groves. Rooster had his fingers into almost every illegal gambling pie in Southwest Florida. He most likely was behind the gambling house that Carlos and Omar burned down over a month ago. It seemed he was determined to operate as many outlets as he could get away with, free of the protection fees levied by Tiny and Post. Compared to the kind of money he was making on the cockfights alone, these fees were nominal. But like most greedy businessmen, Rooster wanted more than his due. After all, police protection in the form of turning a blind eye while obfuscating the truth from potential state and federal officials, not to mention pesky animal rights advocates, was all part of doing business. Whether Rooster was a part of the invisible Dixie Mafia or not, Tiny was determined he would not operate without putting hefty sums in his (and sure, Post's) pockets now that he was cutting himself in for some of Post's action. A ballpark figure for Rooster's net on the cockfighting alone was close to seven figures annually. And all tax free. According to Post, Rooster was only coughing up a paltry 10K for his whole operation. That was going to change starting today. A 2,000 percent increase for good ole Cock-a-Doodle-Do was going to be imposed this day. The heart beneath the deputy's badge quickened with anticipation even as his mind reeled with thoughts of thousands of hundred-dollar bills filling his offshore accounts.

Tiny drove a quarter mile past the junction of Routes 846 and 858, making a right onto a gravel road. He drove another quarter mile to where a thirty-six-foot travel trailer was parked. This was a place maintained by Andre, the pimp for discreet encounters between prostitutes and paranoid johns who didn't want to be seen anywhere in town. Post was there, his maroon Grand Marquis parked by the trailer. He was wearing dungarees and a white polo shirt covered by a light leather jacket. Tiny pulled up by the marquis and unlocked his doors to let the captain in.

"Ready?" Tiny asked. Post looked nervous, fumbling with the seat belt.

"I guess," he replied. "I'm just not so sure this is a great idea. Kinda like walking into the tiger's den, isn't it?"

"Sure is." Tiny smiled and put the Jeep in gear. "Let's get this show on the road!"

"What's the plan?" Post was fidgeting in his seat, looking at the Western sky as the sun set.

"Plan is, there is no plan." Tiny enjoyed the captain's discomfort. "You ride shotgun all night, that's all you got to remember. I hope you're carrying." Post pulled a Smith & Wesson Centennial Model 40, a .38 caliber snub nose revolver with no hammer spur, from an inside pocket in his jacket. The gun fit nicely in the palm of his hand and didn't cause any identifiable bulge in the leather jacket.

"Will this do?" Post asked. "How about you?"

"Naw, I'm just the driver, remember? You stay alert, and if I need backup, be there." Tiny reached over and opened the glove box. He pulled out a wad of twenty-dollar bills. "There's two grand there, one for each of us. We use that for betting money on the first couple of fights. Then we go to the house and talk to Rooster. Leave the security people to me. Just be ready." Tiny drove a few more minutes south on 858 and turned left on a driveway paved with burnt orange interlocking bricks. There was a front gate and guardhouse. The guard waved them through with a bored expression on his slack face. They drove through the twilight down a driveway of two hundred yards, lined with oak and banyans, conveying a sense of pastoral beauty and old Southern-plantation charm. They went by the gate to the house compound and drove another two hundred yards to a parking area where a couple of dozen cars and pickup trucks were already parked. They got out and walked toward the arena. Behind a chain-link fence to the left were dog kennels with at least a dozen pit bulls barking and snarling.

"Looks like there's more than cockfights going on here," remarked Post.

"Seems to be," said Tiny.

Just past the dog kennels and extending out as far as they could see in the rapidly fading light, around the other side of the arena, were dozens of four-foot-high metal A-frame huts. They were spaced ten to twelve feet apart.

"That's the housing for the 'stags' or young males," Tiny explained. "They keep 'em tethered to those hutches until their first molt around two years. Otherwise, they'd kill one another before they ever got a chance to fight." This wasn't the first time the deputy had been to an arena of this sort. They walked up to a gate in a chain-link fence, forming an outside foyer to the arena. A bearded hulk in coveralls stopped them here.

"Hole up, y'all," the man mountain said. "Don't reckon I know you two. Maybe somebody invited you and didn't tell me."

"Yea, somebody like Rooster Babcock," said Tiny with a presidential smirk. "Ever hear tell of him?"

"Tell you what, dump truck," the guard Goliath said, glaring at Tiny, "how 'bout I call Mr. Babcock and ask him?" Picking up a radiophone, he began a call to another security guard but was interrupted by the arrival of a stocky middle-aged man in a sports coat and two tough-looking young men in denims and tan polo shirts.

"It's OK, Lester," Rooster said. He ran a hand through thick auburn hair going a little gray. "These gentlemen are my guests. I simply overlooked telling you they might be here tonight." Still glowering, Lester stepped aside for Tiny and Captain Post.

"Glad you two could make it," Rooster said. "Did you come to watch the action?"

"We came to do a little betting as well," said Tiny.

"Great, be my guests! How 'bout a couple of beers?"

"I'll take a Coke, and Post here favors Dr Pepper," Tiny answered. Rooster turned to one of the two tough-looking young men bird-dogging him and nodded toward a small concession area. The man scurried away. Obviously, Rooster didn't go anywhere without his own private security contingent.

"See that man over there?" Rooster nodded toward a thin seedy character in coveralls and wearing a baseball cap with a Master Bait and Tackle Shop logo on the front. "He'll take your bets. One hundred dollar minimum. I'll be at the house taking care of some business. Come up when you run out of money, and we'll talk." Rooster gave them a smile and a nod and left with his hired muscle.

"Let's go bet on the birds," said Tiny, and he headed toward the arena door.

Inside the arena were maybe seventy or eighty men in every kind of clothing from shorts and tee shirts to jacket and tie. Most were white, but there were few Hispanics. No blacks except Captain Post. This was a private event and required a certain standing and connections in the rural gambling underground to get in. There were virtually no African Americans who qualified. The seedy guy with the hat approached.

"Admission is a hundred apiece," he said. "Wanna bet now too?" He had a Southern drawl oozing out of his lips stuffed with chewing tobacco. Fact is, most of the men had decidedly Dixie accents. Tiny and Post paid the admission fee but declined to bet the first fight. More men were straggling in. A muscular man in his midthirties approached them. He wore the tan polo shirt of an employee. Above the rooster emblem was an embroidered shield with Security Chief printed inside.

"I'm Teddy Grimms, top watchdog here," he said. After shaking the lawmen's hands, he signaled with a hand gesture. A young man in his late teens came up to them, bright blue eyes blazing with excitement. He wore a tan shirt as well.

"Jimmy here will show you around," Grimms said. "I have to get back to work."

"Howdy, my name's Jimmy," the boy said, extending his right hand to Tiny. "Mr. Babcock told me to stay close to y'all and help anyway I could."

"That's mighty white of Mr. Babcock," said Tiny. He turned to Post. "Excuse the expression, Ben."

"No offense taken, Harris."

"They're about to begin," said Jimmy, pointing to a pit enclosed by a wire fence in the center of the arena. Two men entered from opposite sides, one with a red baseball cap and one with a black. Each is holding a majestic bird but with its head shorn of wattles and combs. The heads are angry red bobbing nubs with vicious bills. Nasty curved metal gaffs, two inches long, had been bound like thorns to the nubs of severed spurs. The rooster on the right had a mane of shiny bright orange hackle feathers and black arching tail feathers. "That there's a Roundhead. The other is a Butcher." Jimmy pointed to the left one. "See, the hackles are darker, like burnt orange, and it has splashes of white at the base of its tail." The two men began thrusting the birds back and forth, beak to beak. "That's how they start each fight. It's kinda like a ritual."

"Two on the black tail!" shouted a man in coveralls. All bets are in hundreds.

"Three on the Butcher!" screamed a young man in polo shirt and khakis. There is an uproar of vociferous bellows and cries.

"Gus, he's the referee," Jimmy instructed, "is fixin' to start the match."

"Ready . . . *pit!*" Gus shouted. The birds discharged from their handlers grasp and flew into each other in midair, beak grasping beak, crashing and rebounding from each other again and again, hackles flaring like fur on an angry cat. The betting continued at a fever pitch.

"Two on the orange feathers!" a fat man bellowed.

"One on the black hat!" a senior cried, clutching a bill in a gnarly outstretched hand.

Finally, the Butcher caught the Hatch with a foot spur, puncturing a lung. The wounded cock withered quickly, coughing up blood and rasping in breaths that sounded like tires spinning on gravel. The dying bird was carried out of the pit.

"The Butcher wins, pay all!" Gus hollered.

"OK, Jimmy," Tiny said, "let's go get 'em!"

Two hours later, Tiny gave Post a weary look. "I've had enough of flying feathers and blood. It's time to go see Rooster. You up or down?"

"Guess I'm about five hundred down," replied a glum Post. "What about you?"

"Two hundred up."

"Give me blackjack, anytime," said Post. "I don't care for blood and gore gambling."

"Not exactly dainty, is it?" Tiny said. "Jimmy, lead us up to the house, good buddy."

"Sure, Tiny. Just follow me."

Outside the arena, Jimmy directed them to a four-seat electric golf cart. He whisked them across the parking lot to the gate of the house compound. The gate was steel bars about seven feet high with two iron roosters beak to beak in the center. A voice came over a speaker. "Come up to the house, Jimmy. We're by the pool." With that, the gate swung inward. It was like driving into a well-maintained country club. Floodlights illuminated several acres of the grounds. Palms of every variety—the clustered date palms, tall Florida royal and sabal palms, fan-leafed and gnarly barked Washington palms, and the thick-trunked and plume-topped Canary Island palm—graced the landscape. Oak and banyan trees lined the driveway that passed through the spacious groomed lawns and hedges. There were at least two putting greens that Tiny could see. They rode to one side of the main house, a white stucco mansion enclosing around seven thousand square feet, surrounded by flowers and flowering vines of every description. Another gate, this one wrought iron, gave passage through an impenetrable fence of eight-foot-high red-flowered bougainvillea. The Oz-like brick path ended at a walled-in lanai with a screen roof enclosing a swimming pool, hot tub, and utility cabin.

"Leave the cart here, Jimmy," Tiny said.

"But I have to go back to the arena," Jimmy pleaded.

"Walk." Tiny gave the young man a hard stare, no longer Mr. Good Buddy. Jimmy got out of the cart, gave Tiny a forlorn look, and headed back around the house. One of the young men in khakis admitted them through an ornate metal door in the masonry wall.

"Welcome!" Rooster called to them. He stood up and beckoned them over to the table where he was sitting by a large pool. The courtyard around the pool was immense. There were dozens of exotic plants, particularly rare breeds of orchids. An outer building on the east side enclosed showers and toilets. Near this was a large Jacuzzi with a raised platform around it. A glassed-in area with comfortable-looking leather lounge chairs, a couple of tables, and bookshelves looked out on the lanai. In an adjoining room was a fully equipped gym. *No doubt about it,* thought Tiny. *Ole cock-and-bull Rooster was doin' just fine.*

"How about a drink, boys. Take a load off." Rooster gestured to the vacant chairs around the table.

"Coke's good for me," said Tiny.

"I'll take a beer," said Post. "Bud, if you've got it."

"No problem. Sit." Rooster again with the nod, and his man Friday was getting the drinks. "So how'd you make out at the fights? Exciting stuff, huh?"

"You drug those birds to get them so aggressive?" Post asked.

"No way," replied Rooster. "Good care and breeding produces the healthiest and toughest fighters. That's not to say some of these local yokels don't hype their birds occasionally. But when we find out about it, and we always do, they pay hefty fines and are banned for a couple of months. That puts a huge crimp in their incomes, trust me. It's not a big problem. Remember, we don't *make* them fight really. Their sole purpose in life *is* to fight. You have people in these animal rights groups and our esteemed legislatures, who have never lived a rural lifestyle, trying to impose their values on us. It doesn't mean they're right. It just means there are more of them."

Friday gave the guests their drinks. The two cops sat down at a round table.

"Maybe the laws are made by poodles," Tiny said, "but we're sworn to uphold them. Way I see it, you got several felonies goin' down at once out here. You seem to be makin' a pretty good livin' at it." Tiny rolled his head on his thick neck in a circular motion to take in all of the surroundings.

"Well, now," Rooster said, shifting in his chair and picking up his drink, "that's why I cut you boys in for a piece of the action. Here's to sharing the profits with our illustrious sheriff's department."

"That's what we're here to discuss, Rooster," Post injected.

"What's to discuss?" Rooster asked. "Like I said on the phone, I'm happy to raise my contributions to the Fraternal Order of Police." A very lovely young lady in a bikini approached from the house with a sour face.

"Rooster, Jackie and I want to use the Jacuzzi now," she said with a whine.

"Go back to the billiards room and wait until I'm done here." Rooster was more than a little irate but doing well containing himself. "I'll send one of the boys in to get you later. Now, go!" She turned, her face a pout, and stalked back to the house, her nearly naked backside swaying with provocative allure.

"The amount," said Tiny. "That's what there is to discuss."

"That's not open for discussion," responded Rooster. "I'm donating a liberal amount as is. Don't go getting *greedy*, boys." Post opened his mouth to say something, but Tiny cut him off, the blood beginning to rise through his bull neck to his face like mercury in a thermometer placed in boiling water.

"From what I've seen just tonight and what I know of your other operations," he began, "you're makin' ten times what any other operator is grossing. You're also cutting into turf that don't belong to you. Remember that house fire 'couple months ago?"

"That was an unfortunate misunderstanding," Rooster replied. "As I've said, I'm willing to enter into negotiations with other players, but you can't stop progress." Rooster forced a weasel smile between his lips.

"You're a suspect in at least one homicide," interjected Post.

"Come now, Captain." Rooster drained his glass and handed it to Friday to be refilled. "I haven't the slightest idea what you're talking about, and I don't want to know. You haven't a shred of evidence on me, and we both know it. If you want to shut down a petty rural pastime like the occasional cockfight, go ahead. I'll plea bargain a deal, pay some fines, and be free to go. Let's stop with this arrant nonsense and idle threats."

"Listen, Rooster—," Tiny began.

"No, you listen, Teeny!" Rooster interrupted, deliberately mispronouncing Deputy Harris's nickname. "Don't fuck with me, or you and the captain here will find yourselves wearing orange uniforms inside your own jail. Take this settlement amount and get out." He tossed a small brown package across the table to where Post was sitting.

"Here's the new deal," said Tiny through clenched teeth, his face crimson red. "You're payment is going to 20K a month, starting today. If you try any more expansions without clearance, you pay a 100K fine. If you even hint at threatening either me or Post again, you'll get a lot worse than this." Before anyone could grasp what was happening, Tiny overturned the table, knocking Rooster over. Grabbing Friday by the shirt and belt, he picked him up and heaved him into the pool. Whirling around like a toreador, he faced another bad boy coming straight at him. Tiny stepped gingerly to the side, and using the man's momentum, he cast him into the pool as well. The commotion and Rooster's yells brought two more thugs from the house, both with semiautomatic handguns. Post was behind Rooster now with his .38 in his hand pointed at the crime king's head.

"Tell them to drop the guns. Now!" Post yelling.

"OK, OK." Rooster was furious but a little scared too. "Drop 'em boys." The two did as instructed. "Now, beat the crap out of that ape by the pool."

They charged toward Tiny who likewise came at them, toreador turned bull. Post grabbed Rooster's shirt with his free hand and pushed and dragged him over to secure the dropped weapons. There was a loud *oomph* as Tiny, changing to football tackle, dove into the middle of the lead man. The man's wind went out, and Tiny rolled over him and was back on his feet behind the other bodyguard. The guard turned, coming off his feet, one leg extended to drop-kick Tiny in the face. Tiny rotated to the right, and the foot bounced harmlessly off the deputy's left shoulder. Tiny's fist found his adversary's balls, and all willingness to fight went out of the man as he sunk down with his hands covering his groin, groaning in pain.

It wasn't over yet, however. The tackled man, his wind returned, came behind Tiny, wrapping an arm around his neck. Tiny pried the arm away as if it was a small child's. Taking the right one, he twisted it up, hard, one hand on the wrist, the other at the elbow. There was a loud crack as the bone broke. The man screeched like a jungle monkey in heat and crumbled. Post held Rooster, left hand grasping the back of his shirt collar, the gun pointing at the two reluctant swimmers.

Tiny strode over to the crime boss and smiled. His fist struck out snakelike and landed a tough love tap on the jaw. Grabbing the semiconscious playboy away from Post, he dragged him to the pool. He gave the kingpin a quick blow to the midsection, bringing him to his knees. Grabbing Rooster's head in his massive hands, he forced it into the pool, holding it underwater for ten seconds. Red hair in his grasp, Tiny pulled the gambling don's head out, let him gasp a breath, and then shoved it under again. This time, he didn't let up until Rooster's legs were kicking like a dog chasing rabbits in his sleep. Rooster had taken on a little water and was coughing and sputtering, unable to catch his breath.

"We have a deal?" Tiny yelled in his face. The crime lord nodded feebly, unable to speak. Tiny grabbed his head again.

"No!" Rooster managed to blurt before his head went under for a third time. "Deal. I'll pay what you want."

Tiny and Post stayed long enough to make sure Rooster would survive his near-death experience. Tiny picked up the handguns, removed the clips, and tossed them in the pool. He also grabbed a Nextel radiophone and took it with him. He motioned to the captain; and they went out the back door, got in the purloined golf cart, and sped back to their car.

Rooster, with help from Friday, staggered through the door and down the path through the wrought-iron gate. The other henchmen were already in the open, firing their pistols when Rooster caught up, breathing hard. The lights on the cart the two lawmen usurped were disappearing out the front gate.

"Should we go after them?" Friday asked.

Rooster Babcock shook his head side to side.

"I'll kill both of them," he whispered.

7

Mike Nolan was at the end of his second month in room 112 at the Fireproof Motel. His contact inside the sheriff's department indicated both Sergeant Edwin Harris, a.k.a. Tiny, and his station captain, Benjamin Post, were running some kind of extortion scam in the eastern part of Baron County. Hell, it might go as far as Napolis. Facts were scarce, and even disgruntled deputies failed to come forward. Meanwhile, the two had excellent track records on paper, and Post was on friendly terms with the top law enforcement officer in the county, Sheriff John Gunther. It was time to go out and start shaking some orange trees and see if any rotten fruit dropped out.

Nolan walked over to the motel office to pay his rent for another month. It was just after seven in the evening. Nolan rang the bell, and Morris came to the door with napkin in hand, still chewing. Nolan could hear Pat Sejak spinning the wheel of fortune in the background.

"Sorry to interrupt your dinner," Nolan said. "I'd like to pay for another month, but I can come back later if it's inconvenient now." *Because I'm Mr. Considerate,* he said to himself.

"No, no, it's OK," Morris said. "Business before pleasure, hey? None of the money from the wheel comes my way no matter how many times I solve the puzzle. How's the job search going?"

"Oh, I'm working for the county, part-time, doing housing surveys of migrant workers." Nolan gave Morris the approved cover story for his continued stay in this part of Baron County. If anyone checked, they would find him on the county payroll with an official title.

"Well, I can tell you the housing here is a disgrace," Morris interjected. "Most of those people are living in run-down trailers and shacks, some without running water half the time and most with leaky roofs. And with the exorbitant rents, families have to live double and tripled up. I understand there's as many as twenty men, women, and children in some of those places." Morris looked at Nolan for confirmation of the stories from local newspapers.

"It's as bad as that and worse," replied Nolan, picking up the ball. "If there was a fire in some of those places, half the inhabitants would be trapped. And disease! There's open cesspools all over the county. Listen, I won't keep you any longer, have a good night." Nolan pocketed his receipt and turned to go.

"Good night to you," replied Morris and returned to finish dinner with his wife, Ida, Pat Sejak, and Vanna White.

Nolan saw the Mexicans' truck parked outside 106. Time to put some pieces together. He walked over and waited in the shade of a palm. In a few minutes, the two Mexicans, Omar and Carlos, emerged from Jamie Dorr's room. Nolan knew they were the same two Harris visited at the Rainbow Pines Trailer Park. After they left, he approached the door. He tried the doorknob. Locked. He knocked.

"Who's there?"

"It's Mike from room 112." This was only the second time he'd been over to Jamie's room since movin' in. The first time he came over was to have a piece of Brian's birthday cake a couple of weeks ago. Everyone at the motel was invited to that party.

"Just a sec." There were scrambling sounds from the other side. The latch clicked, and the door swung open. "Hey, Mike. What's up?" Jamie appeared a bit discombobulated.

"Listen, I have to discuss something important with you," Nolan half-whispered. "Can we go inside?"

"I guess so." Jamie didn't sound thrilled, but he made way for Nolan.

Nolan surveyed the scene. There was no incriminating evidence in view, but there was the unmistakable sweet pungent odor of marijuana. No smoke, just the almost-palpable smell.

"Actually, I was wondering if I could buy a lid. I turned Toad on to most of what I bought before." Nolan looked nonchalant. Jamie gave him a long look. A lid was a full ounce. More than most people he sold to could afford.

"Toad thinks you're a narc," he blurted. Nolan smiled.

"I work for the county," he said. "Migrant housing. I just got the job a couple of weeks ago. If I were a cop, I sure as hell wouldn't be wasting time on you. No offense."

"Some cops are just pricks," Jamie said. "They don't care who they bust as long as they get in the papers. It looks good for their department if they throw a bunch of kids in jail for sellin' dope. Or bust some dude just trying to get by. How many lives have been ruined over a few ounces of pot or even less? Ain't the users that are the sick ones but the cops and judges and prosecutors and legislators. But especially the cops."

"I guess you got a point there," Nolan said. "Big guys rarely get busted."

"Too much dough," jumped in Jamie. "They don't touch the stuff themselves. It's all done by proxy. And if they piss someone off enough to get caught, they buy their way out. That's why our prisons are full of guys like me. Guys who just smoke a little."

"I see your point," chimed Nolan. "The local district attorney is always going after the small guy with no funds for decent lawyers. That way, he makes a name for himself. Shows how tough on crime he is. Maybe teams up with some money and runs for governor."

"Probably, some of the money is from the big dealers," said Jamie. "The same rascals he is supposed to protect the children of America from."

"Yeah," went on Nolan. "The United Hypocrites of America." They both laughed. "So how 'bout a little smoke. If I bust you, you can bribe me."

"That's another thing," said Jamie. "Some cops will get the goods on someone and extort money for 'protection.' Happens all the time." Nolan gave Jamie a sympathetic nod.

"You know anyone like that?" Nolan asked. Jamie seemed to be warming to the topic. *Maybe he'll talk,* thought Nolan. He waited.

"Well, there is this guy . . . a deputy in the sheriff's department," said Jamie. "He's like a sergeant or something. A humungous dude, they call Tiny. I hear he's real dangerous. Puts kids in jail and tortures them at that fucked-up camp they have. Gets names and shit from them and weasels money out of a few small-time dealers, especially the Mexicans."

"Is he hitting you up?" Nolan queried, a look of real concern on his face.

"No. He hasn't come near me," Jamie replied. "But why would he? I don't do any kind of dealin'." *Trying to cover his tracks,* thought Nolan.

"Sure. So how much for that lid?" Nolan was being his buddy now. "C'mon." *I'm the reason that big fuck hasn't hassled you. He's made me,* Nolan thought.

"OK. It's three fifty for a lid," said Jamie. "Primo bud." Nolan pulled two one-hundred-dollar bills and five twenties from his wallet.

"I have three hundred," he said. "I'll bring the other fifty over tomorrow. You can trust me. I'm your neighbor, remember."

"No problem, neighbor," said Jamie. They both laughed. Jamie handed Nolan a plastic bag he retrieved from under the bed.

"See you later," Nolan said, walking out the door.

"Adios." Jamie closed and locked the door.

Brian was trying to make a dent in the pile of dirty dishes that were piled around the sink in Toad's room. It was Brian's habit to make himself useful wherever he went. He stopped in for a quick drink with the army veteran and was listening to one of the war stories from his endless repertoire. The room was full of empty vodka and rum bottles, with the occasional whiskey added to the mix. Books lay scattered about on the floor, counters, and bed. The Toadster would never earn any good housekeeping awards.

"So this army intelligence officer shoots this poor kid right in front of the rest of the village," Toad continued his story after taking a leak, "and it turns out he was the nephew of the village mayor. We all had to scramble to get the fucker out before they hacked him to dog meat."

"Sounds like a totally fucked situation, all right," Brian said and finished off his drink. "I should go see what's up with Jamie."

"I'd like to watch you two birds getting it on," said Toad, the booze starting to kick in. "Florida has laws against sodomy, ya know. Are you guys into that?"

"Hey!" Brian was blushing, indignant. "I ain't saying nothing about it, that's our business. And fuck the laws anyway. And fuck you too, Toad."

"I'm not saying there's anything *wrong* with it. Seems pretty natural to me. I mean about 10 percent of every animal species is homosexual from birth. Why should people be any different? Natural selection. Population control. It's actually a *good* thing if you think about it."

"To be honest," Brian said, "I can't help feeling some guilt and shame even though I know it's 'cause I've been conditioned to think that way. But I *do have* these strong feelings for Jamie. Sometimes I just feel like I'm totally crazy." He turned away from the sink and went to the foot of the bed, picked up the half-full Popov bottle, and took a long swig. "Yyaaahh!"

"I'd say if you feel a physical, sexual attraction," Toad lectured, "you're probably gay. You really don't have much choice in the matter. You can abstain, but that won't stop your fantasies. Nobody cares what your fantasies are because that's *all* they are, unless they're *acted* on. That's why I like masturbation. You can think any damn thing you like while you're getting yourself off." Toad lit a cigarette and walked over to the curtain and looked outside. "Hey, Nolan just left Jamie's room. I hope your boyfriend didn't sell him any dope. We better go over and see what's shakin' 'n' bakin' at the dealer's den."

Mike Nolan headed into the one horse town of Bella Villa. He knew Harris was on duty, and he wanted to stalk the dangerous deputy called "Tiny." He switched on his police radio and listened. It took him thirty minutes or so to pick up on Tiny. He was making a stop at the Foo Foo Club, Bella Villa's only disco. He called his contact in the department on his cell phone. David O'Brien had been with the sheriff's department for eighteen years, one year less than Tiny. He had some good contacts, and what he didn't know he knew how to get. Still, Baron was a big county. And Napolis, where the sheriff's main office and the county courthouse were located, was a world away from Bella Villa. Someone picked up.

"Hello, this is O'Brien."

"Hello, David. It's Mike Nolan. What's up?"

"All my antennas. You bein' careful? My impression is Post and Harris know who you are. I don't think any of the other deputies have a clue."

"What are you hearing from the other deputies?" Nolan asked.

"Well, there's been some grumbling. They say there was a reported child abuse case that one deputy thought might be pretty bad, but Harris and Post put the kibosh on any investigation."

"Do you know the name and address of the offender?" Nolan asked.

"That information I don't have, but I'll dig around and see what I can come up with. The other thing ticking off some of the patrolmen is they are being pulled back from patrols where they might intercept drug traffickers. Weekend roadblocks are practically nonexistent. One time, a deputy pulled over a suspect and radioed for backup; Harris shows up and tells the deputy he knows the guy and everything is OK."

"You think Harris is dirty?" Nolan asked.

"I think there is reason to believe something is wrong in Mudville."

"One more thing. What do you know about the Foo Foo Club?"

"Only that it's the only dance joint in Bella Villa. There's some chatter that the owner, Pat Raeford, is gay and into the nose candy. But that's probably true of most of the nightclub owners in the state."

"Roger that," said Nolan.

Nolan drove down the bleak main street of Bella Villa. The most prominent building in town, next to the casino, was Casa de los Amigos, a shelter for the homeless, on the corner of Main Street and County Road 846, the road to Napolis. Taking a right into a minimall with a cigar store, he drove past a 7-Eleven, a Mexican food restaurant called "Carlitos," a fishing gear shop called "Master Bait and Tackle," and a sewing shop called "Eye of the Needle." Separated from these retail stores and set a little back was the Foo Foo Club. Nolan pulled his LeBaron convertible up and parked. He walked in and took a table by the wall. He thought maybe he'd have a beer and check the joint out. It was still too early for any real action. It was pretty much just a big room with tables around the edge, a bar on one wall with stools, and a small stage in the center for go-go dancers. There was some disco music playing amidst a plethora of blinking lights spinning on an overhead wheel. He hated places that were always dark and too loud for conversation. Meat lockers for the young and too often the psychopath who picks up a sex partner, and they're never seen alive again. A pasty-looking girl in her twenties wearing a short black skirt and black nylons came over.

"Hi. Can I get you a drink?" She sounded thrilled.

"I'll have a Coors please," Nolan answered. The girl was back in less than two minutes with a bottle of Coors. "Tell me something, eh, what's your name?"

"Cindy."

Nolan fished a twenty out of his pocket and handed it over to the girl. "Cindy, do you ever see a guy in here goes by the name 'Tiny,' a deputy sheriff?" He waved his hand when she started to make change, indicating none was needed.

"Yeah, he comes in once in a while. I never talk to him. He usually goes in the office and hangs out for a while with Mr. Raeford."

"Could you do me a favor, Cindy?" Nolan smiled, all teeth and charm. "Tell Mr. Raeford a friend of Tiny's is having a drink and would like to see him for a minute."

"Sure." She smiled back "He's usually not too busy this time of night. Who should I say is waiting?"

"Just tell him a friend of Tiny's."

"Yeah, sure." She turned and walked with an exaggerated wiggle of her behind to the back of the large room and disappeared. In the time it took to finish his beer, taking it kind of easy, the girl reappeared with a thin balding man in his forties. She pointed to Nolan, said something, and returned to her station. The man had short dark hair and a thin face. Nolan imagined he was probably considered quite good-looking in his early years. He wore a flowered silk shirt open at the throat. A gold chain circled his neck. He smiled and extended a hand.

"Hi! I'm Pat Raeford."

"John Kelly." Nolan decided to use his standby alias.

"What can I do for you Mr. Kelly?"

"Tiny says you have something for him. He sent me to pick it up." Pat Raeford raised his eyebrows followed by a furrowed brow.

"I beg your pardon," he said. "I haven't a clue what you're referring to."

"Don't be coy with me, Pat. I'm not known for my patience." Nolan didn't know where his bluff was going, but he went fishing anyway.

"Listen, maybe I better *call* Tiny, see what gives." Raeford pulled a cell phone from his belt. Nolan put his hand around Raeford's wrist and twisted it.

"Ouch!" screeched Raeford. "What the hell?"

"Just tell me what you have now."

"OK, OK. Let go please." Nolan let go of his wrist. "You're so macho. Jeez." Raeford gave him a long appraising look. "You're a good-looking man, but your temper destroys your charm and distorts your appearance, dear boy. I have my usual ounce of blow. I can pay Tiny the 'tax' now. But the 'insurance money' I won't have until the end of the month as usual."

Bingo! Nolan thought.

"Is Tiny getting greedy or what?" Raeford asked. "He knows I'm always good for the payola. I can't believe he's sending a sweet thing like you to do his dirty work."

"He wants an advance payment," said Nolan, "in return for skipping next month's premium." Raeford's eyes lit up at the mention of the reprieve. It would mean more toot for him and an opportunity to lure another cute boy to his lair.

"Deal," he said. "But no money changes hands until I confirm this with Tiny. And no more rough stuff, handsome."

"Gottcha," Nolan said. "I'll be right back." He went out the door and didn't return.

Mona picked up her phone and pressed the autodial for Deputy Edwin Harris's cell phone. She was pissed off. She got his voice mail. "Hey, Tiny, where the *fuck* are you? Last I remember we were supposed to go to Napolis and have dinner at the Outback. Let's see, you're only an hour and a half late and no call. Guess I'll just go out by myself and see what I can find. I have a feeling there is a raft of lonely men out there who would love to take me out. Have a nice night, *loser.*" She put down the phone, grabbed her purse from the sofa, and headed for the door. She opened it and stepped back with a gasp. There was a man standing there, grinning like a naughty schoolboy.

"Excuse me," he said. "I didn't mean to startle you. My name is John Kelly. Tiny wanted me to pick you up and take you out. Said he'd try to meet up later. He told me to apologize for the change of plans. You know—police business."

"Yeah, this ain't the first time I heard that sorry tune." Mona gave the guy a quick once-over and liked what she saw. "Well, I'm Mona. Let's go get some dinner. I'm starvin'."

The LeBaron's roof was down. "Roof up or down?" John Kelly asked.

"Oh, a convertible!" Mona said. "How cute! Leave it down. Listen, let's just go to Domino's and get a pizza. I need a quick food fix. We can bring it back to my place. Have a couple of beers. What you think, Mr. Kelly?"

"Sounds perfect. And please call me John."

"Well, Johnny, let's fly!"

About thirty minutes of small talk and banter later, they were back at Mona's apartment eating pizza and drinking beer. "So, John, how do you know Tiny? Are you a deputy too?"

"No, he and I do business together. Investments and real estate."

"Real estate," Mona said. "Do you know Ron Badger? He does a lot of real estate stuff around here. He owns the King Burger in Bella Villa. Tiny does some stuff with him."

"Oh, really?" John Kelly said.

"Yeah," Mona went on. The beer was beginning to loosen her up. And she liked this guy. He wasn't some creepy thug like most of Tiny's acquaintances. "I guess they didn't exactly meet up under the best of circumstances." She giggled and proceeded to tell John Kelly what happened when Tiny caught her with Ron Badger. As the night went on and the beer supply diminished, she told him a few other stories about their mutual friend, Tiny. Nolan got up twice to go to the bathroom and changed the tapes in his mini recording machine. He had enough information to convince him that Tiny was a *very dirty* cop indeed. Still, he had no hard evidence. When Mona started to come on to him, he figured he'd better not push his luck and made an excuse to leave. No sooner had he hopped into the LeBaron, parked discreetly a couple of houses away, that Tiny's Jeep Cherokee pulled into the driveway.

"Rut ro rig rubble," he said to himself and drove off, whistling a Don Henley tune.

"Dude, I can't believe you sold that Nolan guy a lid." Brian was already a little tipsy. *Brian's on another bender,* Jamie thought. *What can you expect hanging out with Toad?*

"I already told you, the guy is some kinda narc," Toad added. "Didn't you ever notice he never wears shorts? Look at his left ankle and you'll see a slight bulge. He's carrying a piece there, probably a Smith & Wesson Centennial or some equivalent. No hammer spur so it's easy to pull and small enough not to be real noticeable. He might just be some redneck jerk, but I don't think so." Toad took a drag on his cigarette and went on exhaling smoke as he talked. "Even if that's *all* he is, you don't want to be doin' business with him." He punctuated the last statement with a loud belch and tipped up his Popov for a swig. He offered the bottle to Brian who took a swallow despite observing Jamie's disapproving glare.

"OK, OK, you don't have to tell me how to run my business," said Jamie. "Even if he *is* a narc, I don't think he's after me. And he won't bust me for one lid. He's looking for bigger fish to fry. But yeah, I need to keep him at a distance. If he's undercover, I have a feeling he might end up underwater as gator bait in any event. That's just how things seem to go around here."

"Let me talk to him, see what I can find out," said Brian.

"No, Bry," said Jamie. "You stay out of this. It would be too devastating if something happened to you."

"I'll bullshit the guy," offered Toad. "If he's a vet, and I believe he is, I might draw him out a little."

"Thanks, Toad," said Jamie. "Everything is cool. No *problema*. Let's fire up a doobie then go get some pizza."

"Sounds like a plan," said Brian.

"I'm going to go over and see if that hermit crab, Vaughn, wants a drink," said Toad. "Save me a piece of that pie."

"You got it," said Jamie. "Let's roll, Bry."

"Seizure!" Toad said.

"Labor pains!" Jamie and Brian chorused.

8

Camilla wrapped the disposable diaper around Billie's freshly powdered baby bottom and fastened the sticky tabs. She slipped on his blue Winnie the Pooh shorts and pulled his striped shirt, with Tigger embroidered on the pocket, over his head. She smiled and kissed his chubby cheek, picked him up, and turned to look at Robert, her smile replaced with a stony glare.

"We are going to your mother's today! Right now! I have had it with this shit! Now get the keys to that heap and let's go and pray we make it to Napolis."

"OK, OK," Robert said. "But how do we even know she's home?"

"I already told you, I called her and asked," Camilla replied. She picked up Billie's rucksack. "We are supposed to be there for lunch at one, so get your ass in gear." Robert opened the refrigerator and pulled out a Bud. "Oh no, you don't. Put that back right now." Robert sighed in resignation, returned the beer to the fridge, and followed her out the door. They went out to the beater Buick, a relic of the early eighties when family cars were the size of cruise ships. They drove west to Napolis past newly gated country clubs where mega mansions *started* at over two million each. Although Robert had a privileged upbringing by any standards, the vast number of multimillionaires with sufficient portfolios to invest fortunes in seasonal and vacation homes never ceased to amaze him.

Constance Valentine lived in the heart of old Napolis, one block east of the Gulf of Mexico. This was a sedate neighborhood of rambling older homes along well-kept, treelined streets extending along the sandy shoreline of the gulf. The house was a large two story surrounded by palm and banyan trees. There was a large courtyard in the back with guest quarters and changing rooms on one side, a garage with servant quarters above on the other, and a large swimming pool in the center. A substantial lawn and flower garden provided the background on the fourth side. The entire area was enclosed with an overhead screen to keep out insects and birds. Robert parked on the street to avoid oil leaks from staining the parquet stone driveway that made a semicircle in front of the house. They walked up to the massive oak door; a carved lion's head was set over a brass plate in the center. A large brass ring passed through the nose of the lion and served as a knocker. Naturally, there was also an electric door chime on the side of the doorframe. Camilla pushed the button, setting off a symphony of church bells. Billy squealed his approval and pointed a pudgy finger toward the button, squirming in his mother's arms to have a go at the device.

Pablo Rodriquez moved swiftly from the patio where he was helping Anna, Constance Valentine's longtime maid, arrange the luncheon table. He opened the front door and smiled at the trio like the captain of the Love Boat.

"*Bienvenido*, welcome!" he said. "What a beautiful baby! Allow me to carry him to the lanai. It's such a gorgeous day we thought it would be nice to eat outdoors. Come here to Pablo, Billie." Pablo took the baby from Camilla with the deftness of someone who has held plenty of toddlers. "Follow me, please."

"Thank you, Pablo," said Camilla. *He's probably got four or five younger siblings he's cared for,* she thought. "It's so good to see you again. How does the garden grow?" That last question came out sounding like a dig, and she immediately regretted it.

"Everything looks radiant like yourself, señorita," he responded. He gave her a look of amused reproach. Something inside her turned over at that moment. This handsome young man—*he must be a few years younger than Robert,* she thought—was someone she could get to like very much. At the same time, an inexplicable sense of sorrow overcame her at his fate and what it reflected about this big dirty world. But there was something else too. Something she wasn't sure she wanted to explore. Maybe it was envy or even jealousy for Robbie's mom. *No, I don't want to go there,* she thought.

They walked through the foyer and large living room toward the back of the house. The floors were polished hardwood. The living room floor was covered with a red-hued oriental carpet of exquisite design.

"It must 'ave taken three or four weavers and a half a dozen kids a year or more of full-time work to make this," Robbie commented on the way through. He had spent a few months in Morocco, so he had an idea of the labor intensity of these things. He was beginning to feel a strange sense of resentment toward Pablo. *This guy is younger than me,* he thought, *and he's taking over the place like some goddamn rooster, strutting around and showing me through the house I grew up in. I don't like the bastard, and he's holding my kid.*

"Here we are," Pablo said. "Please sit wherever you'd like."

"I'll take Billie now," said Robert.

"OK," said Pablo. "Let me get his chair. Your mother had it delivered today just for this occasion." He brought a handmade, ornately carved wooden high chair, gleaming with numerous coats of polyurethane, over to the table.

"Oh my god!" Camilla exclaimed. "Billie, look what Grandma got for you. It's fantastic!"

"Nice," said Robert. "Billie gets to finger-paint with his food in a chair that probably cost as much as a Lexus while we beg for an old car that belonged to my father."

"The VW is not that old," said Camilla, "and we're *not* begging. This is just family business."

"It sure seems—," Robert began.

"Well, well, the gangs all here!" Constance proclaimed, striding onto the lanai. "And look at little Billie. Isn't he the cat's meow?"

"Hello, Constance," said Camilla.

"Hi, Mom," murmured Robert.

"Camilla, Robert," Constance said, taking a hand of each in turn, clasping them with both of hers, and giving them a peck on the cheek. "Let me put Billie in his chair."

"That chair is absolutely gorgeous!" Camilla said as she handed Billie to her mother-in-law. "Where did you get it?"

"You won't believe this," Constance said as she put Billie in the high chair. "But I bought that at Goodwill for one hundred and fifty dollars. It's in perfect condition too."

"Ohhh!" Camilla exclaimed. "That is so fantastic! When Robby and I get a place, I'm going to be doing a lot of shopping at Goodwill and the other thrift stores."

"Yeah, cool," said Robert.

"Why don't we all sit down," Pablo injected. "I'm starving, and Anna said everything was ready."

"Great idea, Pablo," said Constance. "You two don't mind if Pablo joins us?" She looked at Camilla and Robert with a coy smile.

As a matter of fact, I do, thought Robert. "It's fine with me," he said.

"Me too," said Camilla. She smiled at Pablo, and he smiled broadly in return. His good looks rattled something inside her.

"He works so hard around here," Constance said. "He's become almost like family. Let's sit. I had a luncheon brought in for the occasion. I believe we start with lobster bisque." Anna was already at the table with a steam tray. She began ladling bisque into bowls and serving. There ensued a delicious meal of lamb curry, rice, and asparagus. A light California Cabernet was uncorked. Dessert was strawberry shortcake. Pleasant conversation and small talk, much centered on the baby, accompanied the repast. After the coffeepot was passed for the second time and Constance went to powder her nose while Pablo helped Anna, Camilla turned to Robert.

"Well? Are you going to say something about the car or do I have to?"

"Yeah, yeah. I didn't want to be pushy," he replied.

"Robby, we *need* a car. And you need a full-time job. I can't take it anymore."

Constance returned and began to fuss over Billie.

"Listen, Mom," he began. "We were wondering about Dad's VW convertible. We really need a dependable car. I think Dad would want me—us—to have it."

Constance continued to wipe Billie's face.

"I didn't know you were interested in the VW. I was going to let Pablo use it—to run errands and so forth." Robert looked crestfallen.

"But, Mom, our car is totally undependable, and I have to work. It's not safe either. Think of Billie."

"It doesn't seem to me living like gypsies is a way to take care of my grandson," she retorted.

"I *am* going to get a good job once I get wheels—seriously."

"A good job doing what? You've never stay long enough to keep a job. God knows I've bent over backward to help, and all I get is embarrassed by your total lack of responsibility. How many jobs have you quit or been fired from now? You have a great job history for sure!"

"OK, OK. My record's not so hot. But this time I'm going to get into a job and hang in there for Billie's sake. We really need some bread." His face was the picture of earnest self-appraisal. Constance knew her son well enough to know he really meant what he said at the moment, but like a drug addict swearing off, his promises were like smoke rings, solid seeming at first then dissipating to nothingness.

"Tell you what," she said. "If you start going to FGCU full-time next semester, you can have the VW." She held up her hand when he opened his mouth. "And I will help you get financial aid as well as contribute a significant sum myself. I have a check here for five hundred dollars to start the ball rolling and the VW keys." Before Robert had a chance to reply, Camilla spoke, "Done." She cast a look at Robert that said he'd better damn well agree.

"I guess I'm a full-time student," he said. "I'll take the VW to campus tomorrow and pick up some catalogs."

"Thank you so much, Constance," Camilla said. "This really brightens up the day. And now we can bring Billy over more often to see you."

"Yeah, thanks, Mom," Robert added. "I'm really going to work at the school thing."

"Good, good," Constance said. "I'm glad I could help out. And, Robby, don't throw this opportunity away. Remember, you have a family to support now."

"I know, and I promise to do my best."

"OK. Robby, come to my office, and I'll give you the keys, registration, title, and the check, as well as some documents you'll need at the financial aid office. I'll also supply you with the names and numbers of some people to talk to. Keep in mind, this is a who-you-know world."

Camilla sat down with Billy on her lap as Robbie and his mother left to attend to business. Dreaming about their bright future, she suddenly realized Pablo was looking at her from the other side of the table.

"Madonna and child," he said. "It is so beautiful to watch." Camilla smiled, blushing a little.

"Pablo, I didn't see you return," Camilla said. "Constance gave us the VW. I suppose that is a bummer for you. I'm really sorry, but we need wheels too."

"Don't give it another thought. Señora Valentine has already bought me a Honda Civic from her car dealer friend. It's only two years old with low miles. We are going to get it tomorrow."

"Oh, I see." A cloud passed over Camilla's face for a moment but disappeared like a desert rainfall. "That's wonderful, Pablo. I'm happy for you." And she meant it.

"And I for you, Señorita Camilla. I know you are part Mexican and must appreciate how hard it is to get ahead. There are many mouths to feed in my family and of course many more relatives still in Mexico."

"I know, Pablo. I guess I know that you do more for Constance than garden. At the risk of being gauche, and you understand I really like you, how do you do it? I mean she's a grandmother, and you're still a schoolboy." Pablo looked at his sandal-clad feet for a few moments. There was a hint of a blush beneath his copper-colored skin.

"I guess I'm a whore. I want to be honest with you because I want another person to hear, and you are truly sympathetic. Sure, I do it for the money, for my family, for my college education. But I think I like the narcissistic rush I get when she makes love to me. I think I am addicted to that."

"That's a lot like what Jamie, a gay friend of mine, says about making love to another man."

"That may be," said Pablo. "Coincidentally, the man who hooked me up with Señora Valentine tried to place me with an older but very rich man at first, but I said no. Lucky for me the big deputy talked to him and brought me here to meet your mother-in-law." Constance and Robert returned from the study, laughing gaily.

"Look what I've got," Robert said, holding up a set of VW keys. "Cammy, you can drive our new convertible home. It's still registered, and guess what else? Mom says there's a brand-new child seat in the garage."

"You're the man," said Camilla. She went over and gave Constance a hug. "Thank you, again. We'll be back soon. I'll call tomorrow."

"Buzz my cell number, dear," Constance said. "Pablo and I have an errand to run, and I have to meet most of the day with some boring old real estate developers."

"Will do. Bye, Pablo."

"Adiós, señorita."

Once out on the street and headed east, the Buick and VW were passed by a maroon Jeep Grand Cherokee with police antennae on the roof, heading west and turning into the Valentine's driveway.

Tiny eased his massive frame from the driver's seat of the Jeep and surveyed the front of the house. *Yup, nice digs and great location,* he thought. *I especially like that front door.* He walked up and rang the bell. A moment later, Anna answered.

"May I help you, sir?" she inquired. Policemen frightened her. This was a reflection of old country thinking, perhaps, but hard to shake, especially with this cop who reminded her of many Mexican *policía.*

"Hi, Anna. How are you?" Officer Politeness asked.

"I am fine, Señor Harris. Thank you."

"Tell Mrs. Valentine I am here to see her please. Mind if I step in?"

"Of course not. I will get Mrs. Valentine."

"Oh, Anna, I'd like you to give this to Pablo." Tiny handed Anna a manila envelope. "Tell him I'm here now and, if he has any questions, to see me pronto."

"Sí, Señor Harris." Anna scurried away like a mouse from an approaching feline. Tiny walked into the foyer and looked around. There were some paintings by local artists—mostly seascapes. One, a dolphin jumping in the waves and a fishing boat nearby, was by a world-renown painter and sculptor. Wealth and power, it was an almost palpable presence here like the fragrance of curry in an Indian restaurant.

"Well, Tiny, to what do I owe this surprise visit?" Constance entered the foyer. "I assume it's a social call since you are out of uniform."

"To be perfectly honest," Tiny began, "it's more in the nature of business."

"I see," Constance said. "Perhaps we should go to my office." She walked quickly down the corridor to a large room with an enormous desk.

"Nice desk," Tiny blurted. He was making a monumental effort at being polite.

"Yes, I had it made by a local carpenter," Constance said. "It's an oak veneer." Tiny glanced around. There were walls of books, some family pictures, plaques noting public service, and a wall safe.

"I'm not going to mince words, Mrs. Valentine. There is a very rich old fag who is willing to pay a king's ransom for a good gardener. Fact is, he wants Pablo. Andre is pressuring me to return Pablo to the front so to speak. I'm afraid the boy's reputation precedes him. The old goat Andre spoke to is willing to double the boy's salary."

"Consider my payment doubled," Constance retorted. "But you tell this Andre he's pissing in the eye of a hurricane. All hell is going to break loose on him and anyone associated with him if he pushes his luck too far." She gave Tiny a stern thin-lipped look. "Your sheriff's badge will be like a sand castle in a tidal wave if you show your face in my house again, Harris. Now get out!" Tiny smiled, turned, and walked to the foyer where Pablo stood waiting.

"Mr. Harris," he said, "I cannot do this thing." He handed Tiny the envelope. Tiny nodded toward the front door and continued outside. Pablo followed. Tiny didn't stop until he reached the driver's door of the Cherokee. He turned around, took the envelope, reached in, and pulled out a silver-and-gold brooch. It was a beautiful piece of work, costing him over a grand. Built into it was a microphone capable of transmitting up to a half mile.

"Now you listened to me, you dumb spic." Tiny's face was inches from Pablo's. "You are going to give this to your old bag of a girlfriend, and you are going to make sure she wears it tomorrow when she meets with those developers. Because if she's *not* wearing this bauble, you are going to be sucking on some old faggot's dick until you choke." He jammed the point of the brooch pin into Pablo's left forearm.

"Ow!" Pablo yelped, putting his right hand over the wound. Tiny slapped him hard across the face. Pablo staggered back, still holding his arm; but now, his left hand went up to touch his cheek. Blood trickled down the wounded arm.

"Next time, I'll use my fist. After that, you go to jail." Tiny took Pablo's chin between his thumb and middle finger. "And, Pablito, when you get out, you'll see Andre about your new boyfriend. Now get in there and lick some old pussy. You got your marching orders, fairy." He gave Pablo a shove toward the front door, watching him slink back into the house, eyes downcast.

The extralarge deputy got into the Jeep and drove back toward Bella Villa. Bitch-slapping Pablo had turned him on. He picked up his cell and dialed Mona. "Hey, Mona. I'll be there in twenty. Break out that bottle of vino and burn some incense, baby, I'm on fire."

9

Constance, dressed in a blue pantsuit, gave the shirtless Pablo a long lingering kiss on the lips, rubbed off the lipstick with her index finger, and took just a little extra time to insert the finger in his mouth a little. He slid his mouth down the length of the digit, holding her hand in both of his.

"Stop it," she sighed. "I'm getting hot, and I really have to go."

"Wait," Pablo said. "I want you to wear something I had made just for you." He opened a dresser drawer and pulled out the brooch. "A cousin in Mexico made this. I told him what a great lady you were."

"Oh, you darling boy! This is beautiful! But it must have cost a fortune!"

"Don't worry, it was part of a trade for the help I've given him and his mother. Here, let me pin it on you." He pinned the brooch on the lapel of her suit jacket and kissed her on the cheek.

"This will bring you *buena suerta*, good luck, in whatever you do today." She hugged Pablo, to her more like a little boy than a man, held him a moment, turned, grabbed a briefcase, and left the room. Pablo, a young man of seventeen with dark eyes reflecting the sorrow of the ages, looked after her.

Tommy Nelson sat on the edge of the bed picking out the chords to the Traveling Wilburys' "Dirty World." "It's a dirty world," he sang. "It's an effin' dirty world."

"So what else is new?" Julie commented. "Isn't that a gay song? It's about homosexual lovers but metaphorically speaking. Am I right? We can't do that tune around here. No way."

"Sure we can," Tommy said. "None of these crackers are going to catch on, believe me. Metaphor interpretation requires thinking on a *higher* level. The only thing these yahoos know about higher is what they suck from a joint into their lungs. Speaking of which, don't we have a little of the ole Mary Jane kicking around? I'm due for wee bit of the ole *reefer madness*."

"What's with all the fifties lingo?" Julie asked. "You psyching up to doin' some Elvis tunes?"

"Naw, just screwin' around," said Tommy. "Why don't we go up to Tampa next week for Tom Petty. It'll be fun. We'll stay at a real hotel with a swimming pool and sauna. Eat at a good restaurant. We'll go back through St. Pete and spend a few hours on the beach at Fort DeSoto or Treasure Island if you want."

"It *is* starting to get a little boring here, and we've been busting a string playing out," said Julie. "On the other hand, we've got almost two thousand saved, and a trip like that will run us a couple three hundred easy."

"Yeah, maybe we should just stick close to home," Tommy said. "We haven't been to the beaches in Napolis since I don't remember when. Let's get everyone together and go to Wiggins Pass this Sunday. We'll get there early afternoon and get a nice picnic spot with a grill and a couple of tables. Cook us up some of that good ole barbeque."

"Sounds like a plan," Julie said, getting on the bed and giving her man a squeeze. "We can come back here and play music on the porch, a regular hoedown!"

"Yee-ha!" Tommy whooped.

"Let's go round up the troops," Julie said, sliding off the bed. Tommy caught her by the shirttail just as she started to walk away and pulled her back to the edge of the bed. Wrapping his legs around her hips, he pulled her down on top of him.

"Help!" Julie made a feeble effort to escape his clutches.

"Da big bad Daddy longlegs as got hisself a juicy bug." Tommy pitched his voice low and took on a Mississippi Delta drawl. Julie screeched and struggled as he ran his hand up under her shirt. A moment and a hot kiss later, Julie-bug was naked and that bad ole Daddy longlegs was on top and buried deep inside her.

John Vaughn looked at the VW convertible outside of Robert and Camilla's room and raised his eyebrows. He walked over to where Toad sat reading a paperback outside his door. When he got there, he noticed Toad's eyelids were drooping. The obligatory coffee cup sat half-full on the table.

"Yo, Toadster," Vaughn ventured. Toad snapped awake.

"Oh, hey, John."

"Sorry to interrupt your nap. Thought you might want to go see if Jamie has a little something to toke on."

"Sure, we can do that." Toad lifted his cup and drained it. "What time is it? I don't think he's home from work yet. His car ain't there."

"Yeah, guess you're right, but it's close to time for him to be getting back. Mind if I join you?"

"No, sit down." Toad reached under the table and pulled out a liter and a half bottle of Gold Crown Rum. "Thought I'd change my poison."

"Let me get a cup," Vaughn said and retreated to his room, returning with a coffee mug half-full of steaming black coffee. The mug featured a train running over a man's legs and the words "These things too shall pass." He sat at the table and poured a brief shot into the mug. He nodded toward the car parked in front of 105. "Looks like Robbie and Camille finally got that VW convertible."

"Yup," replied Toad. "I'd like to fuck that bitch mother of Robbie's, but I guess she likes her men *very* young and hung." He took a long swallow and wiped his beard and mustache with the back of his hand. "I imagine hookin' up with a woman like that would kinda be like mating with a black widow spider."

"I see your point there," Vaughn said. "But you could probably live pretty good for a while before she stuck the poison stinger in."

"Yeah, I bet some of those young studs think they're the cock of the walk before the fall." Toad slurped a little more rum, pulled out a pack of unfiltered Camels, and torched one.

"Hey, Camels now?" Vaughn cocked a brow.

"Treat." Toad pushed the pack over to Vaughn. "Nolan bought them for me yesterday. We had a little chat."

"Oh?" Vaughn's brows lifted quizzically as he sipped from his cup.

"He's more than a housing inspector, I can tell you that. I don't think he's real interested in busting anyone here if he *is* a cop. Seems to me he's after that big prick of a deputy with the flattop and sergeant stripes. He kept getting back to him when he was talking to me."

"Would he be undercover if he were into internal investigations?" Vaughn asked.

"Maybe. Cops are weird about shit like that though. They don't like to bust their own. Usually, they cover for each other. That's why someone from outside has to come in. That someone could be Nolan."

Jamie Dorr pulled up in front of his room and climbed out of his ten-year-old Honda Civic. He walked over to where Toad and Vaughn sat. He had a six-pack of longneck Bud under his left arm. He looked tired.

"Howdy, guys."

"Yo!" Toad and Vaughn chorused.

"Mind if I set a minute?" Toad gestured to an empty plastic chair against the wall to his right. He proffered the rum bottle to Jamie.

"No thanks." Jamie pulled a bottle from the six-pack and twisted off the cap. "I'm thirsty for the malt and hops." He tipped the bottle and took a long drink. "Rough day."

"You work for an interior design company," said Toad. "How can that be rough?"

"It may seem like just a bunch of girls and fairies picking out flowered wallpaper, but believe me there's much more than that. There's actually a lot of physical work that has to be done like moving furniture, painting, and delivering things. That's where I come in. I mean, I'm *trying* to learn the business, but my boss is just impossible. He never thinks of taking a second to explain anything. He just expects you to automatically know it all. And everything is rush, rush, rush. The man can't give anything a rest. If I go take a leak even, he jumps in and takes over a project I'm working on then says, 'I just did your job for you.' He's the most obsessive-compulsive person I've ever met. Problem is, he's my boss." Jamie took another long swallow from the bottle of Bud.

"Sometimes he's right, and sometimes he's wrong," chimed Toad. "but he's always the boss, hey."

"That's a big 10-4," sighed Jamie.

"Along the lines of relaxing," Vaughn said, "would you have a number we could smoke?" Jamie pursed his lips and nodded his head in resignation. He had long ago realized that because he sidelined in the pot trade, there would always be the inevitable requests for a freebie from friends. As if the stuff was God-given to him, he committed the sacrilege of selling it for money. Well, it came with the territory.

"Yeah, I think there's a few crumbs at the bottom of a baggie somewhere."

"Hell," said Toad, "let's go smoke shake in the dealer's house."

The first leg of Mario's trip from San Antonio was on Amtrak. He purchased a ticket for a private sleeper for the overnight trip to Tallahassee. There was a secure place outside the door for his two duffle bags containing seventy pounds of hermetically sealed marijuana. A chilled complimentary bottle of Blue Nun awaited him in his compartment. After drinking a couple of glasses of wine with snack nuts as he stretched out and read a book, he made his way to the dining car. Dinners on board were quite good and reasonably priced. Adjourning to the bar car after dinner for a couple of drinks, he enjoyed the convivial atmosphere for a while before retiring to his sleeper car. He didn't allow himself the dubious luxury of drinking too much or staying too late. After all, he was engaged in a serious and perilous business. Back in his own compartment, he read some more before pulling down the bed and falling asleep to the rhythm of the *clickity-clack*. The following morning at eleven, the train arrived in Florida's capital.

Mario boarded a Greyhound for Tampa, his baggage going in the buses below deck storage compartments. Completing the second phase of his journey, Mario walked from the grungy bus depot to the street. He was greeted by a blinking multicolor neon sign above a topless bar across the street advertising DOLLS—DOLLS—DOLLS. A seedy bar adjoined the bus station on one side and a greasy all-night diner the other. This was Mario's least favorite part of the trip. He was in a hurry to hail a cab and get out of these environs.

Clutching his bags with a viselike grip, Mario hailed a cab and told the driver to take him to the Frontier rent-a-car office on the corner of Third and Beaumont streets. He rented a Ford Taurus. This was his favorite car to transport dope. It was totally inconspicuous. Also, it had plenty of trunk space and was comfortable. He drove straight to I-75, stopping only for some Dunkin Donuts coffee and chocolate munchkins. Driving south, he reflected on his present status. Once in Bella Villa, he would leave off the merchandise and return the car to Fort Myers. Usually, Homeboy would drive him back to Bella Villa for a free lid of the pick of the crop. It was a good system, one that had served him well for the last couple of years. Then that son of a bitch, Tiny, came along and shot Homeboy, screwing up everything. A shot of adrenaline caused his guts to churn like a sausage blender when he thought of the marauding deputy. He had turned a wonderful life into a nightmare. The Mexicans were right to call him El Diablo. He was as close to the devil incarnate as anyone Mario had ever met. Mario's thoughts spun like a runaway carousel trying to figure a way out of the horrible trap in which he had become ensnared. He sipped his coffee as he sped south in the rental car, passing the second Sarasota exit.

Mario pulled into the driveway of a small two-bedroom stucco house and painted a pastel pink on Burnwood Drive, Bella Villa, just after dark. He got out of the car, stretching. The arrangement he had with Lana, a single mom who lived here with her two-year-old boy, was that they could live here free in exchange for him using it as a safe house to store products. Lana was a friend who was completely out of the business. She didn't smoke pot, drink, or use any illegal substance whatever, which made her ideal. As far as Mario knew, this arrangement was unknown to anyone but him and Lana. He opened the trunk and grabbed the first duffle.

"Have a good trip?" Mario almost came out of his socks. He whirled around to see a stocky middle-aged man standing behind him. The guy was smiling like the Joker in Batman. Mario couldn't think of anything funny. He couldn't see much from the distant light of the lamppost, and per instruction, the front house light was off.

"Who the fuck are you?" Mario asked.

"I'm a business man same as you." The man raised his right arm and clicked a Bic; and two men, young and athletic-looking, appeared from the darkness. "As I see it, you and I have business in common."

"I don't know what you're talking about," Mario said. Perspiration was dripping down his forehead into his eyes. He tried to blink it away. He was nervous. No, he was scared shitless.

"As I see it, you and I are in competition," the man said. "Some people think competition is a good thing—free enterprise and all that crap. But as I see it, competition is just bad for business—*my business*." His voice became harsh, scary with the last words. A moment later, he was all smiles and friendly. "Allow me to introduce myself, I'm Rooster." He extended his hand.

"Never mind that shit," Mario said. "I don't care if you're King Tut. What I want to know is what the fuck *do you want?*"

"Talk, Mario." The man's smile was maddening. He lifted his right hand, index finger pointing, and shook it. Immediately, the man on his right turned and jogged off into the darkness. "I want to offer you help in the form of a merger. And in return, you can help me bag some very big game in the form of a mutually annoying deputy sheriff."

"I don't need any help," Mario said. His shirt was soaking wet; he had to wipe his eyes with the sleeve of his tee shirt. Allusions to Tiny ratcheted up his fear factor. "I still don't know what the hell you're talking about." Headlights appeared in the driveway. A Cadillac Escalade glided in to a stop. For a moment, they were all frozen like deer in the halogen glare. The lights were quickly reduced to the soft glow of parking lights. The man to Rooster's left slipped beside Mario and put a hand on his right arm, just above the elbow, and squeezed. Mario, startled, started to pull away. He opened his mouth to protest, casting an angry glare at the man gripping his arm. Then he noticed it. Glimmering in the Escalade's lights was a very nasty nickel-plated semiautomatic handgun, caliber indeterminate, but most likely the ubiquitous 9mm variety.

Rooster took Mario's other arm. "Let's take a little ride and talk things out." He guided the reluctant black man to the purring SUV. Meanwhile, the driver went back and shut the rented Ford's trunk. "Come, step into the luxury that is Escalade."

"But, Lana." Mario's voice sounded feeble even to himself.

"Call her on your cell and inform her you'll be back shortly," Rooster said. The gunman was in the backseat sliding over. Rooster gave Mario a gentle push and climbed in beside him. He turned to the driver. "Let's go."

Mario sat between Rooster and his gun-toting thug feeling very much alone. The seat was soft leather, and the air blowing on him was cold. Soaked in nervous sweat, he felt a deathly chill creep over him. Suddenly, Deputy Harris, a.k.a. Tiny, seemed like a very distant problem indeed.

Carlos and Omar sat in Carlos's Florida room, a large screened area abutting the trailer, smoking a joint, talking in rapid Spanish. They expected a call from Mario an hour ago. Well, maybe he was going to wait and return the car to Fort Myers in the morning. He did that as often as not. Still, he always called to give them the news, usually bragging in circuitous and zigzagging phrases about the dope he scored. "I had the best seats at the concert," he'd say, or "You gotta see the new shirt I bought, it's boss." Omar was getting itchy for a *cerveza*.

"What do you think, Carlos? Let's have a beer. We aren't going anywhere until tomorrow."

"Maybe," replied Carlos, "but I wanted to get a little something to bring over to Jamie tonight. He always pays cash up front, and I could use a little extra spending money."

"Why don't we just make a quick run over to Beto's? He's always got something going. Hey, maybe we could score a little nose candy too."

"I don't like going there. He asks high prices for shit that ain't that good, for one thing. The other thing, he works for the gringo who runs that cockfighting ranch. Man, once they get their talons into you, they don't want to let go. Beto is creepy enough, but that gringo, Rooster, with all his thugs and guns, man, he *scares me*. It's bad enough we got that devil with a badge on our asses. We start messing with this other guy, we could get in serious trouble. Maybe dead."

"Yeah, like caught in the cross fire," Omar added.

"No shit." Carlos stood up. "We'll have a beer or two or six. If Mario calls now, we just say tomorrow. Let's take a walk, see if we can find a card game."

Constance Valentine relaxed by the pool, most of her second gooseneck martini already coursing through her bloodstream. She felt good. Totally relaxed. The day had gone well. And as it turned out, it was a lucrative one. She had agreed to vote for a wetlands variance and a slight zoning change to make way for another country club of two thousand acres and over five hundred luxury homes and villas on the east side of Napolis. In return, a deposit of three hundred thousand dollars would be made to an offshore account in the Caymans. This was her third deal with the same development company, and it most assuredly would not be the last. Besides, she was all for more golf courses and a fat tax base. She loved the game, and it attracted only the wealthiest of America's retiring and aspiring families. Yes, life was good.

"Señora?" It was Anna.

"Yes, Anna."

"I must leave now. Anything else you need?"

"Tell Pablo I'd like to see him by the pool on your way out please. And have a nice evening."

"Sí, señora. Adiós."

"Adiós." Constance sipped her martini. Pablo came on to the lanai. He was wearing red Speedo swim trunks. The bulge in front seemed to be growing as he came closer.

"Another drink?" he asked.

"No, you beautiful boy. Enough with the drink. Now it's time to eat. Come over here." She reached up, took his hands, and pulled him on top of her. They kissed on the lips. Her fingers were working their magic all over his back. They rolled off the chaise longue; now she lay on top of him. She French-kissed him a full minute, her tongue pushing its way through his full lips, deep into his yielding mouth. She started to move her mouth to his neck. She let his hands go. Lips and tongue swept over his nipples, over his belly, onto the elastic band of the Speedos that could no longer contain their package. Pablo relaxed and let the trunks be stripped from him and expose everything. He opened to her lips and tongue like a morning flower, letting it all go.

The Cadillac Escalade pulled up to a small house somewhere a few miles east of Bella Villa and down a couple miles of gravel road. Mario glanced down at his watch. They had driven for just about fifteen minutes. They waited in the car while the driver went in the house. Mario could hear dogs barking. Rooster opened his door and stepped out. He motioned for Mario to follow him. The gunman exited from the opposite side and came quickly around to join his boss. The Florida night air was hot and extremely humid. Mario, almost dry after the ride in the cool dry air of the Escalade, began to sweat again at once.

"So, Mario," Rooster said. "As we were saying on the ride over, we both share an interest in the demise of a certain deputy who has outgrown his uniform."

"That may be true," Mario said, "but he's pretty much got me by the short hairs at the moment."

"That's only because he's *alive*," said Rooster. "With your help, I am going to see to it that unfortunate fact is altered to the benefit of all concerned."

"Whoa!" Mario backed off, holding his hands up as if to ward off an imminent assault. "I don't want anything to do with murder, *especially* a cop! You're *crazy*!"

"I'm not sure *crazy* is an appropriate adjective here, Mario." Rooster flicked his Bic again, using it to light a huge cigar he was handed by Johnny Gun. The driver came down the porch steps with two pit bulls on choke chains. The dogs were straining forward, growling deep in their throats. When they came into view of the headlights, Mario could see the bared fangs and drool coming off their skinned back jowls. They were growling and emitting short menacing barks. Mario knew all too well they could tear a man apart like a rag doll in a matter of seconds. They tugged forward, coming just a foot away from the terrified herb dealer. They lurched and snapped at him. He tried to back away, but a hard steal barrel poked into the small of his back.

"Stay put," Rooster said. "Don't make any sudden moves or the dogs are let loose." He waved at the gunman, and the pistol was withdrawn. "Now you listen to me. You no longer have choices. I have *chosen* you. And you will do *exactly* as you are instructed." He nodded to the man holding the chains. The dogs were freed up just enough to lunge at Mario, snapping their vicious fangs inches from his belly. He stumbled backward and fell down on his ass. The dogs came straight for his face. His hands went up reflexively to protect himself. He could smell the fetid canine breath and feel the spray of their saliva. His bladder let go, and piss stained his khaki pants. The dogs picked up instantly on the odor of his urine and went into a frenzy so savage the handler could barely restrain them even with the choke chains.

"Enough!" Rooster snapped. The dogs were dragged away. "Are you ready to listen, or do you want to see just how *crazy* I can be?"

"I'm all ears," said Mario, trying to add a bit of bravado to his voice.

"Good," Rooster said. "I'm so glad you've chosen to cooperate. Don't worry, it will be a simple plan, and your part will be no more than picking up the phone and calling me. When you next meet with our favorite deputy, give me the time and place. I'll make all the arrangements."

"I still don't know how you know about me and Harris." Mario stood up, brushing off his pants. The wet spot in his crotch was covered in dust and not too noticeable in the dark.

"I have a *very* large payroll, young man. It's a 'who you know and pay' world, my boy. Let's get you back home where you can clean up and get back to your unfinished business. Oh, take the third seat. We'll all be more comfortable, eh?" Rooster laughed and opened the door to let Mario climb in.

10

Nolan turned the LeBaron convertible into the parking area of Crayton's Market. A couple of old geezers stared at him for a moment from rocking chairs on the porch and resumed their conversation. O'Brien, his police informant, said there were whispers of a child abuse case here that was snuffed by Deputy Harris. Maybe he'd buy a six-pack and sniff around a little. A sign to the right of the door proclaimed this store specialized in meat of every kind, including alligator. (Alligator was legal to sell provided that strict guidelines were followed. The state government issued hunting and trapping permits to those who qualified.) Nolan nodded and smiled at the two rocking chair jockeys who were once again focusing their murky gazes on him. He went through the door into the dark cool interior of the store. This was an old-fashioned mom-and-pop store without the bright lighting of modern convenience stores. The beer coolers were prominent at the back of the store with old neon signs advertising Budweiser, Coors, and Miller. The glass doors, however, were smudged and dirty. Nolan made his way to the back of the store.

"Kin ah halp y'awl?" A dark-haired man with a leathery face approached. One look and you could tell this man was born and brought up within a mile of where he was standing. Nolan could picture his mother giving birth in a rough fishing shack in the alligator-infested Everglades at a time when the great wetland extended from the Florida Straits to Lake Okeechobee without interruption. He probably wore alligator-skin boots from the time he was in diapers.

"Just here to pick up some beer," Nolan said.

"We got it awl, jest 'bout ever kynd." The man has a particular drawl Nolan hadn't heard anywhere else in the South. It was not unintelligible, just difficult to decipher, but no worse than some he'd heard in the mountains of the Carolinas, as well as in Alabama, Mississippi, and Georgia.

"OK." Nolan started looking in the first cooler. "I'll look and see what you've got. Maybe buy a couple different kinds."

"Sure, y'awl tyke yer tyme." Bud walked back toward the register. What Nolan really wanted was a peak behind the rear door with the MEATS sign on it. As soon as ole buddy boy was out of sight, Mike tried the knob on the door. Locked. It was a simple Kwikset lock. He pulled out his trusty Visa card and slipped it in the crack. The door popped open. He pushed on it, and as it swung open, a stainless steel counter with a rack of knives came into view. Directly across the small room, about twelve feet, was another door, apparently to the main house. He was looking at an antechamber serving as meat-cutting room. He caught sight of the three chains with collars screwed into the wall. Two were on one side of the bench near the floor and the other on the opposite side. There was a bowl and spoon near each of the chains. Spoons! No, it couldn't be. Surely these were for dogs kept under the master's supervision and fed scraps of the trimmed meat. But spoons! According to O'Brien, there were three small children here. Surely the children were not eating from these dishes. It must be just a coincidence. Nolan felt a chill shimmy up his spine; he closed the door and looked around to see if he'd been noticed. Apparently he was not. He quickly selected a six-pack of Coors Light and one of Miller Draft. He walked to the front of the store where Bud Crayton stood in the doorway, talking to the two curmudgeons outside. Nolan stopped at the chip rack near the cash register. Bud turned and went over to the counter.

"Y'awl find sumthin' ta drank?" he asked.

"Yeah, yeah, I did." Nolan selected a bag of "cool ranch-flavored" corn chips and put everything on the counter.

"That lyte beer ain't gonna halp if'n y'awl eat'n them cheaps 'long weeth it." Bud grinned, displaying rotten tobacco-stained teeth. Two of the bottom front teeth were missing.

"Yeah, but the chips are for the guy drinking the Miller," Nolan lied for no reason.

"Them's good cheaps, I et 'em awl the tyme m'salf." Bud put the beer in a plastic sack.

"I guess your dogs get plenty of fresh meat with the scraps from your meat cutting." Nolan tried to be casual. But ole buddy boy gave him a hard stare. His friendly mask slipped for a moment as a reptilian paranoia swept over his features. The smile was back in a flash as he regained his composure.

"Only got me one dawg. It's a peit bull, and he does awl riot fer chow."

"Yeah, I bet he does," said Nolan and left quickly.

"Y'awl come byack," Bud called after him.

"OK," Nolan replied half to himself. *I'll be back all right, but not to buy beer and "cheaps,"* he thought.

"Dave O'Brien please." Nolan was on his cell phone calling direct to the sheriff substation. A bit risky, but he was impatient.

"O'Brien here, can I help you?"

"Dave, this Mike Nolan. I need any information you can get from Child Protective Services on this Bud Crayton and wife. Any arrest records, jail time, complaints, investigations, emergency calls, hospital visits, you name it. Get some help from one of the guys in Tallahassee. I'll put a call through to my guy and get as much clearance for you as I can."

"Roger that."

"I'm on my way to check out this Mario Stevens. It seems he's still an active player in drug trafficking. He's the same guy Harris monitors for probation, am I right?"

"That's affirmative," O'Brien said.

"Find out when he's scheduled to meet Harris next. I need exact date, time, and place. Maybe you can ask around and see if there's any location, other than those registered in the logs as designated for that purpose."

"Ten-four. Give me a day or two. I'll see what I can do. Be careful. Diggin' around in Tiny's business can be dangerous." O'Brien sounded nervous and reluctant.

"How so?" Nolan was curious.

"Not only is he a bad-tempered palooka," O'Brien answered, "but he has a reputation in the department as being tight with Sheriff Gunther. Judge Thomas seems partial to him as well. There's a lot of leniency and favoritism coming from the courts. There are rumors too that he hangs out with Councilwoman Valentine. He's got all his bases pretty well covered."

"OK, do the best you can," said Nolan. "And include all those people you just mentioned and any others in a hard copy report, for my eyes only, to be delivered at a time and place to be decided. Over and out."

"Copy that." O'Brien seemed relieved to be ending the communication.

Nolan drove down Flamevine Drive past Mario's place. The Ford truck belonging to Omar and Carlos was in the driveway. Now he could connect the dots to Jamie in the Fireproof. He knew Harris must be involved with these characters in some illegal activity. But how was he going to prove it? Harris was proving to be as hard to get as a groundhog in his labyrinth of tunnels. And surely there must be another major player or two in the county, judging by the amount of drugs found on the streets. For now, he'd better keep a low profile and maintain his cover. He drove to Palm Boulevard and headed back toward the Fireproof. He thought of the Wicked Witch cackling, "All in good time, my pretties, all in good time."

Tiny pulled his patrol car into a parking slot at the Baron County Sheriff's Department Juvenile Boot Camp. He was in a pissy mood. Mona started spouting off about leaving him. She accused him of being a liar, cheater, and blackmailer. And a drug dealer to boot. He had to smack her around more than usual before fucking her. She was becoming a nuisance. She must have been talking with that ole festival of fat Ron Badger. Yeah, Mr. King Burger himself. But who else? He couldn't get anything out of her. Maybe Sam had some department gossip that might shed some light on who was sniffing around. He felt sure there was some hound dog on his trail.

Noticing there was something going on at the "pit and post" in the center of the yard, he took a walk over. A crowd of the juvies and a couple of the officers were there.

"Hey, what's up?" he shouted. "Sam!"

"Tiny," Sam called out. "Just in time. See what we have here—an unrepentant sinner." Tiny walked over to the center; the fatigue-clad squad of delinquents moved aside in a wave, making room for him to pass. A Hispanic boy, fairly short but all wiry muscle with smooth coffee skin, was writhing and gasping for air on the ground by the post. He was stripped naked. It looked like he'd taken a few good blows from a rubber baton.

"What'd he do?" Tiny asked. Not that it made any difference.

"Stole a pan of cookies from the kitchen," Sam replied. "Said he was hungry. Said he wanted to go home, that life in Mexico was better than here." The child continued to gasp for air, hyperventilating, his face turning red. "Now when he has to face his punishment, he throws a hissy fit."

"Sir," one of the boys dared address the sergeant, "I think he has *allergies*."

"Yeah, and I have aller-gators." Sergeant Sam was furious at the impudence of the do-gooder, especially in front of his mentor. "Strip down, mister. *Now!*"

"But, sir—"

"Quiet!" Sam motioned to his chief juvenile lieutenant, and he and two other boys jumped the lad, knocked him to the ground, and tore at his clothing.

"I think I have a remedy for your cookie thief," said Tiny. He bent over the boy, scooped up some dirt, and forced it into his mouth. The boy tried to spit it out, but Tiny placed a large hand over his mouth. The boy gagged and writhed on the ground. His red face turned purple as he clawed at the merciless deputy's hand. His eyes bulged as if they were going to pop out of their sockets and finally rolled up into his head. Tiny removed his hand, but the child-man had ceased breathing.

"What the hell?" Sam peered down at the boy.

"Think we just lost one," said Tiny. He was anxious to get Sam alone for questioning. The boy's demise at his hands was merely a nuisance obstructing his agenda.

"I better try to revive him, or there will be a mountain of paperwork and pesky inquiries," Sam said, bending over the boy, trying to clean out the air passage. He turned to another Hispanic, one of the boy's compadres. "Try mouth to mouth on him."

"*S-sí*, yes, sir," the boy stammered. He began to blubber and shake so much he was completely useless.

"Forget about him," said Tiny. "He croaked. Big deal, another dead spic. Clean him up real good and write it up as an accident. You heard his fairy friend say, he had allergies. He just seized up, stopped breathing. Shit happens. Let his girlfriend there"—Tiny nodded to the sobbing failure of a Boy Scout—"do the work. He's so broken up. And tell everyone else to go back to the barracks and keep their mouths shut, including this faggot." Tiny kicked the seminaked "allergy" wimp in the ribs. "You know the drill."

It was done as the master prescribed.

"Listen, Sam." Tiny settled into the chair in the sergeant's office across from the desk. "I need the scuttlebutt in the department. I think there's some behind-the-scenes undercover operation, maybe." Tiny slid a manila envelope across the desk. "Enough to take a weeklong luxury cruise or put in a nice pool." Sam didn't look so good suddenly. He looked a little shaken and worried.

"O'Brien," Sam said, peeking at the greenbacks inside the envelope. "That's all I know. No who, what, where, when, or whys." He closed the envelope and slid it into the top desk drawer.

"That son of a bitch!" Tiny said. "I should've figured that Irish lapdog had something to do with this." He looked at Sam's fretful face and made a magnanimous offer. "By the way, since I was here during the unfortunate incident, I'll be glad to testify how the boy had a seizure, stopped breathing, and you tried everything to revive him."

"Yeah, OK." Sam seemed to be in a bit of a fog. "Guess I better call an ambulance now."

"Good thinking," said Tiny, getting up. "You got things under control. I'll radio for backup from my patrol car, see if they want me to stick around for a statement. In the meantime, I'll have a quick talk with the bad boys. Make sure they all know it was an accident, period. And if I hear anything different coming from them . . ." He made a fist of his right hand and punched the open palm of his left as he made for the door. Sam picked up the phone and placed a 911 call.

Judge Thomas sat behind his polished mahogany desk, puffing a Hoyo de Monterry, one of Cuba's finest cigars. The cigar was contraband, but the judge bought them by the case using a proxy. He was ensconced in his sanctum sanctorum, the judge's chambers. Across from him, in a leather upholstered chair, sat John Gunther, Baron County sheriff for the past two decades. Sheriffs are elected in Florida's counties, so the office is filled by politicians rather than law enforcement professionals. In Baron County, Republicans run unopposed since Democrats are as scarce as Indian head pennies. Sheriff Gunther was, naturally, a Republican. He too puffed one of the judge's Cuban cigars. The office was lined with shelves of law books and references. To the left of the desk was a small window overlooking an inner courtyard with a flower garden, a fountain, a couple of orange trees, and benches. Next to the window was a wet bar with a couple dozen bottles of liquor and the same number of bottles of wine. A portrait in oil of the judge hung on the opposite wall, next to one of the governor.

"I'm tellin' you, John," the judge said, leaning over his desk, "Harris is becoming a real liability. If we don't put some distance between him and us, we're going to be covered in gator shit when he goes down."

"This'll all blow over, always does," replied Gunther. "No one can corroborate any of the allegations or prove any misconduct. Our boy'll come up smellin' like a rose."

"Oh, I'm not so sure about that." Judge Thomas puffed on the Cuban and picked up a manila file folder. "This here is a secret grand jury probe. Seems one of your little girls in the Explorers claims he raped her, and she's pregnant now. Pregnant! With DNA, it will be an open and shut case. The girl is fifteen."

"Tiny told me she was lying," Sheriff Gunther said, shifting uneasily in his chair. "Told me he has a good idea who the boy knocked her up is. He'll take care of it."

"Also, there's another report he's covering up a child abuse case. So far no substantiating evidence from Child Protective Services, but they're looking into it. And there is testimony from at least two deputies that he gives the appearance of impropriety in the supervision of Mario Stevens's probation, which I authorized by the way. Some say he's soft on drug dealers as well."

"Now that's total bullshit. Check out his arrest record." Gunther got up out of his seat and went over to the wet bar and poured two fingers of Jameson Whiskey. "Let's not get bent out of shape by rumor and hearsay."

"Now," went on the judge as if he didn't hear the sheriff, "there's this nasty business with the boy dying at the boot camp, and Harris just happened to be there. Some reporter is going to sink their teeth into this mess and not let go until the blood is flowing."

"I don't think so," Gunther said and gulped down the bourbon. When he could catch his breath, it came out as hot as that of any dragon. "But I'll have a one-on-one with him and see what's shakin'"

"The sooner the better, Sheriff. Now, I have a hearing on a nasty custody case concerning a twelve-year-old girl, so if you'll excuse me."

"Sure, time to roll anyway." Gunther headed for the door.

"Bry, what the hell are you doing?" Jamie was pissed. "It's not even four in the afternoon, and you're smashed." Brian took a gulp from a can of Budweiser, his drink of choice, and sat down heavily on the bed. "You've been overdrinking with Toad again, haven't you?"

"Aww, quitcherbitchin'," Brian said and burst out laughing.

"What the hell is so damn funny?" Jamie asked. "There's nothing amusing about being a drunk."

"Quitcherbitchin's the name of a cottage on Chance Lake up in Maine," Brian managed between chortles. "Get it? Quit-your-bitch-inn. That's where I need to go now." He began laughing like a lunatic.

"Oh, very funny." Jamie folded his laundry on the other side of the bed. "I suppose running away from all your problems and hiding in a bottle is your idea of escape. But let me tell you something, it catches up to you. And it is *always* worse."

"Yada yada, doncha bodda me." Brian let out another whoop of laughter at his nonsense rhyme. He tipped up his beer can in a defiant gesture and drained it. He belched loudly. "That one's for you, Jamie just the samie don't try to tame me." He laughed again, but there was a note of derision in the hilarity.

"I'm going over and talk to Toad about giving you liquor." Jamie began walking toward the door. "You're not like this unless you go over there and drink vodka or rum."

"Hole on jess' a minute." Brian slurred on purpose, but it wasn't all fake. He was just over the line where losing control of the voice is a symptom of acute intoxication. "Doncha' go schticking your fag ash face in my biznes." He giggled some more.

"What the fuck kind of remark is that?" Jamie was having trouble remembering he was dealing with a sick man, probably an alcoholic.

"I mean," Brian said, "since you were the one who *made* me into a *homosexual,* you should be the lashed to complain if I drinks a wee bit too much whonch 'n a while."

Jamie stood, frozen like an ice sculpture. His mind went completely blank. Anger mixed with an unholy guilt began to rise like volcanic stone, red hot and partially melted in his gorge. His face flushed red, and he clenched his jaw. Words began to form but were squashed while others came and were as quickly recycled. It seemed like an eternity on his internal clock before he uttered a word. His eyes never left Brian's face. Brian, for his part, stared defiantly at Jamie at first; but his gaze soon faltered, shifting down at his lap, and then out the window. His resentment revealed fear and confusion his muddled mind needed to retreat from.

"Now listen, Brian." Jamie's voice wobbled a little as he fluctuated from reconciliation to tearful torment and sorrow, to fury and resentment. By some miracle, he managed to sound reasonable. "I don't know who you've been talking to or what you've been reading, but nobody can *make* somebody else homosexual. Only God can do that. You're either born with those proclivities or you're *not.* If you experiment some and find it's not your cup of tea, you walk away, no harm done. But if it is for you, you will *know* it. Despite what all the religious bigots and self-proclaimed spokespeople of God's word spew to their unwitting followers, only the troglodytes who still live in the Dark Ages believe homosexuality is a choice or willful decadence. It's just as much an inherited trait as the color of your hair or eyes or whether you will get heart disease or Parkinson's or cystic fibrosis. Or for that matter, whether you're an alcoholic or not. Accept what God has given and run with it. God doesn't make mistakes. That's the thing all the twisted preachers and jaundiced cracker heads can't seem to get straight."

Brian lay on his back, legs still hanging over the edge of the bed, arms crossed over his face, pulling his shirt up to expose his belly. It was as if he were making himself physically vulnerable, sexually available, while shielding his mind from what was being said. This was the dichotomy that formed the nexus of his drinking binges. For Jamie, this behavior both turned him on and repulsed him, pushing him further to find solace in the serenity pot brought to him.

It is difficult for even the most die-hard antidrug advocate to find scientific or statistical evidence to support the contention that marijuana is addictive. And in Jamie's case, it didn't make his life unmanageable. The primary danger ole Mary Jane posed to the user was *legal*. And for folks like Jamie, playing on the fringes of the draconian laws surrounding this relatively benign drug had become a lucrative pastime. Lately though, he wondered if it was worth it.

"Come on, Bry." Jamie decided to be conciliatory. "Let's get something to eat, you'll feel better. I'll call out for pizza."

"With pepperoni and jalapenos," said Brian, sitting up.

"Sure, and how 'bout some green peppers too?" Jamie added. "I'll get us a liter of Coke to drink."

"Whatever." Brian watched Jamie make the call as he took off his shirt. He laid back down, arms stretched over his head. "Why don't you take advantage of me while we wait."

"You're soo bad, Bry," Jamie said as he moved toward the bed.

Tiny pulled his patrol car into the Fireproof Motel parking lot. He parked in front of Jamie's room and walked up the steps and stood by the window. Looking between the cracks in the blinds, he could just make out the fag drug dealer sitting on the bed eating pizza. Another fag in underpants came prancing from the bathroom. Cheezus K. Ryst! Maybe they were having a party. A bunch of seminaked queer boys prancing around in a motel room. That would look good on his report. He could turn it over to vice; they might get some mileage out of it. Vice squad. He chuckled to himself. Chasing whores and their johns around the bathrooms in the public parks. Posing as whores themselves. Jesus, they even had *guys* acting like queers to lure in some rube to bust. What a bunch of pathetic fuckin' losers. Still, if it weren't for their diligence, he wouldn't be able to extort protection money and favors from his favorite pimp, Andre. He walked over and tried the door. Locked. He knocked twice.

"Who is it?" Jamie Dorr asked from the other side.

"Baron County Sheriff's Department." Tiny tried to sound businesslike but not threatening. There was total silence for a long moment, then . . .

"What do you want?"

"I'm looking for Jamie Dorr. Is he present?" More silence.

"That's me."

"I have a summons for you to appear in court for overdue parking violations," Tiny lied. "I'm asking you to open the door please." Tiny could hear furtive whispers and scrambling on the other side of the door. He knocked again.

"One minute please."

"I'm asking you one more time to open the door, *now*." Tiny knew the best chance an officer had to uncover something illegal was to rattle the suspect. He used the technique all the time with proven results.

"OK, OK!" Jamie yelled. "I'm fuckin' coming." Managing to slip into a pair of denim shorts, he undid the lock and cracked the door. He peered out at Tiny and recognition flittered across his features. Jamie's eyes glittered in the porch light, reflecting fear in his enlarged pupils. He looked like a dog who just did doody in the corner, and here comes master with a rolled-up newspaper. Without a word, Tiny punched the door with the base of his open palm, slamming it into Jamie's shoulder and knocking him backward. He stumbled and fell onto his ass. Tiny walked into the room and shut the door.

"Nice to meet you, scum bucket," Tiny said. He looked over at Brian who stood seminaked on the other side of the bed. "What's your name?"

"Br-Brian Sutter."

"Just a minute," said Jamie, starting at his feet. He got less than halfway up when, reaching out and grabbing him by the belt, Tiny lifted him up off his feet and pushed him against the wall. Holding him there, his feet six inches above the floor, Tiny stuck his face within six inches of Jamie's.

"You listen to me, Dorr." Tiny's face was turning red with the mercury rising. "You do what you're told and nobody gets hurt or goes to jail, which is where you are going *right now* if you don't keep that mouth shut." He let up on the pressure, and Jamie sank to the floor. Stepping back, Tiny nodded at Brian. "Tell your boyfriend to scram. What I have to say doesn't concern him."

"You better leave, Bry." Jamie was visibly shaken. Brian put on his shorts and headed toward the door.

"And, pretty boy," Tiny said to Brian before he went through the door, "don't be yakking or your ass will be mine."

Jamie sat on the edge of the bed, his knees were too unsteady to stand up, and he was shaking like the color mixer at work.

"I want to know what's up with this Nolan dude that's living here," Tiny said. "He talk to you yet?"

"He's been over a couple of times."

"What did he want? Did he say where he comes from?"

"He just wanted to bullshit. He didn't say where he was from." Jamie realized the big deputy wasn't going to bust him. He was worried about something, worried about Mike Nolan.

"I know what you do, punk," Tiny said. "And I know your little buddies, Carlos and Omar. I'm going to give you a pass. I just want you to find out everything you can about this guy, Nolan. You tell me if he buys any dope and, especially, if he asks about me. *Comprende?*"

"I guess so, but—" The door opened, and Mike Nolan walked in.

"Trouble here, Jamie?" he asked. He looked directly at Tiny, staring at him as if trying to memorize every detail of his face. "Does this officer have a warrant? Because if he doesn't, he has no business in your room."

"There's no problem," Tiny answered. He was glaring at Nolan. Jamie thought he was going to go for him right there. "Guess I had the wrong address." He walked past Nolan, started to say something, changed his mind, and walked out the door.

"Do you want to make a complaint?" Nolan asked Jamie. "I know some people in the sheriff's department."

"No, like he said, just a mistake."

"If he is threatening or intimidating you in any way," Nolan said, "you should let me know. I'll go to the district attorney with you."

"Naw, it's OK, Mike." Nolan looked at Jamie a long moment.

"All right," Nolan said. "But, Jamie, any more trouble with this cop and you come to me. *Comprende?*"

"Sure, Mike. I'll do that."

11

"Tommy," Julie said. Lying on her side behind her husband in postcoital fetal position, her arms around his waist, she was rubbing his tummy. It was early in the evening, *Wheel of Fortune* just finished to make way for *Jeopardy.*

"Ummm . . ."

"I'm worried about Jamie and Brian. As convenient as it is having someone with pot for sale right on the block, so to speak, I think he might be getting a little too close to the fire. And Brian seems confused and unhappy with his sexuality. He may be slipping into a drinking problem the way he's been going at it lately." Light from the setting sun was pouring through a crack in the curtain, dividing the room and the bed with a veil of light. Julie could not see Tommy's feet through the glare.

"Ummm . . . ," Tommy moaned.

"No, seriously, don't you think we should say something?"

"Ummm . . ."

"Tommy!"

"What do you mean *we, Keemosabi.*"

"OK, shouldn't *I* say something, have a talk with them?"

"You worry too much about other people's business. They'll be OK or they won't." Tommy rolled over. "Right now, you better be more concerned about the Lone Ranger here. Tommy poked his tumescent member into Julie's belly. "Stick 'um up, *tonto.* I'm gonna make a squaw outta you."

"What are you, priapic! Didn't we just do this?"

"I'm Priapus with a pryin' prick cryin' for pussy. Now roll over." Tommy helped Julie flip to her other side and quickly probed her honey pot with his warm gun. He brought them both to climax in a few minutes. They cuddled awhile, both his hands covering her firm grapefruit-sized breasts.

"I'm still going to talk with them, you nasty man."

Tommy quoted from "Dirty World" on the album *The Traveling Wilburys.*

"You know, 'it's a dirty world,' Mrs. Wilbury. 'It's a fuckin' dirty world.'"

Leaving her room an hour after Tommy pulled his double play, Julie almost bumped into Mike Nolan in the semidarkness of the porch. "Oh! Hey, Mike!"

"Hi, Julie. What's up?"

"I was just going to see Jamie for a minute," said Julie. Mike Nolan made Julie feel a little uneasy, mostly because of what Toad said about him. *But come on,* she thought, *what does Toad know?* Quite a bit, it seemed, for a certified alcoholic—a registered garden variety drunk. Still with all things said and done, Nolan was an attractive man. "Tommy and I were thinking *picnic* this Saturday at Wiggins Pass. The beach is great there, and they have grills and tables and lots of shady spots. You want to come with us? It'll be a group outing. We'll have a blast. Just say yes."

"Sounds great, but I have to go out of town Saturday. Family problems."

"Oh, I'm sorry to hear it. Anything I can do?"

"No, but thank you. It's nothing *too* serious, just a case of my brother drinking too much and getting into trouble." Nolan flashed her a warm smile and shook his head in a sorrowful "what are you gonna do" way to make his little lie seem more real.

"That seems to be going around lately," Julie said. "For a lot of people, it's terminal." Julie looked out at Camilla's garden, a harvest of shadows, illuminated by a single light post in the motel's courtyard. "Guess it's a good reminder for us to be discreet in our imbibing this weekend."

"Well, have a good time. The weather looks fantastic." Nolan started down the steps to walk across to his room.

"Good night, Mike."

"Good night."

Julie knocked on Jamie's door.

"Yeah?" Jamie sounded hostile.

"It's Julie. Am I interrupting?" Jamie opened the door.

"Come on in, Julie. Not a problem. We just had the *mother of all interruptions.*"

"What happened?" Julie walked into the room and slid into the leather Easy Boy. "Pizza, huh?"

"Still plenty, want a piece?" Jamie brought over the pizza box and held it in front of her. "I can heat it for you in the micro."

"Don't be silly. Umm . . . looks good." She started to lift out a piece.

"Just take the box and eat all you want," said Jamie. "Me and Brian are done." Just then, Brian opened the door and came in.

"Hey, Julie."

"Hi, sweetie. So, Jamie, tell me about this 'mother of all interruptions.' Was it Nolan? I just saw him on the porch." Jamie gave her a quick rehashing of Tiny's unexpected visit and Nolan's fortuitous entry. Julie was thunderstruck and terrified at the same time. "Jamie, you gotta get out of the business *now.* Maybe leave the county. This is *too* scary."

"Yeah, Jamester," said Brian. "Maybe Jules has a point."

"It's something to think about. But my take is, he's scared of Nolan. I think Nolan might be gunning for this Harris guy somehow." There was a *tap tap* at the door, and Tommy walked into the conversation.

"Hey, Jamie, Brian," Tommy said. "What's in the skillet? Any chance of scoring a quarter Z of your finest, Jamie?"

"Jamie doesn't have anything illegal here," Julie said loudly as if making an announcement for any one in the peanut gallery who might be listening. Tommy gave her a quizzical look, projecting his thought. *What the fuck?*

"We just had a visit from that deputy called 'El Diablo,'" said Jamie. "At least that's what Carlos and Omar and some of the other Mexicanos call him."

"Whoa! So that's—" Tommy was interrupted by a knock at the door and the entry of Toad and John Vaughn. Camilla crowded in followed by Robert with little Billy in his arms. And the whole story was told over with a few more embellishments. Lighting a joint in defiance of logical discretion, Toad passed it around. The customary Popov jug was given the rounds as well. Jamie gave Brian a hard stare as his lover poured a double shot. Tommy left for a minute and returned with a twelve-pack and his guitar. He strummed a few strings and launched into "Dirty World" by the Traveling Wilburys. The party atmosphere locked in, and Julie forgot she went there in the first place to talk to Brian about his drinking. But she remembered to tell everyone about the picnic at Wiggins Pass.

"Sunday," Julie informed them, "everybody, on Sunday we go to Wiggins Pass. We'll all go together in Brian's van. The Fireproof is going to the beach!"

"You know your boyfriend's a drug dealer?" Tiny asked. He scrutinized Brenda, the former Explorer, wannabe policewoman, and whining rape victim. They were at a rendezvous in the parking lot of the King Burger, sitting in his Grand Cherokee on the edge of the lot in the shade of a red bay tree, munching burgers. She was claiming to be pregnant with his kid and promising to make *mucho* trouble for one supersized sheriff's deputy.

"What the hell you talking about?" Brenda gave Tiny a look of defiance. You're gonna pay for a lot more than an abortion, I can tell you that." Her face had grown puffy in the last couple of months, a double chin emerging. A red rash of pimples dotted her forehead. No, pregnancy was not going to be kind to her girlish figure and seductive appearance. "You're going to get fired for what you did, you big ape."

"Not so." Tiny stared hard at her a moment. "I'm virtually 'fire-proof.'" A sinister grin spread across his face. "As I was saying, your boyfriend, Roger, am I right? Roger has been dealing in the ole wacky tabbacky." Tiny smiled and shook his head. "He's due to get pulled over by yours truly any day now for a traffic violation still to be determined. A search of his car will reveal half a pound of marijuana and some crack cocaine. He'll be charged with possession with intent to distribute. I can add a witness or two if need be. He'll get a minimum of three to five with God only knows how much probation. You want that for such a sweet boy? I can't even imagine what those hard-core prisoners in the state pen will do to such a cute young thing. Maybe you can."

"What are you getting at?" Brenda looked alarmed, concern and fear etching pimply lines across her brow.

"Just that I'm giving you this." Tiny handed her an envelope. "There's two thousand dollars in there. You go get an abortion. Now. Today or tomorrow. The name of a doctor is enclosed. If you don't, the shit is going to hit the fan for your pretty boyfriend. And soon." He got out of the Jeep and walked around to the passenger side. He opened the door, and appearing the gentleman helping a lady out, he squeezed her arm with a vicelike grip.

"Ow! Let me go, you pig!" Tiny let go of her arm, the beginning of a dark bruise already apparent where his fingers mashed her arm.

"If I ever see or hear from you again," Tiny said in a low voice, "I'll dump you in a canal for the gators. Talk about fast food, you'd be gone in a heartbeat."

Josh knew he had to escape from his parents or perish like his siblings, Alice and Kevin. They were both gone now. His father had locked him in a closet upstairs for what seemed like eternity. No light, no food. He soiled himself. He was thirsty. He was bereft of hope, friends, and any form of love. He knew only the unbearable darkness. The smell of death was everywhere in this house. He was an animal looking for the least shard of human kindness and found nothing but the toe of his father's boot in his gaunt middle. He was alone and lonely beyond human description. Finally, his mother opened the door, leash in hand, and led him from his confinement. Alice and Kevin were simply gone. He started to ask his mother about them but was swatted across the face before he got two words out.

"Don'tcha ever tawk of them agin," she said and took a long pull from a can of Pabst Blue Ribbon. "Yer next, yah don' mind yer *p*'s and *q*'s. Now git in the tub and clean yerself. Yer disgustin'. Y'awl kin et when you're done." She pulled a can of SpaghettiOs from a cupboard and began opening it.

As Josh passed the doorway to the living room, he caught a glimpse of the big man with the uniform and gun. He was poking his finger in his father's chest and saying something in hoarse, angry whispers. No light of hope crossed his face when he saw this man however. Whatever evil possessed his parents guided the one in uniform as well. He sensed there was something terribly wrong in the order of things but had no clue what it was. He knew only that he *must escape*. And do it soon. After bathing and eating, he was taken back upstairs and chained to a metal loop in the baseboard of the closet. He curled up in a fetal position, the smell of his own urine and feces gagging him. He wept and finally slept. He dreamt of a place where there were friends, music, kindness, and love.

"You dumped them in the swamp!" Tiny could hardly control his voice. He wanted to scream and curse this fool of a man. This Bud Crayton, this *idiot*. It would've been nice to reach out and grab him by his scrawny red neck and throttle him. He could feed the moron to the alligators like Bud did his two children. A lot of people got dumped in the Everglades in South Florida. More than anyone imagined. A corpse would disappear without a trace in a day or two. The swamp was a hungry beast and digested everything with a little burp and a fart.

"They was dead, Tiny. What else could I do?" Bud Crayton lit a Lucky Strike and inhaled. "They was seekly keeds anyways." He was looking down at the floor behind Tiny like he was wishing there was a trapdoor he could escape through.

"This is going to cost you another ten thousand." Tiny looked around to make sure there was nobody within earshot. "You're looking at twenty to life now. It's gonna cost me some sweat and blood to cover this up. You get that other boy the hell out of here and put him with some kinfolk 'til this blows over. Let's hope nobody misses the other two."

"But, Tiny, how'm I gonna git that much money. I jest—"

"You can, and you will," Tiny interrupted. "I'm giving you one month to get half of it and no excuses. I don't care if you have to sell this damn store to do it. And I want the money in cash—fifties and twenties. I'll be back in a week to see what you've come up with. If I don't like what I hear and see, the cuffs are goin' on you." Tiny left the house by the private entrance to avoid any of the store's porch cronies. *What a day,* he thought, *first the girl, now this.*

Sheriff John Gunther pulled his white Cadillac Seville into the parking lot at the Witch's Brew, his favorite watering hole. His Caddy was equipped with blue-and-red flashers behind the rearview mirror, rear window flashers, and strobe headlights. He had surprised more than just a few motorists, racing up behind them, lights flashing, pulling them over for traffic violations. They never saw it coming. He invariably wore a navy blue blazer with the sheriff's seal sewn to the pocket. He had half a dozen of the jackets in his wardrobe.

He also wore a black bolo tie with a star clasp and his trademark white cowboy hat. His feet were clad in alligator hide boots. He walked into the dark confines of the Witch's Brew, a tall well-built man with a trace of gut, and slipped into his usual corner booth. He held court here at five in the afternoon on Fridays. All the top brass usually showed up. Gunther would invariably drink over the legal limit for driving and would call a deputy to chauffeur him home. More than once, however, he'd driven drunk with the deputies spotting his route, sweating bullets until he pulled safely into his own driveway. Today, he was meeting Sgt.

Edwin Harris for a very private talk. It was three in the afternoon on a Saturday, and there was hardly a soul on the premises. A skeleton crew of workers was cleaning and prepping for the evening onslaught that would begin in earnest a few hours from now.

"Hi, Mr. Gunther." An attractive young waitress with short hair the color of wet beach sand placed a coaster in front of the sheriff. "What can I get you today?"

"Hi there, Pam. You're lookin' just radiant today."

"Thank you." Pam and the rest of the women at the Brew were used to the sheriff's flirtatious banter. Only Midge had been fool enough to get involved with a married man more than twice her age. Sheriff or not, it was never worth it.

"Bring me a Coors Light and a shot of Jim Beam," ordered the sheriff. Truth was, despite his rank as the high sheriff of Baron County, an elected official, Gunther was nervous about his meeting with Harris. He'd have just this combo of drinks to steel his nerves and no more. The whiskey would be gone by the time Harris arrived, and it would appear he was just sipping a beer—and a light beer at that. He was a model of discretion and decorum all right. How Harris had found out about his ongoing affair with Midge, he couldn't figure. The sheriff was a pillar of the community, a married man for almost thirty years now. If this affair became public knowledge, it could put him out of office in next year's election. Baron County was home of one of the most conservative constituencies on the United States. There were more churches per square mile than barrooms, or almost.

His drinks arrived, and Gunther drained the whiskey in one gulp. He chased it with a sip of beer from the bottle. He put the shot glass on another table behind him. He picked this time partly because he figured it would be almost vacant in the bar and partly because he knew Midge wouldn't be here. He looked at his watch. Harris was due in five minutes.

Twenty minutes later, Gunther was halfway through his second beer and getting ready to leave. He was furious at being stood up. His cell phone rang. It was Harris. He was two minutes from landing, deepest apologies, etc. The man's audacity was appalling. Gunther made up his mind that Harris would have to be dealt with permanently. Problem was the only way he could sink Harris for good was to do it literally in a slough somewhere in the glades. Well, so be it. He picked up his bottle and drained the remaining beer as if in toast to his thoughts. He could order another as soon as Harris arrived and make it look like his first or maybe second. The waitress collected the bottle just before Harris came through the door.

"John, good to see you." Tiny was in civvies, a button-up shirt with palm trees and orchids, and dungarees. His enormous feet were clad in white sneakers. "Sorry I'm late. I was putting one of our little problems to bed, so to speak." Sheriff Gunther gave Tiny a hard look. He signaled to Pam.

"Coors Light," Gunther said to the waitress. "What're you drinking, Harris?"

"I'll have a Coke, light," said Tiny and smiled.

"OK, Harris. Tell me what you're doing about a list of problems of your own making. We're looking at a potentially explosive situation unless it's diffused. And I mean yesterday."

"What, John, no friendly chitchat? I was going to ask you how that little server was doin'? What's her name, Gidgit or Midget? No, wait, just good ole Midge, right?" Gunther's face turned bright red, and the veins on his neck looked like they were about to come through the skin. The waitress returned with the drinks and set them on the table. When she retreated, Gunther spoke first.

"I'm warning you, Harris, don't you mock me. I'll take your badge right this minute, and you'll never be a law officer again. In fact, it would be a miracle if you didn't wind up behind bars yourself."

"Calm down there, Chief. I didn't mean to rattle your cage. Just tryin' on a little levity. Now as to this roll call of troubles. There simply aren't any, period. Everything is under control. Let's go down the list." Tiny held out his left hand and separated his pinky finger with his right index finger, signifying number 1. "The girl will not be pressing charges or making any more allegations. She's fucked half the high school class, and the whole town knows it." Now, he parted the pinky and ring finger for number 2. "The child abuse case just doesn't exist. You can have human services go over and check next week. The Craytons' story is they packed up the runts and sent them off to their kinfolk, and the one boy that stayed is fine. He's a little scrawny, maybe, but look at that buzzard of an old man, bad genes is all." The middle finger joined the other two for number 3. "The death at the boot camp was unfortunate but certainly nobody's fault. I can testify the boy had allergies and was overcome. Shit happens. We can get any number of the boys and staff as well as the camp doctor to back us up. Case closed." He covered all four fingers now. "And as to being soft on drugs, you've got to be kidding. I have the highest bust rate in the county. I don't like the other goofball rookies muckin' up my hard work, so I steer them away from my ongoing operations. That's where the complaints are coming from—bellyaching, plain and simple." Tiny curled his fingers into a fist to signify number 5. "The captain and I are about to smash some illegal gambling rings, and we don't need a bunch of do-gooders tipping off our suspects." Tiny sat back in his seat and took a drink of his Coke. "Now, Sheriff, don't you have something to tell me?"

"I never said this." Gunther took a sip of beer and narrowed his eyes. "There's a joint federal and state investigation going on in this county right now with at least one undercover agent that I know of. Word is he's got you in his sights."

Tiny measured the sheriff a few seconds with his eyes.

"Well, what has this agent turned up so far? And who the fuck is it?"

"So far, not much. I'm kind of out of the loop about specifics. Judge Thomas knows a little more, but he can't risk a special grand jury probe. The assistant district attorney is pushing for one, but our good buddy serving as DA is stalling."

"Well, do you know who the federal agent is?"

"I just know he's been covering Bella Villa pretty close. I haven't got a name. And if I did, I'd do ten years, minimum, if I told you, so obviously, I wouldn't."

"OK, OK. But like I said, everything is copasetic." Tiny grinned like an innocent boy. "Not to worry. Listen, I have to pick up my girlfriend at the mall for dinner and a movie. So if you'll excuse me."

"Sure, have a good night. And tread softly, hotshot."

"Yeah, you too, Sheriff. Oh, say hi to the wife." Tiny walked out without turning back to see Gunther's sourpuss. The sheriff drained his beer.

John Vaughn placed his fishing pole by the door of his room and pulled out his key. He had a woven basket in his left hand with today's catch of bass and catfish, already gutted and cut into filets.

"Hey, John!" It was Julie coming out of her room. She walked over with a big smile. She thought Vaughn was kinda weird, but he was OK. He just liked being alone a lot. She could certainly understand why. "Catch anything?"

"Just a bass and couple of catfish," he drawled.

"I hope you're ready for our beach trip tomorrow. Camilla and I have been cooking all day. We made potato salad and coleslaw and baked brownies. There's no pot in the brownies by the way, so let's not go down that road. It's going to be an alcohol—and drug-free outing. I don't want any hassles with the police. Everybody can abstain for a few hours, I hope."

"I dunno, I'm not much for the beach." Vaughn looked westward, squinting in the bright sunshine.

"Everybody, except Nolan, is going, and that means you, buster."

"Listen, I gotta put these here fish in the fridge, come on in." Julie shrugged her shoulders and followed Vaughn into the room. The room looked pretty much the same as it did when he first moved in, a framed poster art picture of five flamingos in a pond hanging over the bed constituted the only decoration. There was, however, a picture of his son on the dresser. Vaughn put the fish in a glass dish with a lid and stuck it in the small refrigerator.

"So did you hear what I said, John. No excuses. You can bring the fish if you want. I'd like to try some."

"Sure, I kin bake 'um on the coals."

"Sounds good. So have you heard from the family at all?" Julie would like it if John Vaughn would open up a little. She'd like to get to know him better.

She picked up the picture of his son and looked at it a moment. "Nice-looking kid."

"Thanks," Vaughn grunted. "Naw, I'm not ready to talk to the ex just yet. I miss my son, but I gotta give it a little more time."

"Why not bring the boy here for a visit. Me and Tommy will help you with getting around. We could go on a nature cruise and to Caribbean Gardens in Napolis and the water park in Cape Coral. It'd be fun!"

"We'll see. I'd have to get some kind of job right afterward though. It would take almost all my cash stash to fly 'em here plus do stuff. I could live practically another year on that. But yeah, maybe I'll call next weekend and try to set something up."

"You can call right now if you want. I'll get my cell phone." Julie got up to leave.

"Hold on a minute, Ms. Rambunctious," Vaughn chided. "I said next weekend. You bring the phone, and I'll make the call—promise."

"And I'm gonna hold you to that promise, sport." Julie was a believer in miracles, great and small. She was certain this loner could reclaim the happiness of his past.

12

Deputy Sheriff David O'Brien walked out of the sheriff department's North Napolis headquarters on Vanderbilt Beach Road and smiled in the bright Florida afternoon sunshine. The headquarters was west of Route 41, about half a mile shy of the Gulf of Mexico. O'Brien lived less than two minutes away on the six hundredth block of Ninety-fourth Avenue. It was called "Napolis Park," one of the last working-class communities to border the gulf. With property values skyrocketing, the community was falling victim to gentrification. New gingerbread mansions were being erected here and there on the remaining lots available, and older homes were being purchased and bulldozed to make way for their million-dollar replacements. Gulf access brought big money, and many older homeowners were selling out and running with the dough to other parts of the county or state.

Next week, Dave O'Brien was scheduled to go back on part-time road patrol. He had been reassigned to office work pending an investigation involving the use of deadly force. He used his service pistol on a crackhead coming at him with a butcher's knife. Dave barely had time to get his gun out of the holster before the shirtless guy, who looked like a linebacker for the Miami Dolphins, was on top of him with the knife. He shot the man almost point-blank in the chest, perforating his left lung and severing an artery. A witness claimed that the deputy gave no warning and that O'Brien gunned the man down in cold blood. But finally, after a thorough investigation, he was exonerated. Tomorrow, he was scheduled to return to active road patrol. Right now, he wanted to go home and take his two boys, Mike, age eleven, and Timmy, age eight, for a bike ride to the beach. Afterward, he could order pizza for the boys and get a babysitter while he and his wife, Janet, go out to a nearby Macaroni's for supper.

Dave was just pulling out of the parking area when his cell phone rang.

"Hello, this is O'Brien."

"Dave, Mike Nolan. How goes it?"

"What's up? I'm just leaving."

"Yeah, I just called your desk at headquarters. They told me you had just left. I was hoping you had something for me."

"I have something that might light a fire under our favorite barbeque." O'Brien didn't want to talk explicitly on the phone. "We need to talk, face-to-face. Can you meet me at the service area on the corner of Randall over by the Valencia Country Club? I'm scheduled for duty in that area tomorrow p.m. We can take a ride from there."

"Hey! You're back on active!"

"That's affirmative. Let's meet at eight."

"Perfect. See you then."

The problem of Deputy Rat O'Brien was eating away at Tiny. His rage at this meddlesome twerp, who was standing between him and his retirement fund, interfered with his thinking. Something had to be done. Oh yes, and something surely would be done. But what? First things first. He swung by his house, a two-bedroom two-bath stucco affair, ubiquitous in this part of the Sunshine State. In a locked cabinet in the master bedroom, Tiny stored a small arsenal of weapons he'd confiscated from criminals, mostly two-bit hoods and dope dealers, then "forgot" to report. None of the guns was traceable and certainly not to Tiny. After pulling on a pair of disposable latex gloves, he fished out the same snub nose .38 he had given to Carlos and Omar for their burning hot night at one of Rooster's gambling dens. Since he always used latex gloves when handling these firearms, it would still have one or both of their prints on it. It would come in handy in some fashion Tiny had yet to figure out.

He picked up a box of ammunition and loaded the six-shot cylinder with .38 special rounds, flipped it back into place, and stuck it under his belt. He walked back out to his patrol car and put the gun in the glove box and locked it. He headed off to pay Mario a surprise visit. It was getting to the point where he couldn't keep up with all his moneymaking opportunities. Just when he thought he had enough greenbacks coming in, another plum fell his way. At this rate, he could have enough to take early retirement in two more years and move to the Bahamas or Caymans a millionaire with a pension.

A few minutes later, Tiny turned left onto Flamevine Drive and pulled up into Mario's driveway. He called Mario on his cell phone. Mario picked up.

"Hello."

"Mario, my man. How they hangin'?"

"I'm tapped out, man. Whaddaya want?"

"Take a gander out your front window, my little Sambo." A moment later, there was Mario's anguished face in the window. Tiny roared with laughter at his discomfort. "Don't look so unhappy, it's your good buddy, Tiny."

"Aww, man, I can't—"

"Hush up your fat-lipped mouth, Mario. Just step out on your front porch, hands where I can see them." Mario, shuffling, did as he was instructed. Tiny got out of his car and walked up to the first step.

"I can't give you a thing, Tiny. It's still all out. Probably be another week before I have any back." Mario gave the deputy a sulky look.

"Sure it will. I understand." Tiny walked up the first step. His face was now even with Mario's who was standing on the landing. Mario backed up against the door. "Here's the deal, my little chimp." Tiny stepped up on the porch, towering over Mario. "You and I will meet next Saturday night at 8:00 p.m. out on the Old County Road where the old schoolhouse is. Do you know where I mean?"

"Yeah, yeah, I guess so." Mario was perspiring freely from his temples. "There's an orange grove just after it."

"That's it. And one more thing." Tiny was feeling truly inspired.

"What?" Mario was not feeling real anxious to hear what that one more thing was.

"I want you to get one of your nice rented cars, like a Ford Taurus, and pick up your amigos, Carlos and Omar, tomorrow. I want you to wait for me to call you on your cell phone. You boys'll be on call from 6:00 p.m. on." Tiny turned and left Mario sweating on the stoop as he drove off.

Mario, regaining his composure as Tiny's patrol car made a right turn at the corner heading for the intersection of County Road 845, went back into the house and picked up the telephone. He dialed the number Rooster Babcock had given him.

"Hello, Babcock residence," a young female voice greeted.

"Yeah, hi. Is Rooster there?"

"May I ask who's calling please?"

"Uhh, this is Mario."

"Mario?"

"Just tell him Mario wants to talk to him. He'll know who it is."

"Just a minute please." There was a long moment of silence before Rooster's voice came over the line.

"This is Rooster."

"Hey, this is Mario. You said to call."

"Oh yeah. What've you got for me, Mario?"

"I'm supposed to meet Tiny—"

"You mean Harris?" Rooster interjected.

"Yeah. We're meeting next Saturday at the old schoolhouse on the Old County Road at 8:00 p.m."

"Beautiful!" Rooster was almost ecstatic. "That's perfect. I'll be in touch. And don't worry. Like I said, I'll take care of everything. And as a bonus, there will be a nice profit in it for you."

"OK, man. Catch you later." Mario vaguely heard an adios as he hung up the phone. Maybe this whole thing could work out in his favor after all. If they got rid of Tiny and Rooster kept his word, he'd be free to operate without the interference of that greedy gorilla breathing down his neck. Maybe he'd have a little bundle of extra cashola to boot. Mario went to the fridge and pulled out a Heineken to quiet his frayed nerves.

Camilla was up early even before baby Billy opened his eyes. She picked up a wicker basket and went out to salute the morning sun. One of the benefits of living in this part of the country was the morning sunshine almost every day. The indefatigable Toad was already up in his porch rocker smoking a cigarette. Despite his tremendous drinking, he was invariably an early riser. "All in the genes," he said. She walked down the steps toward her garden, waving to Toad. If she didn't go over to say anything to him, she wouldn't get drawn into an unwanted conversation. Right now, what she wanted was some quiet time to tend her flowers, pick some fresh tomatoes for the picnic, and meditate. She passed the camellia and angel's trumpet bushes marking the garden entrance on the hotel side. She knelt by the tomato plants, propped up by stakes, and began plucking the ripest tomatoes. She pulled out a few weeds while she was at it. Weeding always put her in a meditative mood, stilling the flock of thoughts, which always seemed ready to take flight in fear at the approach of every problem.

After spending twenty minutes or so pulling weeds and gathering tomatoes, lettuce, and cucumbers, Camilla stood up and stretched. She looked west toward the road, over the trumpet honeysuckle vines that overgrew a four-foot-high wooden fence on the roadside of the garden. What she saw froze her blood. An unmarked sheriff's patrol car was idling on the narrow shoulder with that abominable asshole deputy sitting behind the wheel, smiling. His aura was bloodred. She stood, transfixed, somehow paralyzed, until the car roared back onto the highway and sped toward Bella Villa.

Camilla picked up her basket and walked back toward the porch, catching sight of Toad, head bent down, snoozing in his chair. He evidently didn't see El Diablo parked there. Instead of the usual sense of serenity that infused her after her morning meditations, she was filled with a portentous sense of dread. But she was damned if she'd let that malicious brute cast a cloud on her day.

"Morning, Robby," she said, coming through the door.

"Morning to you. Been out to the garden already, huh?"

"Sure have. Look at these tomatoes. Nice, huh?" Billy started screaming when he heard his mother's voice. "Oh, Billy Bob wants his mommy, doesn't he, snookums?" She picked up the baby who quit squalling immediately.

"Are we ready for the picnic this afternoon?" Robbie asked.

"Everything's set except the salad, which I'm going to make right now."

"Cool. I'm going to call my mother and tell her we won't be over today. Are you sure about getting a job? We're going to have to figure out what to do about Billy when I start classes next month. Maybe you should wait a little while."

"You're probably right, but I'm sick of hanging out here. There's only so much of Toad a person can take. I don't want him to be encouraged about coming over when I'm alone and he's drunk. It's bad enough when you're around."

"You got a point there. Coffee's ready." Robby poured a cup for himself and one for his wife. "Still, let's wait another month or two until I get settled into my routine."

"Sure, but why don't you bring up the subject with your mom now? She offered to pay a sitter to come to her house."

"That means we'd have to move into Napolis."

"Well, duh." Camilla smiled at her husband, then kissed the squirming infant in her arms.

There was a knock at the door.

"Hey, Cammy, Robbie, it's Julie."

"Come on in, Julie, the door's open." Julie came through the door.

"Hi, guys. How's Billy?" Julie walked over and gave Billy a smooch on the cheek. "I'm going out to buy ice and soft drinks. You wanna come with me, Cam?"

"Yeah, I guess that'd be OK. Robby?"

"Sure. Not a problem. Billy and I will hang out and do guy stuff."

"Great," said Julie. "Camilla and I need to catch up on some girl talk. And it's a good chance for you two dudes to bond. We won't be gone long."

"Bye, Billy." Camilla kissed the baby and flew out the door with Julie.

Jon Vaughn walked over to Toad's rocker. "Hey, you goin' today?" Toad looked up from the book he was reading.

"Yeah," he responded. "Why not? Good food and pretty girls in bikinis. I don't get to see that sittin' here." He nodded to a chair for Vaughn to sit. He picked up the cigarette papers next to the can of Bugler rolling tobacco and reached in the can for some tobacco. He began the ritual of rolling a smoke.

"Mind?" Vaughn asked, indicating the Bugler.

"Help yourself," Toad said. He finished making a cigarette and lit up. A prodigious plume of smoke rose above his hairy head as he exhaled. "I saw that wacko cop pull in the driveway this morning."

"Yeah?" Vaughn lit his own not-so-well-made cigarette. "What d'ya think he wants?"

"He wants to *intimidate*," Toad said, using the emphatic tone he reserved for making a point.

"He seems like a real bastard all right." Vaughn puffed his cigarette.

"He's dirty," said Toad. "And dangerous. He's trying to cover all his bases, but I get the feelin' he's overextended."

"Oh, how so?" Vaughn was amazed sometimes how Toad seemed to tap into the stream of feelings and events without leaving his rocking chair.

"Can't say for sure, but he's much more interested in what Nolan's up to than Jamie." Toad puffed on his cigarette and produced a pint bottle of rum from the small cooler by his chair. He dumped some in his coffee cup. He poured black coffee from a thermos to fill the cup, followed by a generous portion of the rum into the thermos. He sipped the brew. "I'm fixin' to be a wide-awake drunk today."

"So I see," said Vaughn. "You think we have anything to worry about with this cop? Maybe we better have a talk with Nolan."

"Oh yeah. He's trouble all right. He's followed by an evil specter wherever he walks, that one. But I doubt Nolan would ever blow his cover by talking to us."

They sat awhile in silence until Julie and Camilla pulled in from their ice-and-drink run.

"Hey, John, Toad," Julie called. Camilla waved, and both girls walked over to where they were sitting.

"We're pretty much all set," Julie said when they got to Toad's little patio table. "Brian said he'd clean out the van this morning so we could all ride together. We figure on leaving about one o'clock. That'll give us a couple of hours to set up, get the coals started and all that, enjoy the beach some, and have a midafternoon repast at around three. We'll hang out and enjoy the sunset before we split. How does that sound?"

"Are you wearin' a bikini or string suit?" Toad asked.

"I'm goin' naked, Toad." Julie grinned, hips out to the side, arms akimbo. "I suppose you will slip out of your dungarees and go all native too. That is, if you can peel those crusty things off you."

"Matter of fact, I'm washin' 'em today," Toad replied. "When I greet the Gulf of Mexico. But if you get bare-assed naked, I sure as hell will too." He gave her a gap-toothed grin through his thick whiskers.

"Oh, brother, I just can't wait," said Camilla. "You got any ass tattoos, Toad?"

"Not yet, but I'm thinkin' of puttin' a set of smoochin' lips on my right cheek."

"You'd do better to have a boot tattooed there," Cammy replied. They all had a good laugh.

"Hey, Toad," Camilla said as if the fun was only transitory like the sun peeking through the clouds on an overcast day, "you missed that big goober sheriff pulling in the driveway earlier." Toad looked at her and squinted.

"Oh yeah?" he said.

"Yeah," Camilla went on. "He just sat there in his car like a big ugly spider, giving me a creepy grin, then took off. You were dozing I guess."

"Must've been." Toad shot Vaughn a "keep quiet" look. "He's definitely a class A creep, no bouts a doubt it."

"I'll say," Camilla said and shuddered.

"Well, let's just forget all that stuff and focus on having a good time today, everybody," said Julie in her best onstage voice. "Come on, Cam, let's get the ice and drinks out of the car and check up on Brian and Jamie." She looked at Toad and added, "Remember, no alcohol or drugs today." Toad smiled and nodded.

Jamie and Brian were in the middle of cleaning out the van when the girls came around the corner to the side of the motel. They had just returned from their trip to the Circle K for ice and soda. (They had exchanged confessions about having juvenile crushes on the enigmatic Mike Nolan.) Brian's work tools, along with some roofing materials, were piled neatly by the vehicle. Morris Kline, proprietor of the Fireproof, was looking on.

"Well, good morning, ladies!" Morris said through a big grin, displaying what he claimed were all his original teeth. He held his arms open for a hug. He loved to hug the ladies every chance he got. But he was always the model of discretion and didn't overstep the bounds of decorum in his affections.

"Hi, Morris!" the two women chorused. They both gave him a quick hug.

"So, Morris," said Julie, "are you overseeing the lads' efforts to accommodate our picnic entourage? Why don't you come? You and Ida are more than welcome."

"No, no, but thank you," he responded. "I go most days anyway, as you probably know. Me and my buddies do our constitutional walk on the beach in the mornings. I may go into Napolis later today. It's a rare day when Ida is ready to leave the house before three in the afternoon, and she most certainly doesn't go to the beach, ever."

"What's up, Jamie, Brian," Camilla said, looking inside the van.

"Hi!" Brian said.

"Hey, Camilla," said Jamie. "We've got everything out. Now we're going to bolt in a second seat to strap down the baby's car seat and put in an old love seat Morris is lending us for the back. Toad and Vaughn can share that."

"Oh, how perfect!" Camilla said as everyone broke out in laughter.

"Just remember," interjected Morris, "you can't leave all this stuff by the motel after you return."

"Don't worry," said Brian, "I need all of it for work anyway."

"Good job, guys," said Julie. "Come over to my and Tommy's for a cold soda and to pick up the cooler."

"Remember," said Camilla, "we're leaving at twelve thirty. That's in about two hours."

"You got it," said Jamie as Brian snapped to attention and saluted. Everyone laughed, and the girls headed back to their respective rooms, arms locked together, chatting and giggling.

Tiny checked the Sunday roster and discovered O'Brien would be working patrol between Bella Villa and Napolis. Perfect. The rat was probably planning a few information gathering stops at the homes of some of the deputies that worked his substation. Maybe he was even going to rendezvous with the secret agent man. Tiny couldn't allow that to happen as much as he wanted to ascertain who the guy was. He might be able to nip this whole investigation bullshit in the bud by taking O'Brien out of the equation. As it stood, O'Brien was the one busted switch that could derail his retirement train.

Tiny made a quick trip to see Mario. He didn't dare use a phone to pass along his simple instructions. These days, you could never be sure if any phone was secure. Hell, you never knew who might be videotaping from a distance with a mic pickup. Better to err on the side of caution when it came to clandestine operations. He got Mario out the back door of the house, patted him down for bugs, and gave him instructions. "I want you to get the rental car, pick up Carlos and Omar, and put 'borrowed' plates on the car for just a couple of hours. The two Mexicanos should have a spare set of plates or two kicking around from their last job. Drive to the McDonald's at the junction of 951 and 846 and wait. Make sure you're there at 7:00 p.m. All you're going to have to do is drive fast for a few minutes, and your part is over. Don't worry, I'll take care of everything."

When he left Mario, Tiny headed for the "Shit for Shines" Trailer Park to see his little buddies before they hooked up with Mario. He turned in, navigated through the sea of little brown noodle scooters playing in the narrow street, and pulled up to Carlos's trailer. Carlos stepped out on the shaky steps. Tiny rolled his window down.

"Carlos, my friend," he began. Carlos scowled, anticipating something distasteful. "Come over here. I need a small favor."

"What can I do for you, Señor Tiny?" Carlos pronounced the name "Teeny."

"I need to borrow your cell phone for a few hours. I'll return it later today after you hook up with Mario." Carlos did not like this idea very much. Omar came out of the trailer and looked on from the porch.

"But I need this phone, Tiny," Carlos pleaded. He wasn't going to surrender all his contacts and numbers without a fight. "Please, why do you need another cell phone?"

A small crowd of children began to gather at a distance. Adults were sure to mosey over soon. Tiny wanted to avoid a scene at this delicate time. He noticed Omar was wearing a phone hooked to his belt.

"Omar, come here." Tiny got out of the car. Omar shuffled over reluctantly. Tiny held out his hand. "I need your phone."

"But, señor—"

"Just give me the phone, *now!*" Tiny commanded. He left no room for interpretation of whether this was negotiable. Omar complied. Tiny was careful to take the phone without touching it with his fingertips.

"Smart move," Tiny said. He turned to Carlos. "You and Omar go with Mario when he comes. He'll know what's shakin'." Carlos looked baffled.

"Happening—he'll know what's going on," Tiny interpreted.

"*Sí*, Señor Tiny," Carlos said. "El Diablo," he muttered under his breath.

13

"You know, Toad," said Julie, "an occasional shower and laundry could improve your social compatibility 150 percent." Everyone in the van laughed as Brian navigated through light traffic on County Road 846, which went straight to Wiggins Pass State Park and Recreation Area.

"I don't know what you mean," Toad responded. "I take a bath once a year whether I need it or not. Afterward, I throw away my old clothes and put on new ones from the thrift store." There was another chorus of laughter from the front area of the van where everyone crowded away from Toad who was given the love seat and the entire rear portion of the vehicle to share with only the picnic goodies. It had been agreed upon before the excursion that there would be no smoking of any kind for the thirty-minute duration of the trip. After all, there was a baby on board, as well as a couple of nonsmokers.

Tommy, sitting on a rolled-up futon with Julie, started singing a Jethro Tull song: "Sitting on a park bench, eyeing little girls with bad intent, snot running down his nose, greasy fingers smearing shabby clothes, hey, Aqualung . . ." Everyone clapped and laughed. As for Toad, he sat back with a vacant grin and rolled another cigarette against the time when the smoking lamp would be lit.

The van passed through wide-open tomato fields separated from the road by a canal. This canal bordered 846 almost all the way to where it intersected Route 41. The canal disappeared into the Coco River, which ran into an inlet separating Wiggins Pass beach from the landmass. This body of water was connected to the gulf at Wiggins Pass where a state boat landing and park was located. There was a private marina as well with boat storage facilities, but this was doomed to be bought and developed into multi-million-dollar condominiums. They passed through a long stretch where there was little more than cypress and pine forest, interspersed with cabbage palms, bordering a vast sea of grass and wetlands—the Everglades. Within fifteen miles of the Gulf of Mexico, the first of the large developments began. They passed Valencia Golf and Country Club, a middle-class community. Moving west, they passed Twin Eagles, a much more exclusive club where huge mansions sprung up as erratically as mushrooms throughout the vast golf fairways and putting greens. Soon there would be hundreds of multimillionaires living there, mostly as part-time neighbors during the North's cold winters.

Land was being cleared almost every foot of the way, signs advertising new homes and condominiums starting at three hundred forty thousand dollars. Others offered homes starting in the low five hundred to three million. They passed the sprawling new Gulf Coast High School, Crystal Lake, Saturnia Lakes, Huntington Lakes with it's treelined drive, and the beautifully landscaped and exclusive Quail West. Many others, too numerous to mention, were within nine iron distance of their route. By the time they passed North Baron County Hospital and came to the light at Route 41, the conversation turned to the parking at Wiggins Pass. They were less than two miles away now. A few minutes later, they arrived at the gate and paid for parking. The attendant assured them there were still a few places left but going fast. He handed Jamie a parking ticket with the date and time stamped on it. Jamie placed it on the front dash and drove through the gate. They found a spot in the number 3 lot and, with even more luck, a vacant table. Toad lit a smoke as Vaughn helped Tommy kindle the barbeque.

For the first time in a long spell, John Vaughn felt part of something bigger than himself. The Fireproof crew cooked and ate and shared stories and laughter. Someone produced two Ping-Pong-like paddles and a hard rubber ball, and they played beach tennis on the hard, wet sand. They swam in the warm gulf water and lay in the hot near-tropic sun. Baby Billy was enthralled with the sand and the sea. He jubilantly splashed and wallowed naked in the wet sand at the tide line. When the sun was low in the Western sky, Tommy pulled out his guitar and led them in song. Vaughn thought Julie provided a wondrous and beautiful harmony. They sang a song they said came from a group named the Talking Heads. It was called "(Nothing But) Flowers," Tommy said, including the parentheses with hand gestures. It had a Caribbean rhythm, and Julie produced a small bongo drum to complement Tommy's guitar. The lyrics contained many of the sentiments Vaughn espoused, and though not much of a singer, he joined in the chorus parts.

The lyrics of the song alluded to a postapocalyptic world where cars are dinosaurs and rattlesnakes are dinner. The shopping centers and 7-Elevens have returned to the wild—fields, trees, and flowers. "And as things fell apart, nobody paid much attention." The singer misses the conveniences of civilization. The final line of the song, Tommy and Julie stopped playing, and Tommy belted out the words. "Don't leave me standing here." End of music. "I can't get used to this *lifestyle.*" Tommy made the final word vibrate like a verbal poltergeist.

The sun had begun its final descent behind the gulf waters, a round fiery disc smearing the low fog on the horizon with dazzling light. The sky turned a dozen shades of blue from turquoise to indigo to cyan as puffy white clouds began to glow with the multiple colors of burning hot coals. It was a cosmic painting by a creator with incomprehensible artistic flare. In the peaceful twilight, the group gathered their things and boarded the van.

"Beer store!" Tommy yelled once the engine started.

"I second the motion," said Brian. "And as the driver, I have the final word."

"No drinking 'til we get back to the Fireproof," said Julie. "THEN IT'S PARTY TIME!"

They put the gulf to their backs and headed east.

David O'Brien finished the plate of meat loaf and mashed potatoes his wife had prepared for him. He sat at the table in his modest Napolis Park home. He was wearing his gray sheriff's uniform. The table was in a small alcove with a window looking out at the backyard on one end. His two boys were playing in the yard as the setting sun cast long shadows everywhere. He washed down the last bite with a gulp of black coffee and got up from the table. His wife, Kathy, a wholesome-looking woman of thirty with chestnut hair and a smattering of freckles under her eyes, came over to pick up his plate. She had on a light blue blouse that hung loose over khaki shorts. She was a loving wife and mother, supportive in every way. He'd met her at Lulu's Restaurant where she still waited on tables. Asking her out the first time had been a defining moment in his life.

"Aren't you having pie?" Kathy asked. "It's your favorite, apple. I can heat it in just a second, and we have vanilla ice cream."

"Not tonight, honey," David said. "I'll probably meet up with a couple of the guys on patrol in Bella Villa, and we'll hit some local diner for coffee and a bite. I don't want to get bogged down with too much of your good chow at one time." He grinned and gave her rear end an affectionate swat.

"That's my man, always thinking ahead." Kathy smiled and gave him a hug and kiss on the cheek. "I better call the boys in and get them settled for the night."

"I'll get them and say my good nights at the same time." He put on his utility belt and the holster with his 9mm Glock. He went to the back door and stepped out into the tepid Florida twilight. The boys were engaged in a form of kick ball with no real rules or goals. *Two boys at play with a ball as ancient as civilization itself,* O'Brien thought.

"Don! Timmy!" he called. "Time to come in now." They ran to him, screaming gibberish. Don was a head taller than Timmy, with blonde hair like his dad's but his mother's green eyes. Timmy had chestnut hair, freckles, and bright blue eyes, and he looked like his mother. "Easy now. I don't want to get all dirty before I catch any bad guys."

"Daddy, I wanna go with you," Timmy said.

"Not tonight, big guy. Too many bad guys and you've got to stay home and take care of Mom and Donny."

"Aw, Dad," said Don, "I'm the only tough guy here. Timmy's a sissy."

"Am not, you're a bastard, I'll kick you in the butt." Timmy charged his brother.

"Hold on right there, you two roughnecks." Dave O'Brien held them apart. "Timmy, I don't want to hear that kind of language, do you understand?"

"Yes, but—"

"No buts, and no fighting while the sheriff's in town, or I'll bust both of you. And if I get any bad reports while I'm gone, there will be no video games for a week. *Comprende?*" They both nodded their heads, still glowering at each other.

"OK. Let's go in." David herded them through the door.

"Say good-bye to your father, boys, and get ready for bed," Kathy said, returning to the kitchen sink. The boys went up to their father who gave them each a hug and kiss on the cheek and sent them to their rooms.

"And no video games before bed, you two," Kathy called from the kitchen. "Try reading a book tonight."

"Isn't that kinda harsh?" Dave asked.

"No way," said Kathy. "They get too worked up when they play those games. I'll go in later and read a little with Timmy." She came out to the living room to say good-bye.

"Sounds reasonable," Dave said. "Well, I gotta go." He kissed her lightly on the lips. "Love you."

"Love you too, sweetheart. Be careful." She walked out the front door and watched him get in his patrol car and leave. She waved.

It was the last time she would see her husband alive.

Mario parked the gray Ford Taurus in front of the beat-up old trailer Carlos called home. He honked his horn. The sun, low in the west, was turning the sky a fiery crimson. A sea of round brown faces swarmed around the car. The children stared at him, large dark eyes reflecting the sanguine glow on the horizon. At last, Carlos and Omar emerged from the trailer and got in the car. Carlos sat in front. Neither of them looked pleased to be going.

"Me no like dis," Carlos said in his heavily accented English.

"Join the club," Mario retorted.

"Eef El Diablo he eez up to someding, eet wheel be troubles for us." Carlos nodded his head toward the rear seat. "And he took Omar's cell phone. Why?"

"You got me there, amigo," Mario replied. Mario's cell rang. He picked it up from the utility tray in the car's console.

"Hello."

"Mario, my man!" It was the devil himself, disguised as one colossal deputy sheriff and calling from Omar's cell.

"Hey, Tiny." Mario sounded somewhat less than enthusiastic.

"Listen carefully," Tiny said. "I want you to drive west on 846 and turn left on Rock Road. It's about a mile west of where the service station next to the firehouse is. You know where I mean?"

"Yeah, I know the road you mean," Mario answered.

"Good. There's a wide shoulder where that road connects with 846. Just park there and wait for me to call again. Be ready to fly out of there at no less than eighty miles per hour when you get my call. And don't worry, I'll be covering your ass. Got that?"

"Yeah, I guess so," Mario said. "But I don't like the sounds of this."

"Like I said"—Tiny's voice grew hard with impatience—"I'm covering your ass."

"That's what I'm afraid of," Mario mumbled, holding the phone away from his mouth and glancing at Carlos. He mouthed the silent words *We're already fucked.*

"I didn't copy that," said Tiny.

"I said," Mario improvised, "we're ready to rock."

"Then get there as fast as you can. Time's running out." Tiny hung up.

"Ten-four," Mario said into the dead phone.

Brian pulled the van into the convenience store at the juncture of 846 and Randall Boulevard. They were about ten miles east of the beach. "Psycho Killer" by the Talking Heads blared on the van's four speakers.

"I'll fly if y'all buy!" Brian shouted out. A minute later, he had enough for two cases of brew ha-ha. He walked into the store, and the first person he saw, sitting at a table eating a burrito, was Mike Nolan.

"Hey, Mike! What's up? I thought you were out of town."

"Hi, Brian." Nolan was surprised but accustomed to making quick recoveries. "I'm just on my way home matter of fact. Thought I'd stop for a little dinner. How was the beach?"

"Terrific. We're heading back for a little Fireproof party. Why don't you come over and join us."

"Ahh, sure," Nolan said. He looked out at the parking lot. A sheriff's patrol car screamed past, lights flashing. He seemed nervous. "OK, I'll do that."

"Great," Brian said. "We'll see you back at the hacienda." He turned and walked back to the beer coolers. He paid for the beer and put it in the back of the van next to Toad and restarted the engine. "Life During Wartime" came on. "This ain't no party, this ain't no disco, this ain't no foolin' around . . . ," David Byrne sang.

"Hey, guess who I saw in the store?" Brian said to Jamie as an afterthought.

"Who?" Jamie asked.

"Mike Nolan."

"No shit," Jamie said.

"I told him to come over when he got home."

"What the hell," Jamie said. "Why not?"

They were about two miles east of the store when Vaughn said he needed to take a leak.

"Why didn't you go at the store?" Brian asked.

"Didn't think I had to go so bad," Vaughn replied.

"There's a road with an old cemetery about half mile down," Brian said. "I'll pull off there, and you can water the dead."

"Sounds like a plan," Vaughn said.

Tiny waited in the driveway of Gulf Coast High School for O'Brien to come by in his cruiser. Ten minutes later, O'Brien swept by. Tiny pulled out behind him. As soon as he passed the 951 intersection, Tiny called Mario on Omar's cell. "Get ready to take off. Turn into the old cemetery road and pull over. You're about to go on a short police chase. Remember, I got you covered."

"Oh, J-zeus Christy," Mario moaned. He told Carlos and Omar what El Diablo said. The bronze skin of their faces seemed to turn pale as the blood drained out. The phone buzzed again.

"Go, now!" Tiny disconnected.

Mario pulled out onto 846 directly ahead of O'Brien and accelerated to eighty miles an hour as instructed.

"Shit," said O'Brien and turned on his lights. He really didn't want to do this right now, but the fool was giving him no choice. He called it in and pursued the car for a couple of miles. A second officer radioed he was only a few miles behind and would lend assistance. It was Deputy Edwin "Tiny" Harris.

14

Josh Crayton sensed something was different around the house, starting from the time the big man in uniform came after his brother and sister disappeared. He wasn't exactly fed much better, but he started getting more food, just enough to keep the hunger heebie-jeebies at bay. This calmed and clarified his mind to some degree. Also, he was let out of the closet more often to bathe and was given a change of clothing. He was allowed to clean the reeking cave where he was kept. His mother smoked and drank while she watched him work. Despite showing an unwilling restraint in corporal punishment of late, she couldn't get through the process without smacking him with a rolled-up newspaper a couple of times. What he couldn't rid himself of was the constant gnawing fear that this was all in preparation for his future. He was to be taken away. To where, he had no idea. But he just knew it couldn't be good. He had to get away.

Late one afternoon, Josh was taken out of the closet and told to bathe. His father was nowhere in sight. His mother was drunk than usual. She was slurring her words and staggering around. When he finished his bath and came out, she was asleep in an old overstuffed chair, a cigarette dangling from her lips and smoke curling up from a long ash. Josh moved quietly through the house. This was his chance! He slipped into an old pair of sneakers that were kept in a hall closet. They were too small for him, but they'd have to do. Something else was in the closet—a small backpack with a change of clothes for him. So they were intending to send him away for sure. He picked up the pack and, heart thumping like it would explode through his scrawny rib cage, opened the front door. His stomach was doing flip-flops. He glanced back to see if the witch was coming. She hadn't stirred from her roost. He went through the door, a ghost who would never look back.

Brian turned right on the cemetery road, and about ten yards in, he turned right again onto a dead-end appendage. He wanted to be able to turn around easily. Toad cracked open a beer. John Vaughn got out and let loose a stream of urine. There was the squeal of brakes and tires as a car made a hard turn onto the road behind the van. Headlights flooded the road for a second before they were switched off. The car halted about a hundred yards down the road.

"Turn the friggin' lights and music off!" Vaughn yelled over his shoulder. Brian readily complied. A second car's tires protested with a loud screeching as it made a hard turn onto the same road. This time, more than headlights flooded the road behind them. There were the bright blue-and-red flashing variety as well. Vaughn zipped up his pants and hurried around the van to check out what was happening. Just before he reached the juncture of the two roads, there was again the shriek of tires and more flashing lights. This time, they came from the windshield of the squad car and the rear window. Brian got out of the car and slunk up beside Vaughn. Vaughn put his fingers to his lips. "We better stay put until this is over," he said in a whisper.

They looked down the road from behind an enormous hedge of star jasmine. There was no mistaking the figure that emerged from the second patrol car. It was Tiny. The deputy from the first car turned and said something. Tiny walked straight up to the other cop, raised his right hand, and pointed at him. There was a loud booming sound and a flash of fire. The first cop went down.

"Jesus!" Brian gasped. Vaughn clutched his arm. There was a cacophony of voices, both English and Spanish, from the car ahead of the first cruiser. Tiny went over and barked something at them. He handed something through the window. The car pulled ahead and made a U-turn in the road and sped down the road past them to 846. The lawman turned murderer was rummaging in the slain officer's patrol car. A minute later, there was the wail of a siren getting very close.

"Come on," Vaughn whispered, "we've got to push the van ahead."

"What—?" Brian began, but Vaughn shushed him. He put his finger over his lips and approached the others as they climbed out of the van.

"Quiet, everybody quiet!" Vaughn hissed. "We've got to push the van ahead out of sight, *now*! He'll kill all of us."

"Who?" Julie began.

"The devil," Brian answered. "That's who?" Camilla started to whimper.

"I'll put it in neutral," Brian said. Vaughn put his back against the van and crouched, ready to push.

"Come on, everyone." By this time, everyone was outside. They all found a spot and shoved on the van. Slowly it rolled forward into the spectral gloom. Thankfully, there was a slight bend in the road that, with the help of shrubbery, shielded the van from view. They were going to have to settle in here and be very quiet until it was clear to leave. Toad popped another brew, and Brian followed suit. A police car screeched onto the cemetery road. The wail of more sirens could be heard; and very soon, another cruiser pulled in, lights flashing. A minute later, there was another, then another. An ambulance and a state police car showed up. It looked like a carnival was going on in the cemetery. The only thing missing was music.

"It'll be a miracle if they don't spot us," Jamie said.

"You got that right," said Tommy.

"We're gonna *burn*," Brian whimpered and sucked down his beer. Vaughn put his finger to his lips.

"Then pray," Julie urged, "that by the grace of God we'll be *fireproof*."

Tiny pulled up behind O'Brien's cruiser and grabbed the .38 from the glove box. He wore a pair of easy-on disposable plastic gloves. Omar's cell phone was clipped to his gun belt. He got out of his patrol car with the .38 in his right hand. He walked up to O'Brien without a word. He knew this was going to have to be fast. No time for chitchat.

"Tiny, why am I not surprised—," O'Brien began, not seeing the gun in the dark. Tiny pointed the revolver at O'Brien's heart and pulled the trigger from six feet away. The impact knocked the erstwhile deputy back and off his feet. He hit the ground with a *thump*. Smoke and the smell of gunpowder filled the humid Florida night. When the ringing stopped in Tiny's ears, it wasn't the shrill voices of the cemetery ghosts he heard, but cries of bewilderment and shocked disbelief, in a gabble of English and Spanish, coming from the Taurus. He walked over and tossed the gun in the open driver's window, Omar's cell phone as well.

"Both of those and this heap you're driving," Tiny informed them, "are items with fingerprints and DNA linking you three amigos to this horrific crime. Do with them as you will. You are presently 'unknown assailants,' and I'd like to keep it that way. I'm sure you agree. Now, get the fuck out of here before the cavalry arrives. Go!" Still wearing the plastic gloves, Tiny went over to O'Brien's patrol car and found the manila envelope containing the intelligence Deputy O'Bastard intended to hand off to Nolan.

Tiny's story was simple. When the adrenaline-pumped deputies arrived, he'd say he joined O'Brien in the chase of a speeding car. When he arrived at the scene, the car was gone, and O'Brien was dead from a gunshot wound. Probably, it was drug desperados. There were some mean critters out in these swamps—some more dangerous than a hungry gator.

When he saw the taillights of the Taurus disappear, Tiny called for backup. "Officer down. Send an ambulance. Location, Old Cemetery Road, east of Oil Well on 846. Shooter has fled the scene. Probably in dark or gray late model Ford Taurus or Mercury Sable. Consider them armed and dangerous." Taking his finger off the radio's Call button, he said to himself, "Dangerous as three hamsters in a cage."

15

"Jesus! Motherfucker!" Mario turned the Taurus around and sped down the cemetery road. He made a right onto 846 and headed toward Bella Villa.

"Shit!" Carlos said, his Spanish accent making the word sound like what you put on a bed. "What we going to do? We fucked now!"

"The bastard set us up," said Mario. "We have to get rid of the gun and these plates, pronto. I know a back road that goes around the lake and comes out in Corkscrew. We can double back into town, stopping at your trailer to switch the plates. We wipe the gun and cell phone down for prints and toss them in the lake on the way by. You take the stolen plates and lose them where they can't be found. I go home. Anybody asks where we were tonight, we were playing cards at your trailer. Make sure everyone knows the alibi." He paused to make sure Carlos understood everything he said, repeating where necessary.

"If we make it back to your place without being stopped, we might be all right."

Carlos muttered some words in Spanish to Omar, and they both cursed in their native tongue for a couple of minutes. The words, *Tiny* (pronounced "Teeny") and *El Diablo*, stood out as they were repeated often and venomously.

It was almost one in the morning before the last of the emergency vehicles left the cemetery. A display of colored lights—red, blue, yellow, and white—caused a thousand wraithlike shadows to flit across the gravestones before being swallowed by the black night. The constant squawk of radios, voices, and running motors filled the air. The Fireproof crew stayed glued to the van, trying to be invisible. The survival instinct was sufficiently encoded among all of them, so there was very little noise, other than the occasional pop as Toad or Brian opened a beer. Everyone else contented themselves with passing a jug of fresh water they had brought from the beach. Thankfully, Baby Billie, exhausted by the afternoon of fun in the sun, slept soundly in his car seat. There was an extremely tense moment when one of the final patrol cars turned its spotlight down the road they were on. Fortunately, they were far enough not to be noticed around the bend. They waited nearly twenty minutes in the dark quiet of the cemetery.

"Let's get the hell out of here," Jamie said. "I'm driving. Brian, switch seats with me—and no open beers in the van. Put the empties out of sight." Brian offered no protest to being relieved of his chauffeur's position.

"Hold on," said Vaughn. "I'd better go check outside first to make sure no cops are waiting around. We don't want any surprises."

"I'm coming with," said Toad. He grabbed a Budweiser from the cooler. He figured on chugging it while Vaughn checked for signs of hostile life. Unfortunately, he tripped over a rock in his semi-inebriated condition, and his Bud went flying as he waved his arms to regain balance. The can went under some brush on the side of the road, and before Toad could launch a search effort, Vaughn was hustling him back to the van.

"All clear," Vaughn said as he climbed back into the van.

"Let's get the hell out of here," said Jamie, and he backed the van to the access road, turned, and drove out to 846. A car was approaching from the west, but the headlights were plenty far away for him to drive out onto the highway heading east to Bella Villa.

Tiny's was the next-to-the-last vehicle to leave the scene. A road service deputy in a white Ford Ranger pickup with yellow warning lights on the roof was left alone to clean the area up. Tiny turned his spotlight down the service road on the left as he drove slowly by. He thought he saw a red glint like a reflector. It was probably just the play of light and his jangled nerves. He turned left on 846 and headed west. He was hungry and wanted to get a bite from the twenty-four-hour convenience store located a couple of miles away. When he arrived, the store was deserted, except for a lone clerk restocking the shelves. As expected, the rest of law enforcement involved had retreated to the Clock, an all-night diner in Napolis, to powwow. Tiny, like a lone wolf, was left to stew on his own before returning to Bella Villa. He would have a mountain of paperwork to complete before bed tonight, and there would be more questions tomorrow. Still, all in all, things went pretty well. On the surface, it appears they bought his story. He had placed the rubber gloves under the band of his underwear. He was right in thinking they would stop short of a full body search. The gun he used in the execution had the prints of illegal immigrants, which, if ever found, would turn up zip. It was a throwaway, impossible to trace. Besides, unless Mario was stupid enough to get caught, he and his two amigos had most likely disposed of the firearm.

Tiny gulped the last of his Coke and headed back east to Bella Villa. He was about a half mile from the cemetery road when a vehicle pulled out and headed east. "What the fuck," he said out loud. He drove up fast on the vehicle and saw that it was a Ford van. He didn't have to get close enough to get a plate number; he recognized Brian's rattletrap. What in hell's kitchen was it doing on the cemetery road, and how long had it been there? He put on his blue lights. The van slowed and carefully pulled onto a wide area of shoulder about a quarter mile farther down the road. One thing's for sure, he wasn't going to call for backup on this stop.

After finishing his burrito, Mike Nolan checked his watch. It was just after 8:00 p.m. He read *El Milagro*, the migrant and Hispanic newspaper. There was an article by Luis Alvarez, someone who knew just about everybody in the community. Nolan had begun to cultivate a relationship with Alvarez in hopes of getting some good leads. In this particular article, he was bashing a local slumlord, the owner of King Burger, Ron Badger, for some of the horrific buildings and trailers he rented to migrant workers at obscene prices. *That's the ticket, Luis,* Nolan thought, *give 'em hell. If I were really a housing inspector, I'd be all over his ass.*

Nolan checked his watch again. Eight fifteen. O'Brien was a "no call, no show." He wondered if it could have anything to do with the patrol car he saw go by earlier when Brian was buying beer. He went out and got in the LeBaron and switched on his police radio. He heard Tiny's voice. "It's O'Brien," he said. "I think the wound is fatal." Nolan's heart skipped a beat as he put his car in gear and drove back toward Bella Villa, monitoring the police band. Baron County sheriff's patrol cars, coming from both the east and west, roof bubbles blazing in the night, passed him. When he drove by the cemetery road, it wasn't hard to figure out the apex of all the activity. He continued to drive east, stunned and shocked. Was O'Brien's death related to their meeting or just circumstantial? He feared it was the former. By the time he got back to the Fireproof, the implications sent an icy chill down his spine and made his skin percolate with ten thousand bumps. He cracked a beer and returned to his car to follow the chatter.

Jamie's heart nearly bashed its way out of his rib cage, like a sledgehammer going through drywall, when he saw the blue lights come on in his left-side mirror. His stomach heaved, and he nearly let fly his picnic lunch. It was all he could do to keep the van on the road. He slowed and searched for a place to pull over. Sweat drenched his tee shirt. The palms of his hands slipped on the wheel. He had no doubt who was in the patrol car behind him. When he got the van over and stopped on the side of the road, he addressed everyone in the van.

"Listen, everyone!" Jamie gave instructions, talking rapidly. "This is our story: We stopped so Toad and Vaughn could take a leak. We were there two minutes and left. That's it. Period. We're coming home from DeSoto State Park in St. Petersburg where we spent the day, that's why we're out this late. Brian, get the registration out of the glove compartment. Jesus, Joseph, and Mary, here comes the devil himself."

Tiny didn't bother to radio in the license plate or anything else to headquarters. He got out of the patrol car and walked toward the van, holding his flashlight in his left hand. This was some fucking coincidence all right. He wondered if Nolan put them up to this. Maybe Nolan was with them. Wouldn't that be a jumpin' Jehoshaphat ole jack-off party! When he got to the driver's side window, he flashed his light directly into Jamie's face. This had the effect of intimidating or pissing off the driver, either of which brought about a desired result.

Jamie squinted in the bright light. "I have my license and the registration right here." He offered the documents to Tiny.

"Keep 'em," Tiny growled. "I know who you are. What I want to know is *what* you were doing back on the cemetery road." Baby Billie started wailing. "How many of you are there in here?" Tiny panned his light around the back of the van.

"Let's see." Jamie had to count on his fingers. "There's eight adults and a baby."

"I see. Is there a Mike Nolan aboard by any chance?" Tiny didn't figure Nolan was there, or he'd have opened his big fat Irish mouth by now.

"No, sir," Jamie answered. "He couldn't make it."

"Make what?" Tiny asked.

"Our beach party up at DeSoto State Park." Jamie suddenly had to go pee.

"DeSoto? Long trip for a day ain't it?"

"Yeah, well, we started early and stayed late as you can see."

"So what were you doin' on that road back there?"

"A couple of the guys got out to take a leak." Jamie looked over at Brian for support. Brian nodded his head up and down, mumbling something.

"How long were you there?" Tiny put the light in Jamie's face again and studied his expression.

"Just a couple of minutes, that's it." Jamie gave him the most sincere look he could muster. Brian mumbled again and continued to nod.

"Couple of minutes, huh." Tiny panned the light onto Brian's face. "You been drinking tonight." At that moment, Jamie noticed the parking ticket for Wiggins State Park on the van's front dash. It felt like somebody pulled the trigger on his adrenal gland, a shot flooded his bloodstream with nature's own hyper high. His heart began pumping even more furiously against his will, sweat beaded his forehead and ran freely from his armpits. His stomach muscles started twitching. Brian was stammering some reply, but Jamie's only focus was getting rid of that damning evidence in front of him. Toad yelled an obscenity from the back of the van. Tiny turned his light on him and scowled through the window. Jamie's hand went to the ticket on the dash and crumpled it in his fist; God loves a drunk and a fool they say.

"What did you say, buster?" Tiny demanded. Julie grabbed Toad's calf and pinched. Vaughn shook his head from side to side.

"Nothin'," Toad replied. Tiny swept his light over the rest of the passengers, over the dash, and returned to Jamie.

"You can go," Tiny said and walked back to his car. He did a U-turn and went back to the Cemetery Road and turned left. He made the first right-hand turn and stopped. He got out of the car but left it running with the headlights and spot on. Walking along the road, he looked for evidence, a vehicle had been there recently. It was hard to tell in the night. He saw something shiny. He walked over and picked it up. It was an unopened Budweiser can, still cool to the touch.

Judge Thomas ran a lazy finger over the nipple of the budding breast of thirteen-year-old Megan Quinn, a delectable Irish morsel, who had the unfortunate luck to be brought into his court in a foster care proceeding. She lay whimpering next to him, her gorgeous mane of strawberry blonde hair covering the pillow. The old goat had completely exhausted himself, even with the aid of Viagra, on her supple and unblemished, if not totally willing, flesh. Already, his mind was plotting how and when to arrange another "interview." He was so enthralled with Megan's beauty he contemplated becoming her foster father himself. That would be a decidedly dangerous course as it would mean contending with his frumpy wife. But of far more consequence, it would make him completely vulnerable to blackmail, Tiny's favorite pastime. Still, he was obsessed with her and wanted to keep her. At last, his mind returned to the reality of his situation, and he got up from the bed to draw a bath for her. He watched as she got in and submerged herself. He would have to make sure she washed thoroughly, removing all traces of DNA. He sat on a stool he kept in the bathroom for just such events, a thick bath towel and a cordless phone on his lap.

"When you finish," he said, "come over here, and I'll dry you." That sport never failed to resurrect his flagging member. He dialed a number and waited.

"Hello, Rooster," the judge said. "I understand we have a mutual problem."

Constance Valentine took the manila envelope her maid Anna handed her and looked it over. The only markings on it were her first name printed in block letters in black ink. She raised her eyebrows. "Where did this come from, Anna?"

"It was between the front door and the pulling screen, señora," Anna answered in accented English. She said *pulling* because she couldn't think of the word *sliding*. Anna had little doubt El Diablo had left the package, but she kept her opinion to herself. The sudden expression of dismay that came over Señora Valentine's face indicated the same thought just occurred to her.

"Thank you, Anna," Constance said. "I'll be in my study." She turned abruptly and went down the hall to the study, closing the door behind her. Once inside, she went to her desk and switched on the brass lamp with the handmade stained glass shade. The shade was in the shape of a half oval, positioned horizontally over the bulb to shed the light downward while enough escaped to prevent glare.

It was a gift to her late husband from the governor of Florida. The glass was dark reds and greens with an amber outline of a fish in the center. Constance reached for the letter opener and sat in the plush leather executive chair behind her desk. She opened the envelope and pulled out a page of construction paper, a cassette attached with a piece of duct tape. There was no message. Her heart fluttered, and she began to perspire, chills rippled through her flesh. Her sweat had the sour, nervous smell of guilt and fear. She got up and put the tape in the Sony portable she kept on one of her shelves for background music. What she heard made her blood freeze and her stomach heave. Constance listened in agony to a recording of her meeting with the SWF Development Company. In it, she could be clearly heard accepting a large bribe for her vote in favor of a zoning variance permitting their project.

Constance walked over to the small wet bar she kept for business meetings and poured herself a double Chivas Regal. Walking back over to her desk on wobbly legs, she nearly collapsed, but she managed to plop down in her chair. How could that big ape have gotten this tape? She took a large swallow of the Chivas and sat quietly. She reflected on that day until she remembered the brooch. *Oh my god,* she thought, *not Pablo.* Her heart sank. She fought back tears. Finishing the drink, she picked up the phone. She hesitated a moment and dialed.

"Hello, Rooster. This is Constance Valentine. It's about a mutual problem."

Morris tossed fitfully in his sleep. It wasn't the arthritis in his shoulder, which sent burning tendrils of pain through his chest when it flared up, causing the restlessness, however. It was a nightmare, the kind so vivid and clear you wake up in a cold sweat gasping for air and, finally realizing it was but a bad dream, sink back onto the pillow in stunned relief.

In this nocturnal play, Morris was driving east on 846 in his Buick LeSabre. Behind him were the sunny beach and the Gulf of Mexico. Directly ahead, it looked like Armageddon. Thunderclouds black as smoke from a coal furnace covered the sky. They were sending blindingly bright bolts of lightning to the horizon. Another sort of light caught his attention, the blue-and-red lights of a police car. The lights were in his rearview mirror, the car directly behind him. He pulled over and reached to get his registration from the glove compartment when a bolt of lightning struck the car, nearly lifting it off the ground. A violent blast of wind, accompanied by a tremendous thunderclap, shook the automobile. He heard the sound of metal tapping on his side window. He looked over his left shoulder, registration in trembling hand, to see the muzzle of a 9mm pointing directly at him. But it wasn't a hand of flesh holding the gun, but one of bone. He looked up at the gray-uniformed body, past the badge over the left breast pocket, to a skeleton face under a black cowboy hat with a star on it. The muzzle of the gun exploded in a fireball, and Morris's vision went as dark as the storm clouds above. He opened his eyes to find himself lying in Camilla's garden at the Fireproof. "This is where I'm supposed to wake up," he said.

The normally well-tended garden was completely overgrown with weeds. The star jasmine hedge was ragged. Nothing remained of the vegetables or flowers except brown and withered stems and vines. He looked at the motel. It was lifeless. The paint had faded and was covered with mold. Spiderwebs were everywhere, some of the windows broken or boarded up. A large rat scurried across the porch and disappeared underneath. He went to the door of his and Ida's bungalow. Wiping away a veil of webs as a fat spider scrambled to a corner, he turned the knob and pushed the door open. A dark cloud of bats flew past him, their wings flapping in a leathery clamor. He shielded his face as they rushed by, the wind from their beating wings tickling the skin of his face. When he walked in, there was his beloved Ida, sitting at the dining table, her face a mummified mask, her clothes rotting ruins and hanging in tatters. A beetle crawled out of her left eye socket. Suddenly, the television set turned on, and there was Pat Sajak spinning the wheel of fortune. He looked straight at Morris and said, "Our first contestant, from Bella Villa, Florida, is Morris . . . Morris . . . Morris . . ."

"Morris, wake up!" It was Ida. She was shaking him. "Are you all right? Is it your shoulder again?"

"No," Morris said. "It's not my shoulder. A dream, just a dream."

16

Jamie drove a quiet van back to the Fireproof. Except for an occasional whimper from baby Billy, nobody so much has cleared his or her throat. When Jamie got the van parked, he turned in his seat and addressed the group. "I don't know about anyone else, but I need a beer. Anyone who cares to join me, come on over."

"I'll second that motion," Tommy said.

"Sounds like a plan," Robbie said.

"I'm in," Vaughn said.

"Me too," added Toad. "I'm breaking out the Maker's Mark I've been hoarding."

"I've got one side of the cooler," said Julie. "Tommy!"

"Robby, pick up Billy's car seat," said Camilla. "He can sleep in it 'til we go back to our place."

Jamie met Brian at the front of the van and hugged him. He kissed him on the cheek and went up the stairs to open his room. Everyone crowded in, leaving the door open. Toad showed up with the whiskey and passed the bottle. Everyone except Camilla, who couldn't abide hard liquor, took a substantial swallow. Once everyone's nerves were on calmer seas, the beer flowing, they began to talk about what they had just experienced. The first one to speak was Jamie.

"One thing," he said, "please, no one mention this to Nolan, or anyone else for that matter. If that son of a bitch, Tiny, ever finds out we know anything at all and we spilled our guts, we're all as good as dead."

"Thing is," said Brian, "John and I were the ones who actually saw it! Damn, I'll never get that out of my head. How can I live with myself if I don't say something?"

"At least you'll live," said Vaughn. "I'm not sure I want to be involved in this whole mess at all. That cop, El Diablo, is insane."

"Listen, bro," Tommy said, "you're *already* involved. You can't change that."

"I'm scared," said Camilla. "What if he finds out we were there? Or even suspects. God knows what he'll do."

"I think he bought our story," said Jamie. "We all have to stick to it, that's all."

"Oh, I have no doubt he'll be back here," interjected Toad. "He's gonna be shakin' Jamie down for sure. Our only ace in the hole *might be Nolan*. That big bastard's afraid of him for whatever reasons."

"How the hell are we gonna handle this?" Tommy asked.

"I think it'll all blow over," said Robbie.

"You got a baby to think about, Mr. Tough Guy," Camilla snapped.

"Here's the way I figure it," Toad said, walking over by the door, handing the whiskey to Brian, and lighting a cigarette. Brian took another gulp from the bottle. "Jamie, much as I hate to say it, you're going to have to lie low for a while, clean house here. And this goes for everybody, no going out and getting high or drinking then driving back." He pointed to the liquor bottle as he took another drag on his cigarette. "Remember, alcohol and gasoline don't mix."

"But don't forget," said Brian, "no matter how you slice it, there were two actual eyewitnesses. The rest of you just heard stuff secondhand."

"Well, I'll tell you what," said Julie, "it's pretty scary stuff. But we have to have faith everything will turn out all right."

"Karma is going to catch up to that bozo deputy sooner or later," Camilla said.

"Hopefully sooner," Robbie added.

The long day and night caught up with everyone even before the beer ran out. Camilla and Robbie left first, Robbie carrying the baby in his car seat. Julie and Tommy checked out right after. John Vaughn steered the tottering Toad back to his room. Brian looked at the door, shifting his gaze back to Jamie, unsure of what was expected or what he wanted.

"I could sure use some company tonight," Jamie said, taking Brian's hands in his.

"Yeah," Brian said, "so could I, come to think of it." Jamie wrapped his arms around him and pulled him close.

Unable to fall asleep after hearing what happened to O'Brien, Mike Nolan sat in the plastic lawn chair on the porch by his door and smoked a cigar. He puffed pensively, occasionally inhaling a little of the fragrant tobacco. What had begun as an undercover sting operation for drugs had become an investigation of at least one dirty cop. This could get very messy and, considering what just happened to O'Brien, deadly. Any clandestine operation was fraught with peril, but Nolan was confronted for the first time in a long while with the jeopardy his life was in. There was no doubt in his mind Deputy Edwin "Tiny" Harris murdered Deputy O'Brien. Still, Nolan was certain the official report would place "parties unknown" at the center of the investigation. He was equally sure the renegade deputy would hesitate at nothing to remove any threat to his illegal activities. For that matter, he would have to assume Tiny knew about him already. Another surge of adrenaline forestalled any hopes of sleeping soon.

Something else was bothering Nolan as well. The Fireproof was completely abandoned except for Morris and his wife, another odd coincidence. The only light was the large spotlight in the center illuminating the parking area. It cast enough light to create a ethereal world of the motel and its grounds. He looked at his watch, almost 2:00 a.m. It was almost five hours ago when he saw Brian at the convenience store. Where in hell was the Fireproof gang? Surely they wouldn't be at the casino or the Foo Foo Club with the baby. Just as these thoughts were running through his mind, he watched Brian's van pull into the parking lot. He got up from his chair and stepped behind an upright post. The entire crew appeared to be aboard, and they were being awfully quiet. A few words were exchanged, and two of them carried what looked like a chest cooler into Jamie's room. The rest of them, except Toad, easily distinguished by his long beard and hair, followed into the room. Toad went back to his room and, a moment later, reappeared on the porch heading back to Jamie's with the stock bottle in tow. He stopped outside the door to finish the cigarette he was smoking. After tossing the cigarette butt onto the driveway, he lifted the bottle to his lips for a long swallow before he went in.

Nolan slipped off the porch and walked to the back of the LeBaron. He put out the cigar in the gravel driveway. He opened the trunk and fished in the dark for a bag there. He was glad he never bothered to replace the burnt-out trunk light. He intended to be invisible. The bag contained specialty tools of his trade. He felt around until he had what he wanted. He quietly closed the trunk. He glided like a specter across the center court, past the garden, over to the stairs in front of Toad's room. He went up the stairs quietly and, with his back against the wall, shuffled over to the door marked 107, Brian's room. It was next door to Jamie's. At that moment, the door to Jamie's swung in. Nolan turned the knob on Brian's door and pushed. It opened. Slipping inside, he peeked through the blinds and noticed no one came out the open door. They were probably just getting air. He attached a device to the wall separating Brian's room from Jamie's. It used suction cups so no marks were left. It was designed to amplify and transmit sound up to a hundred feet. Nolan had a listening device attached to a mini cassette recorder. He sat down on the single padded chair in Brian's room and listened.

By the time the party was breaking up, Nolan had heard and recorded enough to convince him Edwin "Tiny" Harris had murdered O'Brien. But he did not have that on tape as he missed the first part of the discussion where Harris may have been referred to by name. Also missing was who, among the Fireproof crowd, might have witnessed the execution. He was going to have to ferret out the individual witnesses and convince them to testify. That would take some effort. Tomorrow, he would call his county liaison, Judge Thomas, and ask whether he should go to the district attorney and get warrants now or wait.

Tiny drove back to Bella Villa in an agitated state. If even one of those vermin living at that fleabag motel was a witness to what happened tonight, he was in deep doo-doo. The real problem, however, continued to be the newest resident of that glorified flophouse, Mike Nolan. What an unfortunate coincidence he lives next door to possible homicide witnesses. Any investigation Nolan might be involved in was sure to take a decided turn, leading to big trouble for Edwin "Tiny" Harris. An accident resulting in the death of Special Agent Mike Nolan was imminent. In the meantime, a call to a certain lecherous judge might help keep the lid on events.

When Tiny arrived at headquarters in Bella Villa, Captain Post was just going through the front door. He signaled Tiny to come to his office. Tiny walked in, carrying the clipboard with his notes containing the fictitious account of O'Brien's murder. He closed the door to the captain's office, laid the clipboard on his desk, and sat down in a chair across from Post.

"Too bad about O'Brien," Tiny started. "I got there too late to be of assistance."

"What are you going to do, Tiny," asked Post, "kill half the department, including me? Where is this going to stop?"

Tiny narrowed his eyes and looked hard at Post. His face was contorted in an effort to control his rage. He leaned back in his chair and smiled. His right hand made a sudden move to the holstered Glock on his belt. Captain Post jumped out of his seat, an expression of surprise and terror on his face. Tiny roared in laughter and put his hand back on his lap. "Just testing your reflexes, boss."

"Have you gone completely insane?" Post inquired.

"No, Captain, but you're distorting things way out of proportion. First, for the record"—Tiny picked up the clipboard, waved it in front of Post, and put it back down—"I suggest you read my report when I finish it. You'll see O'Brien was shot by parties unknown. Apparently they slipped away without being picked up, at least not yet. I understand roadblocks have been set up, but it may be too late. Besides, the plates were stolen, we know that much. And there are a million Fords or Mercurys around that fit the description of the suspect's vehicle. They aren't even sure of the color. So keep your shirt on. We're doin' just fine."

"I don't know," Post said. "We better chill out for a while." He looked worried and scared despite Tiny's comforting words.

"Sure, cool down and lose everything. I don't think so." Tiny stood and picked up his clipboard. "There's one more thing. Clear your calendar for Saturday night. I want you along on a pickup I'm making. I have a feelin' I'm gonna need a little backup."

"I can't be going out on these little adventures of yours, Tiny. I'm the captain here, and I don't have the same latitude to move like you do."

"I'll pick you up at seven," Tiny said as if he did not hear Post's protests. "Make sure you bring plenty of firepower, just in case someone gets a smart idea. We'll log it as part of our joint gambling investigation." He gave the captain a mock salute and left. Post sank down in his imitation leather chair and rested his head in his hands.

Rooster sat in his chaise longue by the pool, a good Cuban cigar pinched between the thumb and first two fingers of his right hand. He was in boxer swim trunks soaking up South Florida's afternoon sunshine. Two guards armed with holstered pistols and short barreled shotguns stood by, a discreet distance away. After his run-in with Harris and Post, he wasn't taking any chances. A shapely blonde splashed naked in the pool. She came up to the edge and splashed him with a handful of water. "Come on, lazy," she called, "come in and swim with your little mermaid."

"Now cut that out!" Sandy admonished her. "I'll be in, and when I do, the little mermaid better watch out for hungry gators!" He puffed his cigar and blew smoke at her.

"You're a big meanie," she teased. "I know some tricks that will make pussy food out of you." She flicked a little more water on him.

"Okay, baby, enough with the splashing," Rooster chortled. "You go back to swimming laps so you can keep that girlish figure I adore. I've got a little business to take care of. After that, I'm coming after you." The girl sighed audibly and pushed off the side of the pool with her feet and swam away. Rooster picked up his Nextel radio cell, thumbed a button until the name he wanted came up, and beeped him.

"Jimmy, you there?" It was the young man Rooster asked to chaperon Harris and Post when they had violated his hospitality. He was an excellent gofer.

"Yes, sir," Jimmy responded.

"What's your ETA?"

"About thirty minutes, Mr. Babcock. Santana is on board and very cool." Santana was the name of Rooster's hired gunslinger.

"Very good, Jimmy. When you get here, bring Santana out to the pool and fix him a drink. I'll join you within a few minutes."

"Roger that."

"Adios." Rooster put the phone on a table near his chaise longue and stood up. "The gator cometh! Mermaids beware!" Diving deep into the pool, he swam straight for the naked and giggling demimondaine.

Sitting next to Jimmy in the Escalade, Santana smiled, the gold caps on his front teeth glimmering in the Florida sunlight.

At first light, Monday, after the shooting in the cemetery, John Vaughn put on his backpack loaded with a few essentials and headed out for his woods camp in the Everglades. The disassembled Survivor shotgun made up the heaviest part of his load by far. He was shaken by what he had witnessed and needed some time alone to think things through. He walked almost an hour southwest on Route 29. Traffic was light, the air fragrant in the predawn. He crossed the highway and headed down a jeep trail on the west side of the road. A family of raccoons crossed in front of him, the mother giving him a look of obvious disdain before hurrying her little ones into the marshy woods. Slash pine interspersed with a few sabal palms, royal palms, and cabbage palms comprised most of the dense woods around the trail. He came to a small area dominated by laurel oaks with a cluster of dahoon holly at the far end, its red berries glistening in the morning's first light. At this juncture, Vaughn left the jeep trail and walked along a footpath for some three hundred yards to a small clearing on a hammock, bordered by bald cypress, with a single majestic oak near the center. It was here Vaughn had constructed a crude shelter, using shipping skids for framing and scavenged pieces of plywood he dragged in with the help of a Mexican house painter and his four-wheel-drive Toyota pickup. This amigo, a customer of Jamie's, had supplied Vaughn with enough exterior paint to repel water from the worst of Florida's ferocious summer thunderstorms.

Vaughn stopped short of the clearing at the frightful sound of a wild boar in rut grunting and squealing in rage. It was probably in a territorial duel with another rival for one of the sows in its harem. Still, knowing how aggressive and dangerous one of these three-hundred-pound tusked feral hogs could be, Vaughn dropped his pack and pulled out the three pieces comprising the Survivor. He assembled the shotgun in less than twenty seconds and fished out a round of buckshot and a slug. He thumbed the lever opening the bore and inserted the buckshot into the chamber. He flicked his wrist in a sharp upward motion, snapping the barrel back into firing position. He dropped the slug into his breast pocket. When confronted with larger animals and possible tricky shooting conditions, loading a round of buckshot ensured a crippling blow on the first shot. By ejecting the spent shell and loading a bone-smashing slug—*bahda bing, bahda boom*—the doom of the target was sealed.

As Vaughn stepped into the clearing, firearm at the ready, a small boy, maybe ten years old, emerged, more staggering than running, from the other side. The boy looked emaciated, his clothes were ripped and tattered to rags, his face scratched and bloody. Spotting Vaughn standing there, he ran straight toward him, arms outstretched.

"Help! Help me!" he screamed. At that moment, the wild boar burst from the underbrush behind him, bearing down like an out-of-control locomotive. When the beast noticed Vaughn, it skidded to a halt, about fifty feet away, snorting in rage and defiance, pawing the ground. Yellowed tusks the size of large bananas protruded from its jaw. Beady eyes regarded the humans with malevolence. Running behind Vaughn, the boy clutched his legs in terror.

"Easy there, young fellow," Vaughn said. "Don't trip me up, or we'll both be in trouble." He took the risk of removing his left hand from the gun momentarily to touch the boy's matted hair, patting his head in hopes of calming him. Possibly sensing its opportunity, the boar lunged forward. The boy screamed and grabbed Vaughn's hand. Holding the shotgun with the pistol grip in his right hand, he cocked the hammer with his thumb, pointed it at the head of Mr. Piggy, and pulled the trigger when it was less than ten feet from him and the boy. The firearm exploded with a deafening report and nearly jumped out of his hand from the kickback, torquing his wrist. He grimaced at the pain, pushing the Eject button with his thumb to pop the spent shell part way out. Tearing his hand loose from the boy's grasp and snatching out the fired casing, he pulled the slug from his breast pocket and slid it into the chamber.

Turning aside at the last second, the boar sustained substantial damage to its left flank. It was on the ground, emitting an awful screeching sound, trying to regain its footing. Its entire left side was running red with blood. Vaughn walked up to within six feet, aimed at the head, and fired. There was an abrupt end to the noise, and after a couple of death thrashes, the animal lay still. Vaughn turned his attention to the boy. His matted brown hair looked as if it had never been brushed or combed. Vaughn kneeled so their faces would be on the same level. Tears streamed from the child's dark blue eyes, down his dirt-smudged cheeks, as gaunt as any concentration camp prisoner. His bedraggled clothes looked as if they would fall from his skeletal frame.

"What's your name, son?" Vaughn asked.

"J-Josh," the boy answered through sobs.

"My name is John. How long have you been out here?" Vaughn hadn't heard any news reports about a missing child, but from the looks of him, this unfortunate child most likely have been wandering for a week at least.

"Since I ran away last night," Josh answered. "My brother and sister are dead."

"What happened?" Vaughn asked. "A fire?" He was convinced the lad must be disoriented.

"No food. They just got sick and my pa took them away."

"Away where?" Vaughn asked.

"Swamp, I guess. That's what the big man in gray clothes said. I dunno." The boy started to sob again.

"It's okay," Vaughn said. "You're going to be just fine now. I'm going to roast that nasty ole pig, and we'll have a feast. In the meantime, there's some crackers and canned beans and peaches and applesauce in the cabin. C'mon on, let's get you some chow and a drink of water. Looks like you could use a little lunch, whaddaya say?" The boy nodded. Holding the shotgun in his left hand, Vaughn took the boy's tiny left hand in his right and led him to the rough but cozy shelter.

Inside, there was a single cot, a sink Vaughn salvaged from a house undergoing reconstruction of the kitchen, a small table with two folding chairs, and a large padded office chair comprising the single capitulation to creature comforts. There was room for little else in the twelve-by-twelve dwelling. Vaughn leaned the gun against a wall and led the boy to a chair at the table. Slinging his pack on the bed, the outdoorsman reached over the boy's head to a set of crude shelves fixed to the wall. There were some cans of food as well as jars containing rice, barley, pasta, instant coffee, tea, and powdered milk. A lower shelf held two pots, a frying pan, a couple of plates and bowls, several ceramic mugs, and a plastic container of silverware. At waist level was a shelf with a Coleman stove. Two Coleman lanterns hanging from the ceiling and a kerosene lamp on the small table provided lighting. There was drinking water in plastic gallon milk containers. Runoff water from the roof, collected in a fifty-five-gallon drum, provided water for cleaning up. During the dry season, Vaughn was able to get enough water from a nearby spring hole he had dug out for washing up. The water had a bit of a sulfurous odor to it, but it was useable.

"How about an applesauce appetizer, Josh?" he asked. "Then I'll cook up some barley and open a can of sardines, and we'll have us a mini feast." Vaughn opened the jar of applesauce and put some in a bowl and mixed up a mug of powdered milk for him. He took down a plastic bottle of daily vitamins and gave one to the boy. He started the stove and put water on to boil. The boy practically inhaled the bowl of applesauce and started gulping the milk.

"Easy, not too fast," Vaughn cautioned. "I'm going out to gut that pig. I'll be back in ten minutes, so don't worry. This barley will be ready, and we'll eat." Vaughn put the applesauce away. He was afraid the boy would get the runs if he ate too much of it in his condition. When Vaughn returned from dressing the pig, the boy was staring at a picture of his estranged wife and four-year-old son tacked to the wall.

"Do they live here too?" Josh asked

"Nope, they had to stay where that picture was taken, far away from Florida." Vaughn went over to the makeshift sink to wash the boar's blood off his hands. "Let's have some lunch, and you can tell me all about how you got out in these woods being chased by that mean ole piggy."

After giving him a bowl of barley with creamed corn and beans and another mug of milk mixed with some Swiss Miss chocolate he had stashed, Vaughn sat across from the boy with his own bowl of chow.

"So whadda ya think of my cooking?" Vaughn watched as the boy greedily wolfed down his food. The poor runt was starving and probably had been for quite some time. Josh nodded his head and continued stuffing his mouth. "That good, huh? I sure surprise myself with my culinary skills."

Finally, Josh finished a second bowl, which went down slower than the first. His shrunken stomach must be groaning with the sudden overload. He started telling Vaughn about his brother and sister. With some gentle coaxing, Vaughn heard the whole pitiful story of the criminally negligent and abusive Craytons. The boy was barely able to articulate what had transpired due to the limitations of vocabulary and practice in speaking. The boy was sobbing throughout the monologue, and Vaughn found tears coming to his eyes as well. When the boy seemed ready to collapse from exhaustion, Vaughn got up and knelt by him. He put his arms around the frail and bony child, holding him close. It was the first human touch of compassion for Josh in a lifetime of misery and brutality. The child clutched on to the solitary stranger and, in the comfort of his arms, poured out his anguish in a torrent of tears. At last, he fell quiet and was soon asleep. Vaughn lifted him up—he weighed no more than a rag doll—and gently put him on the cot. He stared at the sleeping boy and thought of the lyrics in that Willie Nelson song: "Like an angel flying too close to the ground." He went out to build a fire for the pig roast.

17

"What's up? You guys moving or what?" Julie was sitting on the bed in Robert and Camilla's room, back against the headboard, baby Billy in her lap. She and Camilla were alone with the baby.

"Yeah, looks that way," Camilla answered. "It's going to be a lot easier if we get a place in North Napolis or Bonita. Robbie will be able to get to the FGCU campus in twenty minutes or so and, likewise, the other way to Napolis where his mom lives. It'll be nice living near places to go out and the beach. I just hope Robbie takes this opportunity and runs with it. Who knows if he'll get another chance? They say as you get older, things get harder."

"Ain't that the truth," Julie said. "Tommy and I are trying to save enough to move to Napolis as well. If we can get weekend gigs there, I can substitute teach, and Tommy can spend his time writing songs. He's got some good ones now, but we need breathing space and exposure."

"Hey! Maybe we can be neighbors!" said Camilla, the excitable girl. "We can look for places together. Maybe this whole thing with that crazy deputy is just the push we all needed to get on with our lives."

Billy fussed in Julie's lap. He wrestled free of her grip and started crawling straight for the edge of the bed.

"Hey, tough guy." Julie laughed. "Where you off to? The abyss?" Billy chortled as if finding her remark amusing and continued for the edge, Julie scooping him up before he went over.

"He wants to be on the go," Camilla said, "and it's going to get a whole lot worse. Another reason for moving, pronto. Let me put him on the floor for a while. I'll have to keep a close eye on him." Camilla walked over to the bed and picked up Billy.

"Then, there are my parents," Camilla continued. "Neither of them has even seen Billy, except for the pictures I send. I want them to be able to come to Napolis and visit with us, stay in our home. That is, if I can ever get my delinquent father out of the Baja and the surf." She gave Billy a noisy kiss on the cheek, blowing air and making a farting sound. Billy squealed his approval. She put him on the floor, and he was off like a greyhound from the gate.

"This whole thing with that deputy," Julie said, "I'm afraid we haven't heard the last from him. I'm scared, to be honest."

"You should be," Camilla responded. "We all should be. That man has the devil in him for sure. He has a very evil aura. I noticed it the first day I laid eyes on him."

"I think we should call the police." Julie got off the bed and walked to the window, peeking through the blinds as if expecting someone to be spying on them. "Maybe the FBI or something. If he is tipped off somehow though, we could all end up as buzzard chow."

"I don't know." Camilla grabbed Billy as he crawled around the corner into the bathroom. The toddler wailed his indignation and squirmed to get free. "Easy, little guy. Mommy's got something for you." Camilla fished out an animal cracker and gave it to Billy to keep him busy. "Robbie thinks we should say something to his mother. She's a friend of Sheriff Gunther and a county commissioner. She could apply some pressure."

"Hey, that's a great idea!" Julie said. "Have him call her as soon as he gets home from fishing with Tommy. What about the school thing by the way?"

"Oh, he went to FGCU to check out the campus and get a catalog and some registration forms. He's going to try to take one course this summer."

"Good for him! He's finally taking some action. Tommy as well. He went to Napolis to see about a Sunday night gig at a new gay bar that's opening."

"Really?" A mischievous look sparkled in Camilla's eyes and crinkled her face. "Aren't you afraid he'll get picked up by some rich dude and whisked away to a new lifestyle?" They both laughed.

"Maybe I'll be the one to get picked up," Julie said. "It's not just a bar for gay men. Napolis isn't nearly big enough for that kind of leap. There'll be plenty gals looking to score as well. I might slip the noose of male chauvinism and go gay."

"Yeah, I can really see you as a lesbian." Camilla giggled. She grabbed a diaper and wiped a mudslide of vomit from Billy's chin and tee shirt. The head of Pooh Bear was completely besmirched. "How would you ever have one of these little darlings?"

"Good point." Julie walked over and gave the oblivious Billy a smooch. He thanked her by holding out a rhinoceros from his cracker box. "Oh, thank you, Billy. You're already sharing. Your generosity at such an early age will become legend, I'm sure." The ladies chuckled some more. Still, the levity was more a diversion from the apprehension they both felt. The maverick deputy was a real and perilous threat. He cast a long and ominous shadow over the Fireproof Motel. He was like a summer thunderstorm pumping up to an anvil cloud, the color of a bruise turning purplish black, obliterating the sun and sky wherever it passed. A knock at the door interrupted a moment of reverie. Both women turned their heads.

"Who is it?" Camilla shouted. Prior to the cemetery incident, she would have just said, "Come in."

"It's the Big Bad Wolf," replied Brian. He pushed the door open and stuck his head in. "Are you ladies decent? Damn! I guess you are."

"Get your cute little ass in here and get some of Mama Cammy's lovin'." Camilla put Billy on the bed and gave Brian a world-class hug.

"Let me have some of that man," Julie joked. She also crushed Brian in her arms.

"Hey," Brian gushed, "don't break the merchandise."

"Why, are you made of glass?" Camilla asked.

"You still like girls a wee bit, dontcha?" Julie teased.

"Only from the back, doggie-style," Brian shot back.

"I bet you do know something about that position, sweetheart," Julie taunted.

"I'll teach you to sass a glass man about his ass, man," Brian retorted. He threw Julie down on the bed, narrowly missing the baby who whooped in delight, and tried to wrestle the wiry woman into submission.

"Careful of the baby, you two knuckleheads!" Mama Camilla yelled. The two combatants disengaged and rolled off the bed onto their feet, careful to avoid little Billy who continued screeching with excitement.

"Wow, Bry"—Julie stood up and grabbed one of Camilla's brushes and ran it through her hair—"you've already been hitting it pretty hard, huh? I mean there are some serious alcoholic fumes in here."

"Yeah, I stopped by at Toad's and had a few nips." Brian rolled off the bed and stood with his back against the wall. "Thing is, I get to feelin' kinda sick and shaky if I don't have a couple beers around noon. I guess I'm developing a serious habit. I don't know if I could quit, even for a week or so."

"Is it interfering with your life much?" Julie asked.

"Seems to be, more and more. Like sometimes I show up late for work or not at all. And I fight all the time with Jamie it seems." Brian looked down at his feet. He sank to the floor, back against the wall, and put his hands on his face. "I can't live with it, and I can't live without it. I don't know what I'm going to do." He started to whimper softly.

"We're going to get you some help," Julie asserted. She picked up the phone directory. "I'll dial the number for AA, and you talk to them."

"Not now." Brian jumped to his feet and walked to the door. "I've got too much goin' on in my head. I'll catch you guys later." He practically ran out the door.

"Poor guy," Camilla said. "He's probably scared shitless of that wacko deputy."

"I think he's just plain scared of life," said Julie, a tear running down each cheek.

"Well, I can tell you one thing," Camilla said. "Robbie better not start going off the deep end with that drinking crap. I'll cut off his balls and feed them to the chickens. That's another reason I'll be glad to move."

"Tommy goes overboard on occasion," Julie added, "but he's usually pretty good about how much he drinks. Thing is, it's a disease. And it needs to be treated, or it gets progressively worse. The only treatment is totally abstaining. Anyway, that's what I read in *Dear Abby*, and she's pretty much got it together about most things as far as I'm concerned." She went over and picked up Billy, who was starting to fuss. She held him over her head, and he laughed with gap-toothed wisdom. "What do you think, Billy? Are we all just full of fear? Are we all sick? Do you need a bottle?" He cooed his assent.

"Comin' massa', Billy," Camilla said. She handed him a half-full bottle of apple juice with a plastic nipple on it. "Go to town, my little man." Momma took her baby and put him on the bed.

"Another thing Abby says," Julie continued, "is people's sexual orientation is pretty much determined at birth, and those bigots who think it's just a sinful choice are living in the Dark Ages. That's something Brian needs to come to grips with if he wants to ever lead some kind of decent life."

"Amen to that, sister," Camilla said.

"You know what?" Julie asked. She looked distressed.

"Uh-huh." Camilla was changing Billy's diaper.

"We didn't get a chance to talk to Brian about going to the police or maybe talking to Nolan. Now he's probably at Toad's drinking more. And who's going to believe a drunk?"

"I'll work it out," Camilla said. "I'll put the pressure on my man, and you nail Tommy when they get back. We'll get Brian sober enough to talk to Nolan tomorrow, and hopefully, Vaughn will be back as well."

"Deal," Julie said.

When Jamie arrived at the Fireproof for lunch, he had a hunch something was askew. Brian's van was in the parking lot, but Brian wasn't in his room. Jamie walked over to Toad's room and knocked. Toad opened the door and a cloud of cigarette smoke mixed with the pungent aroma of marijuana blew out of the dark cave. The glow of the television provided the only light. Apparently, they were watching a movie with a car chase as the sounds of revving engines and squealing tires blared from the tube.

"Hey, Jamie, what's happenin'?" Toad's breath reeked of alcohol. "Me 'n' Brian are watchin' *Bourne Identity*. Matt Damon. Come on in." He stepped back into the room, and Jamie followed. Even in the gloom, Jamie could see the place was a mess. If Ida Kline saw this, she'd make Morris toss Toad in a heartbeat.

"Yo, Jamie," Brian said, a bit sheepishly. He reached for the remote and put the movie on pause. "Early day?"

"No, just back for lunch. Care to join me?"

"Naw, Toad's gonna nuke some popcorn, and we're gonna watch the rest of this flick." He cast Jamie a defiant look and took a swallow of his Bud.

"I thought you were going to finish a roofing job today." Jamie's stomach was fluttering, and he began to feel woozy. He was sick with despair and worry for his friend and lover and for their relationship. Although he was no more than ten feet away, he suddenly seemed on the other side of a huge warehouse, a distant and unknown figure staring at the glow of a tiny screen. Jamie's knees grew weak. This was another world, another dimension, with chimerical images of reality. Maybe this was hell. He had to get out. "Don't come over later if you're drunk," he managed to gasp. Tears were threatening to spill from the dam of his eyelids. He turned and fled the room, the salty waters of grief streaming down his cheeks as he strode into the light. Jamie was no longer hungry. He went into his room, a feeling of emptiness overwhelming him, and lay down on his bed and wept.

"Bitch," Brian said when Jamie was gone. He opened another beer and looked at Toad. "So where's the popcorn?"

Mike Nolan watched Brian go into Toad's room. He wondered if this might be a good time to corner the two of them on what had happened to O'Brien. He started to walk over but changed his mind, returned to the porch in front of his room, and sat in the plastic chair provided by the management of the Fireproof Motel. He took a cheap but satisfying cigar from his pocket and lit it. The cigars were sold out of plastic drink cups at the two gas stations/convenience stores/Subway/Dunkin Donuts on the south and north corners of Baron Boulevard and Daniels Avenue in Napolis. They were a no-name brand, but from the way they smoked and tasted, Nolan guessed they were made with Cuban leaf grown in the Dominican Republic. In any case, they were the finest dollar stogies on the market. He sat and watched awhile. Soon, Jamie drove up in his old but well-kept Civic. He went from his car to his room, over to Brian's, and finally to Toad's room. He disappeared inside for a couple of minutes and came back out looking pretty distressed. He returned to his room, slamming the door. Nolan waited another fifteen minutes, finishing a second cigar. Putting a mini cassette tape player in his shirt pocket, the federal agent walked over to Toad's room and knocked on the door. A tipsy Toad ushered him inside a smoke-filled room; there was no light except that emanating from the television. When his eyes adjusted, he noticed Brian sitting in a chair on the far side of the bed.

"Greetings, earthling," Brian said. "We're watching how a secret operative for some spook outfit in the U.S. outwits his bosses after he forgets who he is."

"You might have some insider intel on that," Toad said, handing Nolan a red plastic cup. There was a look on Toad's face that made it seem wise for Nolan to accept the cup.

"Here's to you two, the Fireproof, and all her crew." Nolan raised his drink, rum with a splash of coke, in a toast. He took a sip and grimaced. "Strong drink, Toad."

"I don't like to waste the Coke," Toad replied. "Sit down and take a load off." He gestured to an ancient padded chair by the door. "I'm sitting on the bed anyway." Nolan sat down and sipped his Coke-flavored rum until the movie ended.

"Pretty cool movie," Brian said. He took a tug of his Bud.

"Not too shabby," Toad joined.

"Listen," Nolan said, "I've got to tell you guys something." He put his hand in his shirt pocket and pulled out a badge. "I'm a federal special agent undercover."

"Are you bustin' us?" Brian jumped to his feet, knocking over his can of beer.

"Sit down, Brian," Toad said, "and let him have his say." Toad appeared untroubled. He suspected Nolan all along and was certain the agent had bigger fish to fry.

"I have good reason to believe," Nolan began, "that one or more of you folks here witnessed the fatal shooting of a Baron County deputy on Sunday night around eight o'clock on the Cemetery Road. If there's someone you're afraid of, I can offer you federal protection."

"What makes you think we know anything?" Toad asked.

"Simple, I heard it on my scanner. When you guys got home, I was coming over to tell you about it and heard some of your conversation. I didn't want to freak anybody out, so I decided to wait to ask you about it." Nolan figured a little distortion of the truth came with the territory.

"Bullshit," Toad said. "I was out smoking and would have seen you eavesdropping. You must have a tape made through the wall in Brian's room." He picked up his cup and drained it.

"What the—," Brian began.

"Okay, you got me." Nolan didn't feel like screwing around; there was more to this Toad than meets the eye. "I do have a tape, and sorry, Brian, I got it from your room. I don't know who the eyewitnesses are, but I know there was at least one, probably two. I need your help here to nail the killer. I suspect the local cops are on a wild goose chase. The real killer is right under their noses." Brian was visibly shaken.

"Wha-whadda you know about Tiny?" he blurted.

"Are you taping now?" Toad interjected.

"No, but I'd like to," Nolan said. He took the recorder out of his pocket.

"I don't think so," Brian said.

"Better let me hold that," said Toad. Nolan gave him a recalcitrant glance.

"Okay, this conversation is over, you should leave now." Toad stood up.

"Wait, wait." Nolan held up his hands. "Here's the tape player." He gave it to Toad. Toad looked at it to make sure it wasn't recording. "Now, Brian, tell me what you saw. And when you say Tiny, do you mean Deputy Harris?"

"Yeah, that's exactly who I mean," Brian said. "He shot the other cop and ditched the gun in another car. I think it was a Ford Taurus, but it was pretty dark."

"That fits the identification of the vehicle the police are looking for. Did anyone else witness the shooting besides whoever was in the other car?" Nolan wanted to know.

"I don't think I should speak for anyone else," Brian said. He walked over to the small fridge and pulled out another beer.

"A man's been murdered," Nolan said, losing his patience. "A good man and a good cop—a father with two young children and a wife. We need to arrest the shooter and get your testimony along with everyone else's on tape as well as a sworn affidavit. And we need you to be sober for it." Nolan held his hand out to Toad, palm up. Toad drained the contents of his coffee cup.

"Too late for that now," Toad informed Agent Nolan. "Better come over early tomorrow and bring this." Toad put the tape recorder in Nolan's outstretched hand. "But don't bring anybody else, and no papers to sign. In any case, the other witness ain't around right now."

"And that would be John Vaughn, I presume," Nolan ventured. Brian looked at Toad who just shrugged.

"Okay," said Nolan. "Tomorrow morning." He started for the door.

"I'll make the coffee, but you bring the donuts," Toad called as the door shut.

Tommy and Robert spent the morning fishing at Cypress Lake. They were on the way back to the Fireproof with a couple of bass on ice. Tommy was driving his '90 Toyota Corolla. It had about 150,000 miles but was still running strong. A lot of little shit like wiper motors and the tape player had worn out and been replaced, as had the alternator and starter motor. It still got him where he wanted to go, but he was afraid its days in his motor pool were numbered. The fishermen had a pretty good pot and beer buzz going, but nothing serious.

"We're gonna have to say something about the shooting to somebody," Tommy ventured. They had managed to avoid the obvious all day.

"Yeah, no shit," Robert said. "Cammy and I talked about it, and I'm going to say something to Mom. She knows the top dog in the sheriff's department."

"It's kind of up to Brian and John to come forward," Tommy said, "but we're all involved to some extent." There was a brief silence. "What about bouncing it of Nolan? He seems to be okay and knowledgeable."

"Let's see what the two witnesses think," Robert replied. "But yeah, we need help here. This is serious shit. We could all be in a lot of danger."

When they arrived back at the Fireproof, Toad was sitting in his chair on the porch, cup in hand. He waved them over and broke the news about Mike Nolan. They agreed Robbie should tell his mother, who could contact Sheriff Gunther. Toad also told them about Brian and Jamie's little tiff. Tommy asked where Brian was.

"Went to the store for more beer," Toad said. He neglected to mention his order for rum and tobacco.

Tiny couldn't believe his luck when he saw Brian pull up in front of the ABC liquor store. He whipped a U-turn in the Grand Cherokee and pulled into the parking lot as Brian went through the door. He picked up his cell phone and called Mona. She answered with a lackluster hello.

"Get your ass out of the apartment now," Tiny said by way of greeting.

"Why?" she asked. "What's wrong?"

"Just do it. Go shopping or over to one of your whore girlfriend's places. But be out in ten minutes." He hung up and waited for Brian to come out.

18

Brian emerged from the package store with a fifth of Ron Virgin and a twelve-pack of Budweiser. He had on a gray tee shirt with Quicksilver silk screened on the back. He opened the passenger side door of his van and put his beverages on the seat. Walking around to the driver's door, he noticed a Jeep Grand Cherokee idling across the lot. It stirred up a feeling of dread although he couldn't quite put a finger on why. He climbed in and started the engine, put the van in reverse, and started backing out when there was a loud bang on the side of the vehicle. A rush of adrenaline shot through him, and his heart raced. Stopping and looking to his left out the open side window, he nearly jumped out of his seat. The grinning face of Deputy Tiny Harris, a.k.a. El Diablo, was peering in at him. Tiny wore a knit white-and-tan golf shirt with an alligator embroidered on the breast pocket. He was holding his badge up in his left hand.

"Well, what do we have here?" Tiny's face seemed to turn into a shining death mask in the dusky light of the late afternoon. "Smells like booze in here. Have you been drinking today?"

Brian wanted to say, "Sure I have, Officer, but just seven or eight beers and a couple of rums so far." Instead, he said, "Just a couple of beers at lunchtime."

"Couple of beers at lunch, huh?" Tiny mimicked. "You want to step out of the vehicle, Mr. Sutter." Brian complied and was immediately shoved up against the van. Tiny slapped a cuff on his right wrist and leaned hard against him, crushing his face into the side of the van and making each breath a struggle. Tiny took his left arm and twisted it up hard behind him. Brian yelped in pain; and Tiny locked up his left wrist, grabbed him by the shoulders, and pulled him away from the van, then slammed him forcefully into the van, putting his weight behind the push. Brian's head was gashed and bleeding now. He felt like he'd just been spun by his heels in circles. He couldn't keep his balance and stumbled. Tiny propped him up with a vicelike grip on his left arm. The errant cop steered him to the Cherokee and shoved him in the front passenger seat. He waved his badge to a couple of baffled onlookers and said, "Another drunk driver off the streets." He got in the Jeep, turned on his blue-and-red flashers for a good show, and took off, shutting his cop lights off as soon as they were out on the highway.

"Am . . . am I under arrest?" asked Brian "Because if I am, you have to read me my rights and shit." Tiny took his massive right hand off the steering wheel and covered Brian's left jaw with outstretched fingers, caressing the skin.

"I'll read you your rights, your last rites, pussy boy. You just shut the fuck up." He pulled his hand away and flicked Brian's left cheek, launching his middle finger off his thumb.

"Ouch!" Brian yelped. "You bastard!" Tiny repeated the assault.

"I said, shut your faggot mouth." Tiny put his hand back on the wheel.

Brian remained silent as they drove through backstreets in Bella Villa. His fear was mounting as it began to dawn on him he was with a cold-blooded murderer. Nervous sweat trickled down his back and down his forehead and into his eyes. He tried to blink the drops of perspiration away. They pulled up in front of a two-story faded pink apartment house. An unkempt hedge of silverthorn ran along the front of the building. Tiny got out of the Jeep and walked around the passenger side. He opened the door and pushed Brian forward, unlocking the handcuffs.

"Now, you and I are going to walk up those stairs just like the good buddies we are," Tiny instructed. "And you're not going to try anything funny." He patted the holstered handgun on his belt. Tiny let Brian get out and then, hanging a meaty arm around his shoulders like they were old school chums, walked him to the stairs. "Go on ahead, I'll be right behind." When they arrived at the covered platform by the back door, Tiny brandished a set of keys and inserted one in the lock. He twisted the handle, pushed the door open, and, with his right hand around the back of Brian's neck, shoved him through the opening.

"What's going on here?" Brian asked, looking around the apartment. "I thought I was under arrest for DUI." He suddenly had to urinate, badly. He was so scared his teeth began to chatter. "Take me to jail. I deserve it. I'm guilty of driving drunk." For the first time, he was desperate for the relaxing formality of jail.

"Shut the fuck up," Tiny said. "You get jail time, and I'll see you do it at Raiford where the guys will eat up your pretty ass and spit it out." Tiny pulled out his gun and unlocked the handcuffs.

"Strip," he said, pointing the 9mm at Brian

"Wha-what do you mean? Why?" Brian took a step back.

"I said take off your clothes now!" Tiny leveled the gun at Brian's face. Brian took off his shirt and tossed it on the floor. He bent over and unbuckled his Teva sandals and stepped out of them. He unbuckled his shorts and let them fall to his feet. Tiny waved his gun at Brian's groin, and the trembling young man pulled his jockey shorts down to his feet as well, kicking his feet free. Tiny walked up to him and stuck the barrel of the gun against his prisoner's right cheek. With the exception of a sporadic whisker, Brian's face was smooth as a beach pebble. Tiny stuck the end of the barrel against Brian's lips. "Open up." Brian's eyes bugged out, his fear was so intense he thought his entire insides were going to come up his throat and out his mouth and all over the deputy's hand. When Brian parted his lips, Tiny shoved the gun into his mouth. "Suck on it, queer boy. You like it? Nod your head up and down." Brian nodded his head. Tiny removed the gun from Brian's mouth but held it an inch away. "What did you see in the cemetery the other night? And don't lie or I'll put the gun back in and pull the trigger. Remember, the truth shall set you free."

"You . . . you shot the other cop," Brian blurted. He started to sob. He forgot he was stark naked standing in a strange apartment. All he could see was the gaping hole in the barrel of Tiny's 9mm gun.

"Who else saw?" Tiny asked. Brian just stood there shaking with fear. Tiny shifted the gun to his left hand and coldcocked Brian with his right. Brian staggered backward, almost falling. His left jaw turned a deep crimson. Later, it would become an ugly purple bruise.

"Nobody else," Brian said, "I swear. They were all in the van."

"Who have you told about this?" Tiny's voice was threatening but also laced with threads of anxiety.

"I said a cop was shot. That's all. I didn't say anything about you—honest." Brian began to improvise, hoping to assuage the fear he sensed in the murderous deputy. "I really couldn't see that well. It was dark and kind of far away." Maybe this was what El Diablo wanted to hear because he lowered the gun and grinned.

"I don't believe you," Tiny said. "Not completely. But you can understand how anything you saw, or think you saw, may be something to put away in a lockbox forever. I especially don't want you talking to Nolan. Understand?" Brian looked shocked at hearing Tiny mention Nolan's name. He must have figured Nolan was an undercover cop. The look on Brian's face didn't escape Tiny's notice. "You've already talked to him, haven't you? What have you told him?" Tiny raised the gun back up to eye level.

"Nothing, I swear," Brian said. "I was just surprised you knew him."

"This is my county. You think I don't know what's going on here?" Tiny said, lowering the gun again. He decided he'd throw some bluff into the pond to muddy the waters, give himself some time and leverage. "One thing you gotta know, Nolan works *with* me." Tiny savored the look of shock and distress that fluttered across Brian's face. "Come over here, I want you to see something." Tiny gripped Brian's left arm and half-dragged him into Mona's bedroom. For the first time, Brian looked furtively around the apartment. It was almost like a hotel suite furniture by Rooms to Grow. A couple of ocean prints on the walls. A TV set and boom box. The bedroom was equally nondescript. The bedclothes and feminine articles on the bureau were proof a woman lived here.

"I have to take a leak—bad," Brian said. Tiny indicated a small bathroom off the bedroom by pointing with the pistol.

"Leave the door open," Tiny said. Brian went in and relieved himself. He took a couple of deep breaths and tried to calm himself. *This could be the end*, his brain kept repeating. When he walked through the door to the bedroom, there was no Tiny. Something very hard and metallic struck him in the back of the head, and he dropped to his knees. He fought for consciousness, everything went all murky, and he felt like he was drowning in a swamp. He just got his head above water when he felt the penetration. He was being raped.

Brian tried to get up, but his head was slammed brutally back to the floor. Tiny's powerful hands gripped Brian's torso like grappling hooks, holding him down. Brian's face was being ground into the bedroom carpet. Brian's eyes cleared enough for him to see a dirty sock under the bed.

"This is the way you're going to be gettin' it every day, pussy boy, you even think about talkin' about what you seen in that cemetery." Tiny growled like a dog and let out a howl as he came. When he finished, Tiny stood up, zipping up his pants. Putting the sole of his size 13 shoe against the whimpering young man's naked ass, he shoved him down on his belly.

"Get up and get dressed," Tiny commanded. "If you know what's good for you, you'll keep your cock-suckin' trap shut."

It was dark by the time Tiny dropped Brian a half mile from the liquor store where his van was parked. He looked at Brian and grinned like a hyena. "I'll be stopping around on official police business to visit you and your cunt boyfriend. Don't worry now"—he pinched Brian's cheek with feigned affection, just below the eye, squeezing hard enough to leave another red mark, which later turned into a black eye—"I'll just be there to make sure my pussy boy is safe and happy. Your drug-dealin' bitch won't have anything to worry about from me." He laughed. "Now get out."

Brian stumbled over to his van, got in, started it, and drove in a state of shock to the Fireproof. He went inside his room, locked the door, and went directly to the shower, stripping off his clothes on the way. He stayed in the shower for a very long time as if the water could wash away the pollution of the last couple of hours. When the hot water gave out, he walked out into the room, took the bottle of rum out he bought for Toad, and took a long drink from it. Opening up a beer, the defiled young man sat with his back against the headboard on the bed, a glazed look on his face. He turned on the tube and sat for an hour watching an MTV special on Elton John without seeing or hearing anything. Finally, he passed out.

When Josh awoke, the stranger who killed the wild animal sat watching him. The smell of meat cooking wafted into the bungalow. The man smiled, got up, and brought him a cup of water. Josh drank thirstily. The man took the cup and put his hand on Josh's head to ruffle his hair. Josh flinched involuntarily.

"Easy, little fella," the man said in a deep soft voice, "nobody's gonna hurt you here. Do you remember what happened?" Vaughn held the boy's hand.

"Yeah, I runned away. A mean pig chased me. But I don' remember your name."

"John. My name is John."

"Oh yeah." Josh nodded. "Now I remembers."

"Good boy. Listen, I cooked a piece of that ole pig that was chasing you. The rest will be cooking awhile longer. Why don't you come outside and eat."

"Okay." The boy followed him out to where the pig was roasting on a spit.

"Pull up a seat," said Vaughn, indicating an aged webbed beach chair. Vaughn pulled up a five-gallon plastic paint bucket turned upside down. "Let's see what we got to eat here." He picked up a metal mess plate and spooned some rice and canned corn and beans from a pot in the fire onto the plate. He put a small chop he'd finished cooking in a frying pan on the plate and cut it into bite-sized pieces. He added a spoonful of applesauce from another can and handed the plate to the lad. Again, the boy attacked the food. "Glad to see someone who appreciates good outdoor cooking." Vaughn watched the boy stuff himself while he smoked a cigarette.

"Now, my little prince," Vaughn said when the boy finished his plate, "we're gonna have to figure out what to do. If I'm guessing right, we share a common foe." The boy gave him a puzzled look. "Never mind that, 'Sufficient unto tomorrow is the evil thereof.' Know what I got? Marshmallows. We'll roast some on the fire for dessert. Afterward, I'll tell you the story of Pooh, Tigger, Piglet, and Roo too."

"Tommy." Julie waited for her husband to open a Bud longneck after he arrived home from his fishing trip before she addressed him. "We have to do something about this mess we're in by being in the cemetery last night. It scares the hell out of me, and Cammy too. We all need to get together tomorrow, in the morning hopefully, when everyone's head is clear and at least partially sober."

"Yeah, I was talking to Robbie, and we pretty much agree." Tommy guzzled some brew from the bottle. "I mean it's pretty much up to Brian and John to come forward. They are the only real witnesses. The rest of us were there, but we didn't see anything. John won't be back until later, so I think the a.m. is out." He brushed his sandy mane back with his left hand.

"Yeah, I guess early evening will have to do," Julie said. "But still, me and Cammy think we should get together and bring some kind of pressure on those two to do something. Meanwhile, Robbie is going to call his mother and tell her what he knows. With her connections, she might be able to help."

"I wonder about that," Tommy said. "With her penchant for young, dare I say underage, boys, she might not want any magnifying glass on her. And God knows what kind of kickback schemes she may or may not have with developers. I understand all the county commissioners pretty much have their hands in the cookie jar to some degree."

"But, Tommy!" Julie protested. "We're talking cold-blooded murder here and of a law enforcement officer."

"Yeah, by another cop." Tommy drank more beer. "And in case you haven't seen the paper today, they're looking for a suspect driving a Ford Taurus or Mercury Sable. That means El Diablo, our cunnin' little Tiny bear, has shifted the suspicion to that car we saw drive out before the cops arrived."

"Anyway," Julie continued, "we need to try everything we can that might help. We're all in this together like it or not. The killer doesn't know who saw what."

"Or if anyone saw anything at all," Tommy added.

"So tomorrow we get together and figure it out." Julie walked over to the end table and pulled out a pad of paper and a pen. "I'll leave John Vaughn a note, and hopefully he'll be back. I'll also make sure everybody else knows about it."

"Good for you," Tommy said, stripping off his shirt. "I'm going to take a shower. When you get back, we can drown out sorrows and fears in lascivious acts of wanton lust and carnality."

"You just said a mouthful, honey buns." Julie pranced out of the room with her note, giving her behind a wanton wiggle.

After a full day of rest and more conversation with the boy, Vaughn decided they would leave the following morning. The boy was already looking better, but the outdoorsman needed to get him to civilization, without being detected, and sort things out. The next morning, Vaughn made breakfast for Josh and packed up as much of the meat as he could carry along with his shotgun. He figured on returning early tomorrow to get the rest of it. On the way, he and Josh talked more about the horrible life Josh ran away from. Vaughn was especially interested in the disappearance of Josh's siblings. It appeared neglect and child abuse may have turned into murder. When they came out to Route 29, Vaughn instructed Josh to remain concealed in the woods for a few minutes until he returned. The boy looked so frightened and confused; Vaughn decided to chance the quarter mile walk with him to the nearest Circle K and phone a cab. It was the best option available. The chance of being seen walking all the way back to the Fireproof was simply too great.

On the side of the convenience store was a large metal bin about five by five by five. There was an open door in the front middle, about three feet square. A sign on the side of the container asked for clothing, canned food, and toy donations for Casa de los Amigos, the area homeless shelter. The shelter provided temporary housing for as many as forty people, including whole families with children. Vaughn was ecstatic to see it was brimming with clothes. While they waited for a cab, he pulled out a couple of fresh outfits for Josh. He could go to the thrift store later if need be to get more. It always amazed Vaughn that despite the enormous wealth of the Napolis community, the two shelters in the county were constantly scrounging for money. The thousands of multimillionaires, who lived either part—or full-time in Napolis, were unable to admit that the poor lived among them.

The cab finally arrived. They drove to the Fireproof, leaving a trail of blue smoke behind. Vaughn thought he'd choke on the exhaust fumes coming into the cab before they arrived. The driver gave Vaughn and the boy a wary look when he left them at the motel but gave no sign of recognizing the boy. As the two approached Vaughn's door, he noticed a note tacked to it with a red pushpin.

"This where you live?" Josh asked.

"It's where I'm hangin' my hat for now," Vaughn answered. Josh looked at him with a puzzled look. "That means yes."

The note was written in neat block letters with a magic marker.

MEETING 7:30 PM
Wed.
CAMILLA and ROBERT'S

Today was Wednesday. Vaughn checked his watch. It was just after 10:00 a.m. He opened his door and gestured for Josh to walk in.

"After you, little guy," he said.

Josh walked into Vaughn's room. The double bed was made, and the room was clean. Only a photo of John Vaughn's son on the bureau gave an indication the room had a full-time inhabitant. There was a stuffed chair by the bed that Josh slid into. He was tired from the walk and his ordeal in the woods, especially the part where he was chased by that ugly wild boar. Vaughn put down his pack. He took out the meat he'd brought with him and put it in the small refrigerator. He removed the shotgun parts, cleaning the barrel prior to placing it on the shelf in the closet. He put the shells in a box up there as well. He looked at Josh, and the frail boy's eyes were shut. Vaughn walked over and listened to the slow rhythmic breathing and, without thinking, bent over and kissed the boy on the forehead. He picked him up and laid him down on the bed, removing the old sneakers. He noticed the boy's feet were swollen and blistered. "Shoes don't fit right," Vaughn mumbled to himself. "Have to fix that right off." There was a knock on the door. Vaughn hustled over and opened it. Toad stood there, coffee cup in hand. Vaughn put his fingers to his lips, stepped aside, and pointed to the sleeping boy on the bed. He pressed past Toad, outside to the porch, and pulled the door shut quietly behind him. Toad stared at him, his face a question mark.

"Got any more of that coffee?" Vaughn asked Toad.

"With or without the rum?" Toad responded.

"Without," Vaughn answered. "I need to keep my head together until I can figure out what to do."

"Ookaay," Toad said, shaking his head with a rueful smile. "One black coffee with sugar, hold the rum, coming up." Vaughn sat down on one of the two plastic lawn chairs on the porch outside his door. Toad returned momentarily with two cups of black brew. He handed Vaughn the mug with the words, "These things too shall pass." Above the words was a picture of a man with his legs being run over by a train.

"Hey, my cup!" Vaughn said.

"Ayup," said Toad, easing himself into the other seat. "You left it here last time. So what's with the little ragamuffin?"

"This is pretty crazy." Vaughn paused and took a sip of coffee. "When I was almost back to my camp, I heard thrashing in the brush. I assembled the Survivor lickety-split and loaded a round of buckshot. Next thing, this little kid comes running out into the clearing and right on his heels, a wild boar. Mean mother too. The kid spots me and runs over for protection. The mean piggy runs into a load of buckshot at close range. I had to finish it off with a slug. I brought enough meat for a barbeque, and there's a bunch still back at camp, pretty much all fire roasted. I'm going back for it as soon as possible—hopefully tomorrow."

"What're you going to do with Sleeping Beauty in there?" Toad loved a good quandary, especially someone else's.

Vaughn shook his head, sipped some more coffee. "I don't know. From what I could get out of the kid and just looking at him, he's been severely abused. But the part that really bothers me, it's been going on a long time. Apparently, there were a couple of siblings who vanished one day. On top of that, it appears our very own deputy sheriff was somehow involved." Toad nodded his head and rolled a cigarette. Vaughn removed his pack of Camel nonfilters. Toad proffered a light.

"It's a tough call," ventured Toad, smoke swirling around his shaggy head. "If you go to DHS, they contact the sheriff's department, and bada bing bada boom, there's Deputy Bad Dog on the scene, who has, apparently, been working some kind of scam with the poor kids' parents or guardians." More silence and smoking.

"I'm thinking," Vaughn finally said, "I'll keep the kid here a couple of days, try to sort things out."

"I hate to say this, but maybe you should talk to Nolan. I have news for you, and I'm sure this will come as no surprise, but it's like I thought, Nolan is a fed."

"How are you so sure?" Vaughn finished his Camel and stubbed out the butt.

"He told us," Toad said. Vaughn gave him an incredulous stare.

"Brian and I talked to him yesterday. He'll be over any minute now."

"What exactly did you talk about?" Vaughn felt a chill run through him, and it came out in the way he asked Toad the question.

"We pretty much told him what happened," responded Toad in a matter-of-fact tone. "Naturally, we omitted your name from the sad story."

"But . . . ," Vaughn prompted. Toad lit a slender joint, inhaled deeply, held a moment, and let out a thick cloud of pungent marijuana smoke. The war veteran suddenly reminded Vaughn of the dragon depicted on the shields of warriors in the Arthurian legends. "Toad Explodes, Poisonous Gases Vented in Pendragon's Castle," tabloid newspapers of the era would've headlined.

"But," Toad finally continued, "Nolan knows about you anyway. Or at least suspects strongly. I think you should come clean with him. This isn't going away, and you *are* a reliable witness. Now if it was me he had to depend on, he might want to look elsewhere."

"Man, I don't know." Vaughn shook his head and took and lit another Camel. "I would like to have some time to think it through."

"Too late for that now, here he comes." Toad nodded toward Nolan's room.

Mike Nolan strode across the lawn from his room. He gave Camilla's small garden a cursory glance, a thin smile stretching his lips. He came up the steps, hand out to Toad. The smell of tobacco mixed with marijuana enveloped the hirsute vet.

"Morning, Toad." Nolan shook Toad's hand and turned to Vaughn. "John Vaughn, I'm Special Agent Nolan." He held out his hand to Vaughn who shook it without enthusiasm. "I hope we can conclude our business quickly and put this matter before the courts. I will personally assure your safety."

"I doubt you can do that," Vaughn said. "The incident in question involves another cop, and it's my observation you will be unable to put a lid on him."

"You probably won't live long enough," interjected Toad, "to even get an arrest warrant."

"We'll see about that," Nolan blustered. "When I get done here, I'm going to Judge Thomas and obtain an arrest warrant for Sergeant Harris. I expect it to be a matter of hours before we can take the deputy into custody. Procedure requires we notify the sheriff as well as the captain of the Bella Villa Division. We will have to reinterview all of you with other agents and possibly someone from the district attorney's office. So where is Brian, Toad?"

"Just a minute, Nolan," Vaughn said. "I'm not all that sure I've got anything of importance to relate. I need some time to think about this. Maybe I better talk to a lawyer."

"I can understand your reluctance, John," Nolan said. "But under the circumstances, I think we need to move quickly. I can arrange to have you subpoenaed to testify under oath, but by that time, everyone in law enforcement, including our boy Tiny, will be privy to what's happening. It's practically impossible to quash something this big without a lot of leaks. Let's get Brian and do this now, John. In an hour, I'll call Judge Thomas and get an arrest warrant, and by tomorrow, we'll be in front of the grand jury."

"All right," said Vaughn and stood up. "Get Brian, and I'll be right there. I have something I have to take care of in my room." He gave Toad a look that said, "Help me out here." Toad stood up and gave Nolan a "let's get down to business" nod of the head.

"Let's wake up Sleeping Beauty," Toad said. He and Nolan walked over to Brian's door.

19

When Brian came to, he was lying on top of the bedcovers in his underwear. His head was filled with spiderwebs. He squinted at the radio clock's illuminated numbers—4:44 a.m. He heaved himself out of bed and shuffled into the bathroom. He stuck out his right arm and propped himself against the wall as he urinated. When he finished, he went to the sink and looked at himself in the mirror. He didn't like much of what he saw. Sitting on the bed, he spotted the fifth of rum on the floor. It was about a third demolished. He picked up the bottle, opened it, said to himself, "Fuck all," and guzzled it to the halfway point. He got up and took a Bud from the fridge and staggered back to the bed. He squinted at the TV still flickering in the otherwise dark room. An old black-and-white *Andy Griffith Show* was playing. Deputy Barney Fife was fishing in his shirt pocket for the single bullet he carried. Meanwhile, bank robbers were about to make off with the fortunes of Mayberry. The sound was off, but Brian knew Barney was wishing out loud his friend, Ange, was there (and, of course, he was). Brian took a swallow of beer and rested the can on the night table. The events of the preceding evening, though not lost to memory, became more like a fuzzy bad dream than reality. He lolled in a semicatatonic stupor for the remainder of *Andy Griffith* and somewhere into another chapter of the Mayberry chronicles. Just as Deputy Fife was giving chase to one of Opie's naughty friends, who was riding his bicycle on the sidewalk in violation of town ordinances, Brian lost all consciousness as the booze, once again, overtook him.

He is on a small hammock of tall sabal palms and shorter Washington palms with their fan-shaped leaves and rough bark. The light is feeble as if the unseen sun is very low in the mauve-colored sky. Black calabash bushes, with their bell-shaped lavender-and-yellow lobes, grow haphazardly, giving the slough-surrounded ground a cluttered feeling. Dahoon holly with bright red berries and date palms cluttered in bunches of ten to twenty were spreading out FA-like from their roots, filling in the landscape. Walking into an open space, he sees a multitude of alligators ripping and tearing at a bloody mangled body. One tears off a leg, another an arm. Yet another rips the head off and slithers back toward the murky water on the opposite side of the hammock. Something shiny glints at Brian's feet; it's a full can of Budweiser. He picks up the can and pulls the tab. It explodes, morphing into a deputy sheriff's badge. Brian looks up to see alligators surrounding him. Toad is over by what's left of the ravaged body; he's taking a leak, an empty rum bottle at his feet, calling out to Brian . . .

"Brian! Brian!" Toad was knocking hard on Brian's door while calling his name. Toad figured Brian was sleeping off the bottle of rum he was supposed to score for him. If true, he would be faced with the unwelcome chore of procuring more alcohol. *Little bastard,* Toad thought.

"Maybe he's at Jamie's," Nolan ventured.

"Naw," said Toad. "I saw Jamie going off to work this morning. His face had the look of a summer thunderstorm."

"Let's try anyway," Nolan said. But Brian opened the door, still in his underwear, and blinked at them.

"Hey, Toad," he said. "I'm 'fraid I did half that rum, but I'm good for it." Brian gave Nolan a stony glance, speaking to an imaginary someone standing behind the federal agent. "I got nothin' to say. Maybe later with a lawyer."

"What happened to you last night?" Nolan asked. "He got to you somehow, didn't he?" Nolan started to push past Toad but was effectively blocked when Toad stood his ground.

"I don't think he's in the mood for company," Toad said, coming to the front for his beleaguered liquor-saving buddy. Toad figured the sooner he got rid of Nolan, the sooner he could quiet his jitters with the distillate of island cane and get to the bottom of Brian's sudden change of heart. "Let him rest." Toad nodded to Brian and pulled the door closed. "We'll see if Vaughn wants to talk. But I think you should wait a couple of hours. Let everyone gather their wits." Nolan looked as pleased as Tiger Woods missing a short putt for first place in the PGA.

"Two hours," Nolan said, "and I'll be back. After that, I call in the cavalry, and things get messy."

"Ahyup." Toad pulled out a pack of Bugler and rolled a smoke as he watched Nolan return to his room. He lit the cigarette and went back to Brian's room. He tapped on the door. Brian opened it a crack and handed him the remainder of the Ron Virgin.

"Later, Toad. Okay," Brian said.

"Ahyup." Toad hoofed it over to tell Vaughn of the new developments.

"Good," Vaughn said when Toad told him the news. "I didn't know what I was going to do with Josh if I had to talk to Nolan. I sure don't want the authorities to know just yet. Guess I'll say he's my nephew from Fort Lauderdale. I actually do have a cousin there someplace."

"I'm going back to see Brian in an hour or so, find out what happened." Toad took a hit off the bottle, still standing on the porch. Vaughn didn't invite him in. "Ahh, that's better. I'm getting some coffee to put this in. I figure on being a wide-awake drunk today." Toad turned to go back to his room, paused, and added, "You ought to talk to Camilla and Robbie. Maybe they could watch the kid, make him feel welcome."

"Just what I was thinkin'," Vaughn replied.

"Oh my god!" Julie exclaimed. She was hanging out with Camilla, drinking coffee while Robbie was at FGCU making arrangements for his curriculum. "John, who is this adorable child?" She got up and stuck her hand out to Josh. "My name is Julie."

"This is Josh," Vaughn said, a little uneasy about asking for help.

"Josh, welcome," Julie said. Taking his hand, she led him over to where Camilla was sitting with Billy. "Josh, this is Camilla." She let go of his hand, allowing Camilla to take it. "And the baby is Billie." The two women exchanged glances. It had become apparent the young boy had been abused, despite his clean clothes and freshly bathed appearance.

"Josh has had some difficult times and needs help," Vaughn started. He gave them a short version of what he gleaned from the boy so far. "I'm going to talk to Nolan, but not on tape. I'll do that later, maybe have an attorney present. If you guys could keep an eye on Josh for an hour or so, I'd appreciate it."

"Not a problem," said Camilla.

"My pleasure," Julie chimed.

"Great!" Vaughn went over and knelt by Josh. "I'm leaving you with these two wonderful ladies, Josh." The boy looked momentarily dismayed, but one glimpse of the compassionate smiling faces of the two women brought a smile to the boy's beleaguered face. Vaughn ruffled his hair, stood up, and gave each of the ladies an uncharacteristic hug. His eyes appeared watery. "See you later," he blurted.

Brian left his room a few minutes after Toad and Nolan departed. He had no intention of talking to Nolan, especially right after what happened to him at Mona's. He didn't much feel like confiding in the Toadster at the moment either. What he needed was to see Jamie. Maybe they could go somewhere and talk. Brian called Jamie from the motel phone in his room (a twenty-five-cent local call charged to his room).

"Gulf West, Jamie speaking."

"Jamie, I . . . I need to talk. Right now."

"Brian, are you okay?" Jamie was clearly concerned. The sympathetic tone broke down Brian's last defense. He started whimpering in the phone and finally burst into a freight train of sobs. He could barely catch his breath.

"No. No, I'm *not* okay," he managed. "I need help." Tears ran freely down Brian's face as he cried openly.

"Where are you?" Jamie asked.

"I'll meet you in the Foo Foo parking lot in an hour, okay?"

"I'll be there," Jamie said. "Just hang on, Bry."

"Bye, Jamie." Brian hung up, pulled himself together, and drove straight to the liquor store. It should be just about opening time, and he owed Toad a bottle, didn't he? Might as well pick one up for himself as well. He couldn't think of anything better than a little hair of the dog to calm the damn jitters.

Jamie's obsessive boss was less than enthusiastic about him leaving early, barring a death in the family. But Jamie persisted, and at last, the disgruntled manager relented. By the time Jamie arrived at the Foo Foo parking lot, Brian had enough rum in him to be feeling mellow.

"Brian, what's the matter?" Jamie asked.

"Let's take your car and go to the beach," Brian said. "Right now. I gotta get out of this town." Jamie saw the desperation in his eyes.

"Sure, Bry. Let's go."

On the way to Napolis, Brian gave Jamie an account of what happened with him and Tiny the preceding afternoon. Jamie was both horrified and furious. At the same time, he felt that sense of helplessness familiar to the powerless everywhere.

"We've got to do *something*," said Jamie. By this time, they were both crying. Jamie pulled into the parking lot at the Strand's Publix, a ubiquitous South Florida Grocery chain. He stopped the car near a Subway shop at the end of the mall. He stroked Brian's hair, giving him a long hug across the center console. Brian continued to weep softly, wiping his tears on Jamie's shirt. "There's a meeting tonight to discuss our options. Let's get a sandwich at Subway and go to the beach for a while."

"I just don't want to talk to Nolan. Not now. I think maybe I should get a lawyer, but I don't have the bread."

"We'll take it one step at a time," Jamie said. "I just want you to know I'm there for you, financially as well as emotionally. Okay?"

"Yeah, thanks, Jamie," Brian said. "I think you're right about the drinking too. I'm going to try to quit."

"That's great!" Jamie almost shouted. "I'll support you all the way."

"But not today," Brian said with a rueful smile.

"Let's get something to eat," Jamie said.

Nolan returned to his room full of frustration and anxiety when Vaughn flat out refused to say anything, on tape, without first speaking to an attorney. Nothing the federal agent said about timing and the danger they were all in could sway the recalcitrant recluse. On top of that, Brian had gone missing. He decided to call Judge Thomas and apprise him of the situation. Maybe they could get the evidence before a grand jury—if only he had the gun and the decoy driving the

Ford. He'd need a whole task force to unravel this. He drove to the nearest pay phone and called the judge.

Judge Thomas was in his chambers interviewing a thirteen-year-old Mexican girl, delicate as a desert blossom, when the phone rang. It was Nolan. He buzzed his secretary and had the girl's social worker come in and take the girl. He would have to continue the session after business hours at his apartment. The judge heard Nolan out. The juices of fear stirred his insides like a corroding acid. Thomas's anxiety was well founded. If indicted, Tiny would drag him into the spotlight along with a dozen others.

"Listen," the judge said when Nolan finished, "try to get statements from the two witnesses. Let me get the names." He picked up a pen and scribbled on a yellow legal pad. "Brian Sutter and John Vaughn, spelled like the star of *Man from U.N.C.L.E.* Call me back in twenty-four hours with any other information. I will be in touch with the district attorney and the sheriff. Keep this classified for now." Nolan seemed reluctant to wait but agreed. When he hung up, Judge Thomas called Sgt. Edwin "Tiny" Harris.

"Get your ass over to my office. *Now!*" Thomas hung up before the deviant deputy could reply.

Santana sat by the pool smoking one of Rooster's Cubans. He wore black swimming trunks. Santana wore black everything. He was a thin man, wiry, with ropelike muscles bulging under his coffee-colored skin. His hair was slicked back like it was painted on his head. His upper lip sported a black mustache. The day before yesterday when he sat here with the gringo, Rooster, he'd been asked to kill a policeman. In Mexico or Columbia, maybe. But in this country, it was *muy peligroso* (very dangerous). He asked to be brought back to the airport. Rooster raised the stakes to one hundred and fifty thousand U.S. dollars, half up front. Santana told the Americano he would sleep on it. He did. He would need much more money than offered. So here he was, still in negotiations. The gringo and two of his women interrupted his reverie.

"Santana, I'd like you to meet two darling girls," said Rooster. "This is Rachelle and Robin." Santana stood and kissed their hands.

"Truly, they are like the first flowers of spring." Santana smiled. His perfect teeth gleamed. The gold caps winked. He was a handsome devil. The girls looked him over and giggled.

"You two fish take a swim while Señor Santana and I talk." Rooster patted them both on the ass. He sat in one of the chaise longues and went through the ritual of snipping his cigar, sniffing it, and lighting it slowly and carefully. Not too much fire in one place. Avoid direct contact between the cigar and the flame.

"I think maybe, Señor Rooster," Santana began in slightly accented English, "I go back to Guadalajara."

"Listen," Rooster said, "I need this done. I'll double the offer. Make it three hundred thousand dollars. I'll wire half to your bank today and the other half when the cop is dead."

"For tree hundred and feefty dousands, I do eet," Santana said. "You have plane ready to go on runway. I no hang around for crazy Amercano *policía* to solve keeling of one of their brothers. I read in periodical they already going loco for one just keeled."

Rooster puffed on his cigar. He picked up his Nextel. "Jimmy! Bring a bottle of Tequila and some glasses." He reached over and shook hands with Santana. "Deal."

The meeting at the Fireproof turned out to be remarkably short and sweet. Brian and Vaughn agreed to hire an attorney referred by Robbie Valentine's mother. In addition, she agreed to pay his fees. She tried to persuade Robbie and Camilla to bring the baby and move in with her immediately. She insisted they could be in imminent peril. They agreed to give it consideration. Brian announced he was going into detox the next day in order to be able to give a sober statement to the attorney. They called Nolan, and he came over for the potluck and music. He agreed to go along with their plan but wasn't exactly ecstatic. He wanted an arrest warrant for Tiny, pronto.

Josh couldn't believe the food. There were hot homemade rolls and fresh salad made from the vegetables of Camilla's garden. John Vaughn and Robbie had driven back to get the rest of the wild boar. They barbequed the already-flame-cooked meat. Camilla and Julie baked two apple and one blueberry pies. He had never seen so much food in his short deprived life. And taste! He thought this must be heaven after each bite. He ate until he thought he would burst and then nibbled a little more. Camilla and Julia fussed over him, constantly making sure he was getting enough, giving him hugs and kisses. Even the scary-looking man called Toad ruffled his hair once or twice. When Josh couldn't possibly hold anymore, he sat in the easy chair and began to doze off. Robbie picked him up and put him on their bed. Josh dreamed his brother and sister were with him in this wonderful place, and they all lived together.

Tiny pulled reluctantly into Mario's driveway. He didn't want to be seen here. It was full dark and after ten when most good folks were safely tucked away. Still, if a patrol car came by and they recognized his Jeep, things could get messy. He might have to play his trump card, implicating Mario in O'Brien's murder. And it was far too early in the game for that. After almost two decades on the force picking up scraps and keeping gutless Gunther off his back, he was about to clean up. Next year, he would retire early with less than he hoped for but more than he previously imagined. At least he would be relatively young and relatively rich. Unfortunately, he needed Mario and the two Chicanos, Carlos and Omar, to come out and play again.

Tiny walked down the driveway, flower-print shirt hanging out over his dungarees, the 9mm under his belt. When he came to the sliding glass door enclosing a screened-in lanai, he pulled disposable plastic gloves over his hands and slid the door open. Walking in, he could hear the Talking Heads, "Life During Wartime," "This ain't no party, this ain't no disco, this ain't no foolin' around." Mario was passed out on the caramel leather La-Z-Boy, feet up in the air, a half drunk fifth of Jack Daniel's on the floor. Tiny enjoyed the aesthetics of the smooth black skin against the leather for a brief moment. He went into the kitchen and took a short thick drinking glass from the cupboard. He returned to the living room and poured a shot of the whiskey. He sat on the couch and watched Mario while he sipped from the glass. In a few minutes, he got up and walked over to Mario, the unfinished drink in his hand. He flung the amber liquid into the sleeping man's face.

"What the—" Mario came awake, spluttering. He saw Tiny standing in front of him, glass in plastic-gloved hand. "Oh, shit."

"Is that any way to greet your best business partner?" Tiny asked. "I'm here to assist you in your present troubles and offer opportunities to earn some extra spending money."

"Fuck that," Mario said, wiping his face with his shirtsleeve. "I was doin' just fine before you busted into my life. Now it's one step ahead and two back. Man, you set us up for a murder rap. I ain't playin' that game with you no more." Mario tried to stand up, but his head swooned. He sat back down and reached for the whiskey. He took a swig from the bottle and started coughing violently, spitting up some of the booze.

"Let me get you some water," Tiny said, hustling to the kitchen. He filled his glass with water and returned, handing it to Mario. "Where's the gun?"

"What?" Mario said. "You've got to be kidding! First you set me up. And when by some miracle I get away, you want me to provide proof for your double cross?"

"It's in the lake, isn't it?" Tiny said. "About as far as you could throw it from shore, and I have a pretty good idea where you threw it from."

"Fuck off!" Mario started to get up again, but Tiny pushed him back down.

"You watch your language talking to me, boy!" Tiny stepped in close and gave Mario a hard backhand across his left cheek. The plastic glove on his right hand ripped but clung to his fingers. Tiny's face was turning red, his teeth clenched. Mario thought he was going to kill him right in the chair. Instead, Tiny stood up straight, and the blood drained from his contorted face. A smile spread like a nervous sun emerging after a brief tempest. Taking the empty glass from Mario's hand and picking up the Jack Daniel's in his right hand, he poured a half glass of the sour mash. He sniffed the strong aroma. "Ahh, there you are, have a drink." He handed the glass to the beleaguered black man. "You and I have some things to discuss, and there's not a whole lot of time. Got any Coke in the fridge?" Mario nodded, and Tiny went out and grabbed a can and returned, sitting on the couch. Mario was sipping the whiskey, a sullen look of resignation on his dark handsome face.

Sitting in the La-Z-Boy, sipping coke, Tiny began to unfold his plan.

"Now, here's what we're going to do," Tiny began.

20

Jamie and Brian spent the night together after the food fest at the Fireproof. When Jamie awoke in the early morning, a few songbirds were celebrating the rising of the sun and the start of a new day. All was not perfect in paradise, however. Brian was gone. Jamie got up and checked the bathroom, then went to Brian's room. He knocked on the door as he pushed it open. Brian was sitting on his bed, drinking a beer, watching Beavis and Butt-head on MTV.

"Yo, bro!" he called gaily.

"You might as well enjoy those," Jamie said, "if *enjoy* is the right word. Because in an hour, we're going to detox."

"I know it looks bad," Brian said, "but I'm not sure drying out is going to help me. I mean, I have a couple of beers, and I feel okay. It's weird, like I feel all sick, sweaty, and jittery when I wake up. But after two or three brews, it all goes away, and I feel great."

"They have a word for that, Brian, it's called *addiction*. In your case, it's alcohol addiction, and it's not a lot different from heroin addiction in its physical symptoms. Brian, you're not going to be able to drink again. You'll have to go to AA when you get out of detox and see how they do it. As far as I know, it's the only place that has any kind of proven track record for arresting the disease of alcoholism."

"I'll be fine once I get a few days under my belt without a drink," Brian insisted. "I'll put the plug in the jug for a month. Afterward, I'll just have a couple after work. It's just a matter of will power. I don't have to drink like Toad. I can be like you and Tommy and Julie."

"Brian, I've seen people try that route and fail over and over. It's an insidious disease. It's usually only a matter of time before those people who start drinking again after sobering up are drinking just like they did before." Brian's chipper attitude became morose as he stared at the only poster in his room, a picture of a young Bob Dylan in a leather jacket and motorcycle tee shirt from the *Highway 61 Revisited* album. His older brother gave him this relic before he was killed in the first Gulf War by "friendly fire." He finished the beer he was drinking.

"Don't look so glum, Bry. Just take things one day at a time. It's like a new beginning." Jamie sat on the bed next to his disconsolate friend and lover. He draped an arm over his shoulders. "You know, people like us—with sexual orientation issues, that is—have a much higher rate of alcoholism and drug addiction than so-called normal people. We suffer from the inside out while enduring a shit storm of abuse from our macho-puritan culture. Even those of us not prone to addictions feel driven to their welcoming arms. Have another beer if you want. We'll leave in an hour."

Brian laid his head on Jamie's shoulder and wept.

The David Lawrence Center (DLC) was located on Golden Gate Boulevard in the part of Napolis called Golden Gate, about five miles east of the neighborhood in Napolis known as the Moorings. While the Moorings neighborhood was the genteel country club set, Golden Gate was the working-class community. The immigrants were crushed into dense housing developments while the better-off skilled workers enjoyed relatively nice developments. Many parcels were two and a half acres and featured huge lawns and exotic shrubbery. These were the people who were involved in the copious construction of new and exclusive high-end developments, a few less ostentatious developments, and shopping malls. In addition, there were the owners of service industries such as landscaping, cleaning, restaurant work, and retail stores as well as their employees. An almost endless proliferation of other homegrown businesses sprouted like mushrooms after a rainstorm to meet the needs of the growing resident population.

For those unable to afford the Willows, a far ritzier establishment, the DLC provided adequate detox facilities of the "spin dry" variety. This consisted of two to five days of supervised medication, nourishment, and education—enough time, in other words, to sober up and be over the worst of the physical withdrawal symptoms of drug and/or alcohol addiction. For those with good insurance or a large bank account, a twenty-eight-day on-site rehabilitation program was available, including outside trips to AA meetings around town and counseling. Jamie waited three hours at the hospital near downtown Napolis where Brian was examined and administered a dose of Librium to ease his withdrawal. Next, Jamie drove Brian to the DLC, holding his hand in the small lobby. When the intake procedure was complete, they hugged and exchanged a kiss on the cheek before Brian was taken through the locked ward by an attendant.

When Jamie returned from the DLC, he encountered Camilla and Julie on the front porch in front of Camilla's suite, sitting in plastic chairs yakking. Baby Billy was in his high chair being entertained by Josh. The girls waved to Jamie as he got out of his Civic. He approached them, a wane yet hopeful smile playing on his lips. They all embraced and cried together for a moment. Josh looked at them mystified. After the huddle broke, Jamie came over and gave Josh a hug too. "Glad you can stay awhile with us, Josh." Nolan had agreed to keep the boy's situation under wraps, at great risk to his credentials, until the mess with Tiny could be resolved.

"Me too," Josh replied. "I want to stay with John forever. Can he be my dad?"

Jamie turned to the ladies for help. Julie came over and knelt by Josh. "We're all going to be your friends for a while, sweetie. Right now, all we know is what each day brings. Why don't you go see if John wants to come over so you two can have lunch with us?"

"Yippie!" Josh yelled in uncharacteristic jubilation. He turned and flew down the steps and over to Vaughn's room, pirouetting in the yard as he went.

"Wow!" Camilla exclaimed. "He certainly is coming out of his shell. It's amazing what can happen to the human spirit given some love and attention."

"Not to mention good food and decent clothes," added Jamie.

"So how did it go, Jamie?" Camilla asked.

"Yeah, what's the local, homeboy?" Julie piped.

"Do you mean as in anesthesia?" Jamie parried.

"No, silly," Julie chided. "I mean as in *news*, dude. What up wid the Bryster?"

"Well," Jamie began, and he gave them the skinny on his boyfriend. He concluded with a plea. "When he gets out, he should be physically withdrawn from the booze. The problem will be *staying* sober. It would be great if everybody agreed not to *enable* him."

"We're revved for nonenabling action," Julie said.

"You can count on Robbie and me to serve nothing stronger than coffee or pop," Camilla added.

"Now, if we can just get Toad on board," Jamie said.

"Don't worry," Camilla said, "Jules and me will turn our *girl power* on the Toad. He'll see things our way." Just as she spoke the words, Toad came out and sat on his chair. He set a pint can of Pabst Blue Ribbon on the small plastic table by his chair and lit a cigarette.

"Looks like he's goin' easy today," Jamie said, "just beer." Toad waved, and they all waved back and smiled. Robbie came out and picked up Billy. Holding the babe in arms, he announced the lunch of tuna fish sandwiches with homemade and homegrown cabbage salad and fresh garden cucumbers was ready to be served.

"Hey, Toad!" Camilla said, raising her voice enough to carry to his doorway. "You want to have some lunch with us?"

"Ayup," Toad answered as Josh came out of Vaughn's room, towing his savior and benefactor by the hand.

"Looks like the gang's all together," said Robbie. "Minus one, of course," he added, looking at Jamie. "I'll go put the coffeepot on."

Driving to the Baron Government Center, location of the county courthouse, Tiny reviewed everything he knew to date. He hooked up briefly with Luis

Alvarez, his snitch at *El Milagro*, the Latino newspaper, just prior to leaving for the government center. Alvarez enjoyed a rum and Coke in a dark booth at the Foo Foo lounge while telling Tiny about Santana. He also told Tiny about Nolan, something he shouldn't have known. Tiny gave him three one-hundred-dollar bills and paid the bar tab. As he drove down 846 past new housing developments pushing ever eastward into the Everglades, he mulled over his increasingly narrow options. It was clear he would have to eliminate Nolan, and quickly. Otherwise, twenty years of work was going down the tubes just as it reached an unbelievable peak. Taking out O'Brien was supposed to forestall a criminal investigation, but the Fireproof crowd had gotten thrown into the mix. Now there was the problem of potential witnesses and the probability the assistant district attorney would impanel a grand jury. The district attorney, a buddy of Judge Thomas, might not be able to quash it. He turned south on 951 and drove to Davis Boulevard trying to think of ways Nolan could be removed from the picture, short of murder, and came up empty. West on Davis, he turned his thoughts to what Alvarez had told him. To top off an already sticky web, that cocky dickwad, Rooster, had imported specialized help to have him assassinated. Judge Thomas was an ace in the hole, but he couldn't be trusted either. He would have to get video footage of the old lecher at work to supplement his audio recordings and the single photo he possessed. Tiny turned his Grand Cherokee from Davis Boulevard south onto Airport, and in a minute, he was in the parking lot of the sheriff department's main headquarters and the county courthouse.

Tiny rode the elevator to the second floor of Baron County's spacious court building. The office of Judge Thomas was located on the west side of the building where there was a view of the Gulf of Mexico. On the south side, the vista was of a bay that formed the south border of downtown Napolis. North and east of the building were man-made lakes serving as centerpieces of country club communities. There was water everywhere in Baron County, which, after all, was part of the Everglades. What was in short supply due to rapid population growth and overdevelopment was potable water. Tiny waited a moment while the judge's secretary buzzed His Honor. The secretary was a sweet woman by the name of Sally with short chestnut hair, blue eyes, and a kind smile. *What this judge needs is an Amazon warrior with a short leash*, thought Tiny, smiling inadvertently.

"What's so amusing?" Sally asked.

"Oh," said Tiny, surprised at being caught enjoying a private joke. "I was just thinking of something a jail guard told me the other day. Nothing I care to repeat in polite company."

Sally raised her eyebrows and nodded to the door leading to the judge's chambers. "You can go in now."

"Thanks," said Tiny and went through the door.

Judge Thomas was in his plush leather desk chair puffing a huge Cuban cigar, illegal on two counts: first, it constituted possession of contraband, and second, smoking in the building was prohibited. Tiny refrained from arresting the judge in his own chambers; it might infuriate the already scowling trafficker in justice. Still, Tiny played the scene in his own mind for entertainment.

"What, exactly, do you find amusing?" asked the judge, noticing the grin on the deputy's face.

"Oh, nothing, sir," Tiny replied. "I was just thinking of something a jail guard told me earlier. I'm afraid it would be in bad taste to repeat it."

"Is that a fact?" the judge scowled. "I've taken the unprecedented action of calling you here to make a suggestion. You would be wise to resign from the force, immediately, and take retirement in Costa Rica, which, by the way, has no extradition treaty with the U.S. I hear it's rather pleasant there and inexpensive as well. You can have your pick of señoritas. I will do everything in my power to stifle any ongoing investigation and see that you get your partial pension." Tiny's smile remained frozen on his face. However, a crimson tide was creeping up his neck, spreading to his cheeks. He stared at the judge a moment before speaking through clenched teeth.

"Thank you, Your Honor, for your sage advice and offer of assistance." Tiny walked over to the judge's desk and removed a cigar from a silver-plated box containing ornate designs. Tiny wondered if Thomas was a multimillionaire yet from the bribes he received from developers whose cases landed in his court. The robust deputy lit the Cuban Puro and blew out a cloud of fragrant smoke. Thomas stood up, his face expressing his indignation.

"I assure you—," Thomas began.

"Fuck you!" Tiny exploded. He regained his composure and strode over to where the judge was standing. He stood almost a head higher than the justice. Thomas looked suddenly old and feeble. Tiny removed the cigar from Thomas's hand and dropped it on the expensive carpet, grinding it out with his foot. He reached a big hand under the now-terrified adjudicator's chin and squeezed his fleshy cheeks until his mouth formed an oval. Tiny placed his cigar into the gap, forcing it in. The mischievous deputy placed two fingers of his left hand on either side of the judge's nose and pinched the nostrils shut. At the same time, he moved his grip down lower on the pudgy neck to render his victim motionless. Able to breath solely through his mouth, the unfortunate magistrate drew more smoke than air into his lungs. He began to choke and gag, his face bright red, eyes bulging. He began to thrash wildly, trying to spit out the smoking stick; but his wind was squeezed off, and he was held firmly in place. His face went from red to white to blue. Tiny relented, letting the nostrils open, while yanking the cigar from his mouth. The minister of justice collapsed to the floor, gasping for air. He vomited over himself and the carpet, covering the extinguished butt with his disgorges.

"We're all in this until I say we're done," said Tiny. He put a picture by the sweaty head of the August judicial administrator. It was a digital photo print of a fleshy older man in a bathing suit, sitting by a pool with a naked girl of about twelve on his lap. It was far from being a good photo, but the man was clearly Thomas.

Tiny left and went directly to Mona's apartment. He felt extremely horny. A quickie before going on patrol was just what he needed.

Camilla looked up from her weeding and saw Mike Nolan approaching across the brief strip of lawn. He was wearing dungarees and a sleeveless tee shirt outside the pants with the Nike insignia on it. She wondered if he had his gun tucked by his buttocks under the shirt. His smile seemed genuine, straight white teeth, sparkling impish emerald eyes. His face was definitely handsome.

"Hey, Cammy, how you doin'?"

"Oh, I'm doing pretty well," Camilla answered. "Just tryin' to keep the weeds from choking the veggies and flowers to death. Gotta keep after them."

"Mind if I sit a minute?" Nolan sat on the grass without waiting for a reply.

"I guess not," Camilla said with a pinch of sarcasm.

"I don't mean to be rude," Nolan said, putting a blade of grass between his fine choppers, "but I'd really like to hear what your take on this mess is." Camilla bent over her weeding, pulling errant plants out of the ground, and heaving them to one side. After a minute, she looked up at the mum federal agent.

"I think it's about time we cleared out of here. Something tells me there *isn't* going to be a lot of movement to put this renegade deputy out of business real soon."

"And why would you think that?" Nolan queried. "You don't trust me?"

"It's not you I'm worried about, Mike." She looked at him and noticed again how handsome and self-assured he looked. He had delicate crow's-feet around his sea green eyes. His walnut-colored hair fell in disarray, almost to his long lashes. *Was she getting turned on?*

"What is it then?" Nolan asked.

"Robbie's mother is a county commissioner, and as you probably know, in Florida, they are the real local power. They have budgets bigger than a lot of countries, maybe a few states. They control development, roads, schools, and the sheriff's department. They employ hundreds of workers." She paused a moment and then added, "And she doesn't think you can touch this guy. There may be more people involved than you think. She said our situation could be extremely dangerous. She wants Robbie, Billy, and me to move in with her. Frankly, I'm scared."

"You should be, this man is a powder keg likely to go off any time. Believe me, I'm sleeping with one eye open as well."

"Why don't you arrest him?" Camilla shook the dirt off the roots of a weed she just pulled. "If he wasn't a deputy sheriff, he'd probably be in jail right now."

"You're probably right. He's got more than the benefit of the doubt being in law enforcement. I suspect he has some good ole boy connections as well." Nolan stood up and smiled at Camilla. He pulled a business card from his shirt pocket. It identified him as a county housing officer. "My cell phone number is on there. You call me anytime, day or night, if you have any information or need help of any kind." Camilla took the card and looked at it. She looked up and returned Nolan's smile.

"How about a drink later," she blurted, "say seven o'clock at the Foo Foo?" Camilla's face flushed; she could barely believe her own audacity.

"You've no obligations at home?" he asked.

"Everyday. But I deserve a drink out, occasionally, with a friend. Robbie can stay with the baby for once." She gave him a mutinous stare. Nolan's smile widened to expose all of his even front teeth and the crow's-feet crinkling around his eyes. Camilla reflected his grin with one of her own.

"I'm sure you do," he said. "See you there at seven. And don't forget, use that number." He turned and walked back to his room. Camilla found herself admiring his backside before she caught herself in the misdemeanor. She returned to her weeding, a long buried excitement turning her insides all giddy.

Nolan went to the pay phone by the 7-Eleven and called his Washington bureau chief in DC. He was told in no uncertain terms to stick to his original mission of finding the sources of drugs and the dealers in the area. He was to leave the O'Brien murder case alone. As soon as his supervisor hung up, Nolan cursed all bureaucrats, slamming the receiver down. A homeless man of indeterminate age and ravaged by alcohol stopped searching the dumpster and looked at him like a timid squirrel, unsure of whether to stand fast or bolt. When Nolan vaulted over the door into his open convertible and squealed out of the parking lot, the homeless man abandoned the dumpster, temporarily, to check the coin return in the pay phone.

21

Santana sped north on Route 658 in his rented black Lincoln Town Car. In Baron County, capital of luxury sedans, he would be as inconspicuous as if he were in a Toyota Corolla anywhere else. He would simply be another of a passel of tourists who frequented the casino. Santana was a big believer in scouting out the territory where his contract of the moment took him. A ride through Bella Villa with an inspection of the old schoolhouse rendezvous site was in order. His drive through the main street revealed not much of note. The most outstanding building was Casa de los Amigos. It was a large old Florida-style frame house with a porch running completely around it. The yard contained sufficient room to kick a ball around as well as a playground. So this was the homeless shelter where hundreds of his countrymen had spent time. Whole families languished here while attempting to find a place in the land of the free and the rich.

Also on the itinerary was a little petty gambling at the casino. He would drive into Napolis later and have a late afternoon meal in Venetian Village where multimillionaires were stacked in luxury condos like bees in their hives. Santana had a *compadre* who lived in one of these; it was called the Enclave, the tallest building in two counties with a single suite occupying each floor. It was right on the beach, but since the building was oval shaped, every condo contained 360 degrees of view through tinted glass windows seven feet high. There was over seven thousand square feet of living space in every unit. He would like to live in such a place or even one like Señor Babcock, but he would have to do it in Mexico. He was still short of making even his first million, but this contract would put him over the top. He drove past the Foo Foo Club, the King Burger, and a Winn Dixie Grocery store with a strip mall attached. This Bella Villa wasn't much of a town. It reminded him of some of the backwaters of Mexico City, just more spread out.

Santana found the Old County Road soon enough, following Rooster's directions. About two miles down the road, on the right, was the old schoolhouse. He pulled off the road into a driveway that was still reasonably intact where it bridged a deep culvert. Apparently, the county road crews were keeping up on the maintenance. A large apron of overgrown concrete with the weeds mowed to stubs spread out for a hundred feet along the road. It most likely had been a parking lot and assembly area. The schoolhouse itself had four large windows in the front, two of which were covered with plywood. The front door was covered with plywood as well. Brick, with badly eroded joints, formed the walls of the structure. The four-sided hip roof was metal with a bell cupola in the center. Getting out of the Lincoln, Santana noticed a couple of well-worn footpaths from the surrounding woods to the back of the schoolhouse. He touched the nickel-plated Beretta tucked under his belt, the cool metal reassuring him as always. In his black shirt and denims, he appeared a modern-day paladin. He even looked quite a bit like Richard Boone from the old TV series *Have Gun, Will Travel.* The sun beat down on his shirt, causing a bead of sweat to trickle down his back and pool just above his wide leather belt. He heard someone cough inside the building.

It was a loud hacking cough, coming from lungs thick with mucus and most likely enfeebled by decades of abuse from cigarette smoke. Santana approached with caution but with the quickness of a cat, not wanting to be caught out in the open. He moved around to the back of the building where there were two more boarded windows and a door bereft of paint, the wood peeling and mottled. He pushed against the door with his foot, at the same time drawing the pistol from under his belt and flipping off the safety. A 9mm hollow point round was already chambered. A grizzled man sat on the floor near the center of a tenebrous room lit only by what sun penetrated the window glass with years of grime obscuring it. There was an old army cot behind the man, and as Santana looked around, he saw at least four more cots and piles of belongings. There didn't appear to be anyone else present. A couple of kerosene lanterns stood like sentries on old classroom desks. A Coleman stove, accompanied by a few beat-up pots and pans, covered a small wooden library table. Empty liquor and wine bottles were everywhere. *A nest for homeless drunks,* he thought.

Santana kept the *pistola* out but pointed at the floor. Homeless these men may be, but not necessarily harmless. As he approached the man in front of him, he could see the man was naked from the waist down. An old soiled tee shirt with an armadillo on it covered the upper half of his body. An awful stench like sewer gas invaded Santana's nostrils. He tried to breathe solely through his mouth. A pair of jockey shorts besmirched with shit lay at the feet of the bearded, unkempt drunk. The man was shaking as he held out a wobbly hand, palm up, as Santana approached. Dried puke, like frozen puddles, lay on the floor around the wastrel.

Larry watched as the man in black approached. He could feel the monster called "withdrawal" inside him, trying to gnaw its way out like the creature in the movie *Alien.* It thrashed around inside him, sending a spasm to every extremity of his body. He felt like puking, but there was nothing left to puke. Sweat poured off his head in rivers. Where did it all come from? He must be turning into a prune. He thought of Mack and Buddy out trying to get a bottle. They just left a few minutes ago but already it seemed like hours. They would help him. A drink. All he needed was a drink, and all this horror would go away. A drink would put the monster inside him to sleep, quiet the insufferable shaking, and bring his drowning mind back to the surface. He would be like a Buddhist temple again, the liquor burning like the fire of a votive candle, warm and serene. He extended his shaking hand in hopes this stranger would take pity, give him some change, perhaps a dollar or two, to donate to the "medicinal" fund. Larry, once a handsome and athletic young man—a boy who the girls called "cute, a living doll" and teachers called "smart and industrious, a winner"—was filled with self-loathing and despair. A drink. A drink would get him to where he could think again and figure out what to do. Go to the hospital, anything, anything but this infernal shaking. He repeated a silent prayer, *Bring me a drink—just one bottle, and I'll quit, start over.*

The man dressed in black was walking away from him now. Larry watched as the man got to the door, spun around with something shiny in his raised hand, a flash. Larry never heard the thunder that followed the lightning. A 9mm hollow exploded through his skull, scrambling whatever useful gray matter was still functional.

Santana walked out into the sunlight and put the Beretta back under his belt. The barrel was warm against his skin. It felt good, soothing, like a massage. It was good to get warmed up on such human trash in preparation for the big game. He had performed an act of mercy, actually, putting that bum out of misery. He felt pleased with himself. Not only were his shooting skills up to snuff, he was a man of charity. A real *santo*, a true saint.

Santana got back into the Lincoln and wheeled it back onto the Old County Road. He drove without pause back through Bella Villa. He already had enough of this town of tears. He headed straight for Napolis and Venetian Village. He picked up his cell and called his friend living on the seventh floor of the exclusive Enclave on the beach and told him to set out two fatties (of cocaine unspoken) and a bottle of tequila. "I must go down to the sea again, to the sunny sea and the sky." Was that something he read somewhere, perhaps in one of the tourist magazines? Oh well, it suited his mood.

Camilla arrived at the Foo Foo at exactly seven. She wanted to be neither late nor early. With some relief, she noticed Nolan's LeBaron already parked near the front door. It had been a nightmare breaking free of home. She hadn't been out for a year and half since she discovered she was pregnant. She hoped Nolan—she should call him Mike—was hungry. *Yucca*, was what the guys called him, or UCA (undercover agent). She smiled. It was Toad's nomenclature naturally. She had fixed dinner for Robbie and Billy but had no appetite herself. There was a bit of a scene when she announced her plans for the evening. Oddly enough, Robbie didn't even mention any romantic motives she might be harboring but seemed stuck on the concept that Nolan was bent on separating the Fireproof clan for the nefarious purpose of breaking them down one at a time. She stuck to her story (at least partly true) of simply needing a night out, away from the tedium of housekeeping. With a sulky reluctance, slumping into his chair in front of the TV, Robbie acquiesced. Camilla dressed with discretion in a white blouse with embroidered flowers on the frilled collar and pressed jeans.

Walking into the dark interior of the Foo Foo, Camilla's anxiety was eased by the Eric Clapton song, "Running on Faith," playing on the nightclub's sound system. Nolan stood up and waved her over to a booth table at the center of the wall, on the left as you pass through the door. A bottle of Miller stood in front of him, half-full. He wore a flower-print shirt and dungarees.

"I hope you haven't been waiting long," Camilla said, sitting on the padded seat across from him.

"Just a few minutes really," Mike said. "Enough time to have half a beer and read the menu. I'm starved. Haven't had a bite since noon."

"Oh, good!" Camilla exclaimed. "I mean, I didn't get a chance to eat either. What do they have here?"

"Well, other than the usual bar food like nachos, chili, burritos, and burgers, they have a pretty good barbeque chicken or ribs. And the New York sirloin cooked on the grill is pretty tasty—that is, if you like red meat or meat at all." He gave her a sidelong glance and smiled.

"I only eat organic meat like that wild pig John shot," Camilla retorted, a sly grin creasing her lips.

"That sounds 'boar-ing' to me," Nolan deadpanned.

"Ugh!" Camilla squinched up her face. "Just for that, I'll have the New York, medium rare, and you're buying."

"Sounds fair to me." Yucca chuckled. He signaled to the waitress. "Would you like a baked potato with sour cream and butter?" Camilla nodded. "And would the lady like a bottle of the house's finest wine?"

"Oh my," said Camilla, "we are going all out. OK, a nice Merlot would please my palate."

"Your wish is my command." Nolan turned to the waitress and ordered, then resumed his conversation with Camilla. "Now tell me why you came to this here cow town and why you're stickin' 'round these here parts." Nolan doing his John Wayne imitation.

Camilla felt like a schoolgirl again, as if dragonflies were tickling her insides. This handsome man was giving her his undivided attention, and she loved it.

Uninvited, a rush of blood flooded to her groin, accompanied by a tickling wetness between her legs.

The first glass of wine on an almost-empty stomach (the waitress put a basket of rolls on the table) made Camilla giddy and lightheaded. She felt like a teenager again on a first date. She and Mike laughed and joked. They shared some of their life histories over dinner although Mike was circumspect about much of his story. As the Foo Foo began to ramp up it's evening nightclub atmosphere, Mike suggested a cruise in the open convertible before returning to the Fireproof. Camilla ordered a wine cooler.

"Let's stay and dance," Camilla said. She gave him a puppy dog look and winked mischievously. "Afterward we can cruise the night fantastic!" She really did feel like a schoolgirl again. But for a second, she saw Nolan the Cop, not her wonderful date, Mike. It sobered her up almost immediately. The drink arrived, and she sucked it through the straw to the bottom of the glass. Mike, her wonderful date, was back, a big grin on his face.

"I'm sorry, Cammy," he said, "but I have some work I have to do tonight, and think of Robbie and Billy without Mama."

Camilla laughed. "Oh my god! The Fireproof has probably burned to the ground by now." They both chortled at the little joke. The waitress came over, and Nolan paid her, leaving a generous tip. As they walked out the door, Camilla bolted toward the parking lot. "Beat you to the car!" She ran to the convertible and vaulted over the door into the passenger seat. Nolan landed right beside her. They looked at each other, a little out of breath, and they both howled like wolves at the same time. Before Nolan knew what was happening, Camilla had her lips on his and her arms around his neck. His surprise gave way to acquiescence, then pleasure. The tumescence between his legs grew to an uncomfortable size, trapped in his jockey shorts, and his body temperature escalated. Before his little head started calling the shots, he pulled away, gently.

"We better get going," he said. Digging the key out of his pocket, his hand met with an old friend, still hard and pulsing. He inserted the key in the ignition and turned over the engine. They were off.

"Let's drive together back to the Fireproof, I'll catch a ride back tomorrow and pick up my car," Camilla said. The air was balmy and the night full of stars as they took the long way home. Camilla sat with her head back looking at the sky, her luxuriant dark hair blowing in the wind. When they got back to the Fireproof, she gave Mike a demure hug and a kiss on the cheek. She opened the door and slid out.

"Thanks, Mike. I had a great time. I'd like to get together again, honestly. We'll talk tomorrow, OK?"

"Sure," he said. "I'd like that." She turned and went up the steps. He drove back onto the highway and headed toward Bella Villa.

Tiny stood at the front door of Constance Valentine's house, dressed in his gray sheriff's uniform, three stripes on either sleeve. The sun was setting over the gulf, just a block away. This posh Napolis neighborhood was one of the first to be built on the gulf this far south. While Camilla and Mike Nolan were dining, Tiny was mining one of his richest veins of gold. Constance stood in the doorway, glaring at the insolent deputy. Tiny held up a mini cassette player and pushed the Play button with his pinky finger, as the others were too large to actuate the tiny control without engaging the record feature at the same time. A recording of the meeting with the SWF Development Corporation began to play.

"I imagine you would prefer this tape recording be kept out of the purview of the district attorney's office." Tiny smiled and beamed like a helpful friend. "You've already heard a copy of it I made especially for your edification. I don't suppose you would care to invite me in for tea and crumpets?"

"How much?" Constance looked defeated but ready to continue the game.

"I'm not a greedy, man. I just want a decent retirement." Tiny put the cassette player in his shirt pocket. "I want you to wire one hundred thousand dollars by the end of next week into an account at a bank in the Caymans. When the wire transfer is complete, you are to call me immediately. In one month from today, you will wire a like amount to a bank in Bermuda. After that, you will hear from me no more."

"How do I know you won't bleed me dry?"

"We'll have a mutual understanding." Tiny's teeth glinted in the portico's light. "You don't tell on me, I don't tell on you. Like 'hear no evil, see no evil, speak no evil.'" Tiny barked out a kind of laughter, like a hyena.

"Very well, you vulture." Constance put every ounce of scorn she could muster in her voice. "You shall have your money, go away from here now." She began to close the door. Tiny put one giant's foot in it to keep it ajar.

"I shall have my pound of flesh as well," he said, mimicking her voice. He shoved hard on the door, knocking Constance back and bloodying her nose. He moved in like a tiger, giving her a backhand that sent her sprawling on the marble floor. He pounced on her, pinning her with his enormous body. The weight of him drove the breath out of her. She struggled to get air in her lungs, blacking out for a moment. Grabbing her by the hair, he dragged her through the house, out to the pool. When she came to, the animal was already ripping her panties off. She realized the futility of struggle. An elf statue holding a pot of lilies stood with a serene smile, declining to help. A moment later, he was inside her, pumping away. When the depraved deputy finished grunting, he got off her, zipped up his pants, tore the remaining clothes off the county commissioner, and, picking her up, dunked her in the pool. Grabbing her by the hair, he plunged her up and down, up and down, like a washerwoman cleaning clothes in the village sump.

"Can't be leaving DNA around like a calling card," Tiny said. He reached down and put the palm of his hand under her chin, his large meaty fingers squeezing her face. "One more thing, *mum*. You tell your snotty son and his whore to be *mum* if you want to keep your grandson fat and healthy." He shoved her down and away, the unholy baptism complete. When Constance came to the surface and had the courage to open her eyes, El Diablo was gone. Salty tears ran down her face, splashing into the chlorinated water of a pool she would never swim in again.

Julie and Tommy walked along the beach at Wiggins Pass, holding hands and talking. John Vaughn and Josh were throwing a Frisbee behind them. Josh would chase the disc into the surf, laughing and calling to John, "You suck!" The four had driven to Napolis together to spend a couple of hours on the beach and watch the sun set. Now, the sun was a great yolklike orb on the Western horizon, running onto the waters of the gulf. A half dozen pelicans, their goofy beaks seeming too large to make maneuvers with, were diving adroitly into the water for unseen fish. Several dolphins were swimming farther out, coming up out of the water for air, their bodies like gleaming arches reflecting the sunlight. Sandpipers dashed in front of the couple like feathery white leaves blown by the wind. The feet attached to their sticklike legs left tiny three-tined fork impressions in the sand. Julie detached herself for a moment from Tommy and turned to watch John Vaughn and Josh. She reached for his hand again and gave it an affectionate squeeze.

"I can't believe how much Josh has changed since he's been with all of us at the Fireproof," Julie said. "In a few days, he's gone from a zombie to a little boy. It's like some kind of miracle."

"Yeah," Tommy agreed, "it sure is. Sometimes we can actually see God at work in our lives. Just look at that sunset. Nobody paints a better picture than his hand, or her hand if you want to call Mother Nature a part of the great mystery. Sometimes, I feel like one of those dolphins, like a cousin."

"I know what you mean," said Julie. "It could be this is where our distant ancestors crawled from the sea to the land. Maybe the Everglades was the bridge in evolutionary history. It does feel like some kind of magic is here. *Ju Ju stick ba'wanna.*" She giggled.

"God is alive, magic is afoot," Tommy quoted. "Buffy Saint Marie. I always got a little tingle when I heard that song or sang it."

"Me too." Julie stopped walking, bringing Tommy to a halt as well. They watched the great star slip beneath the horizon, shimmering eddies of crimson hues on the gulf, the clouds above being ignited to reds and pinks in the reflected light.

"Tommy, I want to have a baby." There it was. The words came out like ordering a roast beef sandwich. Tommy, the dumbstruck musician, stood staring at the Gulf of Mexico like it was the most mesmerizing Wyland mural ever painted.

"Well?" Julie finally asked. "What do *you* think?"

A human cannonball struck Julie, almost knocking her on her ass.

"Hi, Julie! You didn't see me!" Josh screamed. He laughed in triumph over his prank.

"Hey!" Vaughn yelled. "Josh, that's not nice. You have to be gentle, especially with women." He looked at Tommy and Julie. "Sorry if I interrupted. You guys want to go get something to eat?" Josh ran over and held Vaughn's hand. He looked up with a now-timid face, a child looking to his father for forgiveness and direction. Vaughn rubbed the boy's head gently. "Tell Julie you're sorry."

"I'm sorry, Julie," the boy said. He held Vaughn's hand against his face, peering around it at Julie.

"Hey, that's all right, little guy. You just took me by surprise." She went over to him, kneeled down, and held out her arms. He went into them, hugging her tight.

"How about we all go to the Pizza Hut and pig out?" Tommy asked.

"What's Pizza Hut?" Josh asked, squinching up his face.

"A place that makes bread with cheese and sauce and goodies on top," Vaughn said.

"Pizza!" Julie chimed.

"Let's eat!" Tommy shouted.

"Yippee!" Josh yelled, breaking free of Julie's embrace.

"Sounds like a plan," said Vaughn.

"What're we waiting for?" asked Julie. "Last one to the car is a rotten fish!" She sped off across the beach with two men and a boy in hot pursuit. One of the men was thinking he just had a close call. Maybe he wouldn't be so lucky next time.

22

"What the fuck you mean he's gone?" Tiny stood by the counter inside Crayton's Market. He glared at Bud Crayton, his right hand resting on the butt of his holstered gun, his left thumb hooked under his sheriff's utility belt. A Closed sign was in the window; the store was lit only by a Budweiser sign on the beer cooler and the lights behind the glass doors of the oversized refrigerator. After his satisfying encounter with Constance Valentine and a follow-up with Mona, he came to the store after a phone call from Bud whining about the need for an "emergency meeting."

"Gone, tree, fur dyes neow." Bud spit a large gob of Skoal Mint phlegm into a Folgers Coffee can serving as a spittoon. "Jest up an' vanished."

Tiny looked at the idiot behind the counter, barely able to restrain himself from punching him in the face. "Why in hell didn't you call me sooner? Have you told *anybody* else about this yet?"

"Nope." Bud looked at the jar of Tootsie Roll Pops on the counter like a sullen student being reprimanded by his stern instructor. "Figgered he'd be byack by an' by. Ain't no plyace fer him t'go tah."

"Guess you 'figgered' wrong, huh?" Tiny could barely conceal the anxiety he was feeling behind the posture of anger. "If that sorry bag of bones shows up, living or dead, you're going to be in some hot water that I might not be able to cool down for any money. And I'll tell you something, if you try to drag my name into this mess, you'll end up the same place as your two other pups."

"Reckon he's already dyead and eatin' by one varmit or t'other." Bud spit another gob of chew into the tin spittoon.

"If I find him alive, I'll make sure he disappears forever," Tiny said. Picking out an orange Tootsie Roll Pop, his favorite, he unwrapped it and started for the door. "And I suggest you do the same," he called over his shoulder. He stuck the lollipop in his mouth and left.

Mike Nolan drove back to the Foo Foo after leaving Camilla at the Fireproof. He had a date with Luis Alvarez, which was the motivating force, more than altruism, in getting Camilla out of there. When he walked in, the cover band was playing a version of the Talking Head's "Psycho Killer." He walked to the farthest booth in the left corner of the restaurant lounge. Alvarez was there already. Had he been there while he was with Camilla? Nolan didn't think so but couldn't be sure. Alvarez was a small thin man with oily hair and a mustache. His dark skin was stretched tight over his bones as if it stopped growing before his skeleton finished enlarging. He chain-smoked Camel filters. He reminded Nolan of a ferret for some reason, a ferret wearing a Sears cream-colored sports coat and button-down shirt, open at the collar.

"*Que pasa?* What's happening, amigo?" Alvarez said, holding out a diminutive hand. His English was tinged with only a faint accent. "Can I get you a drink?" Alvarez was drinking a Corona with a lime. He lit a cigarette.

"Same as you," replied Nolan. Alvarez waived at a waitress, pointed to his bottle, and held up two fingers. "So tell me what you found out about this Mario guy Harris is in bed with."

"I'd hardly call it something that intimate." Alvarez smirked. "Fact is, it's a relationship of financial gain for Tiny and an unwelcome partnership for Mario. As you recall, there was a shooting just before you arrived here at what was allegedly a drug dealer's house."

"Wasn't that the one where a black dude from Hartford was shot when he pulled a piece on Harris?" Nolan asked as he reached for his wallet. The waitress arrived and placed the beers on the table. Nolan gave her a ten. "Keep the change, honey."

"Thank you!" The pretty young girl beamed a bright smile and headed back to the bar with a wiggle in her walk. Nolan watched her retreat for a moment before turning his attention back to the snitch.

"Gracias," said Alvarez, holding up the beer. "Life is difficult for so many these days, including Chicano reporters. The old cliché rings truer every day, 'The rich get richer, the poor get poorer.' And there is one who is becoming rich on the blood and souls of his victims, and that is Tiny. He is a dangerous and unpredictable devil. Indeed, meeting you here is a grave risk for me."

"A contribution for your favorite charity," Nolan said to Alvarez, sliding three folded C-notes across the table. "How is Tiny tied into the drug business? Bribery? Or is he holding this Mario by the short hairs and extorting money from him? Maybe he's ripping off product and selling it through this guy?"

"All of the above," replied Alvarez. "Mario is someone Tiny practically owns outright. He bailed him out after that shooting. They pinned everything on the guy that was killed. Mario was let off the hook. But Judge Thomas put Mario on probation with Tiny as his keeper. Mario has been pretty much working for him since."

Nolan drank from the longneck bottle. He wondered if it was possible Thomas was involved with Tiny in some way. He shuddered. Leaning over the table, he beckoned Alvarez to do likewise, their faces inches apart. The music drowned out most conversation, but Nolan didn't want to take any chances. "Do you think there was any conspiracy between Tiny and Mario in the shooting of Deputy O'Brien?"

"Absolutely," Alvarez replied. "There were also two Mexicanos involved. Here's the thing though, nobody knew what was going to happen except Tiny. From what I understand, the three thought they were being used to draw this policeman away from his duties for an unspecified reason. They are terrified of El Diablo and unable to speak up because he's holding their lives in his hands. The Mexicanos are especially susceptible because they have families and are here illegally. And who's going to believe drug dealers over a veteran cop?"

"And these Mexicans, who are they?" Nolan took a cigarette from the pack on the table and lit up.

"Ah, sources are sacred," Alvarez replied.

"I have a pretty good idea who they might be anyway. What do you think is going to happen next?" Nolan asked.

"I think there is something going on with Rooster Babcock at the Red Rooster Ranch." Alvarez looked around the room like he was making sure he wasn't being followed. "Everybody knows they have cockfights there. And dogfights too. Lots of money changing hands. Somehow, Captain Post and Tiny are trying to shake down the operation like they do every other gambling ring in the county."

"Are you tellin' me Post is involved in all this too?" Nolan felt the icy hand of fear touch his guts. This may be too big for a single agent. He suddenly felt his own life was in immediate jeopardy. Camilla and the Fireproof fellowship were also in the line of fire. And they were virtually defenseless against a brute like Harris.

"I am certain of it." Alvarez lit a cigarette and inhaled deeply. "Post has been running a large ring of gambling places for well over a decade, and Tiny has his hands in that pie, as well as drugs and everything else. He's been up to petty extortion for close to twenty years now ever since he came to the department. He'll be up for early retirement in the spring next year—March, I think. So he has only ten months to go. Then *poof!* Gone—the captain as well. Post already has twenty-five years. They move to California or the Caymans or Costa Rica if there's too much heat, probably as millionaires. They'll also receive their pensions unless there is incontrovertible evidence of criminal wrongdoing. And look at the people they're dealing with: drug dealers, illegal gamblers, pimps, prostitutes, adulterers, juvenile delinquents, thieves, and drunks. What jury in one of the most conservative counties in the United States would be likely to convict? What prosecutor, given the likelihood of malfeasance in that department as well, would be crazy enough to press charges against decorated veteran police officers?"

Nolan finished his beer, looked at the snitch, who had put on glasses to review documents produced from inside his cheap sport coat, and decided the ferret had shape-shifted into an owl, at least for the moment.

"Yeah," Nolan said, "you're probably right on."

"Here is something else," Alvarez said, pushing the papers toward Nolan. "Our beloved top gun, Sheriff Gunther, has been called on twice to do an internal investigation of first Harris and then Harris *and* Post. In the first case, an informer supplied information and agreed to testify before a grand jury. The witness, never identified to the public, was, according to what I found out, a fellow deputy sergeant on the force. That deputy died in what was called an automobile accident. It was a single car crash on a desolate stretch of State Road 29. Gunther, who occasionally plays golf with the governor, by the way, quietly shut down the investigation, and all pertinent paperwork was shredded or deleted from computer files. In the second investigation, two deputies filed complaints against Harris and Post for pulling them off drug-smuggling details just before they made a major bust. Both officers were discredited by Gunther and dismissed from the force. But not before their wives and children were harassed and intimidated. They were promised good recommendations if they kept their respective mouths shut."

"This is much worse than I anticipated," said Nolan. "There's trouble in paradise all right, and I have a feeling this Lone Ranger might have to ride alone to save the day. Here"—Nolan passed another bill across the table—"buy yourself some good scotch. I've got to go. I'm getting a case of claustrophobia in here."

"One more thing," Alvarez said as Nolan started to slide from the booth. He rested his arms on the table and leaned toward Nolan to make himself heard above the music without shouting. "There may be a grand jury investigating the shooting of O'Brien, and Tiny's name has been brought up again. I think, maybe, Judge Thomas is trying to snuff things this time. Just rumor there, though I'm looking into it."

My god! Where does it end! Nolan thought.

"Thanks, Luis," Nolan said. "I gotta go. Be careful." He had to get out, get some fresh air, clear his head, and assemble a battle plan.

Tiny left Crayton's store and headed for the Foo Foo. *I'm gonna have to hit up that fag Raeford for more cash due to unexpected expenses,* thought Tiny. He parked his police cruiser in the yellow lines in front of the Foo Foo and surveyed the parking lot before he started in. Noticing Nolan's LeBaron, Tiny experienced a flash of anxiety. He went in the doorway and stood shrouded by the gloomy lighting and pressing patrons, trying to be as inconspicuous as possible for a man his size, in uniform, no less. The music was loud and strange. Tiny couldn't identify what kind of sound it was exactly, a kind of calypso disco. On stage, a local band called The Swamp Monkeys did their best to imitate the Talking Heads.

"This ain't no party, this ain't no disco, this ain't no foolin' around," sang the lead, a young guy wearing an oversized suit with a tie. Tiny tried to focus on finding Nolan without being seen. More lyrics swam into his ears. "We got computers, we're tappin' phone lines, know that ain't allowed. We dress like students, we dress like housewives, oh, a suit and a tie. Changed my hair style, so many times now, I don't know what I look like."

Tiny spotted Alvarez first as he was facing the front of the club. It dawned on him it must be Nolan whom Alvarez was talking to. *That fuckin' little spic weasel reporter is hooked up with Nolan,* he thought. *He's probably spilling his stinkin' guts right now. Can things get any worse? This shit has got to end—now.* Tiny slipped out the door, slid into his cruiser, and sat thinking a moment. He picked up a cell phone registered to a phony name and address he kept on hand for just such an emergency. After using it tonight, he would toss it.

"Hello, Mario, my man," Tiny began. "Listen carefully, I want you to go get Carlos and Omar and 'borrow' the Ford 550 truck parked at Gadillo's Farm. The wetbacks will know exactly what I mean. Call me back as soon as you're headin' south. My number's on your caller ID." He hung up before Mario could say anything.

Tiny drove his car around back, radioed the dispatcher he was going for a break, and waited. He could see most of the parking lot from where he parked, cloaked from the lights and view in a shadowy spot under the sprawling canopy of an enormous oak tree. Nolan emerged first from the lounge. Hopping in his convertible, he took off. Returning to his fleabag motel, Tiny guessed, from the direction he headed. Five minutes later, the sedulous reporter came forth from the den of iniquity and lit a cigarette. Tiny watched him get in a Ford Escort and head for his weasel's burrow. The conscientious deputy sheriff, mindful of his duty to protect the motoring public from alcoholically impaired drivers, followed the Escort for a mile until they were on the street where Alvarez lived. Deputy Harris turned on his blue lights and pulled him over.

Robbie was sulking in the recliner, the baby asleep in his crib, when Camilla came in after her short evening out with Nolan. "So did you spill your guts after a couple of drinks?" he asked. Camilla burst out laughing. It was so ridiculous. She wished Robbie could see the humor in it.

"What's so damn funny?"

"You," Camilla said. "What d'ya think this is, a James Bond movie?" The effects of the booze were wearing off fast now. She needed a nightcap. She went to the fridge and got a Budweiser, the only alcoholic beverage available.

"I'll tell you what I think this is," Robbie said. "It's bullshit. I don't like it." Camilla thought she heard a hint of jealousy in his tone.

"Robbie, are you jealous because I went out with another man for dinner and a couple of drinks?"

"Fuck no!"

"What's all this shit about then?" Camilla asked. "If I went out with Julie or Tommy you wouldn't mind, would you?"

"That's not the point," Robbie countered. "They're trusted friends, and this guy is a *narc* for Chris's sakes. And let's face it, he ain't that hard to look at."

"Oh, sweetums, you *are* jealous! Listen," Camilla said, "you haven't a thing to worry about. Besides, ain't a man alive cuter than you, except maybe Billy, and he hasn't had a chance to strut his stuff yet."

She put her half-full bottle of beer on the table and walked over to Robbie and slid easily onto his lap. Her feminine charm was in high gear. "Wait 'til our little boy gets to be a teenager, he may outshine the old man with the ladies." She gave him a beery kiss. Her left hand went under his shirt; her right hand caressed his neck and wandered through his hair as she kissed him again. His icy demeanor was melting fast in the erotic heat generated by her body. Something pushed against her bottom. The sleeping dragon between his legs was coming alive, seeking warm wet places. Now, all resistance and reason would evaporate in the coming passion. "Nobody could replace my Robbie." Her tongue went French, and a minute later, she was on her knees in front of him, bobbing for apples at their own private party.

Constance dragged herself out of the pool and walked naked back to her room. A brief sense of betrayal washed over her as she passed the smiling—or was he smirking—elf statue. She averted her eyes from the sculpture and trudged, dazed and bewildered, to her bedroom. The room was done in lavender with an ornate canopied king-sized bed. Simple watercolors of wading birds done in off-whites, dark hues, and pinks adorned the walls. There was a single tropical wood bureau with a mirror. A large walk-in closet and dressing room eliminated the need to clutter the master bedroom. Opening her nightstand drawer, she removed her late husband's .38 revolver. Its gleaming black metal looked oddly comforting. It seemed enormously heavy. The round six-chamber cylinder was loaded with the thick stubby bullets characteristic of the potent caliber. She was dimly aware of admonitions against keeping a loaded gun in an accessible place. Her husband, she remembered, kept the bullets stashed separately as a safety precaution. He could have the gun loaded in a matter of seconds, he claimed. Suddenly, she missed him as she sat naked on the edge of her bed, dripping chlorinated water, his gun in her hands, alone when she needed someone most. She was a lying, cheating, corrupt, and evil woman. Her own dear son and grandson were in imminent danger, and she could do nothing to help. She thought of Pablo and the others before him. She felt like a worthless tramp.

Constance laid the gun on the bedspread where a dark wet stain was spreading and removed a prescription bottle of Valium from another drawer and opened it.

Picking up the gun, she stood up and left the room. Still nude and in shock, she made straight for the wet bar in her office. Laying the gun down again, its weight like an anchor to her tumultuous mind, she poured a tumbler full of Dewer's. She tipped up the dark prescription container and poured all of the remaining caplets, about twenty ten-milligram doses, into her mouth. She lifted the glass and drained the scotch, only pausing once to catch her breath.

Constance shambled back toward the pool, toting the .38. When she reached the elfin flower holder, she pulled back the hammer on the pistol and the cylinder rotated, making a clicking noise as it locked into place. Holding the gun in both hands, she aimed at the head of the ungrateful and brazen imp. She remembered to *squeeze* the trigger. The statue's head blew apart in a shower of plaster as the report from the center-fire round echoed through the house. A cloud of sulfuric gun smoke drifted out over the pool. The recoil had nearly torn the gun from Constance's grip. She dropped anchor where she stood, sinking to the floor, as the booze and pills overtook her senses.

Robbie and Camilla were sleeping, snuggled in each other's arms, when the phone rang. They both groaned, and Camilla rolled over to grab it before the baby woke up.

"That better not be another one of your boyfriends," Robbie joked. But Camilla's face went as white as fine ash a moment after putting the phone to her ear.

"Oh my god!" Camilla threw off the covers and sat up, her legs over the edge of the bed. "Thanks, Pablo, we'll be right there."

"What? What is it, Cammy?" Robbie was scared now.

"It's your mother. She's at the hospital in a coma."

"What happened? Who called?"

"It was Pablo. All he said was 'drug overdose.' He hung up before I could ask any questions."

"I'll go," Robbie said. "You stay here with Billy."

"But I want to come with you." Camilla looked at Billy and back to Robbie. "Maybe I could get Julie to come over."

"No, don't get them up. It's late, almost two in the morning."

"They're used to being up late," Camilla said.

"Still, I don't want to bother them." Robbie was pulling on his dungaree shorts and looking for his shirt. "We don't even know what's going on. I'll call you from the hospital. Everything will look different in the morning." He opened a drawer and took out a clean shirt. The logo Quicksilver was embossed on the left breast and in larger letters on the back. He started out the door.

"Oh! I left the VW at the Foo Foo, Robbie," Cammy said. "You'll have to use the Buick." Robbie shook his head and sighed. "I love you," Cammy said.

"Love you too." Robbie pulled her to him and kissed her on the lips, turned, and bounded to the car.

Camilla went back and sat on the bed. She got up after a minute and took another bottle of Bud from the fridge and poured a glass full. After taking a sip, Camilla lit an incense stick to drive away evil spirits and a votive candle to mark a vigil. She went back to the bed, sitting with her back against the headboard, glass of beer on the nightstand, and said a prayer.

23

Luis Alvarez cursed and pulled his Escort to the curb. His annoyance at being pulled over so close to home for no apparent reason gave way to gut-wrenching fear as he peered into his side mirror and recognized the hulk in uniform walking toward his car. By the time Tiny reached his driver side window, sweat clung like morning dew to his temples and the small of his back. His hands trembled as he fumbled for his license. He needed to urinate, and his stomach threatened to spew what was left of dinner and the booze on the deputy's shoes.

"Hey now!" Tiny said. "If it isn't my little buddy from the spic press. How are you tonight, Señor Alvarez? Have you had anything to drink tonight?"

"Tiny—I mean Officer Harris, I'm fine, really. Yes, I think I had, maybe, three drinks with dinner. But over a couple of hours."

"Oh, I believe you, Luis. Let me have your license please. Keep the registration. I know this is your car."

Luis willed his hand to remain steady as he extracted the license from his wallet and handed it to Tiny. "As you can see from the unflattering photo, it's me." Luis smiled weakly with his attempt at levity. The light from a street lamp glinted off Tiny's teeth as a brief Cheshire cat smile flashed, disappearing on moth wings into the humid night.

"Why don't you come with me a moment," Tiny said, "and sit on the front seat of my car. I will be able to make an appraisal of your condition and whether I need to administer a sobriety test." Tiny walked back toward his police cruiser.

The thought of escaping to his house and locking himself in, calling his editor, his mother, anyone but the cops, flitted like a bat across Luis's mind. Reluctantly, he got out of his car and followed Tiny back to the Crown Victoria, which sat purring like a large jungle cat. As he entered that inner sanctum of officialdom, crowded with instrumentation and the tools of law enforcement—large flashlight, shotgun locked to the dash, spare handcuffs, laptop, radar, radio, and summons books—Luis could smell the fear of those who had ridden in the cage behind him. He felt a cryptlike claustrophobia overwhelming his senses. It was difficult to swallow. Speech seemed impossible. He heard Tiny speaking from far away through dense fog. "Luis, take out your cell phone. I have a call I want you to make. Afterward, we're going for a little ride. I'm going to give you an exclusive. Only problem is, you're not going to be able to report any of it."

"Wh-whaddaya mean?" The words came out as if Luis was half-choking on them.

"Allow me to be candid with you," Tiny replied. "You're going to call somebody and say exactly what I want you to. Then we're going to hang for a while, dude." Another Cheshire grin was accented with a maniacal gleam in his icy blue eyes. "Maybe, you'll call him more than once. If you're a good Boy Scout, you get to live. Otherwise . . ." Tiny shrugged his massive shoulders and held his baseball-glove-sized hands out, palms up.

"Who am I calling?" Alvarez squeaked, hoping it was one of his many Hispanic contacts Tiny wanted to use for his own avarice.

"Your buddy, Nolan," Tiny said. He put the tip of his middle finger against the tip of his thumb like making an OK hand signal, reached over while making a buzzing sound, and released the digits, flicking the frightened reporter on the left cheek.

"Sting!" Tiny said and laughed. A red splotch welled up where all color had previously drained at the mention of Nolan's name. Luis Alvarez knew his life hung in the balance, and the odds were stacked against him.

Mike Nolan drove back to the Fireproof, trying to enjoy the fragrant Florida night in the convertible despite Alvarez's troubling news. He pulled up in front of his room and turned off the engine. He looked over at 105. The Valentines' lights were out. He sighed and shrugged his shoulders. *Focus on reality, fool,* he thought. *First, she's married with a baby. Second, your line of work doesn't include a place for legitimate romance. Third, she's not your type. She's practically a hippie for Chris's sakes!* Nolan went into the room and secured a Romeo y Julieta from his cigar stash. It was a genuine Cuban. One of the few luxuries he allowed himself. He went out and settled down on his plastic chair, clipped the end, and lit it. He looked up at the starry night. It seemed both beautiful and indifferent to his predicament. A gibbous moon shone a baleful light in the clear sky. The mosquitoes seemed to be on holiday tonight. In any case, the cigar was producing enough fragrant smoke to keep anything but the most determined pest at bay. He was almost done with the cigar when his cell phone rang.

"Señor Nolan, this is Luis Alvarez."

"What's up, Luis? Something you forgot to tell me?"

"Yes. I mean no. This is something else, Mr. Nolan. I just got confirmation from a reliable source that a major drug shipment is coming ashore on Chokoloskee Island this very evening. As you know, that is in the parameters of the Baron County Sheriff's Department. And guess who is on patrol down there right now?"

"Harris," Nolan said.

"You got it—our friend, Tiny. And he sure as hell is not going to be there to bust them. My source says he is directly involved in the smuggling and distribution of the product, which happens to be cocaine. I understand there is also some marijuana."

"When is this supposed to go down?" Nolan was out of his chair.

"The operation is scheduled for 3:00 a.m. You may be able to catch the fox in the henhouse if you head there now. But don't call any other law enforcement, or Tiny will be alerted."

"You expect me to make a bust in unfamiliar territory, where there's an unknown number of suspects without backup?" Nolan was already heading for his car.

"I'm leaving myself right now," Alvarez said. "I have a couple of friends in the sheriff's department, deputies we can trust. I'll call them from my car and apprise them of the situation. There is no love lost between them and Tiny. I think we can count on their help. I will call you in thirty minutes with more details. Are you going?"

"I'm on my way," Nolan said. He checked his 9mm and ankle pistol. He went to the trunk of the LeBaron and pulled out a twelve-gauge shotgun and placed it across his backseat. He pulled out on Route 29 and headed south for Everglades City and Chokoloskee. The road stretched before him, smooth as flight, black macadam into blacker night.

Camilla needed to talk to somebody. She didn't want to leave the room for fear of missing a call from Robbie. Of course, there was Billy to think about as always. She sat in torment sipping her beer. After ten minutes of silence, she picked up the phone and called Julie. After a brief explanation, Julie agreed to come over. Fifteen minutes later, she tapped on the door, a bottle of Chardonnay in tow.

"Julie, I'm so glad you could make it." Camilla embraced the other woman, holding her tight a moment. "I was feeling so scared and lonely." She noticed the wine bottle. "Oh, thank God, another drink of beer and I'd look and feel like a bullfrog's throat. Let me get some glasses, and I'll fill you in on this crazy night." The two women talked for over an hour.

"I think you should call the police," Julie finally said. "I think you, and maybe all of us, are in over our heads here."

"But what police do I call?" Cammy asked, visibly distressed. "What if they send that big goon over that was here before? And what exactly would I tell them?"

"I don't know." Julie looked perplexed as well. "Maybe we should wait until morning. Our heads will be clearer, and we'll know more." She split the remainder of the wine between the two glasses.

The phone rang. Both of the women's faces went white at the sound, their hearts beating despite the depressive effect of the wine. Billy stirred in his crib and started to cry. Camilla picked up the phone.

"Oh, Robbie, thank heaven. What's going on?" Camilla listened, nodding her head for five minutes. "I love you," she said and hung up.

"What's up?" Julie asked. "How's his mother?"

"His mother is in the intensive care unit. But they think she's going to make it. Robbie's going to stay all night but said I should wait and come in the morning. He asked me to see if you'd give me and Billy a ride."

"Of course I will," said Julie.

"There's something else," Camilla went on. "The police say she was raped. A gun is missing, and they're looking for Pablo. He brought her to the hospital but split right away."

"Oh, dear God," Julie said.

"I don't believe for a minute Pablo has anything to do with this," Camilla said. "And the police were asking Robbie all kinds of questions about who Pablo is and what he does for his mother and making insinuations and snide remarks. Can you believe it?"

"If that big ape that came here is any example," Julie replied, "then, yes, I believe it."

"Robbie's going to talk to his mother's lawyer tomorrow," Cammy said.

"First good idea I've heard in a while," Julie said. "I think maybe we all should talk to him." She gave Cammy a hug. "I gotta hit the sack. Call or just come over in the a.m. when you're ready."

"Sure thing. Thanks, Julie." Camilla closed the door behind her friend and headed toward the bathroom. The phone rang.

"Hello," Camilla said.

"Cammy, it's Mike. I'm in trouble, I need your help."

"Mike, what is it?" Camilla asked. "Where are you?"

"I'm in my car, on—" There was a loud screeching sound followed by silence.

"Mike, hello, Mike. Mike, can you hear me?" She heard a screeching of brakes and a loud crashing noise. A moment later, there were what sounded like gunshots, followed by someone yelling. There were more gunshots, a long silence, and finally, a voice on the phone. It wasn't Mike Nolan. Fear, like an autumn frost, settled over her skin, chilling her to the bone.

Mike Nolan crossed the bridge to Chokoloskee Island with no idea where he was going. Two calls to Alvarez went to the reporter's voice mail. If he didn't hear from Alvarez in the next five minutes, he'd have to abort. Still, he may as well take a look around now that he was here, not that he could see much. It was like a ride back into the fifties; there was very little in the way of street lamps and no other sign of gentrification. Looked pretty much like a fishing village of blockhouses and frame homes on stilts. He'd have to check the place in daylight. Right now, he was feeling particularly vulnerable. His cell rang. He hit the Talk button. "Yeah, this is Nolan."

"Señor Nolan, it is Luis Alvarez."

"What's the deal, Alvarez? I've been trying to touch bases for the past hour."

"There is no deal. That is the problem."

"What the hell are you saying—you sent me on a wild goose chase?"

"No, well, I guess so." Alvarez sounded odd, hesitant, almost like he was being coached. Nolan was already nervous; he didn't like this. "I mean the operation was postponed for a day. I just found out. That's why I haven't been answering. I've been on my landline."

"Balls on a heifer!" Nolan said, falling back on an old expression his dad used. "Now what?"

"Go back to your motel, get some sleep," Alvarez advised. "I'll call you in the afternoon and apprise you of the situation. I should be able to bring you up to date on who will be involved and who our friends are. It might have worked out for the best. This way we can put together an actual plan."

"Roger that. I'm out of here." Nolan swung the LeBaron around and headed for the bridge. A sense of foreboding, of something being askew, came over him. It was the feeling the hero in Westerns always gets right before an ambush.

Mario picked up Carlos and Omar at their trailer and made sure they had charged cell phones with them. He brought them to the road leading to Gadillo's Farm. On the way, in simple English, he explained where they were to go and meet Tiny, the deputy they called El Diablo. They protested, begging for him to go with them. They were terrified. "Two's a company, three's a crowd," Mario said.

"Why you say dat?" Carlos asked. "Dere much room for tree in beeg truck. Omar sit in meedle. You, 'shotgun,' okay?" He pulled a pint of tequila from somewhere under his shirt and opened the bottle.

"Wait," said Mario. "No drinking until later. No *borracho*. You must be sober. It will be *muy peligroso*, very dangerous, otherwise. Go now." They got out of the car looking crestfallen.

"We call you later," Carlos said.

"You can't call me, my cell battery is dead, and I won't be home tonight," Mario lied. "*Buena suerte*, good luck." Mario headed back to his house where there was a fifth of Myers's Rum with his name on it.

Tiny parked his patrol car at the intersection of U.S. 41 and State Road 29. There was an abandoned filling station on the south side of 41 that afforded a perfect stakeout location. If all went according to plan, Nolan would cross the intersection and head north back to Bella Villa. If he chose to head northwest to Napolis or southeast to Miami, Tiny figured he'd just have to improvise a new plan. Maybe sacrifice his *bien amigo*, Luis Alvarez, who was sitting in the front seat, sweating despite the air conditioning in the Crown Victoria.

"Out of the car, Luis." Tiny said as he opened his door and started around the front of the car. Alvarez sat frozen, his insides knotting up, leg muscles turning to Jell-O. Tiny opened the passenger door, reached over, undid the seat belt, and wrapped a huge hand around the diminutive reporter's right bicep. The deputy's middle finger easily touched his thumb as he tightened his grip and yanked Alvarez out of the cruiser. Tiny was forced to hold up the much-smaller man as Alvarez seemed unable to make his legs work. "Fuck it," Tiny said, slamming his captive's head against the roof over the door as he wrestled him into the caged rear seat and closed the door.

"Any problems you might cause, duckweed, are now minimized," Tiny said to the dazed and terrified newsman.

Nolan drove across the intersection of U.S. 41 and Route 29 heading north to Bella Villa. He felt tired, drained by the rush of adrenaline that comes from getting pumped up only to be let down with no action. It's like the chemicals are still floating in the bloodstream, turning toxic after not being burned up. His muscles were stiff and spasmodic, and his head throbbed. He felt hungover. He wanted to get back to his room and get horizontal on his bed. The road back ran through a wetland wilderness, straight and flat, where nocturnal creatures posed the sole traffic hazard. With his vehicle the only one on the road, he accelerated to ninety miles per hour. As he approached Copeland, one of three stage stops on the way back, he noticed the dim twinkle, like a star, of headlights in his rearview mirror. The car would be several miles away. The lights seemed to be growing brighter at an alarming rate, however. He looked at his speedometer—eighty-eight. The car behind must be doing over a hundred to be catching up to him. He pushed down on the pedal—ninety-five. A minute later and the lights behind were still gaining. In fact, they were coming up fast. That put the pursuing vehicle at a 120 or 30 miles per hour. More adrenaline began to pump into his beleaguered system as he realized what that probably meant, barring someone joyriding in a Porsche or Corvette. About a minute later, as he slowed to eighty-five, his suspicions were confirmed just as he passed through Jerome. Blue flashers accompanied by strobe headlights came on behind him.

Sitting disgruntled and morose in the two-ton flatbed Old Chevy they had heisted from Gadillo's Farm, Carlos and Omar passed a joint and inhaled deeply, coughing and wheezing from the pungent smoke. Carlos, ignoring Mario's instructions, took out the bottle of tequila and tipped it up for a hit. He passed the bottle to Omar, who had some as well. They had driven as instructed, south on Route 29, with no idea what they were doing until they were pulled over by El Diablo. He instructed them to go a mile up the road and turn *izquierda*. "*Is kay hair da* left," he said. They got a laugh out of his stupid gringo pronunciation—after they were out of his earshot, out of his sight, for that matter. Carlos backed into the road and turned off his lights as instructed. When the big policeman called, he was to drive the truck across the road. He did not like doing this thing. He was afraid, as was Omar. In Mexico, this is the way the banditos stopped cars at night to rob and rape travelers, mostly *turistas*.

The lights filled Nolan's mirrors, the patrol car's headlights now only a few feet from his rear bumper. Still, he kept the accelerator down, humming along at eighty now. There was no question who the maniac driving the cruiser behind him was. No way was he going to stop. If he could make Bella Villa, he would call 911 for help and let the chips fall where they may. He had a sudden inspiration. If he could get Camilla to call for help, report a break in, a robbery in progress, there would be cops at the Fireproof when he got there. Let them sort things out when he showed his badge and told his story. If nothing else, it would postpone a showdown where there were no witnesses on unfamiliar turf.

The Crown Victoria's reinforced front bumper struck his rear bumper. The much-lighter LeBaron shuttered but held the road. Nolan sped up. The lunatic was trying to push him off the road. The flashing juggernaut came up on him again, ramming his bumper. Nolan could barely control his old convertible or see the road ahead with the intense light behind blinding his night vision. He had installed Camilla's number on his phone. He removed his 9mm and placed it on the passenger seat. He picked up the phone and managed to push the star and two digits to dial Camilla. The car behind kissed his rear bumper. He swerved, losing speed but shaking the unwelcome impact. Camilla answered as the lights behind dropped back.

"Cammy, it's Mike. I'm in trouble, I need your help."

"Mike, what is it? Where are you?"

"I'm in my car, on—" A large truck pulled out directly ahead of him across the road. He dropped the phone and slammed on his brakes. Realizing he wasn't going to stop in time, he tried to swerve around it. He almost made it, but the corner of his rear bumper caught the front bumper of the truck, sending his car flipping end over end like a gymnast doing cartwheels. The LeBaron tumbled down the bank like a carnival ride let lose from its moorings, landing upside down in the brackish water of the canal on the west side of the road. Nolan's seat belt held him in the car, but everything else—phone, handgun, shotgun, and a Trendy's bag containing empty chili containers—was thrown out of the disintegrating LeBaron convertible.

Tiny pulled his cruiser up near the truck and parked it with headlights pointing at the canal, near where Nolan's slut buggy went in. Donning disposable latex gloves, he opened the rear door, dragging a groggy Alvarez out, the reporter's forehead oozing blood from a nasty gash. Tiny told him to man the cruiser's spotlight. Grabbing a flashlight, he went hastily toward the canal where he spotted the undercover cop's handgun halfway down the slope. Picking up Nolan's Beretta, he snapped back the slide, injecting a round into the chamber of the pistol. He commenced firing at the sinking car. After emptying the clip, he tossed the gun into the water. He removed his own handgun and fired a clip at what he perceived was movement on the other side. There was no way of knowing whether the badge-bearing scumbag would surface dead or alive. In either case, assuming sufficient damage, the scavengers would make short work of him. He imagined more than a couple of gators would tear him apart, fighting over a meal. What they left behind, buzzards would clean up. If, however, he somehow escaped relatively uninjured, wounds of another nature need be inflicted. Tiny scurried to the edge to get a better look at the bubbling water where the car went in.

"Raise the spotlight and point it toward the water!" he yelled back to Alvarez. "Then pan it around." After a couple of minutes passed, Tiny almost stumbled over Nolan's shotgun. He picked it up and pumped a round into the chamber. Looking up, he saw movement. "Alvarez! Over this way! Hurry!"

"That's him! I see him!" Tiny yelled. The spotlight reflected red in Nolan's eyes like a snapshot photo. Tiny let loose with the shotgun. A flash and the report of a firearm came from the other side. Nolan was armed. There was only the one shot. Tiny returned fire in the direction of the powder flash. The two law officers were about fifty yards apart. Tiny gauged the snub nose ankle pistol Nolan was wielding would hardly be accurate, whereas the distance allowed the buckshot enough spread to assure a hit while remaining lethal. "Move the light up, he's running." Tiny pumped and fired several more rounds at the fleeing figure, emptying the twelve gauge's magazine. In the murky light, Nolan appeared to go down. "I think I hit him. Alvarez, where's my light?" Tiny turned in annoyance to see Alvarez slumped by the car. "What the fuck?" He walked to the pathetic figure hunched down by the car, his back against the front tire. Alvarez sat with a blank stare, both hands over his guts, blood flowing between his fingers. Nolan's wild shot must have struck the journalist. Alvarez's mouth opened and closed like a fish out of water. He looked up at the towering deputy and saw no look of pity or comfort.

"H-help me," Alvarez gargled.

"Sure," Tiny said. He pointed the shotgun at the critically wounded informant and blew his head off. Blood, bone, and brains splattered the fender and tire of the Crown Victoria. "That's a mess I don't look forward to cleaning up, Edward fucking R. Morrow Alvarez."

Tiny tried to put the spotlight back on Nolan, but he was gone. He decided to make the two wetbacks go across the canal to look for him. But on his way over to the truck, he spotted headlights coming from the north, still a good ways away. He stooped to pick up a blinking device a short distance from the truck. It was a cell phone, still connected. He read the name and number illuminated on the screen: Camilla and Robert Valentine.

"Hello, slut," Tiny said. The disconnect icon lit up. He smiled, pocketing the phone as he sprinted the last few yards to the truck. "Move over," he barked at Carlos. Tiny climbed behind the wheel and parked the truck on the east side of the road. Racing back to his cruiser, he pulled up behind the truck with his blues and reds flashing. A minute later, a late-model pickup pulling a center console powerboat passed. It was just a couple of fishermen looking to get in the water at Everglades City before first light.

"Take the truck back," Tiny said to Carlos. "I'll call Mario and tell him to pick you up."

"He no answer," Carlos said.

"He'll answer if he knows what's good for him. Don't worry, he'll be there. Now, va-moose. Go!"

"Sí, señor," Carlos said. He'd didn't care if Mario picked them up or not. He was more than willing to walk home as long as it meant getting away from El Diablo. He put the truck in gear and started back to Bella Villa.

Nolan, for his part, was half-shocked by the suddenness of his changed environment and half-amazed by his apparent survival. He struggled to undo his seat belt as he hung upside down, holding his breath in the soupy water. The car was floating for the moment, and the canal was deep. Both of these factors had certainly contributed to his being alive. He freed himself from the restraint and swam to the surface. Luckily his head bobbed up on the side of the canal away from the road, so the car blocked him from view. The car was sinking fast, however, and he needed to get out of sight. The truck lights came on, casting light to his right as he faced the road. More light from the patrol car partially illuminated where his car sank. Shots rang out as the last of the car went under, and bullets whizzed all around him. He went under the water and made for shore. He bumped into a frightened alligator trying to flee as well. The gator ignored him and dove deeper toward the bottom. Another gator splashed into the water to his right, drawing gunfire. Nolan moved to the left and scrabbled to shore. He lay low in the weeds and started to squirm slowly backward. There were flashes of burning powder and reports from a semiautomatic pistol and more bullets all around him. Then silence.

Nolan waited, barely breathing, inching away from the bank. He reached down to his ankle; he could feel the weight of his .38 still miraculously holstered there. He unsnapped the strap and pulled it out. He could make out a bulky figure near the canal bank and behind him a much-smaller man near the spotlight by the front door of the police cruiser. He heard something that made his blood go cold. It was the *ka chunk* of a pump shotgun chambering a round. He had to move fast. There were several thunderous reports, each followed by *ka chunk* as buckshot blanketed the ground all around him.

"Alvarez, over here. Hurry!" he heard Tiny bark. The spotlight from the cruiser panned the far shore. It landed on Nolan who was still on his stomach, staring across the thirty-foot canal. He was transfixed by the light, frozen in its beam. Before he could respond, he heard Harris yell, "That's him, I see him!" Nolan jumped to his feet quicker than he thought possible and fired a shot from his pistol as he turned to run. There were several reports from the other bank as he dashed toward the cover of thick brush only ten yards away. Just as he reached cover, buckshot pellets slammed into him, knocking him off his feet and sending him headfirst into the coppice. Just before losing consciousness, he could feel the warm wet sensation of blood oozing from several places on his right side.

24

Brian spent a fitful last night in detox. Everything he learned in the last few days whirled like a carnival carousel inside his head. He spent forty-eight hours on a decreasing dose of Librium to ease the withdrawal from alcohol. He slept through a good deal of it and felt better on the third day than he had since he was a teenager. Tomorrow, he would go home free of the physical craving for booze. He attended three meetings brought to the detox by recovering alcoholics in AA. He suffered from a disease, he was told—a disease not only of the mind and body, but also of the spirit. The "phenomenon of craving" would return after a single drink. Just as a pickle could not return to being a cucumber, he could never drink safely again. Recovering alcoholics attained a way of living, free of booze "one day at a time." They came to testify there existed *hope* based on a spiritual way of life. There was, indeed, life and happiness in sobriety.

At bedtime, Brian knelt down to pray, hands together forming a steeple. He felt a little silly, self-conscious, and unsure what words to use. After all, the last time he remembered getting on his knees like this he was just out of kindergarten. Still, he prayed because the other recovering alcoholics he met in the last three days told him it was what they did to stay sober. And every one of them had drunk longer and harder than he did and had fallen to greater depths of ruin and despair. "Thank you, Lord, for bringing me here for a second chance at life." He prayed out loud those simple words and no more. He lay back in bed, vowing to ask for help in his morning prayer. He didn't even know if he believed in God. What he *did believe* in was the magic of *the human spirit*, and that would have to do for now. Brian drifted to sleep.

Jamie came over to the bed, naked, and slid in on his left side. There was mischief playing on his lips, a smile showing his dimples and teeth, lighting up his hazel eyes. Brian could feel the heat of his skin, an erotic furnace, even before it made contact. Now, Jamie's hand was touching him between the legs, his fingers moving with a familiar dexterity, coaxing him to rigidity. Their lips touched momentarily, and Brian could feel Jamie's wood against his thigh. Jamie looked up, stretched lazily, and rolled over, his back to him. Brian's sister-in-law and dead brother joined him on the right side. They were both wearing drab army green flannel pajamas. Their names were sewn over their breast pockets. His brother's wife cradled his head and stroked his neck with hands that were all bones. "Don't forget us," she purred. "We want to play too."

"Wake up call," a female voice intruded. Brian half-opened his eyes to see a pudgy Latino woman standing in the doorway. She wore the large identification badge around her neck of the rehabilitation center staff. He recognized Gabriella Ramirez. "Breakfast in twenty. Let's go, Brian, you're checking out today, amigo."

After a quick shower, Brian returned to his room to gather his wits and to pray. He hoped he had the courage to make the changes necessary to remain sober. While he was physically free of the need to drink, the mental obsession lingered, buried for the moment, perhaps, but still vital. How had those AA people described alcohol? *Cunning, baffling, and powerful.* He would need a lot of help.

An hour after breakfast, there was a tap at the door. "Your ride's here, Brian," said Gabriella. "Time to check out and start a new life."

Tiny pulled into the Baron County sheriff's substation. He was exhausted and disgruntled. The events of the preceding three hours left a bad taste in his mouth. Right now, he just needed a shower and some rest. After disposing of Alvarez's corpse in the canal, he went to a manual car wash and scrubbed the cruiser's left front fender and tire. Considering the blood and gore, he figured the gators probably tore the duplicitous reporter apart in short order. Nolan's last-second swerve had cost Tiny a clean kill and the attendant corpse. He could lay to rest most of his present problems with Nolan's dead body. Now, however, there would be the aggravation of *not being certain.* His experience as a law enforcement officer told him there wouldn't likely be any remains left to discover if Nolan expired from either the crash or bullet wounds. Predators and scavengers of every description abounded in the Everglades. Perhaps, a few scattered bones in the next few years would come to light. He checked his log while still in the cruiser. He would include a report about pulling over a truck belonging to a local tomato and vegetable farmer. He would place the truck a couple of miles from where the Nolan incident went down. Those fishermen wouldn't likely remember much, other than they saw a sheriff's car and a truck on the road. Now, it was a waiting game for Nolan's disappearance to be confirmed. There were a few loose ends at that cockroach motel to snip and back to the endgame.

Tiny was out of the Crown Victoria, squinting at the just-rising sun, his hand on the open door, when he heard a shout, and a shot rang out. The safety glass in the rear window beside him spiderwebbed and caved inward, making a small hole near the center. He looked to his left and saw a man with a revolver standing in front of an Indian Hawthorne hedge near the headquarters building, pointing the gun at him and screaming, "You bastard! You bastard!" Tiny dove back into the car just as another shot rang out. He heard the bullet hit the doorjamb as it swung shut behind him. Another shot hit the driver side window, the safety glass again absorbing the impact, caving inward. The bulky deputy scrabbled across the equipment-packed front seat of the cruiser, trying to keep his head down. He pushed the passenger door open and slid out, face-first, on all fours. A fourth shot went through the driver's window and damn near took off Tiny's left foot, slamming into the lower door hinge and knocking the door out of the casing, just as he exited the besieged patrol car. Pulling his Glock from its holster, Tiny crouched behind the rear of the car. He raised his head over the trunk of the car and saw the man was only thirty feet away, advancing with the gun in front of him.

"Bastard!" Pablo Rodriquez yelled again. It was Constance Valentine's young paramour.

Pablo's eyes were on fire with resurrected Latino machismo. He swung the .38 revolver snatched from the floor next to his comatose lover and fired the fifth round at Tiny's head. The bullet whizzed over Tiny's right shoulder so close it actually ripped his uniform and scratched his skin, bringing a trickle of blood to the scene. Tiny ducked behind the cruiser and moved quickly to the front of the car, both to put the engine block between him and a bullet and to draw fire from the Crown Vic's gas tank. He held the 9mm at ready and chanced a look beneath the car. He saw Pablo's calves and feet almost to the car, walking toward the rear. He fired twice at the feet, and Pablo went down with a yelp. Tiny figured there was still a sixth round in the chamber, but when he circled the car, he could hear the misguided youth dry fire the six-shot revolver. Pablo was lying on the pavement, propping himself up with his left arm, his right leg a bloody mess near the ankle. He swung the gun on Tiny. Confident the boy's pistol had no ammunition, the deputy stepped out and pumped four rounds from his 9mm into the wounded and wide-eyed would-be avenger.

Brian walked up to Jamie, and the two men embraced. Jamie kissed Brian on the cheek and whispered, "It's going to be all right, Bry, we're going home."

"Hope you got plenty of ice cream and soda," Brian said. "I'm feelin' a real sweet tooth comin' on."

"Don't worry," said Jamie, "we are going to stop at the store on the way back to the Fireproof and buy all kinds of food. We're all getting together for an alcohol—and drug-free cookout tonight to celebrate your return to the fold. And I've decided to give up my side business to keep an environment you can feel comfortable in." Brian looked a little confused but smiled briefly before looking away from his friend and lover.

"Well, let's get going," Brian said. "You can fill me in on all the latest on the ride home."

"Roger that," said Jamie.

Brian followed Jamie around looking a bit disconsolate as they went up and down the aisles of the Winn Dixie Supermarket. Finally, while they were unpacking the groceries in Jamie's room, Brian summoned the courage to speak.

"Jamie, we need to talk."

"Sure, what's on your mind? You can talk to me about anything, you know that, Bry."

"Look, the first thing is, I really appreciate you guys getting the party together for me and all. But what I need to do is call someone and go to an AA meeting tonight. I mean, I can still eat before I go and maybe spend some time with you later, but it was suggested I go to a meeting the first night out of detox. I'm serious about staying sober, Jamie. And that means there are certain things I will probably have to do different from what I did before."

"I understand, Brian." Jamie looked a little crestfallen but managed a sympathetic smile. "I knew you'd probably want to hook up with a support group. I just didn't know it would be right away. We aren't going to be drinking tonight, and Toad has been warned to be on his best behavior or skip the party."

"I just think it's important I get off on the right foot," Brian said. "I'm going to call one of the numbers I got from the guys who came in to detox, see if I can hook up for a ride to an eight-o'clock meeting. One of the guys I liked is a retired doctor. 'Doc John,' they called him."

"Sure, Brian, like I said, whatever you have to do." Jamie felt a knot begin to form in his stomach. He recognized it as that old nemesis, *fear*. The wheel of change was turning, and there was no telling where it would take his love. He must be careful to not stand in the way and be run over. Rather, he would step aside and let the wheel take Brian where he had to go. The focus should be on Brian, what was best for him. He was savvy enough to realize that trying to hold on to someone or smother them was the fastest way to drive them away. If there was love, the relationship would endure. If not, there was nothing he could do anyway.

"Jamie, there's something else." Brian looked at his feet, sitting on the edge of Jamie's bed.

"Go ahead, Brian. I'm listening." Jamie dreaded what Brian was going to say next because he knew what it was already. He'd heard it all before from at least two other lovers.

"I think we should cool our relationship." Brian looked up at Jamie as he spoke. "At least for a while. It's not that I don't care about you, there have been a lot of good things in it for both of us, I think. But you know I'm still uneasy about the sex part. It feels good when it's happening, and I do get turned on. But afterward, it somehow doesn't seem so right. I don't know exactly how to explain it. It's kind of a mixed-up jumble in my head. Like it or not, I have some kind of puritanical hang-ups on the morality of it. It's embedded like a fossil in my consciousness."

"I guess it's hard for a lot of gays to overcome that indoctrination, Bry." Jamie came over and sat on the bed next to his friend; he put his left arm around the newly sober young man. "I really think we are prone to drink and do drugs to escape the guilt that has been shackled to us like a ball and chain. The image of Sodom and Gomorrah, so powerfully invoked by the Pharisees throughout history, as well as some obscure sentence in Leviticus, branding men who lie with each other as abominations, are meant to intimidate and drive undercover those of us who, by no fault of our own, are attracted to members of the same sex. If their God is so all-powerful, how is it he has perpetrated such an egregious error on mankind. Isn't it more likely homosexuality is part of an omnipotent God's divine plan? A great Jewish rabbi and prophet said what God *is* if you choose to believe it. *God is love.* Therefore, treat your neighbor as you would be treated. All previous rules and traditions are predicated on this primary edict. Keep it simple. *God is love.*"

"Jamie, I know you're probably right"—Brian put his head on his friend's shoulder—"but I think my plate is full, just trying to stay away from a *drink* right now."

"You just do what you have to do, Brian." Jamie stroked Brian's hair, starting to feel a tumescence between his legs despite his best intentions. "Just remember, I'm here for you, whenever you need me. Take however long you need to sort things out." Jamie pulled a little away from Brian and put his best face on, an act of courage in and of itself. "I love you," he said, looking his boyfriend in the eyes. The two men embraced and held each other tight.

Tiny slept on an old leather couch in the break room. Maria, the day dispatcher, switchboard operator, public relations officer, and coffee maker, woke him with a fresh cup of her brew. "The captain wants to see you," she said. Tiny went to Post's office, coffee in hand.

"There's just one thing I'm not clear on," Post said. Tiny sat across from him in the small office. "Why did Pablo Rodriquez want to kill *you?*"

Because I raped his sugar mamma, you dumb nigger, Tiny thought. "I was a friend of the councilwoman, and I helped Pablo get a job there to pay for college." Tiny shrugged his massive shoulders. "Maybe in his distraught state of mind, he made me the bad guy out of a sense of helplessness. I really don't have a good idea, Captain. But it seems like no good deed goes unpunished."

"Well, since we can't really interview Pablo at this point"—Post smiled, a sardonic expression twisted his dark features—"we'll call the case closed." He gestured for Tiny to pick up his gun and badge on the desk. Captain Post declared the shooting of Pablo Rodriquez well within the parameters of rightful use of a firearm by a law enforcement officer.

"There's something I'd like to remind you of, Captain," said Tiny, picking up his Glock and sergeant's badge.

"What would that be?" Post asked.

"We have a date to go out for a couple of laughs tomorrow evening around seven. Bring plenty of punch to the party. We may need it."

"You picking me up?" the captain asked.

"Absa-fuckin'-lootly," said Tiny as he left the room.

Having showered and changed into civvies, Tiny drove the Grand Cherokee out to the old schoolhouse in order to survey the scene of what he believed was going to be an ambush. His plan was to ambush the ambushers. He pulled onto the old parking apron and got out of the Jeep. When he rounded the building, an unusually belligerent crowd of mendicants greeted him, smoking rolled cigarettes and passing around a jug of Gallo Port. Tiny counted about ten at first glance. They drew together at the sight of him in a menacing formation but backed off when one of them pointed at the gun on his belt and the deputy's badge clipped there as well. "Cop," the apparent leader croaked, and they backed off.

"What's going on here?" Tiny asked. "Is there a tramp convention going on I didn't hear about?"

"You hear about our murdered brother?" the leader asked. He was a rangy man, standing 6'2" or so with a full beard and long dirty hair, maybe blonde, but looking darker now. He was looking pretty fit despite his choice of fermented fruit drinks. He stepped forward, hands on hips. "We can take care of our own, we don't need no cops." Just so there would be no confusion about who was running the show, Tiny drove a fist into the solar plexus of the unfortunate kingpin, knocking his wind out with an audible *oomph*. His companions held him up lest he collapse at Tiny's feet. There was no question now as to the identity of the law enforcement officer standing before them.

Someone whispered, "El Diablo." They stared in terror at Tiny. Finally, one brave heart nodded his head toward the schoolhouse door. Tiny walked to the door and entered the darkened room. At the far end, several candles were burning around a bunk with a prone body on it.

"He's dead," said the disheveled doyen, having regained his breath. "Murdered. He was our friend. Everybody liked him. He would never harm anyone. Always ready to share."

"What's your name?" Tiny asked.

"Ray."

"Sorry about the love tap, Ray," Tiny said as a ploy to placate the misfits before roping them into his newly improvised plan. "I get a little nervous sometimes. The man who did this will be back. I know who he is, and he kills for the fun of it.

He'll shoot everyone of you, one by one, hunt you down like vermin, even bring in dogs if he has to. You're all good as dead right now if you don't do something."

"What the hell we gonna do?" Ray asked. There was a tremor of fear in his voice.

"I'm gonna help you guys out," Tiny, the magnanimous, said. "First thing, you bury your friend right off. Another day and there'll be a stink in here that'll make your BO seem like perfume. No use to report it, bring in a bunch of cops and reporters. They'll end up kicking you out of here, then where'll you go? I'll send someone over with supplies. We keep this in the mum bum book. Don't worry, I'll be looking out for you guys."

Tiny went back to his Jeep and drove home. He called Mario from a pay phone on the way and told him he'd be over in one hour. Tiny, wearing latex gloves, dug out four handguns from his confiscated gun collection at his house. These were part of the weapons cache he never reported and were virtually untraceable. He loaded them and put them in a black gym bag before taking them to Mario's.

"Here's what I want you to do," Tiny said to Mario. "Deliver these guns to the crowd of losers at the old schoolhouse and tell them to use them for self-protection. Tell them the desperado who murdered their friend will be back tomorrow sometime, and they should shoot him on sight. Assure them they will not get into trouble if they kill him. Show them this." Tiny pulled out a deputy sheriff's badge he lifted years ago from storage before anyone paid much attention. "And to sweeten things up, bring along some bread, cheese, and a couple gallons of vino. That'll give 'em a sportin' chance." Mario started to say something, but Tiny put his finger to his lips and shook his head. "I gotta fly now. So much to do, so little time."

Tiny left Mario holding the bag and headed for Mona's apartment. He needed to release all the tension inside with a little rough sex and, hopefully, a short nap.

25

Nolan regained consciousness in the fairy light of early morning. A spiderweb covered in dew spread across part of the wild myrsine bush he was buried in. His leg and butt throbbed, and his briefs and right thigh were covered in sticky blood. He sat up and looked back at the canal, trying to get his bearings and restore memory to the organic computer behind his bloodshot blue eyes. What he saw sent a shot of adrenaline through his system, bringing him back to full awareness. About thirty feet away and twenty feet apart on the bank of the canal were two alligators. They were clearly eyeing him, perhaps on the verge of striking. Sooner or later, one would clamp on him with one thousand pounds per inch of force, teeth digging deep into his flesh and bone, dragging him into the water and rolling under the surface to drown him. These two, and perhaps others, would fight over the kill, tearing him apart, then swimming to their respective dens to stash the meat for a couple of days for ripening. This was the time of day they would be feeding. Alligators rarely feed when the temperature is below the midseventies. The temperature, already into the eighties, was prime.

The largest of the gators to his left advanced about ten feet. Nolan could see the lizard blink its eyes. He estimated it to be about nine or ten feet overall, nine hundred to a thousand pounds. Looking around for his gun, Nolan realized it must be behind him where he plunged headfirst into the bushes before losing consciousness. He began to work his way backward, keeping his can to the ground and his eye on the larger gator. He was about where his head had been, partly concealed in the brush, when the larger alligator lunged to within ten feet of him. The other reptile advanced as well but maintained a greater distance, no doubt in deference to its larger competitor. Nolan's heartbeat was in a steadily increasing rhythm and sweat streamed down his face as he blinked desperately to clear his vision. The flowered shirt he wore on his date with Camilla, which now seemed like sometime last year instead of last night, was still wet. It was ripped and filthy as well. Mike Nolan took a deep breath and did the hardest thing he had ever done since joining the Navy SEALs at age nineteen.

Nolan took his eyes off the closest gator and cast his gaze about for the .38 Model 40 he kept as an ankle backup. By the grace of whatever powers rule the fate of men, he saw the black beauty almost touching his left hand. He grabbed it, transferring it to his right hand as he looked to check the green knobby beast closest to him. He saw it blink as if understanding what the gun meant. The alligator lunged forward at startling speed, mouth wide open. Nolan fired into the gaping jaws just as they were about to shut on his arm. At the same time, he hopped awkwardly backward, still on his butt. The jaws snapped shut so close they knocked the gun from the shaken lawman's hand as the large lizard thrashed wildly, emitting a kind of barking sound. Nolan looked to see the other predator slide back into the canal. He retrieved the pistol just as the wounded gator lunged again, bloody mouth wide. Nolan fired three more times until the five-shot chamber clicked empty. The gator swirled like a dervish, the end of its long tail slapping into Nolan's head, knocking him over and putting out his lights for a few minutes.

Nolan came to at sunrise with a god-awful throbbing in his head. The muscles in his right buttocks and thigh were stiff and pulsing with pain; movement was unbelievably difficult. He stood up and assessed the damage. By some miracle, he ascertained there were no broken or shattered bones. He limped toward the canal, realizing he would have to cross it to reach the road. He could only hope for yet another miracle, safe passage to the other side, despite his wounds and the necessity of a slow and agonizing pace. He worked his way down the bank, slipping once and falling on his ass. A wave of torment swept through his lower body, causing a momentary blackness to shut out the world. He opened his eyes and looked around. About a hundred yards down the canal, he spotted number 2 gator, half in and half out of the water. His wounds began to seep blood again. *Great, just great. Fresh blood for Gus Gator to get all stirred up about,* he thought.

Pushing himself up, Nolan began to move down the slope again. He realized he lost his gun on the ground somewhere when the dying gator knocked him out. He patted his front pants pocket to see if he remembered to put a couple of extra .38 rounds in with his change. Nothing. "Oh, shit!" He said out loud. Damned if he was going back for the gun now. He limped to the canal's edge and looked down the water's edge to see the beady eyes of his unwelcome companion fixed in his direction. There was no way the reptile could see this far, but he may well be able to detect motion and smell the blood. Thinking he'd probably die of infection from the plethora of bacteria inhabiting the water even if he made it across the canal, Nolan gritted his teeth and started.

Although he promised himself he wouldn't look, Nolan cast a reflexive glance at Gus. He saw him slide back in the water and head like a log rushing downstream in his direction. Once again, the adrenaline pumped into his system faster than amphetamines from a junkie's needle. He began to swim frantically for the far shore, all pain forgotten. The canal was less than thirty feet across but unusually deep. His car had disappeared entirely. Nolan knew alligators could run at amazing speeds for short distances. He hit the other bank and turned on his backside. The gator was about ten feet away, the bumps on top of its gnarly head blinked. Knowing its prey was wounded, it would take its time. Nolan kicked off his sneakers and slid his pants off as quickly as he could. He hoped the bloodstained pants would act as bait for the rapacious reptile. He stood with some difficulty and scrambled up the slope in his skivvies and flowered shirt, pain be damned.

Gus Gator made straight for the pants, clamping down on them and retreating backward. Realizing the trick as it went under the surface, the furious gator shot up on the shore like an arrow launched by an invisible bow, coming up on Nolan just as he reached the road. Picking up the first thing he saw, an old pine bough lying on the shoulder, Nolan shoved it into the tooth-lined mouth. The jaws snapped shut. Remembering something he read in a newspaper article, he punched the gator as hard as he could in the nose. Amazingly, ole Gus backed off a few feet and spit out the decaying wood. *Guess he doesn't need the fiber,* Nolan thought with a crazed bark of laughter. This being the day of miracles, a battered old school bus, carrying a load of migrant workers to the fields, coughed and sputtered to a stop, discharging a horde of screaming and gesticulating Mexican laborers. The surprised alligator opened its jaws and, with gapping maw, charged at the offending interlopers. The intrepid immigrants stood their ground, screaming and kicking the gator. The scaly monster quickly turned tail and scurried back to the canal when it saw the two-legged creatures weren't running. Two of the Latinos grabbed Nolan's arms and, with wide smiles, shepherded him back to the bus.

Inside the bus, they sat Nolan in the second seat. They watched him, smiling and nodding, speaking in spitfire Spanish. The bus doors closed, the engine roared, and in a cloud of black smoke, they were off. "Gracias, muchos gracias," Nolan said. "I need to get to a telephone. *Teléfono,*" he repeated in Spanish. He tucked his three middle fingers into the palm of his hand, extending his thumb and little finer out; he pretended to hold a receiver to his ear and talk. The Mexican men chuckled and nudged each other. A moment later, three of the men were offering Nolan their cell phones, competing to see which one had the phone Nolan would choose. These phones were obviously a great luxury and a sign of prestige among the migrant workers. The three men held their phones out with more nodding and smiling. Nolan picked the phone in the middle. "This'll do. *Gracias.*"

He called Camilla and Robert's room at the Fireproof.

"Hello?" a female's yawning voice answered.

"Camilla, this is Mike. I need your help."

"Mike? What's going on? Where are you?" Nolan could picture her walking to the window in a skimpy nightgown, maybe naked, and looking out through her blinds at his room.

"Listen, I've been hurt." The bus was hot and sweat streamed down Nolan's face. He was suddenly exhausted, ready to collapse. He was soaking wet. "Is Robbie there?"

"No, his mother is in the hospital. He went last night. Awful things are happening. Is it because of that crazy cop?"

"I can't talk right now. Hold on." Nolan put his hand on the speaker and turned to the Mexicans who were still smiling with reassuring nods as the old bus rumbled over the smooth roadway. "Where do you work? *Donde trabajan?*"

"Gadillo's," several of the men answered at the same time.

"Pick me up at Gadillo's," Nolan said into the phone. "It's a tomato farm, probably some oranges, and who knows what else. One hour from now. I'll need a doctor."

"Gad—what?" Camilla asked.

"Gadillo's," Nolan repeated. "Cammy, I'm counting on you."

"I'll be there. But—"

"Gotta go." Nolan hung up and passed out.

A scraggly band of grungy men met Mario as he walked up to the old schoolhouse. He was touting the black gym bag Tiny had given him and a large canvas bag with bread, cheese, and wine in it. He wore the badge on a chain around his neck as Tiny instructed and a black tee shirt that had POLICE stenciled on the back and front.

"We ain't doin' nothin' wrong here, just talkin'," a tall thin man blustered. He appeared to be the ragamuffin's leader. "We're comparin' notes to see if the dumpster with Krispy Kreme donuts is better than the one with the Dunkin Donuts. That oughta be a topic you'd be real interested in, Officer."

"Maybe he's the dude ole Deputy *Diablo* said he'd send," a short stocky man with black hair and a thick gristle of beard conjectured. "I just didn't expect anyone with such a dark tan."

Oh, brother, Mario thought, *it's Laurel and Hardy.* "You got that right, my brother. Now you guys listen up. I'm not here to listen to a bunch of drunks make funny. I got a few items you might want to keep handy if that killer comes back." Mario put down the two bags, groped inside the gym bag, pulled out a Ruger .38 revolver, and handed it to the head honcho. The gun was loaded with just two rounds. Handing these guys loaded weapons wasn't Mario's idea of something any too smart to do. He had to rely on his policeman facade to deter any high jinks, like for instance, someone shooting him. Mario, who had a vested interest in seeing Tiny killed, had unloaded all but two rounds in each weapon. This would give the assassin a fighting chance to finish the devil's own deputy. If, on the other hand, Tiny survived, Mario would appear to have done as instructed. Reaching into the bag, he pulled out two .22 revolvers of some foreign make.

He gave these to the two nearest bums. Now there was a pushing and shoving as the other men came forward to get a gun.

"I have one more," Mario said. He pulled out a .32 semiautomatic.

"Gimme that one." "Hardy" pushed down the fellow who was reaching for the gun and snatched it from Mario's grasp. Taking off for the woods, he stumbled and fell. There was the muffled sound of a gunshot. The man remained motionless on the ground.

"Oh, for the lovin' Christ." Mario ran over to the man, the band of gypsies on his heels. He knelt beside the fallen gun thief and turned him over. A large splotch of blood spread across the front of his filthy shirt. He gurgled as if drowning in blood, spitting up a tiny fountain of the sanguine water of life before his dark eyes went lifeless.

"Dead," Laurel said. "Right through the ticker. That makes two now."

Clutching the empty gym bag, Mario hustled back to his car. Spewing gravel from his tires as he peeled out of the parking apron. He headed back to Bella Villa and a stiff one or two or three.

"Jimmy, get Mr. Santana another margarita." Rooster Babcock, chief operating officer and owner of the Red Rooster Ranch, sat with a lovely lady on either side. The two goddesses were similarly attired in leopard G-strings. The use of tops was frowned upon here in the privacy of Rooster's mansion. "And make sure to use that special Sammy Hagar stuff I got in Puerto Vallarta. Hell, Jimmy, might as well make up a pitcher of it. You ladies will be imbibing no doubt?" He looked at both ladies, his head turning from one to the other.

"Sure," they both cooed.

"Good, good, we'll all be having a drink together." Rooster turned his attention to the small man with dark hair and mustache wearing deeply tinted polarized sunglasses. "So, Santana, will you be leaving us tomorrow? I can arrange to have a lady give you a relaxing massage tonight." He winked.

"Señor, my plans must remain my own. As you know, we are *ajunta*, joined in deleecate negotiations. The slightest unknown could cause disastrous reepple effects." He looked at the two women and smiled. Two gold-capped teeth flashed in the afternoon sunlight. "Eef you will excuse me, I need to make some plans and get some rest. I'm afraid more alcohol ees out of the question. Oh, one theeng."

"What would that be?" Rooster queried.

"I would like to have Hymie drive me in the Lincoln later."

"That's doable. Jimmy?"

"I'll be ready, sir."

"Good," Santana said, looking at Jimmy. "There weel be a *prima*, how you say—bonus." He stood up and left his client and the toothsome women with their drinks. On the way to his quarters, he seriously thought of getting in the Lincoln and driving straight to the airport with the money Rooster had already given him. He considered the heat he would take for the assassination of a policeman, even a dirty one. In the end, greed won over prudence, and he retired to his quarters. He needed to rest and check his weapons before this evening's work.

"Excuse me a moment, ladies," Rooster said. He signaled Pots, one of his security men, to walk to the other side of the pool with him. "I want you to keep an eye on our Mexican cleaning man and radio back to me his movements on the Nextel. And for chrize sakes, don't let him catch you on his tail." The man nodded and left for the main house.

"Is there anything else I can do, sir?" Jimmy asked.

"As a matter of fact, there is." Rooster sat back on his chaise longue and took a quick sip of his drink. "Umm, well done, young James. This is as fine a margarita as I've had anywhere."

"Thank you, Mr. Babcock."

"Call me Rooster, Jimbo. I've told you that a thousand times."

"Okay, Mr. Bab—I mean, Rooster, sir."

"Yes, well anyway, go down to the arena and check with Teddy about security for tonight's events. Tell him I want everything buttoned down extra tight. You hang with him so you can learn more about how things work. He can call me on the Nextel when he's done or if he has any questions. I'll be down there a little later to check things out."

"Yes, sir!" Jimmy bolted for the garage area where the golf carts were kept.

Deputy Sam Troy, commander of the juvenile boot camp and friend of Deputy "Tiny" Harris, drove his Chevy Malibu on State Road 29. He found the spot his erstwhile master in the ways of juvenile discipline had described. He pulled his vehicle off the road to the extent possible, given there was very little in the way of shoulders. He got out of the car, clothed in jogging shorts and armless tee shirt. Examining the scene of the crash, he noticed the presence of tattered clothing, but no bodies. He walked back to his Malibu and donned rubber gloves. Taking a trash bag down to the canal, he proceeded to clean up any remnants of clothing, plastic car parts, or human body parts that might arouse attention. He figured he had an hour or so before the next patrol passed by here. He should be gone by then. Ascertaining the place the car went into the canal, he headed up the slope to where Nolan was supposedly shot. He found the wild myrsine hedge the federal agent had collapsed in and some blood, but no body. Looking around more carefully, he spotted the .38 Smith & Wesson. Checking the cylinders, he noted the weapon had been fully discharged of its ammunition. There was no sign Nolan had been dragged to the canal by alligators. The creatures invariably killed their prey by drowning. When he finished up with his ghoulish task, he called his mentor.

"Tiny, Sam here." Sergeant Troy continued to scour the bank while talking into his cell phone. "Mr. Clean Jeans has finished up. There are no cockroaches visible but no indication they have been exterminated. Evidence is inconclusive as to their disappearance. Advise follow-up sanitization." Sam smiled, proud of his finesse with spookspeak.

After an unusually rough session with Mona and a refreshing nap, Tiny decided to put into play a plan to increase his income. During this period of high expenses, attributed to the cleaning-up process necessitated by Nolan's meddling, Tiny realized the easiest target for quick cash, besides Foo Foo owner Pat Raeford, was Ron Badger, the portly owner of two King Burgers and a convenience store, not to mention hundreds of acres of land increasing in value at exponential rates. Mr. Badger was a known womanizer and whoremonger. God knows how many young girls, who had the misfortune of working for him, he'd raped and traumatized over the years. Tiny went down to his Grand Cherokee and grabbed a small digital video camera. He went to Mona's room and hid the camera in such a way that it would film the bed area in a wide-angle shoot. After giving Mona his instructions, he turned the camera on and left to hide his Jeep.

Mona called "Ronnie Ranger," her name for Badger, and sweet-talked him into coming over for an afternoon quickie. She assured him Tiny was out of town on department business. Uncomfortable as Mona felt with the charade, she feared Tiny's wrath should she not comply with his demands. The horny burgermeister came trotting over for a freebie, congratulating himself on his charm and lovemaking savoir faire. Hopping into bed with the curvaceous courtesan, he was captured on disc with his pants down, chattering with sufficient dirty talk to make even a pornographer blush. After a few minutes, Mona rolled out of bed and pulled up the blinds.

"What the fuck," Badger began. An instant later, Tiny was up the stairs and through the door. He snapped a flash picture of the buck-naked entrepreneur, both to disorient him and to punctuate his plight in the blinding light. The whir of the self-winder on the camera accentuated the silence.

"Looks like we got to make us a whole new deal," Tiny said. "This entire session has been recorded." The deputy pulled the small camera out from its hidey-hole and held it up, a huge shit-eating grin spreading across his face. "Why don't you get dressed, and we'll talk dollars and cents. Does that make sense?" Tiny guffawed at his pun and the red and twisted face of the infuriated Badger. Tiny turned to leave the room as Badger put on his underwear. "I'll wait for you in the living room, schmuck. I'm thinking of a monthly number that begins with ten and ends with three zeros." Turning to see the fat King Burger's face, he looked straight down the barrel of a pocket .32, a gun as anemic as the pitiful man wielding it.

Tiny shut the door quickly, stepping to the side as he did so. The report of the gun and a small bullet punching through the hollow core door ensued. Badger charged out the door in a panic, wielding the small firearm, only to be blinded by the flash of a camera at close range. Tiny grabbed the hand holding the gun and forced the barrel toward the floor. He slammed his right fist into Badger's face, likely breaking his jaw. The gunman went down like a jet out of fuel. Tiny dragged the semiconscious king of burgers to the head of the outside stairwell and kicked him in the gut. There was an *oomph* from Badger as the air was driven from his lungs, and he dropped over the top step. The fleshy merchant rolled down the stairs like a lump of Jell-O. Tiny went to the moaning heap at the bottom of the stairs and gave him another quick kick in the midsection. Badger barfed on the deputy's steel-toed shoes.

"About that new figure we were discussing," Tiny said, "it just doubled."

26

Camilla was hoping Julie would let her use her car *plus* take care of Billy. She headed toward the singer's room. She didn't think telling Robbie about Nolan's call would be a good idea at this point. Truth is she felt a kind of thrill, like a child going to an amusement park. Not only was this an adventure, but there was also that odd rush of feeling one gets when sexually turned on by another person. A flush of hot passion mixed with a tipsy recklessness spread from her groin down to her toes and up through her face. Add to that the feeling of being needed, crucial to the well-being, maybe even life, of some person you desire to nurture, and you have the green shoot of a tenuous new growth. She tapped on Tommy and Julie's door.

"Hey, it's Cammy." She pushed the door open.

"C'mon in, girl," Julie said. "What up?"

"Hey, Cam," Tommy said, sticking his head around the corner of the bathroom, half his face still covered with shaving cream. "What's the news on Robbie's mom?"

"I guess she's stable," Camilla replied, "but still out in a coma. Robbie says no sense going there right now. He's going to hang out awhile." She paused a moment and looked at Julie. She didn't want to lie but didn't want to tell the truth either.

"Something's on your mind," Julie said. "What is it?"

Both women instinctively glanced at the bathroom door to see if Tommy was listening, but he was already back finishing his shaving. He'd spent enough time around the fair sex to know that look when men weren't particularly welcome.

"I need a big favor right now," Camilla said. "I need to use your car for a little while, maybe an hour or two." Julie opened her mouth, but Camilla added quickly, "I can't tell you where I'm going either. It's got something to do with that monster cop and Nolan, that's all I can say right now. Okay?"

"Yeah, sure," Julie said, handing her the keys. "But, Cammy, don't go getting yourself mixed up in something that's going to get you killed. Remember, you have a family to look after. Speaking of which, what about the baby?"

"Well," said Camilla, "that's kind of the second part of the favor."

"Oh, I see," Julie said. "Let me talk to Tommy a second. I'm sure it will be fine." She disappeared into the bathroom. A moment later, she reappeared, nodding. "We'll take the little tiger, but you have to promise to bring your ass back in one piece, and soon."

"Deal," said Camilla. "I won't let you down."

"We'll go over and hang with the Billster at your place," Julie said. "You just go before the little darling sees you and sends out a wail of alarm."

"Done," Camilla said, throwing her arms around her friend. "And thanks."

"You remember what I said about getting back!" Julie yelled as Camilla got in the Corolla. Camilla waved her right hand, index and pinky fingers raised, the two middle fingers folded into the palm and covered by the thumb.

The sweat ran down Mike Nolan's face into his eyes and mouth. He could taste its briny flavor accompanied by the stench of the canal water, clinging like a greasy fart to his clothing and hair. He sat with his back and head against the trunk of an oak tree, mercifully shaded from the broiling Florida sun. It had been hotter than usual for April in this almost-tropic paradise, great for tourists, not so great for those working outdoors. And it was doubly not good for wounded federal agents. His wounds were throbbing. One of the Mexicans had brought him a pair of khaki work pants, a clean wet rag, and some water in a Coke bottle to drink. He tried to clean up some of the caked blood and inspect his backside but couldn't really see anything. He figured at least three, maybe four, buckshot pellets hit him. Both his right ass cheek and upper thigh were hammered. He drained the water from the soda bottle and laid his head back against the trunk to wait for Camilla.

He was running across an unkempt field with scattered patches of long grass mixed with patches of sand and weeds. There were dandelions here and there, some already gone to seed, their tops all puffy and gray white like dirty snow. He was scared, but not terrified. Mike Nolan, age ten years, looked over his shoulders and saw the large dog was closing the gap. Foam dribbled from the peeled back lips of the snarling predator. Mike could see the merciless glint in the yellow eyes as the beast drove forward, feet barely touching the ground. The hound was nearly the height of the boy with the snout and teeth of a jackal. A massive leather collar with steel spikes circled its thick neck. Its fur, the color of an old penny, was short and bristled out like a hairbrush. Ahead was stake fencing about seven feet high with wire mesh. Beyond was a large brick house where the Goddard family lived.

Judy Goddard was a special friend of Mike. They often slipped into a nook outside their school at recess and smooched. It was kind of neat until Jimmy Lawson caught them going at it the last time and brought his gang of five over to beat the crap out of Mike. The future cop fought like a devil but was no match for five tough punks. That is, until Owen Roman stepped into the fray. Owen was a gentle giant with light coffee-colored skin and a dislike of bullies. He flung the boys off Mike and knocked Jimmy on his ass with a solid right to the jaw. End of engagement.

The gate to the fence was wide open. If Mike could make it there, he might have time to close it before the mutt could get its fangs into him. He saw Judy at the gate. She was waving him on. She stood by the gate holding the door half-open, ready to slam it on the Anubis at his heels. He made it through the gate, and the door slammed. He was safe, gasping for air. He turned to thank Judy, to hug Judy, to kiss Judy; but she was gone. Instead, his sister stood by the gate with a cruel smile and a dog leash. Before he knew what was happening, she opened the gate and turned to him.

"He won't hurt you," she said, "if you're not afraid. He can smell the fear on people." The dog came straight for him and lunged. Mike kicked hard at the animal's chest and fell backward, hitting his head on a tree. Judy was back, shaking him. "Mike, Mike . . ."

"Mike, Mike, wake up," Camilla said.

Nolan opened his eyes to see the angelic visage of Camilla's face looking with grave concern at him. Their eyes met, and he smiled.

"My god!" said Camilla. "You're hurt, Mike. What happened?"

"Looks like I just got my ass kicked on the playground, and the bully got clean away."

"Don't joke. This looks serious. Where's your car? Was it an accident?"

"Nope," Nolan said. "I mean yes, sort of. But it was an intentional accident. An ambush is what you'd call it." Camilla looked nonplussed. "Right now, I need to see a doctor, but not in a hospital. It has to be off the record, or Harris will find out. I'm putting my chips on you, lady. Can you help?" He reached over and took her hand. Camilla thought she was going to melt right there. A wounded man who needed her help. The Florence Nightingale buried in the roots of a woman's soul came flying forth to the rescue. Few bonds are as rapid to bind with such quiet strength as that of caregiver and patient.

"Listen," Camilla said, "I know a guy I think can help. He plays golf with Robbie's mother occasionally. We met him at her house a couple of times. He's really sweet. He's retired and lives in the Vineyards Country Club. Dr. Skillman, John Skillman. He's a recovering alcoholic. He told me that when I asked what he was drinking once. It was kind of a cocktail party, and he said, 'Diet Coke.' I looked at him funny, and he said, 'I'm in recovery from alcoholism. I've been sober two years.' So I asked him if he still practiced medicine, and he told me he was retired but still had his license."

"Perfect!" Nolan said. He winced as a bolt of pain racked his leg. "We'll have to stop and grab a bottle of booze on the way. I don't imagine he'll have a wee drop about the house." He smiled and started to get up. "Oww." Nolan's face squinched up in pain.

"Here, let me help you," said Camilla. She squatted beside his right side and got him under the arm. "Okay, one, two, three, up!" She stood using her legs to thrust them up. "I'll pull the car right up to you, just wait."

They headed west for Napolis as fast as Camilla dared drive. She certainly didn't want to be pulled over by anyone in the sheriff's department. Nolan told her to use 846 all the way to Airport Pulling Road so he could have her grab a pint of Jack Daniel's at the Albertson's. After a couple of hits on that beverage, he was feeling a little better. Camilla called Dr. Skillman from a pay phone without explaining the exact nature of the visit, except to say it was very important. Luckily, he wasn't out on the golf course. The good doctor left their names at the gate, so they had a green light into the golf community. Camilla put a restraining hand on Nolan's arm as he was about to sip more whiskey.

"Easy does it, tough guy," she said. We don't know what's coming up in the way of painkillers. Don't want to lose you from a drug interaction."

"Ah, good point, nurse." Nolan gave her a smile and put the bottle down.

They approached the door, Camilla helping Mike to walk. Dr. John Skillman, a stout but athletic man with a kind face and thick white hair, answered the door. He gave Camilla a brief embrace before noticing her companion was wounded.

"That's why we're here," said Camilla, noticing the expression change from delight to surprise and concern on Skillman's face.

"What the hell happened to you?" Skillman asked Nolan.

"Pleased to meet you too, Doctor. I'm Mike."

"I'm sorry," said Skillman. He held out his hand. "I'm John. Come in, come in. I'm calling the hospital. You need to go straight to the emergency room from the looks of your legs and backside."

"Sorry, Doc," Nolan said, "the hospital is definitely off-limits. These wounds aren't from a car accident although that is part of the story." Nolan grimaced again in pain, and his already-pasty complexion turned a lighter shade of pale. "I gotta lie down, Doctor John." Nolan stumbled forward. Camilla and the doctor rushed toward him, grabbing either arm.

"This way," said Skillman. "There's a spare bedroom. We'll lay him down on the bed."

"Gotcha," said Camilla. "He's been shot, Doctor Skillman. I don't know how bad."

"Camilla, grab some linen from that closet by the door and throw it on top of the bedspread, or *my* wife will shoot *me*." Once the linen was spread, they helped Nolan lie on the bed. Dr. Skillman looked at Nolan and shook his white-maned head.

"We should call an ambulance and the police," Skillman began.

"No!" Nolan came to the front and spoke with authority. "*I am the police.* In my wallet, front left pocket, Doc, leather billfold." He laid his head back on the pillow, exhausted. "You will find I think three wounds of double ought buckshot. The bastard shot me with my own shotgun. The pellets are roughly the size of a pea. They didn't bust up any major blood vessels, or I'd be dead now. Still, it's like being shot three times with a .38 handgun."

Doctor Skillman examined the badge inside the wallet and the other ID. "I'm not sure what's going on here, but you need attention immediately." He looked at Camilla. "I'll get my bag. Take off as much of his clothing as you can, and we'll cut off the rest."

"Doctor," Camilla said, touching his arm.

"Please call me John."

"John, please don't call anybody. He really is a cop, and we'd both be in serious danger if certain people knew where we are. I need you to trust me right now. We'll try to explain everything later. Robbie's mother is in the hospital now in critical condition because of these same people. You can call and check on that if you want, but let's get Mike fixed first."

Skillman took Camilla's hand and gave it a reassuring squeeze. "Let's get to work." He left to get his black bag.

Camilla removed Nolan's shoes and socks. She unbuttoned the same shirt he'd been wearing on their date. She managed to wiggle the shirt off him. She admired his well-muscled chest and arms. When she unbuttoned his pants, she could feel a surge from her groin. It was unwelcome and fraught with guilt, but there it was.

"Okay," said John Skillman, coming back into the room. "Let's get started." He handed Camilla a pair of very large and sharp scissors. "Cut off those pants, they're far too bloody to remove otherwise."

"Right," Camilla said. *Please, God,* she thought, *don't let me get turned on. Think nurse and patient—a little professionalism here.* Cutting off the pants, she did get turned on, but only a little. The doctor's curt and conscientious procedure sobered her up from the hormonal outpouring coursing through her blood vessels.

Doctor Skillman removed a prepackaged syringe, found a vein on Nolan's right arm, and injected him. He looked at Camilla. "Morphine, for general pain and comfort," he remarked. "Now go into the bathroom. Under the sink there should be a shallow pan. Fill it with hot water and grab a washcloth and towel from the closet where you found the sheets. We need to clean him up, he's a mess." Camilla did as the doctor instructed, returning in a few moments with everything. Meanwhile, the doctor checked the patient's vital signs. "He's in pretty good shape, considering. Let's get to work with the washcloth, help me turn him over. We'll need to cut off the jockey shorts." The lady did as instructed.

Nice ass, Camilla thought inadvertently. *At least one side of it.*

Once the blood and muck were cleaned with warm water and a swimming pool of antiseptics, Dr. Skillman inspected the injuries. While there were numerous cuts, abrasions, and bruises from the accident, the right buttocks and thigh exhibited, by far, the most exigent trauma. Nolan's entire right side was swollen and the color of a ripe plum. There were two entry wounds on the right buttocks and one on the right thigh. The doctor injected Xylocaine, a local anesthetic, near one entry site in the buttocks and, after waiting a minute, made a small incision on the first wound. Using a straight Allis clamp, he opened the puncture and probed for the pellet. Finding it buried deep in the tissue, he grasped it with stainless tongs and extracted it. He covered the open cut with more antiseptics and sterile gauze and taped it down. He repeated the procedure twice more, removing the other pellets. When he finished, they turned him over on his back, the doctor discreetly covering his private parts with a cloth.

"Camilla," Skillman said, "bring me two glasses of water, one for me and one for him." He covered the injured agent with a blanket. Lifting his head when Camilla returned with the water, the doctor helped the semiconscious patient take a drink. Afterward, he gave him two 500 mg tablets of Ampicillin, a powerful antibiotic. "I'm writing prescriptions, Camilla, for Zithromycin, a broad spectrum antibiotic, and Percoset for pain. Just follow the directions on the label. I'm also writing one for crutches. He should keep the weight off that side of his body as much as possible."

"Hey, Doc, you're terrific."

"Well, I was a surgeon for special ops in naval intelligence when I served," he fibbed.

"Wow! Really!" Camilla beamed.

"No, but it sounds good," Skillman said. "I was in the navy but before med school. I guess I qualify for some kind of special agent status now though. I want you to realize what I'm doing is totally illegal. I could lose my license or pay a hefty fine or be incarcerated or all three. So I urge you to use the utmost discretion, and I will pray for your friend's return to health and repute in the law enforcement community."

After Nolan had rested for several hours, he dressed in a pair of the portly doctor's oversized shorts and a white tee shirt with the words "Upon Awakening, We Came to Believe" printed around an open arched window looking out on a beach with the sun on the horizon. While eating a light lunch, John Skillman related part of his story, first as an active and now as a recovering alcoholic. He told them how, at the end, he was sucked into such a quagmire of morass and demoralization that he was playing Russian roulette with his .38 Smith & Wesson.

"Do you still have that gun?" Nolan asked.

"As a matter of fact, I do," the good doctor replied. "I keep thinking of getting rid of it but just leave it packed away in the closet."

"Doctor," Nolan said, "if I could borrow that pistol for a few days, it would be enormously helpful."

"I don't know," Skillman said. "It's registered in my name."

"Doc," Nolan said, raising his right hand, "I promise you won't get into trouble. You've just assisted a federal officer in trouble. You may very well be saving Camilla's life, not to mention mine and several others." He looked Skillman in the eye, and the doctor saw truth.

"Okay. I'll get the gun along with half a box of ammo. Then I'm afraid you two will have to leave. My wife is due back in thirty minutes or so, and I'd rather not alarm her."

"You got it, Doc," Nolan said. "And thanks again."

"Yeah," Camilla added. "Thanks, John."

"De nada," Skillman replied, using half of his Spanish vocabulary.

Camilla parked the Toyota in front of Nolan's room. Waving to Toad and Vaughn, who were sitting out on the porch while Josh played in the yard of the Fireproof, Camilla walked around to the passenger door of the Toyota and helped Nolan out of the car. He gave her his keys, and they hobbled up the steps, him with one crutch and Camilla with the drugs. She opened the door and followed him in. Toad and Vaughn, as well as the boy, came over to see if their assistance was needed, but more to satisfy their curiosity. Camilla dismissed them at the door, saying simply that Mike injured his leg and she'd be over and talk with them in a few minutes. She shut and locked the door and pulled all the blinds. Nolan sat on the bed while she plopped down on the one stuffed chair. They were both quiet a few minutes.

"Looks like you don't go much for home decor," Camilla finally said. "Have you done anything to this room since you moved in?"

"Nope. It suits me the way it is. I don't like to get too entrenched."

"How 'bout a poster or plant or something?"

"Okay, transplant me a flower from your garden, and I'll try to keep it alive."

"Deal." Camilla looked at him, worry lines creasing her youthful face. "Whadda ya think we should do? We're in some deep shit, ain't we?"

"You mean with Deputy Harris? Or maybe some other way?"

"Of course I mean Harris, Tiny, El Diablo, whatever the fuck his name is."

Nolan smiled before turning serious like a cop again. "I think you are all in danger, yes. There's a distinct possibility he'll be around looking for me. Everybody else should get out of here."

"No way that can happen right now, buster." Camilla looked both tough and sexy to the wounded cop. "We'll have to set up a night watch and be ready to call 911. I'll get Julie's cell phone for you to use. We can call you, and you can call whoever. I'm sure she won't mind." Camilla stood up. "You look like you could use some water and maybe some of that pain medication."

Nolan fell forward off the bed onto the floor. He rolled conveniently left to avoid landing on his wounds. Still, there was pain, and he grimaced and yelled out softly. Camilla rushed over and kneeled beside him.

"Oh my god! Are you all right?" Her face was close to his, and he put his hand around the back of her neck and pulled her face toward him. There was no resistance.

They kissed on the lips, at first tentatively, then passionately. She pulled away several times only to return to his mouth again.

"Mike. Oh, Mike. Uh-oh, Mike. We can't do this." Then back for another dose. "I'm married with a baby. This is crazy." He had one hand on her breast, the other touched the thigh where her shorts ended. "You were just shot." His hand was under her blouse. Her hand slipped under the waistband of Doc's oversized shorts. Her agile fingers found something long and hard. "Not a good idea with your injuries." He had her shorts unzipped. His hand found the mound of magic covered in velvet pubic hair. It wasn't just wet between the lips, it was streaming. She pulled his shorts down to free the beast, then stood up and kicked off her shorts. She straddled him, mindful of his injuries. "Ohh, Mike, we shouldn't . . . Oh, God . . . ummm . . . !"

27

Toad rolled Bugler tobacco in the white cigarette paper with well-practiced fingers and a deliberate style. His smokes were firm, but not too tightly wrapped. "Gotta have good air flow," he told Josh who was watching him with wide studious eyes, "but you don't want it fallin' apart on you either."

"Never mind teachin' him that," said Vaughn. "That's one habit you want to steer clear of, Josh. Just about anybody that smokes or used to smoke will tell you that."

"Still, if you're gonna do something," Toad said, "do it right, whether it be for good or ill. As for me, after survivin' Nam, I figure every day I'm livin' is on borrowed time. So I don't much care about livin' a long life. I'll probably die with a cigarette in one hand and a bottle in the other. And if I get any pussy along the way, so much the better. I've already logged over thirty years of life from the time I shoulda died." He lit his cigarette and inhaled deeply. Picking up his coffee mug, he held it in the air. "Here's to a long and healthy life for my little friend, Josh." He tipped the cup for a long drink of the strong spirits contained therein and settled into his rocker with a gap-toothed smile.

"My mom drinks beer," Josh said. "But she scares me when she does. She is awful mean sometimes."

"Josh," said Vaughn, "I want you to know I love you. And I'm going to do everything I can so we can stay together. I talked to my wife today, and we're going to get together again. See how things go. You can come with me and be like an older brother to Alex, my little boy. Would you like that?"

"Really? Yes! Yippie!" Josh leaped from the porch to the ground and danced a little jig, ran up the steps, and wrapped his thin arms around John Vaughn.

"You'll have a real family who loves you, not like the place you ran away from."

"Yeah." Josh nodded and clasped his hands together. "And I'll be a good brother to Alex too. I'll share all my stuff with him, and he can come with me wherever I go."

"Just don't go to war," Toad injected. "Shootin' people is not a pleasant pastime for boys or girls."

"Okay," said Josh. "I won't take Alex to a war unless John says it's all right."

"Let's stay with the battle we have right now, which is getting you ready for supper. Go in now and clean up." Josh skipped down the porch and into Vaughn's room.

"I wonder what's up with Camilla and Nolan?" Toad wondered out loud.

"I'm kinda wonderin' myself," said Vaughn. "Julie told me Robbie called a couple of times looking for her, and now she turns up with Nolan, who looks like he's been in a fight with one pissed-off alligator."

"You ain't kiddin' about that," Toad said. "Him bein' a cop and all, it makes you wonder if it's not tied somehow to Tiny. That deputy would be one mean son of a bitch to cross, and that's just what Nolan's been up to."

"You got to figure something's up, that's for sure. After what Brian and I saw that night, him shootin' that other cop in cold blood and what Nolan already knows, it seems likely. I'm going to head out for my camp later and pick up a few things I left there. I figure we better get with Nolan and tell him everything Monday, with legal counsel present, so I can move out and find a safer place. I recommend everyone else does the same. It's time we tell Morris what's up as well."

Toad took a final drag on his cigarette and put it out. "You got that shotgun here?"

"Yup, it's disassembled right now. Course there's nothin' to puttin' it together."

"And the shells are where?" Toad asked. "Just in case."

"They're on the top shelf of the closet in a wicker basket," said Vaughn. "There's both buckshot and slugs. The lighter loads I keep—"

"Toad, John," Julie came rushing over with Billy in her arms. "You won't believe what I just saw on the tube. Pablo was shot and killed early this morning by that awful cop. I guess he had Mrs. Valentine's gun and was shooting at the big bastard. He was waiting for him at the sheriff's station in town. Can you believe it? Wait 'til Cammy and Robbie find out." She followed Toad's gaze and looked over to see her car parked in front of Mike Nolan's room. "What the hell? Where's Cammy? What's going on? Is she at Nolan's? Something isn't quite right here."

"I'm all ready for dinner, John," said Josh, crashing back into the group. "See, my hands are all clean and my face too." He held up his hands for Vaughn to see.

"Good boy," Vaughn said. "Just hold onto your britches a minute and be quiet."

"To answer your first question," said Toad, pausing to sip spirits from his mug, "yes, Cammy is at Nolan's. As to what exactly is going on, you'll have to ask her. All we know is, she came back with a very beat-up fed and helped him into his room. Neither of them was inclined to have us help or hang out."

"Now, what's all this about someone shooting at our favorite deputy?" Toad brought out his tobacco and commenced to roll another cigarette.

"Right now all I know is what I saw on the tube at Robbie and Cammy's," Julie said. Tommy stuck his head out the door of room 109.

"Hey, Tommy! Come out and join us." Julie shifted Billy to her other arm. "Constance Valentine's young stud was killed by our *numero uno* bad guy, Tiny, this morning. Shot four or five times."

"No shit! Are you serious? What happened?" Tommy looked over toward room 112. "Hey! How come our car is over at Nolan's room?"

"Because Cammy is over there," Julie said. "And Toad says Nolan is in pretty bad shape. Pablo was shot by the way. I'll tell you what I saw later. I'm going to suggest we all adjourn to Jamie's room for a powwow."

"I second the motion," Toad said, picking up his jug.

"No liquor, Toad," Julie said with her sternest schoolmarm look. "You *know* Brian just got out of detox. And I can tell you he's plenty worried about Tiny." Toad poured a liberal libation into his cup, looked Julie in the eye, and drained the contents in one gulp. He took a drag on his cigarette.

"Ahhh!" Toad exhaled dragon's breath. The smoke seemed to billow out in a fog that threatened to envelope the entire motel. "Let's shake a leg." He led the gang to Jamie's room. "I better knock in case their givin' each other blow jobs."

"Toad, don't be so crude," Julie chastised. "And don't forget there's a child present. We need to be serious about all this."

"Ahyup."

Jamie brought two cups of freshly brewed coffee over to Brian, who was sitting in the easy chair in his room, and handed him one. He set the other on the nightstand and sat on the edge of his bed. "Brian, I think you've done the right thing by going to detox and getting involved in AA. I don't see though why that should impact our relationship." Jamie sipped his coffee, light with sugar.

"It's just I'm still confused about the whole sex thing, especially the gay scene, and how it ties in with spirituality and all that." Brian looked uncomfortably out the window. "Like I've said before, I still have traditional religious beliefs I need to separate from my own conception of God. I just can't shake them yet. I don't think I want to be locked in a relationship I feel unsure of. And that's pretty much where we're headed, isn't it? A relationship, I mean."

"I certainly was hoping so." Jamie stared morosely into his coffee cup, trying to summon the courage to do the right thing.

"I was wondering," Brian said, "you never told me about your first experience, how you knew you were gay." He sampled the black coffee in his cup and looked at Jamie.

"I can honestly say there was no clue in my childhood." Jamie lay back on the bed, resting on his elbows. "In fact, I was quite fond of the little girls when I was a kid. And I was totally into playing army with the other guys. I loved *Big*

Time Wrestling as well. Dick the Bruiser, Haystacks Calhoun, Stan the Man, and all those guys were part of every Saturday. After watching, we'd go out to homemade wrestling rings and practice the moves, much to the consternation of all our mothers. When I was about twelve or maybe thirteen, I was sleeping over at a friend's, someone with whom I spent many long idyllic summer days with. Together, we went fishing and camping and hiking all over the woods. We got ourselves into a few jams as well." Sitting up, Jamie tasted his coffee. "I was in bed late one morning, lying on my stomach, when he came in and jumped on top of me. I can remember the incredible heat of his body, how good the weight of it felt on me, how when I wiggled he squirmed with me, intensifying the contact. I felt my penis growing hard, inflating, throbbing against the mattress. Still, he laughed and thrashed on top of me, his genitals pressing against my ass. I had my first ejaculation in my skivvies and didn't even know what it was. But I knew I liked it and wanted more. The rest is history, I guess. I was married twice as you know and have two kids. I even had one pretty good relationship, but I just couldn't fake it any longer. I knew in my heart of hearts it was *guys* I really liked. And there wasn't a damn thing I could do about it."

"So"—Brian broke into an impish grin—"now I know why you like to lay on your tummy with me on top doing the old squirmin' mermin.'"

"Quid pro quo, want some more joe?" They both laughed as Jamie got up to refill their cups.

"Hey," said Brian, looking out the window, "looks like company." There was a *rat a tat tat* at the door.

"*Pase a dentro*, come in," Jamie called.

"Listen," said Nolan, sitting up against a pillow, smoking, while Camilla was drying off after taking a shower. "I've got to get out of here for a few days, go to a motel in Napolis and report what went down to my people in Tallahassee and DC. Tomorrow, sometime in the afternoon, can you give me a ride in?"

"I guess, Mike. You think that monster might come looking for you here? Shouldn't you get out right away? What about the rest of us? He's on to Brian and John."

"I don't know, but right now, I gotta rest." Nolan's face contorted in pain. "Hand me a couple of those Percosets please. The pain is really coming on now." Camilla brought over the pills with a glass of water. "And for God's sake, don't tell Toad I have pills, or he'll be over to snag some." They both laughed. Camilla looked both sad and radiant. She bent over and kissed her federal agent man on the lips softly.

"I gotta go now, Mike. My mother-in-law is in the hospital, and the lunatic responsible is on the loose. And worse, he's wearing a badge and seems to be untouchable."

"Trust me, Cam, nobody is untouchable. I'm going to bring him down."

"I hope so, Mike. For all of us, I hope so."

"So where's Cammy and Robbie?" Jamie asked.

"That's partly why we're here," Julie said as she gave Brian a big hug and kiss on the cheek. With one arm around his waist, she went on. "I think we're all going to have to get together with Mike Nolan again to assess how we stand. It may not be safe to stay here if the wacko cop knows there are witnesses. And he does *know*, does he not, Brian?" Julie stepped away from the newly recovering alcoholic but held onto his hand.

"Yeah, he knows," Brian acknowledged. "I think he wants to get rid of Nolan somehow. But he will definitely fuck over anybody who gets in his way. Right now, that's mainly Nolan and maybe John and me."

"I think we need to go over and see Nolan right now," Tommy said. "I mean, maybe we need to all take turns on some kind of watch and be ready to call 911."

"Why don't we give him a call on his cell phone before we go over?" Julie suggested.

"I'll call him on my cell," said Jamie. "I put his number in at the last meeting."

Before Jamie could scroll down his numbers, there was a knock at the door, and Camilla came in. "Hey, everybody, what's shakin'?" She looked a bit abashed. "How's my little boy!" She went over to give Billy a kiss on the forehead. "Mama's home, sweetie." Camilla picked up the indifferent tot. "Julie, did Robbie call from the hospital?" She went over and kissed Brian on the cheek and gave him a one-arm hug. Julie slipped her arm around his waist.

"Wow!" Tommy said. "You're suddenly the ladies' favorite, Brian. Maybe I should go into that detox center and quit the ole barley malt."

"I don't think you're a candidate," said Brian. "At least not yet."

"To answer your question," Julie said, "yes, Robbie called and said Constance is in stable condition but still unconscious. He was wondering about you."

"I had to go get Mike," Camilla reported. "He has been seriously wounded by gunshots *and* a car accident. Our local Barney Fife on nuclear steroids is responsible."

"We need to see him," Jamie said.

"Can we go over now?" asked Julie.

"No way." Camilla appeared flustered for a moment. "He took some pain medication and is resting. He needs to get his strength back enough to leave. He thinks we better do the same."

"I second that," said Brian. "But how are we to know what's going on? It seems like it would be a good idea if we all stayed together."

"Let's all hang on until tomorrow," Camilla said. "We'll let Mike communicate to his boss and see if we can get witness protection or something."

"We'll have to set up a watch," said Toad, who had been uncharacteristically quiet. "I'll start at six and go to midnight. We'll have two per shift to sit out on the porch with Jamie's cell phone." He turned to Vaughn. "John, you keep first watch with me."

"I can keep part of the watch say eight 'til midnight. I've got to go out to my place in the woods and gather a few things. Looks like we'll *all* be leaving soon."

"I'll give you a ride out to the Circle K," said Jamie. He looked at Brian. "It looks like events have overtaken us, but we'll stick to the dinner plan." Looking around the room, he announced, "Dinner at six for all who can attend. Grilled steaks on the barbie. No booze please."

"A ride would be great," Vaughn said. "I ought to have plenty of time to get my stuff together and be back by eight or earlier." He went over and stooped by Josh and gave him a hug. "I'll be back in a couple of hours. Love you."

"Let's go right now then," Jamie said.

Vaughn looked at Camilla and started to speak, but she cut him off.

"Don't worry, I've got the little rapscallion." Camilla came up behind Josh and put one arm over his shoulders, still holding Billie with her other arm.

"We'll be glad to do backup," said Julie, shooting a look at Tommy.

"And I'm available as well," Jamie chimed.

"What's a 'rapsillon'?" Josh asked.

"It's an onion that sings rap songs," Tommy quipped.

"It's a feisty little boy who everyone loves," Julie corrected. She bent over and kissed him on top of the head.

"I'll meet you at your car in about ten minutes," said Vaughn, patting Jamie on the arm as he walked by him to the door.

"I'm ready," said Jamie. "Bry, you want to ride with us?" He cast a meaningful look at his boyfriend. Brian correctly read it as, "We still have a lot to talk about."

"Sure, I could use a little scenery," Brian replied.

"Okay," Jamie said, "let's rock and roll."

The impromptu meeting was over.

Santana, dressed in a black long-sleeved shirt and black denim pants, placed a small hard-bodied suitcase, only slightly larger than a briefcase, on the backseat of the Lincoln Town Car. Inside were five large manila envelopes containing thirty thousand dollars each in hundreds and fifties. The money was layered between pages torn from old manuals or junk mail. The envelopes were sealed and addressed with the appropriate postage. This technique proved effective in discouraging custom officials from probing the contents. He slid into the passenger seat and nodded at Jimmy, sitting behind the wheel in denim shorts and a black Metallica tee shirt with skulls printed on the front. Jimmy, who had no idea where they were going, sat with a smile, hands on the simulated woodgrain and leather wheel. Santana wore his Beretta in a shoulder holster under his left arm. A spring-loaded device strapped on his right arm held a two-shot .22 Magnum derringer. Although he had practiced with the weapon often, he had occasion to use it only once when a cocaine smuggler in competition with another dealer, who happened to be his client, got the drop on him.

That was a bad day with lessons to be learned. He had been drunk the night before, not knowing the next day would bring an early confrontation. The upstart dealer, armed with a gun, stepped out of the alley next to his favorite breakfast haunt in Puerto Vallarta. After relieving him of his Beretta, the fool made the mistake of ordering Santana into the alley, no doubt to murder him out of sight. Santana made a show of being so afraid he was in danger of wetting his pants. He offered the cocky assassin a very large sum to spare him, slowly turning around with his arms still up. While the dullard spent time savoring the apparent groveling of his enemy, Santana brought down his right arm pretending to scratch his ear. He cast a look toward the street to distract the dope-dealing degenerate. In one quick motion, he straightened his arm, releasing the derringer with a flick of his wrist. He fired point-blank into the man's face. The .22 Magnum hollow point went into his left eye and exited behind his right ear, leaving a hole the size of a nickel. There was no return fire.

Santana smiled at Jimmy and nodded his head forward to indicate it was time to leave. "When you get to the end of the driveway, turn right and pull off the road immediately."

"Why do you want to stop?" Jimmy asked.

"Do exactly as I tell you, Hymie, and there weel be a very large bonus for you. But please, no questions."

"You got it, Mr. Santana." When the car stopped, Santana was out the door and opened the trunk in less time than it takes to say, "Fried eggs."

Santana removed a .223 rifle with a scope and laser tracer. The infamous round used widely around the world to kill people in warfare would be perfect for this job as well. The bullet was small, about 50 percent larger than a .22, but very fast, traveling in a flat straight trajectory over a long distance and packing a wallop when it hit. The shape of the bullet caused it to tumble after initial impact, often zigzagging or breaking up inside its unfortunate target. He walked back to the driveway and dropped to a kneeling position, right knee on the ground, left knee up, left elbow on left knee to steady his aim. He quickly sighted down the driveway at one of the Dodge Durangos reserved for Rooster's flunkies. Santana could see through the scope it was driven by the one called 'Pots.' He fired three shots in rapid succession at the vehicle's radiator, followed by three more into the center of the windshield. He didn't really want to hurt the fool driving, not for any sentimental or moral motives, but simply because he didn't want to piss off Rooster and jeopardize the remainder of his fee. The windshield spiderwebbed and caved inward, and the Durango swerved suddenly to the right and off the road. It bounced into and out of a drainage ditch and struck an oak tree head on. Santana shot out both tires on the left side as added insurance. He returned the rifle to the Lincoln's trunk and got back in the car.

"What happened?" asked Jimmy.

"Remember what I say about questions?" Santana looked at Jimmy and smiled, gold caps twinkling. But there was nothing amusing in the copper glint of his eyes. "You do want that *prima*, no?"

Jimmy suddenly realized that the *prima* wasn't optional. It was do or die. Perhaps, driving Mr. Santana wasn't going to be much fun after all.

28

Robbie sat in the hospital room holding his mother's hand and staring at her drawn and sagging face. An oxygen hose was fitted over her ears into her nostrils. An IV dripped fluids into a vein from a bag hanging overhead. A monitor screen blipped with her life signs. This vital woman, his mother, so alive the last time he saw her, looked a decade older and on the verge of death. The doctor said if she didn't come out of this coma in forty-eight hours, it was hard to tell when, if ever, she would. He thought of his life as a child, the care and love she had bestowed upon him, an only child. Where had his father been? He could scarcely recall the man. He was always on the go between his business affairs and public duties. His mother, also a busy socialite, had nevertheless been around to make and share dinner, at least in his preteen years. It was she too who came to all his school functions like the plays he was in and the baseball games when he played first base for the Cougars. After his father died, his mother seemed to go a little crazy, having affairs with men, boys really, much younger than her. In fact, some were no older than he was. What was that all about? Maybe he should have talked to her about it. Maybe he should have talked to her about a lot of things.

Robbie stood up and walked over to the bedside table and poured a glass of water. The doctor told him to go home to his wife and baby. He would call him as soon as there was any change. He *was* tired and starting to ripen a bit. *Yeah,* he thought, *guess I'll go home, get cleaned up a bit, and catch a nap.* For reasons everyone who has attended the sick and dying can understand, he felt reluctant to leave, almost guilty about it. Without really thinking about what he was doing, Robbie got on his knees by his mother's bed and prayed to a god he had all but forgotten until now. He prayed out loud in a low whisper. Tears welled in his eyes and spilled over the lower levee. They streamed down his cheeks as his nose began to run as well. He realized he was crying for the first time since he lost his father. And those were almost reluctant tears. When he was done, he felt better somehow, like everything was going to be all right. He felt like there was *hope.* He stood up and walked out of the room and went outside to a bright sunshiny Florida day. *This must be what faith is all about,* he thought.

On the drive home, Robbie felt a sudden attack of horniness. It began to crowd out the fatigue. He shifted uncomfortably in his seat as his restive penis sought freedom to grow inside the confines of his jockey shorts. The force of procreation, the affirmation of life, is a widespread reaction to the death or injury of a close relative or friend. Pictures of Cammy in assorted lingerie paraded through his mind. Before he knew it, he was back at the Fireproof. It looked quiet. Toad looked like a lone sentry at his post, jug under the small table.

"Hey, I'll catch up with you in a bit," Robbie called out to Toad. The veteran waved.

Entering the room, Robbie saw Camilla was asleep on the bed, Billy standing in his crib with a bottle. He held out a chubby hand to Robbie and shrieked while flinging the bottle to the floor. Robbie wanted to jump his wife's bones in a big way, but instead, he went over and picked up the baby.

"Is my little man taking care of Momma?" Robbie asked Billy as he nuzzled his cheek.

Camilla, half-wakened by Billy's outcry, opened her eyes. "Hi, honey," she said. "How's Constance?" She stretched and yawned like a lazy feline.

"I think she's going to be okay," Robbie answered. "The doctor says he expects her to come out of the comatose state in a few hours. He's going to call me, said I should get some sleep." He put the baby back in the crib and retrieved the bottle for him. Lying down next to his wife, he expected the toddler to howl in protest; but he remained strangely quiet, watching his parents as if he was some kind of jaded voyeur. When Robbie glanced at Billy, he could have sworn there was a gleam of encouragement in the little guy's eyes. He snuggled close to Camilla and put a hand on her breast as he moved his hips against hers. He started to kiss her on the face, then the lips.

"Robbie, I really can't right now," Camilla said. "I'm sorry, honey, but I just need to rest." She was still unchanged and without a bath from her escapade with Mike Nolan. "I'm going to take a hot shower, and then I suggest you do the same." Her voice was as cold as autumn frost. She got up from the bed and went into the bathroom, leaving Robbie and his bulge on his own. He looked at Billy who, having abandoned his bottle, threw his plastic rattle at him.

"A fine warm fuzzy home this turns out to be," Robbie said to Billy, tossing the bauble back in the crib. Pulling off his clothes, his love stick swelling, he went into the bathroom and opened the foggy glass shower door. "Okay, we'll do this like a couple of jail inmates, lassie."

"Robbie, please," Camilla said. She just couldn't have intercourse with her husband so soon after Nolan. It seemed obscene.

"What's wrong?" he asked. "I'm horny for my honey cup." She squirmed away from him but reluctantly consented to give him oral in the shower stall. Not all that pleased, Robbie agreed to this half measure, it being a far better option than dealing with his now fully tumid member with a soapy hand. Still, he sensed that something had changed since he left for the hospital to stand watch over his comatose mother. There is an almost-palpable psychic barrier that comes between close lovers when one has strayed into the bed of another. When the shower was finished, the couple lay down together on the bed.

"Robbie." Camilla was lying with her back to her husband.

"Yeah?" The plastic rattle flung by Billy glanced off Robbie's forehead. The baby whooped with delight. Robbie tossed the missile back into the crib, whereupon the baby, enthralled by this new sport, promptly heaved the noisemaker back at his father.

"Is your mother really going to be all right?" Camilla asked.

"At this point, nobody can say for sure. We can only pray." Camilla couldn't remember ever hearing her husband mention prayer before.

"We should probably go somewhere tomorrow." Camilla rolled onto her back. "Maybe stay at your mom's place until she gets better and this thing with the cop gets resolved. Mike Nolan thinks it's too dangerous to stay here. And I agree."

"You've seen him recently?" Suspicion tinged his tone.

"Yeah, he was hurt in a car accident." Camilla left out the wounded-by-buckshot part, not wanting to explain too much. "He says someone was trying to kill him."

"Someone?" Robbie held the plastic noisemaker in his right hand. "That crazy cop?"

"That would be a reasonable assumption," Camilla replied. "Robbie, I'm scared. And we have Billy to consider." As if on cue, the disgruntled toddler bawled and reached out toward Robbie, who threw the boy's toy back into the crib, causing the crying to turn to jubilation as Billy thrashed after the gewgaw.

"We'll wait for a call from the hospital," Robbie said. "If Mom comes around, we can all go there and stay at her place. In any case, we'll leave tomorrow for Napolis."

"Mike's still in his room, hurt with no car," Camilla worried out loud. "Hopefully, Jamie and Brian can get him someplace. It's Brian and John who are the actual witnesses here. They're the ones most at risk." A colorful clapper landed in Robbie's lap.

"At this point"—Robbie tossed the now-annoying baby bauble back into the crib—"I would say anyone crossing Deputy Mad Dog's path is in peril."

"I think I'll have a beer," said Camilla standing up. "Want one?"

"Why not." The amazing flying rattle bounced off his ear.

"On top of everything else," Sheriff Gunther said, "I've got this Greek geek, a Yankee transplant, trying to unionize my deputies." He sat across the round table from Judge Thomas, umbrella up for shade. They were having martinis and cigars on the screened lanai at the judge's country club home. The judge's wife was on a cruise with three of her lady friends and would be gone three days. They sat by a kidney-shaped pool with five statues of scantily clad girls baring breasts like flour biscuits just rising, hardly larger than the rosebud nipples crowning them, posed around it. A token male cherub circulated the pool water through his small penis. It was very cute, very artsy.

"You can put the kee-bush-bahsh on that easily enough." The judge sipped his drink and leaned back. "Or is there something I missed?

"Oh, I've already got a couple of my good ole boys on that detail," Gunther responded. "I'll use subtle threats about job status, transfers, and layoffs. The usual bag of tricks employed in such matters. If none of that brings results, we'll tail and harass his old lady and kids. That never fails to back them down."

"So," the judge said, taking a drag on his Cuban Cohiba, "what about our mutual friend, that thug, Tiny? He's become a real pain in the ass. Can't you get rid of him?"

"It's not that easy." Gunther downed the rest of his drink.

"Start with some kind of probation," the judge offered, "like administrative leave. Get his captain involved. Surely there are options."

"Mind?" Gunther held up his empty glass.

"Help yourself." The judge nodded toward the small outdoor wet bar. "There's a pitcher of it in the fridge."

"A little birdie tells me we may not have to worry about him after this weekend." The sheriff strolled over, pulled out the pitcher, and filled his glass. He reached over and picked up a pair of tongs and plopped a couple of olives in the glass.

"I'll drink to that," said the judge, and he did. "This business with the missing kids is causing a stir in Child Protective Services. There are a couple of deputies who claim they were told not to file reports by our esteemed deputy, that it was being investigated. I've backed him as far as I can."

"Like I said"—Gunther lit a fresh cigar, strolling to his seat—"we are looking for a new sergeant for the Bella Villa substation. The truth is, I'm getting tired of covering up for him too. If not for my connections in Tallahassee, we'd all be in the ringer now." Gunther took a large swallow of the martini. "I am hopeful there won't be another fiasco. I've all but given up on trying to rein him in. I think the implementation of a 'final solution' is our best and only strategy."

"Then, so be it," the judge ruled.

John Vaughn carried three pictures of his son, as well as one of his estranged wife, in his backpack. Prior to leaving, he sat smoking a cigarette in his cabin, reflecting on the unpredictable path fate steered his life. He mumbled a short prayer for his son, his wife, and Josh. He wept silently a moment before departing.

Trudging out the path from his camp in the presunset woods, he speculated on their reunion. In addition to the pictures, he carried a notebook used for drawing and making cryptic notes, as well as five hundred dollars in cash he had buried in a sealed plastic bag inserted in a coffee can. Vaughn emerged from the woods where his tiny makeshift bungalow lay hidden from the noise and confusion of the outside world. A truck rushed passed him, causing his hair to blow about his head as he began his five-mile hike to the Fireproof. Several cars sped by at excessive speeds. He had grown to truly dislike this modern world, but he realized disengagement wasn't the answer either. Like it or not, his experience at the Fireproof demonstrated his desire to be with people, to care for someone, to need and be needed, to share with others. He longed to be reunited with his son and to bring Josh into a loving family. It was worth making an effort to reconcile with his wife.

The sun was low in the evening sky. Twilight was approaching, the pine trees and scattered palms and oaks casting long hobgoblin shadows across the pavement. Ahead, on the opposite side of the road, he could see the large black shapes of two vultures. As he advanced, more of the coal-colored fowl swooped down. These grotesque birds, common in Florida, were kept well fed and plentiful in numbers by the abundance of roadkill appearing daily along every artery. Vaughn imagined, just going on what he had personally witnessed, it would be possible to fill a very large dump truck every day with the dead animals appearing on Florida's highways and byways. Ugly creatures, these winged kings of carrion stood almost three feet high with a nasty curve at the end of their beaks and long sharp talons. They were jabbing and clawing at something on the side of the road. By the time Vaughn was across from the scene, the numbers had grown to well over twenty of death's flying angels competing for what remained of a large raccoon. Vaughn watched for another ten minutes as the feathered feasters ripped and tore the meat from the carcass until there was nothing but pieces of fur and a few bones. *I wonder how long it'd take to reduce a human body to that state,* Vaughn wondered. He turned with a shudder from the grisly scene, fancying the eyes of the sable fowl were appraising their next meal, and hiked briskly toward his destination.

Putting his rented Altima in reverse (he'd recently developed an aversion to the Ford Taurus), Mario started to back out of his driveway. His plan was a simple one. He would leave his car here to indicate he was still around, just off with someone selling dope or whatever, while he gave the devil of a deputy the old slipperoo, making off with what cash he had left, not to mention his life. Just as his car reached the edge of the driveway, however, a black Lincoln pulled up behind him. Mario came down hard on the brakes, bringing the Altima to a stop an inch or two short of the rear fender of the Lincoln. A small man, looking like a pint-sized version of Richard Boone dressed as "Paladin," emerged from the passenger side. Dressed all in black, wearing a shoulder holster housing some kind of semiautomatic pistol, he was smiling, the glint of gold flashing in the late afternoon sun. Mario pulled his own Brazilian-made Taurus 9mm from between the seats. Paranoid of being caught off guard, he had chambered a round just before placing the gun in the center console. As the stranger in black approached the car, Mario rolled down the window, his left index finger on the electric switch and his right near the trigger. He kept his gun hand out of sight.

"Buenas días, amigo," said Paladin.

"What up?" Mario was trying to sound cool, not scared shitless.

"Mr. Babcock, he say you come with me. We go together to the OK corral. OK?" Santana laughed out loud at his little joke.

"Tell Mr. Ass-cock I've got other commitments." Mario tightened his grip on the handgun, putting his finger on the trigger.

"I no sink so, Meester Mario." Santana used his worst English, all smiles. "Pleeze, you come wiz me."

"Get the car out of my way," Mario said. He tried to stare daggers at the man in black but nervous sweat dripped into his eyes, making him blink.

Santana scratched the back of his head with his right hand. "I give you count of three to get out of car. One ... two ..." Mario raised his gun hand. Santana straightened his right arm with a snap at the wrist. The derringer came into his hand, and he fired from two feet away into Mario's face. The .22 Magnum hollow point penetrated the skull just above the left eye, mushrooming into a jagged piece of shrapnel; it scrambled a fairly decent amount of brain tissue before exiting behind the left ear lobe, leaving a ragged and bloody opening large enough to poke a magic marker into. Mario's eyes rolled back into his head as if to say, "Give me a break," and the unfortunate young smuggler slumped dead in his seat.

Santana reached into the car; and taking the dark right hand of the expired driver, he shook the gun loose, and guiding the hand to the ignition, he turned off the engine. A wet swooshing sound accompanied by a terrible stench told Santana the corpse had released the fecal matter stored in its bowels. He pulled his head out of the window, took a deep breath of fresh air, and returned to the Lincoln.

"You see, *chico*," the gunslinger said to Jimmy, "Santana knows what goes in the dark man's heart." The terrified boy put on a brave face. Driving the assassin was turning into a real nightmare. "Let's go to the school, eh?"

"Yes, sir, Mr. Santana," Jimmy said.

Paladin smiled, reached into a pack on the floor, and reloaded the derringer.

Jamie brought the steaks in from the barbeque grill and put them on the table. Everyone but John Vaughn was there, including Morris Kline, the motel owner.

"Help yourselves, people," Jamie said. "There's two medium rare and the rest are medium. If you need them better done, the coals are still hot, so go for it. Anyone wants it rare, they better have a time machine. There's potato salad and coleslaw on the table. Coke and ice tea are in the large cooler by the TV."

Morris sauntered up to Brian. "It's wonderful what you're doing. Believe me, you won't be sorry. My wife and I pray you will stick with the program." He gave Brian's arm a squeeze.

"Thanks," said Brian. "I appreciate all the support. Everybody's been great." Morris smiled and ambled over to the table to fix a plate.

When everyone had feasted, Tommy and Julie broke out guitars and began to play music. Brian and Toad stepped out to smoke a couple of small cigars someone in detox had given Brian. They leaned against the porch's uprights.

"How you feelin'?" Toad asked. He held out his lighter for Brian to fire up his cigar. Although he had a few drinks during the day, Toad was unusually sober.

"I'm feelin' better than I have in years." Brian puffed the cigar while Toad lit his.

"No craving or compulsion?" Toad asked. "That's what always gets us drunks even after we quit and the physical compulsion is gone. We still have that mental craving. We just aren't ourselves without booze in the blood."

"I gotta tell you," Brian said, "I don't feel quite like myself. I need to remove myself from the party even though there's no booze. It brings on the thirst. Anyway, someone is coming by any minute to pick me up for an AA meeting."

"I guess if that's what you need, you gotta do what's right for you." Toad puffed his cigar, went over, and sat on a plastic porch chair.

"One of these days," Brian said, staring off toward the road, "when my head clears, I'm gonna figure out this whole sex thing before it drives me back to the bottle." He stood watching as the sun disappeared below the tree line.

"Let me tell you something," Toad said. He leaned forward and squinted at Brian. "I know you're mixed up with social mores and religious strictures concerning homosexuality. Nobody's saying being queer is any easier to accept than being alcoholic. But *none* of those constraints, either imposed from outside or by your own unease, will stand in the face of love and passion. They will be blown away like a straw hut in a hurricane. So all your fretting will come to nothing in the final act. I'm sure you know what I'm talking about. That said, I need a drink." He stood up and stuck his hand out. "Good luck, my friend. You *can* beat the booze thing if you have the *willingness* to do it. I don't." They shook hands, and Toad headed for his own porch chair and his bottle.

Rooster looked up from his body massage on a table by the pool. Teddy Grimm, his chief of security, came through the screen door into the patio enclosure.

"What's up, Teddy?" Rooster groaned as a lovely blond, sitting on his towel-draped buttocks and wearing only a G-string, dug her hands into his shoulders. "You wouldn't be here if there wasn't trouble."

"It's Pots, Mr. Babcock. He's been injured in a car accident in the driveway. He's unconscious. I took the liberty to have two of the men drive him to the hospital in North Napolis." Grimm looked sternly at Rooster. "Did you send him on a detail without notifying me first? I'm asking because there were bullet holes in the radiator and windshield, and the tires were shot."

"I told him to check in with you before leaving," Rooster lied. "Can you tell me anything more about what happened? Any witnesses?"

"Not that I know of, but Mr. Santana's car is gone. I surmise he was involved somehow. Pots was no doubt sent to tail him."

"That's right, Teddy. Obviously, Santana knew and tried to kill him." Rooster let out a long sigh as the girl moved down his spine. "That's good for now, Nikki," he said to the bombshell. "We'll catch up later." The girl dismounted and held up a robe for the pudgy kingpin. Rooster slipped into the white terrycloth robe with the rooster emblem embroidered on the two pockets. "Go in and bring me a hot towel, cupcake." He kissed the masseuse on the cheek, and the girl left, her naked hindquarters swaying in a silent siren song.

"I don't think Santana really wanted to harm anyone," Grimm said. "I'm sure Pots would be dead now if Santana wanted to kill him. My guess would be it's just a warning to stay out of his business. My concern is Jimmy. I'm told he left with Santana, driving his car as a matter of fact. I don't much care for that idea."

"Neither do I," Rooster said. "I've developed a liking for the boy. Still, I suppose he has to step up to the plate sometime. I guess his time has come."

"I'm not sure the boy is ready for somebody like Santana and his kind of hardball," Grimm said. "In any case, there's nothing to be done now, is there?"

"I reckon not, Teddy, I reckon not." Rooster offered the security chief a cigar.

Grimm shook his head. "No thanks." He watched Rooster light his. "I think it would be advisable to double up on the security for tonight's fights."

"Whatever you think, Teddy. Better to be safe than sorry, eh?"

"Well, I better get to it." Grimm turned and bustled out the door. Rooster watched him go, his brow furrowed. Nikki came out with a steaming towel.

"Never mind the towel," Rooster said. "Make me a Dewer's on the rocks with a splash of soda. On second thought, make it a double."

Tiny decided to take a drive by the Fireproof to see if there was any sign of Nolan. He was wearing dungarees and a sheriff's department vest, POLICE stenciled with large letters on the back, as well as a baseball cap with a large sheriff's star on the front. The renegade deputy felt uncomfortable after hearing Sam's report.

Failing to find a body or proof of the federal agent's demise didn't mean he wasn't deceased; it just meant there was no absolute proof of death. He pulled into the parking lot and drove slowly around. He saw no vehicle or sign that Nolan was there. On the other hand, the bastard could be in there now drawing a bead on him. Tonight, after disposing of his most pressing threat, Rooster's hired gun, he could return and check the room by coming on foot from the back side. The only one moving now was a little boy playing on the porch next to that stationary and staring fool called Toad. Tiny would like to go over and squeeze the drunken sot's neck under his disgusting whiskers until his eyeballs popped out. *Discretion is the better part of trash removal,* he thought. The boy turned his straw-colored head in his direction, and Tiny saw the smiling face of Josh Crayton. He put on the brakes and scrutinized the boy a moment in shocked disbelief. The crazy drunk stood up and said something to the boy, who scooted across the porch and ducked into a doorway. The besotted moron started to wave his hands and yell obscenities at Tiny. He started down the stairs on unsteady legs, and Tiny whipped out of the driveway, spewing gravel in Mr. Toad's direction.

Turning south on Route 29, Tiny sped off with the notion of turning around and driving by the motel again on his way back to Bella Villa. However, a mile up the road, he noticed a solitary figure walking north on the west shoulder. John Vaughn looked up at the sky just as Deputy Harris sped by. Tiny, recognizing one of the two star witnesses to the O'Brien shooting, saw a golden opportunity laid at his feet or, more accurately, his right foot. He stepped on the gas and drove far enough up the road to turn around without being noticed. He checked the rearview mirror, nothing. From the south, nothing. His Grand Cherokee was fully equipped with leather interior, air conditioning, cruise, tilt, and full power. A state-of-the-art CD player, cassette deck, AM/FM radio with a six-speaker system, provided a dynamic sound for the driver and passengers. Tiny slipped in a Frank Sinatra CD, put on "My Way," and cranked the volume as he put the pedal to the metal.

29

Despite his intrinsic understanding of the natural order of things and the place vultures had in it, the rotting flesh feeders sent a chill up Vaughn's spine. They made him feel vulnerable somehow. It was as if they were reminders of what could be waiting for all of us at the end of the line. Vaughn looked up at the sky just as an SUV whizzed by. The road was almost completely engulfed in dusk. The sun must be near the horizon, about an hour or less from setting, he figured. *They've probably finished dinner by now,* he thought. *Hope they saved a little for me.* He figured he was about a mile from the Fireproof. He should be there in about fifteen minutes at his present pace. He resumed his daydreaming about his future life. He would reunite with his wife and son. And Josh would be a part of the family. Maybe there would be one more child at some point. No more than three though. Three was plenty to care for. Besides, two of his own blood would make a sufficient contribution to the world's population explosion to ensure Armageddon. He stopped for a moment to light a Camel. He heard the crunch of tires on gravel behind him and started to turn.

Tiny checked his rearview mirror and noted the road behind was clear of vehicles. Likewise, there was open road to the front. Could he get any luckier? He steered the Jeep over the centerline, his eyes focused now on the figure walking on the opposite side of the road. He brought the Grand Cherokee up to sixty miles an hour and aimed the left corner of his bumper at Vaughn's meager ass. The forest denizen paused to light a cigarette. Tiny noted a puff of smoke, just as the four-thousand-pound juggernaut he was piloting clipped the future cancer patient on the right buttocks. John Vaughn flew out of his sneakers and pants and launched forward and to the left. The impact shattered his pelvis and broke his spine in three places. He died instantly. His lifeless body was thrown eighty feet through the air until his head made contact with a large Caribbean pine, pulverizing the skull. A few days later, literally nothing was left of the body after feathered, furry, and/or scaly scavengers finished with it. His disappearance would remain yet another unsolved mystery littering the police blotters of South Florida.

Tiny, barely feeling the impact inside the Jeep, swerved back to the right-hand lane and headed for Captain Post's house in Bella Villa. He picked up his cell phone and punched Captain Post's home number on his autodial. "Be there in ten," he said when Post answered. Actually, he was there in nine.

Captain Post was not exactly thrilled to see his business partner and supposed subordinate arrive. He didn't have much stomach for facing down dangerous and armed criminals. In the case of Santana, a hired assassin, he was especially loathe to go on a mission without a SWAT team at his back. Instead, he was going into hell's fire with Tiny, a psychopath, whose usefulness was now eclipsed by his reckless behavior. He thought of simply shooting Tiny and being done with it. Truth is, he didn't have the nerve for that either.

Tiny was bouncing like Pooh's friend Tigger when he hit the captain's steps. His recent dispatching of Vaughn, half the potential case against him if things went south, buoyed him. The other half, a queer drunk, would be easy to dispose of. He rapped on the door, and Post let him in the foyer, holding a finger to his lips. A bead of sweat glistened on his ebony skin near the left temple. He was dressed in his gray deputy's uniform, his Glock holstered on his belt.

"My wife's in the kitchen," he whispered, "keep it down."

"Yeah, okay," Tiny tried to subdue his voice. "Let's go outside." They went out on the porch where the setting sun cast every hue of red, orange, and pink across the turquoise South Florida sky. It was like a watercolor canvas done by an uncommonly gifted artist. A single date palm with a dozen scaly trunks caped with fronds growing in a clump gave the front yard a tropical hue. The two deputies, however, were not inclined to appreciate nature; Tiny saw the sky only as an impetus to hurry.

"We better shake a leg, Captain. We'll be totally in the dark soon." Tiny headed for Post's Crown Victoria cruiser. "You got a riot gun on board?"

"Twelve-gauge pump, loaded and ready," Post responded. "It's in the trunk."

"Rifle?" Tiny asked.

"Ditto. In the trunk. Thirty-ought-six semiautomatic. Also loaded."

"Let's roll," Tiny said. They both got in the car, Post behind the wheel. "Step on it, Captain. Daylight's burnin'."

"We're going to have to call this in if there's gunplay," Post said as they sped toward the Old County Road.

"Oh, we're going to call it in all right," Tiny said. "Two police officers being fired on in the course of duty. You bet we'll call it in. What we *don't do* is connect Santana with Babcock. At least, not right off. First, we make Rooster pay a ransom. A fee to stay free." Tiny chortled at his rhymes. "I'd make a hell of a rapper, eh, Captain? You blacks don't have a copyright on it."

"I wouldn't quit my day job," Post riposted.

"We'll both be quittin' soon if we pull this off." Tiny checked his Glock, pulled back the slide, and injected a round into the chamber. "We'll both be *retired*, living the good life. Rooster is dangerous, but that just makes him a bigger fish. We can take him for all we need and get the hell out. Drop every other operation. It's getting a little sticky anyhow. In the end, he'll survive and just get richer. His kind always does."

They turned on the Old County Road and were approaching the old school building when Tiny undid his seat belt. "This is it, Captain. Stop here. Open the trunk, I'm taking the shotgun with me."

"What's up?" Post looked at him, a bewildered expression crinkling his face.

"Simple plan," said Tiny. "You go in the front door, I go in the back door. I was hoping Mario would be here as a distraction to make him think our original plan was going down. But the stinker won't answer his phone, and there's no time to go looking for him."

"What the hell do you want me to do?" Post was a little disconcerted. "Drive up and ask if there's anybody home?"

"Stay by the car and call for backup as soon as shots are fired." Tiny walked back and took the shotgun and a shoulder bag with ammunition. He had two extra 9mm clips as well. He came back around to Post's side of the car. "Go to the back of the car and open the trunk when you get there. Be ready to use the rifle. Keep down and in radio contact with me using the shoulder mic and earphone. *Let's do it!*" Tiny took off into the woods by the road, leaping over the drainage gully. A well-beaten footpath about a hundred feet into the glade ran parallel to the road and right into the homeless hostel. Post watched him disappear into the foliage. Reaching into his glove box, he retrieved a flask containing Wild Turkey Bourbon, favored for its taste and potency; he took a healthy pull. Returning the container to its resting place, he proceeded down the road.

Jimmy pulled the Lincoln onto the old school building's apron. They arrived a full two hours before eight, the time given by Mario for the meeting.

"I call you on eet when I want to be peeked up," Santana said, handing Jimmy a cell phone. "Put these phone in your pocket, it ees set to vibrate instead of reeng. Eef, for any reason, you need to call, poosh number 1. Eet auto-deals. Okay?" He smiled, his gold tooth emitting a mirthless sparkle.

"Yeah," Jamie said, "but where should I go?"

"Up the road, one mile," Santana said, "ees a place where Los Mexicanos, dey drink and eat burritos, tostados, enchiladas, you know, all that Mexican food." He chortled at his own sardonic humor. "You wait dere. If anyone say anyding, you tell dem you work for Santana. Dey know better than fool with you. Now, open dee trunk." Santana took out the rifle and grabbed his satchel with extra rounds for both rifle and pistol. From the backseat, he took a canteen full of water, a can of bug spray, a twenty-foot section of two-hundred-pound test nylon rope, and some beef jerky. He placed all the items in the pack. If he had to run, he would take only the ammunition he could carry in the large pockets of his fatigue-style pants. He intended to set off a flare inside the bag to destroy all evidence. The Boy Scouts of America would do well to be as thorough as Santana was on any of his assignments. He waved Jimmy away, and the boy who would be a gangster's gopher drove off.

Santana started for the building but was confronted by a lanky man holding a snub nose .38. There were five other ill-dressed and grungy-looking desperados; three of them were also packing heat and pointing the barrels at Santana. The other two brandished nasty-looking knives. They began to drift apart. Paladin flashed them some gold; dropping the satchel and throwing down the rifle, he rolled—drawing his Beretta as he came up on his feet four yards to the right. The ragged band of gypsies began shooting in a panic. He started sprinting, firing his handgun as he went. They were out of ammunition almost immediately, thanks to Mario. None of their shots came particularly close to the fast-moving target, but the authentic Mexican pistolero managed to place every shot into human flesh. The tall leader and another ragged soldier, though wounded, flung their pistols at him in desperation, screaming as they charged him. A knife hit Santana, handle first, in the left shoulder but barely distracted him. Santana cut them down with two shots apiece, almost point-blank, in their chests. He was impressed by their bravado. In the time it takes to say, "That's the real *enchilada*, Señor McCoy," Santana bagged six gringo cowboys, though some were still squirming. He dispatched the two still showing life with shots to the head from twenty feet away. No sense moving closer and giving them an opportunity for a lucky shot if they were capable. He was not aware they had used all their bullets before he shot them in the first place.

Changing the clip in his Beretta while still moving, Santana ran in a crouch to the corner of the building and peeked around. A wide grin erupted on his tense face at the scenario. Another five or six of the hapless homeless were streaking for the cover afforded by familiar forest paths. Still, he used caution in entering the old edifice of education. There may be stalwart students of life yet present but not accounted for. Finding no Johnny-come-lately learners, Santana went back out to retrieve his rifle and pack. He also took time to hide the corpses. He didn't think the shots would be noticed by anyone as the closest house was half a mile away. If someone did hear shots, they would be muffled and distant, nothing anyone in this hick town where gunshots were common would think twice about. Nevertheless, he used caution moving back to the front parking area. Seeing no signs of life, either on foot or motorized, he moved quickly to drag the bodies into the brush. It was a hot sweaty job, and Santana was glad he brought the canteen and the bug dope. After taking a drink, he checked the rifle. The scope couldn't be relied on for accuracy after taking a direct hit on the pavement, so he removed it. Probably wouldn't be good light by the time his quarry arrived in any case. At these distances, he wouldn't need it. Besides, he would have greater mobility without the clumsy addition to his firearm.

Santana went back into the building and took up a position on the second floor by the only window not boarded over. From it, he had a commanding view of the front parking area. He tied his rope off to an old desk and wedged it under the windowsill. He might need an escape route should he be unlucky enough to get trapped. He checked the time, applied some more bug spray, lit a cigar, and settled in for the brief wait until showtime.

Captain Post stopped before reaching the old schoolhouse and retrieved the rifle from the trunk. He placed it in the backseat and drove to the paved apron where he parked passenger side facing the building. The reluctant station commander got out of the car, keeping his head down, and grabbed the rifle from the backseat. He put in his earplug and turned on the police radio. He sat with his back against the rear door, a glum expression on his dark face. The sun was below the horizon now. It would be pitch-dark in thirty minutes or so. He checked his watch; it was ten minutes after eight. If there were going to be an ambush, there would probably be someone hiding in the school building. Otherwise, they would be somewhere in the woods surrounding the building, in which case, Tiny was likely to run into them. Post was tempted to call for backup right now, but he would look pretty foolish if there were no assassin. At the first shot, he would do a Mayday.

"Captain, you read me?" It was Tiny on the radio.

"Roger, I read you," Post replied.

"Hang tight, I'll be inside the building in one minute. No sign of vagrants. Anybody visible where you are?"

"Negative," said Post. "It's quiet here." A series of rifle shots boomed from the second floor of the old schoolhouse. They came in rapid succession and were striking the patrol car behind the rear tire. Suddenly, the gas tank exploded. Post was thrown several yards from the car as it erupted in flames. Stunned and deafened, he got to his feet without thinking. His legs were as unreliable as any well-lubricated drunk's might be. Trying to regain focus of his eyesight, he spotted the rifle lying by the burning car. He started to stumble toward it, hoping the heat wouldn't prevent him from getting close enough or cause the ammunition to explode. Instead, his head exploded as two bullets from Santana's rifle scrambled his brains and punched out the back of his skull. The captain of the Bella Villa Substation fell to his knees as if to plead with God to be merciful although he was no longer capable of anything but evacuating his bowels and bladder into his gray uniform pants. He pitched forward on his face.

Tiny, hearing the gunfire and subsequent explosion, broke out in a full-speed dash for the building. He stopped at the side of the door, back to the wall, and caught his breath. He called 911, gave the operator his badge number, and told her there was an officer down, suspect armed and extremely dangerous. He gave her the location and hung up. He really wasn't in the mood to listen to a lot of annoying questions. Riot gun ready, he burst through the door, sweeping the room. He heard somebody move upstairs. The only way up was a rickety set of steps on the east wall of the building. He approached the steps quickly but with stealth. He heard footsteps above him. He raised the twelve gauge and blasted several rounds of buckshot overhead into the upper floorboards. Dust and debris rained down on him. He moved to the wall by the foot of the stairs and waited, silently reloading. A gaping hole from the shotgun blasts appeared near the head of the stairs. There was still too much dust to see clearly. He caught a shiny glint, followed by a muzzle flash. A bullet tore into his left shoulder, slamming him back against the wall. Recovering in a heartbeat, he let loose a series of blasts from the shotgun. He heard a man cry out above. He fired up through the ceiling in the direction of the sound and heard another shriek of pain and some rapid-fire Spanish. *Cursing in his native tongue—that's a point for the home team,* Tiny thought and smiled despite his wound.

When he saw the black cop bite the dust, Santana figured his real target would be coming inside any second. He wiped the rifle down, sticking two magazines for his Beretta in the large pockets of his black fatigue pants. He flicked a Bic to light the flare when a very loud boom, followed by another, shattered the tranquility of his sniper's nest. Buckshot and wood splinters were flying everywhere. Dropping the flare, Santana ran to the head of the stairs, only to be thrown back by another series of shots, practically removing his feet, sneakers and all. He moved like a panther, spotting a large nebulous shape move against the wall at the foot of the stairs. He pointed his pistol at the fluttering figure beyond the cloud of dust and debris filling the room and fired. The man flinched—a hit! Then the shotgun barked. A buckshot pellet blew his left big toe off as he moved toward the window. He yelped in pain as another blast from below tore through the decrepit flooring. A pea-sized pellet slammed into the pistolero's left butt cheek. He let out a stream of curses in Spanish but made it back to the boarded window where his bag was stashed.

Santana aimed his pistol at the stairwell while picking up his cell phone and making a quick call to Jimmy. Again he clicked his Bic, lighting the flare inside the bag. Santana tossed the pack into the stairwell, where it rolled down in a ball of flame, lighting the night fantastic. The rounds inside began exploding. With great pain, he climbed out the window where he had secured the rope. Once outside, he called Jimmy again on the cell phone. He instructed him to pull all the way up to the building on the north side. His foot was throbbing with pain and bleeding profusely. His left ass cheek was also bleeding down his pant leg and was beginning to cramp up. There was nothing he could do about either wound right now. With some difficulty, the hired gun limped to the corner of the building and hunkered down to wait for his escape vehicle. He hoped to nail the bastard cop as he came out of the already-burning building.

Tiny burst at full speed through the door, making straight for a nearby pine. A shot rang out, almost decapitating him just as a black Lincoln, headlights glaring, pulled up to the other side of the building. The deputy saw a small figure in black limping rapidly to the passenger door. Running forward, Tiny fired the shotgun as the door closed. The car roared backward, tires screeching. He raced out to the road and fired another couple of times, hitting the getaway vehicle but doing little more damage than breaking a taillight. The hunter, turned quarry, was speeding away into the darkness of the now fully arrived night. There was a wail of sirens in the distance.

30

Santana pulled out the tails of his shirt. Using a switchblade that was part of his everyday equipment, he cut a strip of cloth to wrap his foot. He cut another piece to wrap around his thigh as a tourniquet to slow the blood flow. Meanwhile, he instructed Jimmy to drive the speed limit and head back to the Red Rooster. He checked his pistol, ejecting and reloading the clip. He removed a perforated cylinder from his bag of tricks and screwed it onto the barrel of the Beretta.

"What's that for?" Jimmy asked. He knew damned well what it was—a state-of-the-art silencer. It would make the 9mm sound no louder than a baby's fart.

"In case there are any unanticipated surprises." Santana grinned at Jimmy, flashing the unnerving gold-capped teeth.

When Jimmy pulled the Lincoln up to the guardhouse leading to the ranch's main compound, the guard waved them through with a smile. Santana rolled down the electric window on his side of the vehicle as they approached the mansion. Jimmy opened his door and bolted from the car as soon as he stopped in front of the house. The naive boy, in a fit of irrepressible loyalty to his employer, beat feet for the front door, thinking he could warn Rooster. Half-expecting a foolish move, Santana leaned out the window and, with a soft popping sound from his pistol, brought the fugitive down just inside the portico. Too bad. He'd hoped he wouldn't have to harm the young man. Getting out of the car, he limped over to the prone body lying facedown. He squatted down and helped the boy roll on his back. Jimmy's eyes blinked, and he gasped for breath. Blood trickled from the corner of his mouth. He looked up at the last face he would see on earth, and he saw regret and sympathy in the warrior's cold eyes, but no mercy. As a token of respect, Santana ambled to the front door where Jimmy couldn't see him and placed a bullet through the top of his head.

Santana hobbled as fast as his wounds allowed toward the back of the house. An impenetrable hedge of bougainvillea, rife with large red flowers, barred the way to the backyard. A wrought-iron gate, eight feet high and six feet wide, secured the only opening. Santana tried the gate; it was locked. He shot the latch and pushed through the opening, continuing until he stood next to the locked door of the lanai. Peeking in, Santana saw only one man. Shooting through the screen, he put a bullet into the head of the security guard as he talked on his radiophone. The muffled *thump*, like the sound made by squeezing a plastic bottle, went undetected. He shot the bolt off, securing the door to the lanai, and entered, hobbling with wrapped and smarting foot over to the dead guard's body. At the same time, a second sentinel, having seen the black-garbed figure on a monitor, notified Rooster of the breach. Charging with his M16 on full automatic onto the lanai, the heroic soldier of fortune sprayed a shower of bullets in the assassin's direction. Santana, seeing the adversary come through the door, dove to the floor next to the expired first guard. Rolling the body on its side and using it as a shield, he fired twice at the lunatic with the spurting gun, taking him out with a bullet through the heart on his second shot. Not wanting to take the time to see if he killed the man, Santana simply put a bullet in his head and proceeded to Rooster's bedroom.

Tiny called dispatch on his portable radio and told them to send a car and ambulance, as well as the forensics unit, to the old school building. He had no idea at the time that six bodies besides the captain's would be found at the crime scene. Tiny assumed the squatters had run off at the first sign of trouble, leaving the gunslinger to do his dirty work. Probably, the perfidious pot dealer, Mario, had double-crossed him. Tiny was convinced the assassin wasn't one of Rooster's thugs or some second-rate hack. This was somebody with reputation and experience, a real pro, charging large fees for his work. It was the money that caught Tiny's ever-avaricious imagination. And it would all be in cash. Good ole U.S. greenbacks. He had to get out to the Red Rooster Ranch and stop the routed assassin from fleeing with the loot. He decided not to alert his brothers in arms of the situation. No need to connect Babcock to this and kill his golden goose. A squad car roared up to the apron, lights flashing. A deputy got out on the other side, gun in hand. Tiny put down the shotgun and walked toward the car.

"Police officer!" Tiny yelled to the deputy getting out of the car. He was holding his badge up in plain sight, the other hand raised above his head. The cop, holding his handgun at the ready, stayed behind his vehicle as he focused his spotlight on Tiny. Recognizing his superior, he came over to where Tiny was standing. He was a young rookie, two years out of high school with an associate's degree in criminology from Edison College in Fort Myers; his name was Duncan Little, and he thought he had the inside track on law enforcement. His boyish face was flushed in fright and incredulity. He was in the thick of events they didn't teach in books, a potentially life-threatening crime scene. He looked at the burning patrol car and at Post, lying dead on the ground. Smoke poured out the open window of the schoolhouse, and the flickering of firelight could be seen within. The wail of the ambulance siren was growing closer.

"What the hell?" Little blurted.

"Secure the scene here," Tiny instructed. He picked up the riot gun. "Wait for forensics and the ambulance." Tiny started toward the still-running patrol car. "I'm taking your car."

"Wait!" Little cried. "You can't leave the scene, Sergeant. It's against protocol."

"I'm going after the bastard who did this," Tiny said. "Fuck protocol. Go look for anybody else who might be wounded. There's usually ten or twelve vagrants hanging out here."

"I'm going to have to call this in, sir. Sorry, but I'll need permission from headquarters before I let you use my vehicle."

"Who do you think is acting commander with the captain dead, dipstick?" Tiny was in a hurry and didn't want to wet-nurse this greenhorn. "Just follow orders." He tossed the shotgun onto the passenger seat of the patrol car.

"I can't do that, Sergeant." The nit-picking patrolman was right behind him. Tiny turned, viper quick, and slammed Deputy Little in the chin with a right hook. The neophyte cop's gun flew out of his hand. He was out cold before his head hit the pavement. Tiny's shoulder was a flare of pain, but his adrenaline allowed him to pretty much ignore it. His natural endorphins were kicking in to help dampen the flame burning beneath the red spot above his stenciled badge. Roaring out of the parking area, Tiny passed an ambulance arriving on the scene. Putting the police car through its paces, he drove to County Road 846, bringing his speed up to a hundred miles an hour. Slowing enough to make the turn onto 858, he barreled the next few miles to Babcock's spread, the Red Rooster Ranch.

The gate was closed, and a guard stood by it with his handgun drawn, the spotlights rendering him an apparition. He hesitated to shoot when he saw it was a police car. Tiny crashed through the gate without slowing down. He drove straight to the main house where the Lincoln was parked, taillight broken, and its body full of holes made by the buckshot. The house and environs were lit with bright lights. The arena, on the other hand, was shrouded in darkness, no more than an obscure outline in the distance. Tiny chambered more shells into the magazine of the twelve gauge, checked to make sure he had an extra clip for the 9mm, and slipped out of the cruiser's door, keeping low to the ground behind the car. He heard gunfire coming from the back side of the house, probably the pool area. Running in the direction of the sound, he stopped short when he saw Jimmy lying in the portico, blood spotting his face. There was a large exit wound in the boy's chest. His black tee shirt, covered with silk-screened skulls, was ripped open, with a large wet stain surrounding the gapping hole. He didn't look too good.

After receiving a call from the front gate, Teddy Grimm ordered the arena lights doused. He went on the public address system to inform all participants in the evening fights to remain calm; there was a temporary electrical failure that would soon be fixed. He signaled two of his best men to get carts and go with him. Their first stop was the estate security headquarters, located about a hundred feet from the arena. Grimm unlocked the door and went to a steel vault. This was the armory for security. Normally the guards carried no weapons (except Grimm) during actual sporting events. Since no weapons were allowed into the arena, Grimm relied on the muscle of the guards and the pepper spray they carried to maintain order. The two men were handed 9mm pistols and holsters with an extra clip. In addition, they were armed with an M16 carbine, also with extra clip. They headed for the main house, with Grimm in one cart and the two guards following in another. The security chief's radio beeped en route.

"Grimm," he answered. "Go ahead." He listened, frowning as a house guard appraised him of Santana's arrival and Jimmy's murder. He stopped his cart and let the two men in the other cart pull alongside.

"Santana murdered Jimmy right by the front door," Grimm told his two-man posse. "Security cameras picked up the whole thing. He's somewhere outside on the west side of the house. We have to move fast, meet Mr. Babcock at the east side door, and take him to the Wrangler in the east garage. You boys go ahead and cover the door while I swing in to pick up the boss."

Grimm's main concern was getting Rooster out of the house and into a four-wheel-drive Jeep Wrangler with oversized mud tires, kept ready to roll in case things went south in a hurry. The getaway vehicle was garaged east of the main house. From there, it could be driven three miles down a muddy four-wheeler trail leading just over the county line to a grass landing pad. This tactic served the purpose of confusing jurisdictions while, at the same time, the treacherous road eliminated pursuit in most vehicles. A small helicopter was kept in a sheet-metal hanger for Rooster to make a quick getaway. With a five-hour gas supply, it could make close to six hundred air miles before landing. Within that radius, Rooster had over a dozen bolt-holes. Grimm picked up his Nextel as they arrived at the side entrance of the house and called the guard in charge of the four-man house detail.

"What gives, Brad?" Grimm asked.

"The boss is getting some things from his safe. He told me to stay by the pool. You're to pick him up at the east door."

"Roger that," said Grimm. "We're there now. Where are the other men?"

"I have one here, two are with Rooster. We have all the outside spotlights going."

"What about the girls?" Grimm held his gun pointed up, ready to shoot.

"Locked in the west bedroom," Brad replied. "They were hysterical."

"Roger that," Grimm responded. "Santana will most likely go to the lanai door, so stay alert." Silence. "Do you copy, Brad? Brad? Oh, shit." Grimm looked at the two men standing on either side of the door. "I think Santana's inside."

"We've got to talk," Julie said, taking her husband by the hand. They were helping Jamie clean up after Brian's welcome-home dinner. Cammy and Robbie took their baby home, leaving Josh with Julie and Tommy until bedtime. Brian had already left for his AA meeting. Josh was out on the porch, pestering the increasingly inebriated Toad.

"Jamie, could you keep an eye on Josh for us?" Julie asked. "I don't know where John is, but I'm sure he'll be here soon, probably starving. If for some reason he doesn't show up in an hour or so, bring Josh over to Cam and Robbie's. Tommy and I need to talk." Julie looked at Tommy who nodded agreement.

"No *problema*," Jamie said. "Send him back over on your way to the conference room."

"Thanks." Julie went over and gave Jamie a hug and kiss on the cheek. "And thank you for the wonderful dinner. I hope everything works out for you and Brian. You're both super dudes. Tomorrow, we will all be drifting off our separate ways because of El Diablo. Maybe we needed some kind of push to get us going."

"There may be truth to that. I have to tell you though, I'm plenty scared about this crazy cop, especially for Brian. I just hope Nolan knows what he's doing."

"Don't we all," Julie said.

"You got that right," chimed Tommy.

"C'mon, tough guy, we need a powwow."

"Right," said Tommy. "I'll plow and you wow." Julie yanked him from the room. On the way to their room, they stopped at Toad Hollow.

"Yo! Toadster!" Tommy said to the smoking Toad.

"Hey!" Julie said. Toad nodded.

"Josh"—Julie knelt by the child—"you hustle over to Jamie's and wait for John to get back. If he doesn't show up soon, Jamie will bring you to the Valentines'." She kissed him on the cheek, stood up, and steered him in the direction of Jamie's room. He walked a few steps and turned around.

"John'll be back," Josh informed them. "He said he would be." He turned around and sprinted to Jamie's door.

"Later, Toad," said Julie, tugging her husband's arm before he could engage in a conversation that was sure to lead to a few drinks and, probably, hours of bullshit.

"Later," Toad agreed.

Inside the door of their room, Julie embraced her husband tightly and began to cry.

"Whoo," said Tommy. "What's this all about?"

"I'm scared, Tommy. Aren't you?" Julie looked up at Tommy's face, still holding him tight. "We have to leave tomorrow."

"I know," said Tommy, giving her a squeeze. "It'll be OK. I promise you. Together we're golden. Nothing can hurt us."

"Tommy." Julie disengaged from him but held on to his hands. She tossed her head to move a loose strand of blonde hair and fixed her blue eyes on his. "I want a baby."

There it was. Tommy had no place to go, nowhere to hide. He looked at her, looked away, then back again. After a moment of absolute silence that seemed to stretch into infinity, he said, "Let's do it!"

Julie shrieked in delight and jumped into his arms. He almost fell backward. He picked her up and put her on the bed, covering her supple body with his own. Their lips locked together in a very long and sensuous kiss. His hands began to wander, and so did hers. For the first time in a very long while, they took their time undressing each other, using their teeth, tongues, and toes, as well as their fingers. Tommy growled, and Julie groaned. They milked the foreplay for as long as Tommy could bear it (which wasn't all that long), then set about the serious business of baby making. They danced the dance of eternity. Tommy plowed, and Julie wowed.

The two lovers dozed off in each other's arms. It seemed like only minutes but was perhaps an hour later when they awakened to gunshots, accompanied by screaming, and more gunshots.

"What the . . . ?" Tommy sat up.

"Oh my god!" Julie cried.

Rooster Babcock took two guards and left the pool area as soon as he heard what happened to Jimmy. He truly regretted the death of his young helper. He had taken a shine to the boy. Both of his sentries were outfitted with shotguns and 9mm semiautomatic handguns. Rooster preferred a good old-fashioned scattergun at close quarters. Rooster went straight to his bedroom where a safe containing the other hundred and twenty-five thousand dollars he owed Santana was stashed. In addition, he had about thirty thousand in cash he kept around for "ready" money. He could only surmise the attempt on Tiny's life was unsuccessful, and the greedy gunslinger had returned to take the unearned half.

Instructing the guardsmen to remain on alert in the hall, the crime czar unlocked the door. The master bedroom was really a suite with an anteroom that served as a den. It was furnished with a black leather couch and two matching stuffed leather rocking chairs with accompanying ottomans. There was a home entertainment center on one wall and an oil painting of a cockfight on the other. A wet bar occupied the wall by a door that led to a bathroom larger than many living rooms. On the other side of the bathroom was Rooster's sleeping chamber.

Grabbing a metal briefcase by the wet bar, Rooster went over to the entertainment center and swung it out on hidden hinges to reveal a floor safe. Removing the cash and a few jewelry trinkets worth more than many working people made in a year, the castle's lord stuffed the cache in a metal briefcase. He also took out a snub nose .38 he kept "just in case." He slid the entertainment center back in place and went into the bedroom. Inside his boudoir of about six hundred square feet, not including a 120-square-foot closet, he donned a light cotton khaki field jacket, putting the small handgun in his right pocket. Opening a dresser drawer by the ornate king-sized brass bed, he drew out a Colt .45 Government along with an extra clip. Rooster hurried back to the hall.

"Vinny, take this," Rooster said, handing a third bodyguard the loot case. "Go out to the Escalade. Call Grimm and tell him I'll be at the east door in one minute. Oh, and get the briefcase from the Town Car with the money I gave to that Mexican miscreant. Put it in the Escalade as well and get the hell out of here. I'll get in touch with you on the Nextel as soon as the dust settles."

"Gottcha, boss." Vinny started down the hall toward the front door.

"Hey, Vinny!" called the crime boss.

"Yeah?" Vinny stopped and turned.

"Tell Grimm to let the pit bulls loose."

Tiny pushed through the gate of the bougainvillea hedge, whirling around with the shotgun and covering both sides of the gate. There was no one waiting to ambush him. He moved on to the lanai door and saw the lock was shot off. He peered cautiously into the lanai. He could smell gunpowder. He saw two bodies lying on the floor, a fair amount of blood on and around both of them. He noticed a trail of blood splotches leading from the door to both bodies, then into the house. Santana was either wounded or had stepped in Jimmy's blood. The latter seemed unlikely given the persistence of the trail. Tiny's lips twisted in a wicked grin. Following the trail, he went through the sliding glass door into the house, moving cat quick, spinning to pan the sides of the door. He heard gunfire coming from the east side of the house and ran in its direction. He looked through a small window in the east door and saw a body on the ground. There was a golf cart speeding away down a gravel path toward an outbuilding, apparently chasing another cart just arriving at the structure. The second cart, in turn, was being chased by what looked like five or six pit bulls that appeared to be out for blood.

Santana, limping into the house with almost no concern for safety, heard voices in a hallway. He started toward them when he heard a door slam. Moving as fast as his wounded foot and buttocks would allow, he arrived at the east door. Taking a quick peek through the greeting card-sized window, he saw Rooster and another man, probably Grimm, speeding away on a golf cart. Pulling out behind them, a second cart with two men armed with M16s began down the gravel drive. Santana could hear the sound of the pit bulls' maniacal barking. Bursting through the door, he fired at the driver of the second cart, only wounding him due to haste. The cart swerved to the right and stopped just before colliding with a ficus tree. The other man turned and commenced firing a volley at Santana. The black-clothed assassin fell to the ground and rolled. The poor light at this level would render him almost invisible. Santana shot from a prone position. Fire spit from the sound suppressor on his pistol, giving away his position. It was too late for the mortally wounded guard to shoot back. Santana stood up as the sound of savage barking seemed to be growing much closer. The other wounded security man made a feeble effort to get out of the cart and behind the tree, but the dark marksman brought him down just as he set foot on the ground. Santana, starting to feel a little dizzy, limped to the cart and started in pursuit of Rooster, his foot bleeding into the saturated rag and becoming one son of a bitch of hammering pain.

With their master's scent before them and the blood scent of an enemy between them and him, the ferocious fighting dogs tore down the driveway after Santana. Before Santana could reach the garage, the dogs were on top of him. He was forced to make a quick turn to the right to evade the pack, his gun spitting fire. He managed to dispatch two of the dogs before they were in the fray, but a third leaped up and grabbed his left arm. The Mexican pistolero fired point-blank, shooting its brains out with a bullet to the head. Blood splattered across his shirt and arms. Snapping his switchblade out, he turned just in time to disembowel another dog as it went for his face. One of the two remaining dogs went for his right arm, but he stuck the knife in its neck, shooting it in the left eye before it hit the ground. The final fighting dog took hold of his mangled foot in its vicelike jaws and began to savage it. Santana wailed the cry of the damned and gnashed his teeth. He shot the dog in the hindquarters, barely able to focus through tears of pain. He fired again as the yellow-eyed demon dropped away. He fired his gun into the writhing hell's spawn again and again, several rounds after the animal stopped moving, until he ran out of ammunition. He was panting and covered in blood; the stench of death filled the air. He looked up to see the Wrangler on its oversized tires trundling toward a narrow opening in the woods.

Tiny ran back through the house and out the front door to his commandeered cruiser. He arrived just as the Escalade with Vinny and the money came through the garage door. He ran out in front of the vehicle, holding his riot gun in one hand and his badge in the other. The escaping security guard accelerated, steering the SUV directly at Tiny. The deputy leaped aside, pumping two blasts from the riot gun as he went down, landing on his left shoulder with an excruciating stab of pain. The Escalade went off the driveway and crashed into an oak tree. The lights stayed on, but the vehicle didn't move. Tiny decided to forgo an investigation of the driver and the potential cargo he intended to escape with in favor of pursuing Santana. He wanted to kill the assassin not only to quench his thirst for revenge, but also to save his golden goose, Rooster Babcock. Returning to the purloined patrol car, its roof bubbles still flashing, he tossed the shotgun in the backseat. Slipping behind the wheel, he put the car in gear and the pedal to the metal. His left shoulder was on fire with searing pain. Roaring around the house and onto the brick road leading to the east garage, he saw the taillights of the Jeep Wrangler disappear into the woods. That would most likely be Rooster, he figured. His headlights picked up the usurped golf cart and its besieged occupant. He witnessed the execution of the last pit bull as he aimed the cruiser for the bloody shooter.

Santana was far from finished. He slammed his spare clip into the Beretta and took aim at the windshield of the approaching squad car, placing three rounds into the safety glass, causing the window to cave in. The devil of a cop swerved and kept coming. Santana stomped the "go" pedal of the cart in an effort to move out of the way of the two-ton missile bearing down on him. He almost succeeded. Unfortunately for him, the left corner of the Crown Vic's bumper kissed the rear bumper of the cart, sending the gunslinger flying like a rock out of a catapult about thirty feet into a hedge of flowering oleander.

By the time Tiny arrived on foot, gun ready, the cruiser's spotlight on the hired gun, Santana was sitting on the ground. His face was so covered in blood the features were scarcely recognizable. His clothes were ripped and torn in a dozen places with blood oozing from as many wounds. He grinned at Tiny, white foam in an ocean of red and a glint of gold. He raised his right hand as if in a gesture of supplication to the imposing figure of the deputy. Tiny saw the reflection of metal and kicked at the assassin's hand just as the derringer spit fire. The wee gun went flying even as the determined deputy felt a ripping pain in his left bicep, accompanied by the warm flow of blood. Tiny's brain was flooded in a torrent of rage. His neck bulged beyond its already trunklike size as a crimson tide flushed his face and flooded his brain with madness. He dropped his handgun and lunged at the slimy black snake before him. Reaching down, Tiny grabbed the bantam Mexican by his extended right arm and yanked him to his feet. He put his right hand around the hit man's neck and began to squeeze. He bent the right arm back until he heard the snap of a bone breaking. A blood-curdling screech from the combatant barely pierced the maniacal cop's hearing as he let go of the arm and put both hands around the small Mexican's neck, blocking the passage of air. Santana jerked as if he was passing out.

A searing pain stabbed Tiny high in the right ribs. Letting go of death's dark angel, he stepped back. Blood soaked his shirt; he was bleeding from yet another wound. He looked up at Santana to see the mocking grin with its signature of gold. The assassin was holding a bloody knife in his left hand. Bellowing like a bull buffalo, Tiny charged the barely standing Mexican, oblivious to possible harm. When the knife moved to strike his gut, he grabbed Santana's arm at the wrist and twisted until the knife dropped and went on twisting until he broke that arm as well. Santana's cry of pain was cut short as Tiny struck him in the windpipe. Taking hold of the gunslinger's shirt with his left hand, the demented deputy began to pommel his face with a hammerlike right fist. When nothing was left of Paladin's facial features, he wrapped his massive hands around the neck and squeezed what remained of the life out of him. He let the corpse drop to the ground and kicked it a half a dozen times before the anger completely drained out of him.

Tiny staggered back to the patrol car and leaned against it to catch his breath. He examined the wound in his side and found it to be relatively superficial. The knife had not been thrust with a great deal of force and had glanced off a rib. He looked up into the night sky as the *thump thump thump* of a helicopter's rotors announced the departure of the once and future kingpin. Tiny was pretty beat up but still had enough juice to set right his plight before midnight. After all, the only loose cannon was a queer boy at a wastrel's way station called the Fireproof Motel.

31

Tiny walked over to the Escalade with his pistol ready. The driver's door was open, the occupant lying with his back on the ground, one foot still propped on the SUV's floorboard. He looked like a drunk who fell out of his vehicle and passed out where he lay. However, this man was not inebriated. Rather, he seemed to be dead from gunshot wounds to his head. It appeared two or more of the buckshot pellets from the riot gun had struck his face. There were copious amounts of blood on his clothes and on the Escalade's leather seats.

Pressing the button on the open door to unlock all the doors, Tiny walked around to the passenger side to retrieve a metal briefcase. It was locked, of course, and no key could be found on the guard. It made sense that Rooster wouldn't trust a lackey with a latchkey. Taking out his handgun, he shot off the locks. He was not disappointed when he lifted the cover. There were wads of hundred—and fifty-dollar bills. He noticed another similar case on the backseat. Could he be luckier still? Opening the second case, he found Santana's manila envelopes and their contents. The wounded law enforcement officer returned to the patrol car in a giddy daze. He had practically forgotten his wounds. He was rich beyond his greatest expectations! Retirement was just around the corner. Who needed backup to ruin a moment like this? He grinned despite the injuries he received. He was still alive, and the night's work held promise. He needed only to punch the last hanging *chad*, and he would be home free. There would be a lot of explaining to do later. There would be a mountain of forms to fill out and the usual administrative leave "pending investigation" and so on. But in the final analysis, he would be vindicated and reinstated.

Turning on the festive bubble of lights, he sped toward the Fireproof in anticipation of sealing the envelope on any legal proceedings that might expose him. *Murder* was such a harsh word. *Clean up* seemed a more appropriate nomenclature, as in removing evidence that might compromise a mission. And his little butt buddy Brian qualified as a bona fide smudge in need of scrubbing. Tiny called in on his radio to headquarters, reporting he was returning to the old schoolhouse after losing the fleeing car. He turned the radio off before there was a reply. He neglected to mention he would be stopping at a certain "bedbug-ger" motel on the way back.

Josh was hanging out at Jamie's, watching a show on the Discovery Channel, waiting for John Vaughn to return. Brian had not returned from his AA meeting yet though the time was getting late, almost ten.

"Josh," Jamie said, "it's getting late. I don't think Julie is coming back to get you. We're going to have to turn off the set and go over to the Valentines' room. That's where you're sleeping tonight."

"But I'm waiting for John. He'll be here any minute. Can't I stay just a little longer? I know he'll be here 'cause he said he would."

"I think it's better if we go now before everybody goes to bed. You'll see John in the morning. I know he'd want you to go to bed. Something unexpected may have come up to make him late."

"Why wouldn't he call Camilla and Robby?" Josh gave Jamie the kind of look that says, "Something is wrong, isn't it?"

Jamie felt a little worried too. The look of fear on Josh's face made his already-queasy stomach roll in empathy. Jamie was concerned about John, but the unexpected turn his relationship with Brian seemed to be taking was giving him the jitters as well. This feeling was exacerbated by Brian's overdue return from his outing with his newfound AA buddies.

Jamie knelt by the abused runaway. "Listen, Josh, I know you are frightened because John hasn't returned when he said he would, but things happen, probably more often than not, that we can't predict." Jamie ran his hand through Josh's hair, giving him a hug and kiss on the cheek. "Come on, let's roll."

"Okay!" Josh bolted out the door.

"Hey, hold on partner!" Jamie called. He went out and took the waiting boy by the hand. "Let's go together." They walked down the stairs and passed the dozing Toad, arriving at room 105. Jamie rapped lightly on the door. A moment later, Robbie opened the door; he was wearing nothing but an unbuttoned pair of khaki shorts and holding a beer.

"Hey, guys, come in, come in." They drifted into the room as Cammy emerged from the bathroom pulling a tee shirt over her head.

"Sorry to barge in on y'awl," Jamie said. "I just figured it's time for Josh to get ready for bed. He *is* staying here, right? I mean he can stay with me otherwise. No *problema*."

"Not to worry," Robbie interjected. "Josh is already part of the family. Hey, we're all done with the first round and ready for one more if you care to join us." He held up his empty bottle. "Cammy, get Jamie a brew."

"No thanks," Jamie said. "I feel like a little sobriety wouldn't kill me for a change." A car pulled up in front. The sound of voices and a car door slamming carried into the room on the night air. "It's him!" Josh shouted. "It's John!" He rushed out the door onto the porch, Jamie following.

A late-model Cadillac pulled away, and there was Brian standing by the stairs.

"Hey," he said to Josh while smiling and waving to Jamie. "Why the long face? You look like you just lost your best friend and it's my fault." Cammy and Robbie walked over and gave Brian a squeeze. Even Toad lifted his head and squinted at the recovering alcoholic.

Josh turned around and held Cammy's hand. He leaned against her, his head pressing against her hip. "I thought it was John," he mumbled.

"What's up?" Brian asked.

"John hasn't returned yet, and we're a bit worried," Cammy replied.

"Some of us are more anxious than others," Robbie added, nodding at Josh.

"So, I see." Brian smiled at Josh with a wink to demonstrate his sympathy.

"So how was your meeting?" Cammy asked.

"Just what I needed," Brian replied. "The ride there and back was even better, more of an opportunity to talk one-on-one."

"Glad to hear it," Cammy said. "I have a feeling things are going to work out nicely for you, Bry, if you stay sober. I think you're going to make it."

"Thanks for the vote of confidence," Brian said. "I've got a good feeling about my future too." He cast a meaningful glance at Jamie.

"Let's all go back to our room," Cammy proposed, "and have a cup of tea together. We may not have the opportunity to see each other again after tomorrow. I'm sure going to miss you guys." She gave Robbie a "no more booze" look, and he nodded agreement. Putting a hand on Josh's shoulder, Cammy steered him back to their room. "I have Mandarin Orange Spice and mint tea as well as green tea and regular old Lipton. So we do have choices."

The hound of Hades, Anubis, with his hyena head, yellow eyes, and mouth of sharp teeth snarling at Nolan took a step forward, saliva drooling from its lower jaw. A leather collar with studs encircled its neck with a gold five-pointed star dangling like a dog tag in the front. It was a Baron County sheriff's star, no mistaking that. Nolan backed up a step; the growling fiend advanced. Nolan was looking around for something to defend himself with and his hand knocked over a broom leaning against a porch post. Nolan leaned over to pick up the broom as Anubis leaped, mouth wide-open. Nolan swirled, lost his balance, and fell. Skidding to a stop, the beast fishtailed around and bit the special agent on the right ass cheek. He cried out in pain. As the death demon went for his throat, Nolan grasped the broom like a spear and jammed it into the gaping chamber of teeth. The yellow eyes turned blank; the deranged dog staggered. Nolan shoved hard on the broom. Suddenly the straw end burst into flame, and Nolan rolled away. The skewered canine turned to a pile of ashes and blew away, some of the debris stinging the agent's eyes, causing tears to well behind the levees of his lower lids.

Mike Nolan awoke with a start, eyes watering and leg throbbing. He was sweating although the room was cool. He tried to grasp at straws of the dream, but they seemed to vanish like dust in the wind. He was left with a sense of imminent danger, the need to get moving. Trying to stand, his leg was unwilling to support his weight, and his ass was stiff and sore. He spotted a broom in the corner of the room; something prickled his skin like an eidolon whispering. Grabbing hold of his crutch, he rose to his feet. Picking up the .38 revolver, he tucked it under his belt and clipped on his badge as well. Taking a cigar from the top drawer, he poured a shot of Jack Daniel's and threw it down. He went out on the porch. There was a fog beginning to cover the ground and a slight chill in the air. He lit the cigar and took a drag; he exhaled the fragrant smoke. Truth was, he found a good cigar relaxing. The liquor started to kick in, and Nolan found himself coming around. Looking over in Toad's direction, he saw the sentry snoring in his chair, head down, apparently deep in his cups. Nolan, crutch under his armpit, hobbled slowly down the steps, starting across the yard for the motel office. Deciding it was pastime to apprise Morris of the danger they were all in, he would try to persuade him to close the Fireproof for a while and to take his wife someplace safe until events ran their course.

Nolan rang the bell. He could hear the TV. Morris was likely watching reruns of *JAG* or *CSI: Miami* while Ida fussed in the kitchen, cleaning and polishing. "Sit, Morris," Ida said. "I'll get it." She scuffed through the threshold to the tiny office no more than a counter with a thirteen-inch TV and a single couch. Peeking through the outside door blinds, she recognized Mike Nolan. Opening the door, she saw the crutch and the cuts and bruises all over him. "Oh, my gosh! What happened to you? It looks like you've been in a train wreck. Have you been to the hospital?"

Nolan flashed a wan smile. "I have some disturbing news, Mrs. Kline. Is Morris around?" Going into the humble space shared by Morris and his wife, Nolan pointed to his badge and began to unfold for them the predicament they all faced.

Tiny drove past the Fireproof to the gravel driveway of a demolished farm house about twenty yards farther north. He pulled in far enough to not be easily seen from the road. He turned off the lights. Taking his 9mm and an extra clip, Tiny set out for the motel, clinging to the darkest path as much as possible. Locating the incoming phone cable, he cut it with a razor-sharp pen knife on his key chain. This would take care of all the landlines at the motel. As for cell phones, he trusted the element of surprise would work in his favor. He knew Nolan's cell, for one, was out of commission. He made his way across the yard to the side of the L where Nolan's room was located. He glanced at the drunken fool sleeping in the chair with nary an eyelid fluttering. Drawing his service pistol, he tried the knob, twisting it slowly. It was open. He attempted to put his left hand on the gun as well, but his left arm had become too sore and stiff to be useful. He shoved the door wide, charging into the room. It was a grave risk but necessary. He spun covering the blind spot by the door. It appeared there was nobody home. The stale reek of cigarettes, the whiskey bottle, blood on the unmade bed, all testified to the recent presence of a wounded deer. Tiny went to the bathroom door, slightly ajar, and kicked it open. It was vacant as well. Going through the drawers of the dresser, he came upon a box of .38 ammunition about half-full.

Wavering, unsure of what course of action to take, Tiny picked up the bottle of Jack Daniel's and took a slug, pouring most of what was left over his wounds. Clearly, his nemesis was still alive and most likely here at the motel. Also, he had been able to arm himself somehow. The most logical thing would be to do a room-to-room search. Tiny didn't like the prospects of that option. He decided the risks outweighed any benefits. If worse came to worse, he could discredit Nolan somehow. First things first, however. He had a primary target in that sissy Brian. Afterward, let the chips fall where they might. He hoped to be off the grounds of the motel and back in the cruiser again before all hell broke loose. He left the room with as much stealth as possible, again clinging to the murky spots. Looking over at room 108, he noticed the chair where Toad had sat napping was empty. A sudden surge of adrenaline told him to shake the lead out.

Toad saw the hulking figure trying to slip unnoticed across the yard. The hombre was definitely armed and dangerous. There was no mistaking his identity; it was the diabolical deputy. If he were in Vietnam, this adversary would've been vulture chow by now. Feigning sleep, Toad waited until the bastard was inside Nolan's room and bolted for Robbie and Cammy's. He was well aware that Nolan was with Morris and Ida at the moment. He didn't bother to knock but burst unannounced into the tea party. Baby Billy commenced to squall.

"He's here in Nolan's room right now," Toad blurted. "Brian, you get out now and hide in the woods out back. It'll be you he's looking for. Robbie, take Cammy, the baby, and Josh into the bathroom and lock the door." Toad seemed utterly sober in the crisis. "Jamie, where's your cell phone?"

"In my room."

"Go get it and lock your door. Call 911. After you're there, I'm going outside and try to distract him while Brian makes a run for it. Vaughn isn't back yet, and I don't think he's coming back either. Sorry, Josh."

Josh burst into tears and began to scream. "He is so coming back! He said he was! He is! You're a big fat drunk liar!" He ran at Toad and started to hit him with his fists. Cammy grabbed his arm and tried to pull him gently away.

"Josh, never mind that right now," Camilla said. "Toad is just worried. He didn't mean it." She gave Toad a plaintive look.

"Yeah," Toad said, "I'm just worried, that's all."

Gunshots blasted through the night, rattling the glass and shattering Toad's plan.

Mike Nolan wrapped up his story and stood up to leave. Morris continued to sit with a worried and distracted look on his face.

"I'm truly sorry this has come home to roost at the Fireproof," Nolan said. "Hopefully, it will all be resolved in a few days, and you can resume your lives. In the meantime, go stay with your relatives in Maine and have a vacation." He extended a hand to Morris who took it absently, then gave Ida a peck on the cheek. "I'll see myself out." He got as far as the door to the office when Morris called out.

"Wait, Mike." Morris stood up from his chair and came over. "Let me walk you back to your room. I want to go over and see my guests before they leave."

Mike Nolan and Morris stepped out of the motel office and started down the walkway toward the motel rooms, Mike stumping with the crutch. A gunshot, accompanied by a bright flash, came from near the porch in front of Nolan's lodgings. A bullet whizzed by the federal agent so close he could hear the sound of it as it passed by.

"Get down!" he yelled to Morris. He turned to see Morris was getting down all right, falling down, with a red spot on his chest.

"Shit!" Nolan dove for the ground as another gunshot rang out and another. He pulled the revolver from his belt and fired off a round in the direction of the shooter, hoping to at least send him seeking cover. The shots ceased for a moment. Nolan knew he had to get out of the open, pronto. He had no choice but to try for the relative safety of the motel office. He must take Morris with him as well. He simply couldn't leave the old fella to bleed to death or be murdered without a chance. He hustled to the injured man and, leaning on the crutch, grimacing from the pain caused by his protesting leg, helped him up. "Let's go, old buddy; the "wheel" is spinning." By some miracle, Morris was able to stumble along with only Nolan's verbal support and a hand on his elbow. Ida opened the door for them. Mike Nolan had a déjà vu, but he was not stopping to think about it.

"My god! Morris! Morris!" She looked at Nolan, white with terror.

"Get inside, quick." Nolan pushed Morris through the open door. "Call 911."

"The phone is dead!" Ida shrieked, helping with Morris.

Another gunshot, Nolan lurched forward, blood spewing from his mouth like a stream of vomit. Ida screamed, her breasts covered with Nolan's blood. Letting her husband fall, she slammed and latched the door.

"Tommy!" Julie screeched, pulling on her panties. "Stop! Get away from the door!" Tommy was opening the door, still naked from the lovemaking session. She ran up to grab his arm as another gunshot rang out. Tommy slammed backward into her, a large bloody spot opening under his right arm as a bullet passed through the flesh, shattering the mirror over the dresser behind him. "Tommy! Oh, Jesus! Tommy!"

"I'm OK," Tommy said. He flung the door shut. "Call 911." Holding his hand over his wound, he plopped onto the bed. "It must be that fuckin' cop." He lost consciousness.

"Oh my god! Tommy! Tommy!" Julie went over and took his pulse. He was alive, just unconscious. She scrambled to the phone. The line was dead. She took a sharp knife from the utensil drawer and cut a long strip of bedsheet to make a rough bandage for Tommy, wrapping the strip around his torso several times. "Vaughn's gun," she said to herself. Steeling her nerves, she dared a peek out the door. The maniacal cop was crashing through the door into Robbie and Cammy's room. She bolted for Vaughn's room. The door was open. Thank the living bejesus!

Tiny was starting down the porch steps from Nolan's room when he saw his target come out of the motel office. *Nolan's got the old Jew bastard by his side, and he's using a crutch! He's been hurt for sure,* Tiny thought. Without hesitating, the corrupted cop brought the Glock to position and fired. Morris spun away from Nolan. He fired again, missing as Nolan hit the dirt. He shot a couple of more rounds. There was a muzzle flash and report from across the yard, and a bullet passed within an inch of his beleaguered left arm. The delinquent deputy began to move closer, getting low behind Camilla's garden fence. Nolan was up and helping the old fool into the bungalow just as Tiny raised his head over a staked tomato patch. What an idiot! Tiny stood, pointed the gun at Nolan, and let fly. Nolan crashed forward through the door like he just got kicked by an ornery Mexican mule. "Looks like a hit," Tiny snickered. Turning, he ran toward Jamie's room, halting when he saw Tommy looking out the door, butt naked. Throwing a shot at the curious nudist, Tiny watched him pop back into the room, a splash of crimson on his right side. Seeing nobody in Jamie's room, he continued along the porch until he reached to the Valentines' room. The door was locked.

"Open the fuckin' door!" Tiny bellowed. He began hammering it with his fist. "Police! Open up!" When there was no answer, he delivered a hard kick to the door. The old wood of the doorjamb gave way with a loud crackling sound. He kicked again, and the dead bolt gave way, the door banging open into the suite. As he charged in, a phantom slipped by him on the right side and out the door. Sweeping the room with his gun held out at arm's length, he saw only the queer dope dealer.

Jamie was standing by himself next to the sofa in the small living room part of the suite. Tiny squinted at him. Looking around the empty room, the wounded lawman saw teacups and plates on the table and smiled. "Having a little Mad Hatter party, are we?" The smile deliquesced to an ugly scowl. "Where are the others?" He approached Jamie and stuck the muzzle of the pistol under his chin. "Tell me, you fuckin' faggot, or I'll give you a face-lift with this nine millimeter."

"I think they went out to a bar," Jamie squeaked.

With a quick and experienced motion, Tiny bitch-slapped Jamie on the left cheek with the barrel of his gun. Jamie went down on his knees from the force of the blow, his vision smeared by tears of pain. Tiny gave him a severe kick on the ribs. The sound of bones breaking was ensued by a bloodcurdling scream from Jamie. A baby's wail came from the bathroom.

"Leave him alone, you crazy freak!" Brian emerged from the bathroom, the door shutting behind him like it was hung with a tight spring.

"Ahh." Tiny was all smiles again. "My little pussy is bristling his fur. The concern for your sweetheart is touching. Also, deadly." He raised the gun and pointed it at Brian. "Bye-bye." The depraved deputy almost dropped the gun as intense pain jolted his groin. Jamie had delivered a hard punch to the balls from below. Rushing in, Brian tried to wrestle the gun from the much-larger man before he could recover. Despite having only one useable arm, Tiny flung Brian off, sending him reeling across the room into a small desk next to the couch. Brian's head cracked the glass of the framed picture of the Three Wise Men.

Reaching up, Jamie grabbed Tiny's gun hand. Using the weight of his body, he was able to bring the arm down until the gun pointed at the floor. Tiny, unable to use his left arm, lifted Jamie to a standing position with his good arm and shoved hard, thrusting him into his staggering boyfriend. With his face contorted and flushed with rage, Tiny advanced on the two men, jabbing Jamie's already-broken rib and, in a snakelike strike, cracked the gun hard across his temple. Jamie dropped to the floor like a sack of sand and remained motionless. Tiny pointed the gun at Brian, who was about six feet away now, cringing near the couch. A commotion in the doorway caused Tiny to come about, confronting a shotgun-wielding Toad.

Toad had crouched by the right side of the door, back against the wall next to the doorjamb. Just as the door flew open and Tiny crashed into the room, Toad had slipped past him, head down, body low, and out the door like a ghost. Then making a beeline for Vaughn's room and finding the door wide open, he went in. Julie was inside, sitting on the floor with the shotgun out in pieces, trying to assemble it. With tears streaming down her cheeks, she was attempting to put the barrel and stock together.

"He shot Tommy."

"Let me." Toad hefted the pieces and assembled them, fitting the stock and barrel together and locking them with the hand screw. Pushing the thumb lever, he broke open the shotgun. Reaching onto the top shelf of the closet, he clutched a small wicker basket containing twelve-gauge shotgun shells. Toad picked out one marked with a 00 and loaded it into the breech. He snapped the gun closed.

"Loaded for bear," he said, grinning a gap-toothed but mirthless smile. "We'll need a few more of these and a couple of the other," he muttered, taking out a couple of shells marked Slug. "Is Tommy still breathing?" Julie nodded her head. "Good, go to Jamie's room, find his cell phone, and call 911. Tell them there's a federal officer and state trooper down. Take the phone back to your room and stay with Tommy until help arrives."

"State trooper?" Julie scrunched up her face. "What state trooper?"

"The imaginary one that's going to bring the state police onto the scene in case 'federal officer' doesn't work. We sure as hell don't want just the sheriff's department here. Now, shake a leg, missy."

Julie gave Toad a look of awe. "Good luck, Toadmeister," she said, grabbing his hand a second before fleeing the room. Toad followed behind, stopping at his chair for a prodigious gulp of fortifying spirits before hustling to battle.

Toad thumbed back the hammer on the shotgun, stopping by the window to the Valentines' room. He saw Tiny with his right side facing the door, ready to execute Brian. He went around the corner through the door but stumbled, perhaps from the adrenaline-booze combination. Pitching forward brought the shotgun's barrel down even as Toad fired, blowing off the deputy's right knee. The report sounded like the pent-up thunder of an exploding volcano inside the room. Tiny let out a howl of rage and pain almost as loud. He collapsed to the floor, the bottom of his right leg completely separated from the top part. His pant leg was shredded, a sanguine river of life saturating the denim. Toad, regaining his balance, broke open the shotgun, fumbling for a shell in his pocket. Tiny, still hanging on to the pistol, brought it up to blast Toad.

Nolan appeared at the door with the doctor's .38 and fired a round into Tiny's chest. The fallen colossus of a deputy, coughing up blood, changed targets, bringing his gun to bear on Nolan. The federal agent fired again, ducking back as Tiny's gun spat sparks of brimstone. The 9mm round plowed through the door molding and struck Julie in the shoulder. She spun, tumbling down the porch steps, dropping Jamie's cell phone. Her return to the action couldn't have been more ill-timed. Nolan came back around the door and fired a third time into the deputy, who was again aiming at Brian. Nolan shot twice more, using his last round. This time, El Diablo looked at him, smiled a bloody smile, and died. Nolan, his back against the jamb, slid down until he was sitting on the floor. A crimson stream ran from his nose and mouth over the stubble on his chin. He closed his eyes.

32

The state police were, in fact, the first to arrive on the scene in their two-tone black-and-tan cars. When they saw Nolan's badge and the dead county deputy, they closed off the area with crime tape and assumed charge of any investigation. Ambulances arrived at the scene, and the dead and wounded were carted to the hospital. The state troopers did manage to get statements of dubious clarity out of the delirious victims. No charges were brought against any of the residents of the Fireproof Motel during the initial investigation. It would be several months before the district attorney's office, the state police, and the sheriff's department released any findings. Nolan and the Fireproof crowd felt a lot more confident of justice being served with the staties in charge.

By the time everyone awoke the next day, it all seemed like a nightmare. Nolan was airlifted to Tampa, his wounds too egregious to be treated in Napolis. Morris remained in critical condition in the Napolis hospital for twenty-four hours, after which his condition was upgraded to serious. The doctor told his wife, Ida, he was one "tough old bird." Julie was hospitalized for three days with a broken clavicle due to a bullet wound and loss of blood. Tommy was treated for a flesh wound and was released. Jamie remained unconscious with a concussion for twelve hours. Brian stayed at his side the entire time. The level of worry he felt was equal to the level of affection he had for his friend and lover, which, it turns out, was a great deal.

Robbie and Camilla practically moved into the hospital's family room. A bed was set up in his mother's room. They visited their hospitalized friends while keeping a vigil on Constance, who came awake for an hour on the same morning as the others were admitted for treatment of their battle wounds. She fluttered her eyelids and tried to focus on Robbie, who was holding her hand. Robbie tried to give her water, but she was unable to swallow. The nurse told him to give her ice chips, which he did, lovingly inserting them between her parched lips. Finally she managed to croak out two words: *sorry* and *photos*. She slipped back into a coma and died the following day. Robbie and Camilla puzzled over what she might have meant by *photos*. They would find out two years later when they were assembling a family album. A key to a safety deposit box was found tucked behind a photo of Robbie's father in the back cover of an old scrapbook. The key opened box 444 in the First National Bank of Naple's downtown branch. In the box were the numbers and names of two Cayman Islands bank accounts.

The Valentine family, soon after the Fireproof shootings, numbered four. When the truth about Josh finally came out, the Craytons were arrested and held on child abuse and murder charges. The Department of Human Services Child Protective Unit was quick to recommend the Valentines be allowed to adopt Josh. This deflected a lot of the negative press the agency was receiving about the state's negligence in this whole affair. Although it later came out there were complaints the department did not even try to investigate, they blamed the dead deputy for the cover-up. The proceedings impugned the reputation of Robbie's parents to a point where they appeared to be as villainous as the deceased deputy. They were crucified in the press and by other officials for the primary purpose of making them scapegoats for the ubiquitous corruption that plagued every level of county government.

The *Napolis Daily Bugle* launched an investigation into the whole sordid affair surrounding the shooting of two sheriff's deputies, a federal undercover agent, and the apparent suicide of a county commissioner alleged to be corrupt. The sheriff's department, the state police, the FBI, and the state attorney's office launched separate inquiries, often giving conflicting information to the newspaper. In the final analysis, they all came up with similar conclusions to wit: the dead parties, Tiny and Constance, were found to be acting on their own. The *Bugle* did imply Captain Post might have had some role but tread lightly on that particular ground under intense lobbying by the sheriff's department and the district attorney's office. The official spin was these were isolated crimes with no other individuals involved. Some questions were raised about who else might be culpable in the case where Constance apparently accepted bribes for giving zoning variations to a large development corporation. Unknown to the general public, and the *Bugle* at this time, was that Judge Thomas, Sheriff Gunther, and the state district attorney were all financially involved in the same venture as Constance Valentine. They had been accepting large amounts of stock in a golf course and sports arena without investing their own money. These options would reportedly be worth in excess of a million dollars for each of the players in this scam. Also, there were a number of no-interest loans that were to expire without ever being paid back. In addition, there were the perennial campaign contributions.

The sheriff's department gave Captain Post a burial fit for a fallen hero. Since Tiny, acting alone, had been guilty of these heinous crimes, Post and the top cop of the county, Sheriff Gunther, were exonerated. It has become the norm of these times for the notion of "the buck stops here" in administrative hierarchies to be turned into "pass the buck" at all levels of both business and government. Sheriff Gunther, a Republican, was in fact easily reelected the following year for his fourth term. He ran against an unknown and ineffective candidate in his party's primary and unopposed in the general election. Democrats don't even bother to run candidates for public office in Baron County; it is so prodigiously Republican.

Judge Thomas was returned to the bench by popular vote. Judges in Florida retain their seat on the bench by approval of the voters during general elections. A year later, while forcing himself on an eleven-year-old girl in his custody, he accidentally strangled her in an attempt to shut her up when she started screaming. He finished on the corpse what he started with the living girl. He washed the dead body in the tub to remove DNA evidence. The cadaver was found hours after it was dumped by the side of the road in the Corkscrew Sanctuary. A tourist couple from Minnesota, hiking in that part of the park, stumbled on the body. The girl was naked and had bath water in her lungs. When the judge was notified, he claimed he let her go on an unsupervised visit with her mother. The mother's boyfriend, who had a history of domestic violence, was tried for the crime and found guilty. Judge Thomas took early retirement. Soon after, he was arrested at a local Denny's at two in the morning with a fifteen-year-old prostitute.

Robbie, Camilla, Josh, and Billy moved into Constance's house. After taxes and lawsuits were settled, as well as fines leveled on the estate by a plethora of government agencies, the couple was left with barely enough to keep the house out of lien. Fortunately, a scholastic trust fund had been established for Robbie that the government couldn't touch, and he was able to continue with his education.

Julie recovered fully from her shoulder wound with the exception of a little soreness during cold, damp weather. She and Tommy rented a small place in Bonita Springs, a growing community on the northern border of Baron County and North Napolis. She became a full-time substitute for the elementary schools in town. Talking to Cammy about her new home, she described Bonita as a community with a large Hispanic population. Much of the housing was still affordable although that would likely change with the crunch of multimillionaires moving into the area. Land and housing speculation were sure to drive prices through the roof as in Napolis. Already there were half a dozen new country club, golf, and housing developments catering exclusively to those with portfolios in excess of several million dollars. "One would think," Julie said to Cammy on the phone, "by the amount of real estate selling for over seven figures in Southwest Florida that every millionaire in the country was setting up a winter nest here."

Tommy landed full-time employment playing and singing nights at a restaurant/bar in North Napolis four nights a week, Wednesday through Saturday. Julie joined him on Friday and Saturday nights. At last, the two managed to make enough to buy a modest home and a new car. Tommy hooked up with another guitar player, and they started a band called Fireproof. They added a percussionist who played African congas and a bass player who retired to Napolis at age forty after a successful career as a British rock star in a group named the Rust Buckets. They cut a CD that became popular in South Florida and caught the interest of a major label. Negotiations are still underway. A year later, Julie and Tommy were married on Bonita Beach in front of Doc's Roadhouse Restaurant. The entire Fireproof crew, with the exception of John Vaughn, made it to the celebration. Three months later, Julie gave birth to a baby girl, Kaley Nelson. The two happy parents literally glowed with pride.

Toad returned to Maine as soon as the police cleared him. He married and moved into a comfortable home he bought with a small inheritance. He continued to drink until he suffered a stroke. He quit for a couple of months, resuming the tippling at a slightly reduced rate. He continued to drink and smoke still, interlaced with sobriety binges. Occasionally, he drove other disabled vets to the veterans hospital in Togus, Maine.

Brian and Jamie stayed together for a month, though not as lovers. The situation became too strained for the both of them, and they parted friends. Brian hooked up with a Christian group who insisted his homosexuality was caused by a demon inhabiting his body. He could be made whole and heterosexual by letting Jesus into his heart and exorcising Satan's spawn. Brian convinced himself this worked and married a lovely young lady in the congregation. Problem was, certain men still turned him on, and he felt constantly filled with remorse and guilt. Finally, he had enough and divorced his naive and brokenhearted wife two years later. Amazingly still sober, he returned to take up residence at the old Fireproof Motel. Jamie bought the establishment from Morris and Ida, who moved to a condo in Napolis with the money from the motel. He changed it into a quaint and beautifully renovated gay tourist destination, which he renamed the Pink Flamingo. He fell in love with one of his guests, and they set up house in Morris and Ida's cabin. Brian signed on as a handyman and was given a small cottage to live in. In the years that followed, he found a loving and generous god he could pray to. He grew in spirit, faith, and willingness, reaching out to help others suffering from the disease of alcoholism. He returned to college part-time and received a bachelor of arts degree. He became a minister in the Unitarian Church, forming a small congregation in Bella Villa.

Mike Nolan made a slow and painful recovery from a wound that required a lung to be removed, as well as back surgery. He was discharged from the DEA, his official employer, with a full disability pension. He became addicted to pain medications and soon found himself part of the unfortunate crowd he used to target. He was arrested by another DEA agent for possession of a narcotic, OxyContin, without a proper prescription. Due to his service record, he was treated leniently and was sentenced to a rehabilitation facility for twenty-eight days and probation. He was required to attend Narcotics Anonymous meetings as part of his probation. The odds against anyone in alcohol and/or drug recovery making it past a year before relapsing are something like ten to one. There is no accurate source for such data. Addiction is a disease for which there is no cure, only a reprieve from the symptoms on a daily basis. When he was released, Mike Nolan set up shop as a private investigator in Fort Myers.

As for the money Tiny left in Deputy Duncan Little's patrol car, it was never found by the authorities. On the way to the motel with another officer, Deputy Little spotted his car where Tiny left it and got out to investigate. He waved the other patrolman on and stashed the loot before hoofing it to the crime scene at the motel. Little would later hook up with Rooster for a mutually lucrative relationship.

Epilogue

Julie and Tommy walked hand in hand down Napolis Beach toward the pier. They now lived next door to Robbie and Camilla, only a couple of blocks from the Gulf of Mexico. Tommy was wearing khaki shorts and a white silk shirt. He had streaks of gray in his full head of sand-colored hair; his face was tan and slightly lined. Julie, wearing a blue flower-print summer dress with a hemline just below her knees and a white cotton blouse, looked at her husband of twenty years and smiled. Barely a wrinkle, only the faintest of creases could be found on her radiant face. She wore no makeup of any kind.

"Can you believe it, Tommy?" Julie clutched her husband's arm.

"It seems like a dream, out of time or space." Tommy shook his head.

"Turn around, turn around, and you're a young girl, going out on your own," Julie sang. The words and melody were from a seventies song she heard in a Kodak ad on television when she was around ten years old. The ad depicted a life in photos reviewed by the parents of a girl from the time just after birth until she had children of her own.

The two had been married for twenty years, and now, they were going to attend the sunset beach wedding of their daughter, Kaley, and their best friend's son, Billy. As they approached the Napolis Pier, they could make out individual members of the wedding party. Kaley, who just graduated with honors from Florida Gulf Coast University, looked resplendent in her wedding gown. Her blonde hair fell in cascades around her elfin face. The green eyes of the Emerald Isles were shining with a pure light. "Hi, Mom! Hi, Dad!" She came over and hugged them both.

"Where's the groom?" Julie asked.

"Right behind you." Kaley pointed at a rugged man with raven hair and of medium height, who happened to look very much like a younger Robbie sporting a white tuxedo. "You guys go say hi. I don't want to jinx anything." Julie and Tommy walked over to the spot near the Napolis Pier where a gently aged Camilla and Robbie Valentine stood with their son, Billy. The young man turned and fixed them with eyes like the summer sky. The blue gave a startling contrast to the dark curls. He smiled broadly and hugged both of them.

"Good to see you, Mom and Pop."

"Well, it looks as if things have come full circle," Camilla said.

"And how," added Julie. "But we still have a few minutes before we become officially in-laws, so be on your best behavior, young man." She fixed Billy with a stern look, and they all laughed.

"It seems like just a month ago," Tommy said, "when we were all on this same beach but up at Wiggins Pass. We were just out for a day in the sun before our lives changed forever that night on the way home."

"A night of infamy," Robbie said.

"The thought of that cop still gives me the heebie-jeebies," said Camilla.

"I'll second that," said Julie.

"And so will I," said Jamie, arriving on the scene. "Whatever you said." He gave everyone a hug and kiss on the cheek. Jamie was a kisser.

"Where's Brian?" Robbie asked. "We need a pastor to officiate."

"He'll be here soon," Jamie replied. "He wanted to bring his own transportation so he could go to a meeting later."

"Josh couldn't make it?" Julie looked at Cammy.

"Breaking news," Camilla answered. "Josh and his wife have a new baby. They didn't want to travel so soon. Plus, he just got a job working with abused children in San Diego. We're going out to visit next week."

"Wow!" Julie gave her friend a hug. "That's so fantastic! Boy or girl?"

"It's a baby boy, and they've named him John Vaughn Valentine."

"Oh my god," said Julie, "that's so awesome."

Brian arrived on the scene, smiling and hugging his old friends.

"Are we all ready?" Rev. Brian Sutter asked.

"Well, it's time to do it," Billy said. He went to his lady; and taking her arm, they strolled to the water's edge for the ceremony. As the sun slipped away, it cast a reflection like embers from a hot fire upon the placid water of the gulf. And just as Billy said "I do," there was a flash of green on the western horizon.

THE END